# THAT NIGHT

## ALSO BY CHEVY STEVENS

*Always Watching*

*Never Knowing*

*Still Missing*

# THAT NIGHT

## CHEVY STEVENS

ST. MARTIN'S PRESS ❧ NEW YORK

This is a work of fiction. All of the characters, organizations, and events portrayed in this novel are either products of the author's imagination or are used fictitiously.

www.stmartins.com

Library of Congress Cataloging-in-Publication Data

Stevens, Chevy.
  That night / Chevy Stevens. — First edition.
    pages cm
  ISBN 978-1-250-03460-1 (hardcover)
  ISBN 978-1-250-03461-8 (e-book)
  1. Women ex-convicts—Fiction.   2. Judicial error—Fiction.   3. Reputation—Fiction.   4. Bullies—Fiction.   5. British Columbia—Fiction.   I. Title.
  PR9199.4.S739T53 2014
  813'.6—dc23

                                                            2014000124

St. Martin's Press books may be purchased for educational, business, or promotional use. For information on bulk purchases, please contact Macmillan Corporate and Premium Sales Department at 1-800-221-7945, extension 5442, or write specialmarkets@macmillan.com.

First Edition: June 2014

10  9  8  7  6  5  4  3  2  1

*For all the people around the world*
*who dedicate their lives to helping animals,*
*whether it be working in shelters, volunteering,*
*forming rescue groups, or fostering animals in need.*
*Thank you.*

# THAT NIGHT

# CHAPTER ONE

## Rockland Penitentiary, Vancouver

### March 2012

I followed the escorting officer over to Admissions and Discharge, carrying my belongings in a cardboard box—a couple pairs of jeans, some worn-out T-shirts, the few things I'd gathered over the years, some treasured books, my CD player. The rest, anything I had in storage, would be waiting for me. The release officer went through the round of documents. My hand shook as I signed the discharge papers, the words blurred. But I knew what they meant.

"Okay, Murphy, let's go through your personals." The guards never called you by your first name on the inside. It was always a nickname or your last name.

He emptied out a box of the items I'd come into the prison with. His voice droned as he listed them off, making notes on his clipboard. I stared at the dress pants, white blouse, and blazer. I'd picked them out so carefully for court, had thought they'd make me feel strong. Now I couldn't stand the sight of them.

The officer's hand rested for a moment on the pair of my underwear.

"One pair of white briefs, size small."

He looked down at the briefs, checked the tag, his fingers lingering on the fabric. My face flushed. His eyes flicked to mine, gauging my reaction. Waiting for me to screw up so he could send me back inside. I kept my expression neutral.

He opened an envelope, glanced inside, then checked his clipboard before dumping the envelope's contents into my palm. The silver-faced watch my parents had given me on my eighteenth birthday, still shiny, the battery dead. The necklace Ryan had given me, the black onyx cool to the touch. Part of the leather cord had worn smooth from my wearing it every day. I stared at it, felt its weight in my hand, remembering, then closed my fingers around it, tucking it securely back in the envelope. It was the only thing I had left of him.

"Looks like that's it." He held out a pen. "Sign here."

I signed the last of the documents, put the belongings into my box.

"You got anything to dress out in?" the officer said.

"Just these." The officer's eyes flicked over my jeans and T-shirt. Some inmates' families send clothes for them to wear on their release day. But no one had sent me anything.

"You can wait in the booking room until your ride gets here. There's a phone if you need to call anyone."

I sat on one of the benches, boxes by my feet, waiting for the volunteer, Linda, to pick me up. She'd be driving me to the ferry and over to Vancouver Island. I had to check into the halfway house in Victoria by seventeen hundred hours. Linda was a nice lady, in her forties, who worked with one of the advocacy groups.

I'd met her before, when she'd taken me to the island for my unescorted temporary absences.

I was hungry—I'd been too excited to eat that morning. Margaret, one of my friends inside, had tried to get me to choke something down, but the oatmeal sat like a lump in my stomach. I wondered if Linda could stop somewhere. I imagined a Big Mac and fries, hot and salty, maybe a milkshake, then thought of Ryan again, how we used to take burgers to the beach. To distract myself from the memory, I watched an officer bring in a new inmate. A young girl. She looked scared, pale, her brown hair long and messy, like she'd been up all night. She glanced at me, her eyes drifting from my hair, down to the tattoos around my upper arm. I got them in the joint—a thin tribal bar for each year behind bars, forming one thicker, unbroken band that circled my right biceps, embracing me.

The officer yanked the girl's arm, pulled her to Booking.

I rubbed my hands across the top of my head. My hair was short now, the middle spiked up in a faux-Mohawk, but it was still black. I closed my eyes, remembered how it was in high school. Feathered and long, falling to the middle of my back. Ryan liked to wrap his hands in it. I'd cut it in prison after I looked in the mirror one day and saw Nicole's hair, thick with blood, and remembered holding her broken body in my arms after we found her that night.

"You ready to get out of here, Toni?" A friendly female voice.

I opened my eyes and looked up at Linda. "Can't wait."

She bent down and picked up one of my boxes, grunting a little as she lifted it. Linda was a small woman, not much taller than me. I was just a shorty at five feet—Margaret used to say a mouse fart could blow me over. But Linda was about as round as she was tall. She had dreadlocks and wore long flowing dresses and Birkenstocks. She was always railing at the prison system. I followed her out to her car, my box in my arms, as she chatted about the ferry traffic.

"The highway was clear all the way out to Horseshoe Bay, so we'll make good time. We should be there around noon."

As we pulled away, I watched the prison grow smaller in the distance. I turned back around in my seat. Linda rolled the window down.

"Phew, it's a hot one today. Summer will be here before you know it."

I traced the lines of my tattoos, counting the years, thinking back to that summer. I was thirty-four now and had been in custody since I was eighteen, when Ryan and I were arrested for my sister's murder. We'd been alone with her that night, but we hadn't heard Nicole scream. We hadn't heard anything.

I wrapped my hand around my arm, squeezed hard. I'd spent almost half of my life behind bars for a crime I didn't commit.

The anger never really leaves you.

# CHAPTER TWO

## WOODBRIDGE HIGH, CAMPBELL RIVER

### JANUARY 1996

I skipped my last class and met Ryan in the parking lot behind the school, where the "shrubs," the kids who liked to party on the weekends, hung out. Other than the coffee shop at the arena, it was the only place we could smoke off school grounds. The nearby residents didn't like it, but they didn't give us too much hassle unless someone was revving their engines or had their stereos blasting. Then the cops would come by, checking to see if we were drinking or smoking pot—and someone usually was, but I never did, not at school anyway.

Woodbridge High was old, and in need of a serious face-lift. The siding was washed-out blue where it wasn't covered by graffiti, which the janitor was constantly trying to remove. There were about five hundred kids at the school, which went from grade eight to twelve. My graduating class had about a hundred and twenty kids, and I didn't give a crap about ninety-nine percent of them.

There were a few of us that day, clustered around our vehicles in groups. The girls with their long hair and bangs teased up, wearing too much dark makeup and their boyfriends' jackets. The guys with their Kurt Cobain hair and the hoods up on their trucks, talking about carburetors and Hemi engines. Most of us were dressed grunge, flannel shirts, ripped jeans, ragged sweaters, everyone in darker colors.

Ryan was leaning on his truck, talking to a couple of his friends. He smiled when he saw me, passed a smoke. "Hey, babe."

I smiled back, took a drag. "Hey."

I'd been going with Ryan Walker since last July when we hooked up at the gravel pit, which was where the guys went on the weekends to four-wheel-drive and have bonfires. He drove a badass Chevy truck—which he worked on all the time, the only thing we ever fought about. I'd known who he was for a while, always thought he was cute, with brown shaggy hair and thick brows, almost-black eyes, long eyelashes, a killer smile that made his mouth lift up on one side, and this way of looking at you from under the brim of his baseball cap that was super-sexy. But he had a girlfriend for a few months, a blond chick. After they broke up he didn't seem interested in anyone else, like he'd rather just do his own thing or hang out with the guys. He had a reputation for being tough, which was hot. He didn't fight for no reason, but if someone tried pushing their weight around or was talking shit about his dad, who'd been in and out of jail since Ryan was a kid, he'd take them down. Mostly, when he wasn't with me, he spent time with his friends, working on their trucks, fishing, dirt biking, or four-wheeling.

There wasn't much else to do. Campbell River's a small coastal town on the northern part of the island, population who-gives-a-shit. I'd grown up there, but Ryan's family had moved down a couple of years earlier from northern BC. Everyone in Campbell River either worked as a logger, at the pulp mill, in the mines, or on a fishing boat. Ryan worked part-time at one of the outdoor stores. I used to go there sometimes, pretending to look around but mostly trying to catch his eye. He was always busy helping some customer, though, so I'd given up.

One night last summer, I'd been at the pit with friends, smoking a joint and taking it easy, when Ryan came over and started talking to me, asking how my summer was going. I tried to play it casual, like it wasn't a big deal, but my heart was pounding like crazy. He said, "You want to go for a drive?" We flew up the gravel hills, spraying mud out behind us, the engine as loud as the music—AC/DC, "Back in Black." I laughed, feeling alive and excited. He said, "You're some cool chick." Later we shared sips of Southern Comfort around the fire, his arm warm behind my back while we talked about our families, my constant fights with my mom, his problems with his dad. We'd been together ever since.

I took a drag of the smoke. Ryan watched, giving his lazy smile as he leaned against his truck, one eye half closed, his hair winging out from underneath his ball cap. His friends had drifted off. It was the first week of January, and cold, but he wasn't wearing a coat, only a thick brown sweater that made his eyes look like dark chocolate. He tucked his fingers into the front pocket of my jeans, pulled me close so I was leaning against him. He didn't work out much but he did lots of physical labor—his body was hard, his stomach muscles tight. He was already six feet, so I had to reach up to give him a kiss. We made out for a while, the smoky, bitter taste of tobacco tangling on our tongues, his unshaved chin scraping against mine. We stopped kissing and I buried my face in the warmth of his neck, smelling his boy smell, feeling an ache all down my body, wishing it was just us, all the time, like this.

"Can you come over tonight?" he whispered in my ear.

I smiled against his skin. "Maybe."

Even though I'd turned eighteen at the end of December, I still had a curfew on weeknights. Weekends, my parents were a little easier—I just had to call when I got where I was going, to let them know I was okay, and I couldn't stay out all night unless I was sleeping over at a friend's, but my mom was a hard-ass if I was even a minute late. I tried to spend as much time as possible with Ryan, going for drives, messing around in his truck, his basement, wherever we could be alone. We'd gone all the way after dating a couple of months—he was the first boy I'd ever been with. His dad had been at the bar, his mom, a nurse, working late at the hospital. We smoked a joint, then made out in his bed, Nirvana playing softly in the background, the sweet scent of a candle mixing with marijuana. I was excited, my head spinning from the pot, my body grinding against him, our naked chests warm against each other. We took off the rest of our clothes, shy under the blankets. "Do you want me to stop?" he whispered.

I said, "No," and stared in awe at his face, wondering how a boy could be so beautiful, the way he spoke, his voice, soft lips, dark eyes, everything so damn sexy. And I felt beautiful too, a real woman, the way he looked at me like he couldn't believe I was there, in his bed. I was nervous, awkward, then my body just took over, pushing and pulling, grabbing at him. He moaned into my mouth and I caught my breath, holding it against the pain. Our eyes locked. I felt him move inside me, knowing that he was the only boy I ever wanted to be with, would ever do this with.

He was sweet about it afterward, asking if I was okay, bringing me a towel and a glass of water. We cuddled, my head on his chest. I traced my fingers along his ribs, the fine sheen of sweat in the candlelight, kissed the scar on his side from when his dad pushed him out of a truck, and he shyly said, "I love you, Toni."

I heard laughter and looked to my left. Shauna McKinney and her girls were sitting on the tailgate of one of the guys' trucks. I hated it when they hung out back. Kim, Rachel, and Cathy weren't as bad as Shauna, but together they were some serious bitches, the I-don't-give-a-crap-about-anything-especially-not-you kind of bitches. Shauna was popular and pretty, with her long auburn hair and big blue eyes, played lots of sports, and had a super-athletic body.

She always seemed to have the latest gadgets or clothes and was the first kid in our class to have a decent car, a white Sprint her dad bought her. She exuded confidence and had this way about her, like she wasn't intimidated by anyone. She was smart too, got really good grades but made fun of teachers behind their backs so the other kids still thought she was badass.

Most of the girls in our class either feared her or desperately wanted to be her friend, which I guess was kind of the same thing in the end. Rachel Banks was her main henchwoman. Rachel used to be chubby when we were little kids and got picked on a lot, even after she lost the weight in high school, but then she started hanging around Shauna and people stopped messing with her. She was still curvy, with thick, straight brown hair, always wearing baby doll dresses with tights or short plaid skirts and knee-high socks.

Kim Gunderson was a ballet dancer and tiny, about my height. She wore a lot of black clothes, leggings with oversized sweaters and cool boots, and talked really fast. I'd heard rumors that she was gay, but no one knew for sure. Cathy Schaeffer was almost as pretty as Shauna, with long white-blond hair, pale green eyes, and a serious rack. Cathy was crazy and funny, always doing wild shit at parties. She also smoked, which was why the girls came out back.

I'd known all of them as long as I could remember, even used to be friends with Shauna. When we were twelve or thirteen, she liked this game where we'd call a girl up and ask her to come over, then call her a couple of hours before and say we didn't want her to come anymore—sometimes we'd just take off before the girl arrived. Shauna was also really good at mimicking people—she'd call a boy and say she had a crush on him using a different girl's voice.

When I told Shauna I didn't want to play the games anymore, she stopped talking to me for a week. I was devastated, especially when she and our friends walked by me in the hallway like I no longer existed, whispering and rolling their eyes. I went home crying every day. Finally, Shauna came up to me after school and said she missed me. I was so relieved I forgot what had even started the fight in the first place, forgot I didn't like how she was treating people.

Shauna was the daughter of a cop, Frank McKinney. Everyone knew him. He coached baseball teams and hockey teams, stuff like that. McKinney, as most people called him, wasn't around Shauna's house a lot when we were kids—he was usually at the station. Shauna's mother had died in a car accident when Shauna was five, and her grandma looked after Shauna but she wasn't very with it. At birthday parties she'd serve up a bunch of chips and hot dogs, put in a movie, then disappear into the other room for hours. Frank McKinney and his wife had had Shauna when they were eighteen or something. He was a big guy but not fat, just muscular and tall, and he walked with a confident swagger. He had a Tom Selleck mustache, a deep voice, wore sunglasses, and chewed gum, snapping it between his teeth. You could tell he was a cop even when he was in casual clothes by the clipped way he spoke, using short words and acronyms. And you could also tell his job was really important to him—he sent his uniform out to be dry-cleaned, kept his shoes polished, and his police cruiser was always clean.

Sometimes I got the feeling he was kind of lonely—he spent a lot of time sitting by himself, reading a book in the kitchen or watching the news. I don't think he dated much, and the few times he had a girlfriend they didn't seem to last long. We all felt bad that Shauna didn't have a mother and we knew it bothered her too, the way she would talk to our moms when she was at our house, polite and sweet, helping clean up after dinner, like she wanted them to like her.

Most of us kids were kind of scared of McKinney, but it wasn't like that for me. I just felt sad for him, though I was never really sure why. Whenever I thought about him, it was always that one image that held fast, him sitting in the kitchen for hours, the newspaper or a book in front of him, a cup of coffee, and the way he'd look up and out the window like he was wishing he was out there in his car, on patrol. Like he was wishing he was anywhere but in that house.

When we got to high school, I was getting tired of the way Shauna was constantly trying to play the rest of us against each other, saying one of us had talked about the other, leaving someone out of an invite, or making mean comments about our clothes and hair, then adding, "Just kidding!" The next day she'd tell you that you were her best friend and give you one of her favorite items of clothing, jewelry, or a CD she made just for you, which would make the others jealous. It felt like every week there was a flare-up and someone was upset. I was also getting tired of not being able to wear what I wanted—jeans and T-shirts, not skirts and blouses, which Shauna had decided should be our uniform.

When we were in ninth grade I mentioned to Shauna one day that I liked a boy named Jason Leroy. She told me she'd help. She threw a birthday party at her house and invited a few boys. Her dad was working and her grandma was supposed to be supervising, but she vanished into the TV room with a glass of something and a vague "Have fun, kids." Before the party, Shauna told me she heard Jason liked me but he was into "real women." She said I had to give him a blow job, and if I didn't, I was a chicken—they'd all done it. I was nervous at the party, but Jason kept smiling at me and asked me to go into one of the bedrooms. After we were necking for a while, he hinted that he wanted a blow job. When I balked, he said Shauna had promised him I'd do it and that's why he was there with his friends. If I didn't go through with it, he'd tell everyone he had a threesome with Shauna and me.

After the party, when I told Shauna what he'd said, and what he'd made me do, she was furious. She called Jason and said if he told anyone what had happened, she'd tell everyone at school that he had a small penis. We never heard a word more from him, but later that night Shauna started giggling and admitted that none of them had ever given a blow job to a boy—I was the first one.

I was really angry that Shauna's lies had set me up, but I tried to let it go because she'd stuck up for me. Part of me even relished my role as the now sexually advanced member of the group. A month later, though, Shauna developed a crush on Brody, a boy in my woodworking class. We'd often stay late to work on a project, and one day she walked by when we were laughing about something. I wasn't into Brody, not like that, but it didn't matter. After school, all the girls acted like I didn't exist. So I asked Shauna what was wrong.

"You were flirting with Brody."

"I was not! I don't even think he's cute."

"He's *totally* cute—and you've been crushing on him for weeks."

They were all standing there, glaring at me.

I knew what she wanted. I'd have to apologize, then they'd ignore me for a while until they decided to forgive me. But I was sick of Shauna, the power trips, the games. I'd had enough.

"Screw you, Shauna. Believe whatever you want, but it's not my fault Brody doesn't like you. Not everyone thinks you're hot, you know." I walked away. Behind me I heard her gasp, and then angry whispers.

I knew she'd retaliate but didn't realize how bad it would get until I went to school the next day. Turns out, Shauna had spent the evening spreading rumors that I'd been born with a penis—and tried to make out with her. She also told every single person anything bad I ever said about them—most of it stuff I never actually said myself, I'd just agreed with Shauna. After she was finished, I didn't have any friends for months, endured whispers and stares. I was so ashamed of my new loser status that I didn't say anything to my family, even when my mom kept asking why the girls weren't calling anymore. Nicole, who was younger than me but went to the same school, knew something had happened and asked me about it, but I didn't tell her either. My sister was the only person who talked to me at school, and if it hadn't been for her I'd have been even lonelier.

Finally, after gym class one day I dropped my shorts in the girls' bathroom and told them all to have a look. One of the girls, Amy, thought it was hilarious. She was a cool chick, dressed tomboyish like me—since Shauna had dumped me I wore whatever I wanted, camouflage pants and a tight-fitted black T-shirt, or big army boots with faded jeans and one of my dad's work shirts. The next day at lunch, Amy dropped her tray beside mine and said, "I've always liked girls with penises." We'd been best friends ever since, but I had a harder time trusting girls after the way Shauna had treated me—I was more comfortable with boys.

After that, Shauna moved on to other targets, made friends with Cathy, Kim, and Rachel—who instantly moved up the social ladder—and didn't bother me for years. Sometimes she was even halfway friendly, saying hello or smiling when she walked past. But then I started dating Ryan. I found out later that Shauna had been going to the pit every weekend hoping to hook up with him. He'd given her a ride home once when she was super-drunk but nothing had happened, although she tried, and then Ryan and I connected the next weekend. She'd hated me ever since, even more than when I dissed her about Brody.

I'd only run into Frank McKinney a couple of times since my friendship ended with Shauna. He gave Ryan and me a hard time when he caught us out at the lake one night but he just dumped out our booze and told us to go home. Ryan had also gotten caught siphoning gas off a logging truck that summer. McKinney didn't write up a report, just took him to the jail and gave him a tour, told him to smarten up, and said he'd be watching him from now on. And we knew he meant it.

I'm pretty sure McKinney didn't know what Shauna did with all her free time after her grandma died, probably thought she was home studying. She must've done enough to keep up with her grades, though she didn't have to try that hard, which pissed me off, but mostly she was hanging out with her friends or partying.

The girls were all watching me now from their perch on the other truck, whispering to each other, giggling.

I snuggled closer to Ryan and pulled his head down for another long kiss. I got really into it, wrapping my arms tight around him, loving that his hands were on my butt, smiling against his lips when I thought of Shauna watching.

When I looked back up, Shauna and the girls had left.

The next day after school, I was in the parking lot, waiting for Ryan by his truck and having a smoke, when a car pulled up so close it almost hit me. Shauna, in her white Sprint.

"Hey, bitch," she said as she got out. Cathy and Kim climbed out of the backseat, Rachel from the front. They all circled me.

"What's your problem?" I said.

"You're my problem," Shauna said. The girls laughed. I glanced over at them. Rachel had a mean scowl on her face, and Cathy had one of her big stupid smiles. Great. Nothing like being a chew toy for some catty bitches.

"I haven't done anything to you," I said. "Not my fault Ryan doesn't like skanks."

She got right in my face, so close I could smell her perfume, something fruity, like tangerine.

"You better watch your mouth."

"Or you'll what?" I said.

She reached out and gave me a shove. I stumbled into the truck.

I dropped my smoke and pushed her back, hard. Then we were going at it, fists flying, pulling hair. I could hear kids yelling as they ran over, cheering us on. The girls were screaming, "Kick her ass, Shauna!" Shauna was bigger than me and had the upper hand, but I managed to get free and was about to punch her in the face. Then an arm was around my waist, lifting me up.

"Cut it out," Ryan's voice said in my ear.

I was still spitting mad, wiping hair out of my face as he sat me down on my feet. Another guy was pulling Shauna away. Her friends were shouting insults at me. Ryan hustled me into his truck, threw my packsack in the back.

He started up the truck and tried to reverse out. Shauna was still standing by her car.

"Why don't you let Toni finish her own fights?" she yelled.

He yelled out the window, "Shut up, Shauna."

She gave him the finger.

We went back to Ryan's place. His mom was working another night shift and his dad, Gary, as he told me to call him, was sitting bleary-eyed in front of the TV.

He glanced up as we came in. "Hand me another beer, Ry."

Ryan gave him one and said, "We're going to my room."

His dad winked. "Have a good time."

That made me cringe, but it was nice not to be hassled, not that his dad didn't give Ryan a hard time about other shit. Most of Gary's arrests had been bar brawls or stealing stuff when he was drunk. Ryan said his dad didn't have sticky fingers, he had whiskey fingers. When he was really drunk, he'd get rough with Ryan. They'd come to blows a few times this last year—now that Ryan was bigger and tougher, his dad seemed to want to take him down even more, prove he was still the man. Gary had a job as a logger, which was seasonal, but Ryan did all the chores around the house and helped his mom out. I don't know why she didn't leave Ryan's dad. Her name was Beth; she seemed like a nice woman, worked a lot but was still caring, always smoothing Ryan's hair back, asking him if he'd had enough dinner, needed money for school. And you could tell she really liked her son by the way she laughed at his jokes and looked at him proudly.

We went to Ryan's room and I threw myself onto his bed while he turned on his ghetto blaster.

"You can't let Shauna get to you like that," he said.

"She started it." I'd told Ryan the basics of the fight on the way to his house.

"So what? Ignore her."

"Right, like *you* ignore someone who's giving you a hard time?"

"It's different with guys, usually when someone beats the crap out of someone, the other one backs off, but Shauna gets off on making you mad, so you're just giving her what she wants. If you ignore her, you'll piss *her* off."

I thought about what he'd said, staring up at the ceiling. It was true that the more I reacted, the more Shauna seemed to enjoy it.

"Maybe you're right. Maybe she'll run out of steam eventually."

He dropped down beside me, turned his baseball cap around backward with a cheeky smile, and started nuzzling my neck. He slid his body over mine and reached under my shirt, his rough hands scraping against my skin, sending shivers down my spine that made me want to curl into him. I let myself be carried away, by the hard beat of the heavy metal music, his touch, his warm mouth. I wasn't going to think about Shauna, wasn't going to let her win, but I couldn't help but feel a whisper of doubt. Was she *ever* going to leave me alone?

# CHAPTER THREE

## ROCKLAND PENITENTIARY, VANCOUVER

### MARCH 1998

The transfer van pulled up in front of the prison. I was in the back, in cuffs and leg irons, trapped in a metal cage like an animal. The doors of the van opened and the correctional officers let me out, their hands tight on my biceps. I shuffled forward, staring in terror at the imposing building. It was all gray concrete, the blocks stained in big streaks, like giant tears had swept down the sides. Razor wire wrapped around the top of the twelve-foot metal fence that circled the entire building, and guards in uniforms stood on towers, carrying machine guns.

Fifteen years. The words echoed in my head, but I couldn't fathom them, couldn't make myself grasp the reality of what that amount of time meant. As soon as I heard the judge's words and knew all hope was lost, something inside me had snapped off and disappeared way down inside. I felt removed from everything, like I was watching a surreal movie. They'd brought me over to Vancouver on a plane and I'd remembered how Ryan and I had planned on traveling the world. It seemed like a lifetime ago that we sat in his truck and dreamed of our future, of our big escape. We had wanted out of Campbell River so bad, and now I'd give anything to go back, even if it meant staying there forever.

I watched the officers' mouths move but couldn't focus on what they were saying, and they had to repeat themselves. I stared at my ankles as they led me inside. Shuffle. Shuffle. I was aware that my legs and wrists hurt but I didn't care. All I could hear was the whooshing of my heart and the words *fifteen years*.

They took my photo and gave me my ID badge. Next I was asked a bunch of questions while an officer filled out forms. "Have you had any thoughts of hurting yourself?" "Are you on any medications?" I answered no to all of them but I was only half listening, only half there. In another room two female officers ordered me to take off my clothes. I just stared at them. The mean-looking one with the bad haircut said, "Take *off* your clothes."

I'd been through this before, at the detention center when I was waiting for my bail hearing. I'd cried like a baby that time, sobbed in shame when they barked out their orders: Pick up your hair, stick out your tongue, lift up your breasts, bend over and cough. But this time, as I saw the annoyance and disgust on the officer's face, I started to wake up from shock, feel reality beginning to sink in at last. My sister was never coming home, and I was in prison. And then I found something I could grab on to, something I could feel with all my heart. I could feel anger. It rushed through my blood, hot and heavy and thick.

I stripped. I spread my cheeks. I coughed. And I hated them. I hated every person in that place who assumed I was guilty, every person who sat in the courthouse watching our trial like it was a show, and every person who'd lied on the witness stand. But most of all, I hated whoever had killed my sister, who'd taken her away from our family, taken away her chance to grow up, to have a future. I clung to the hate and wrapped it tight around me, a fierce blanket. No one was going to get inside my rage. No one would ever hurt me again.

After I had a delousing shower, they handed me my new clothes: four pairs of jogging pants, four sports bras, four pairs of underwear, four gray T-shirts, two sweatshirts, and one pair of running shoes. I was also given a bag of bedding and a small package of hygiene supplies. It was late at night and all the other women were in their cells. We walked down a cold and drafty hallway, the floors painted gunmetal-gray, the air smelling musty and stale, like death. I was coiled like a tight spring but I kept my head down, didn't look at any of the cells we passed. I could hear women's curious whispers, feel their stares.

My thoughts flitted to Ryan and I felt a sharp stab, an ache under my rib cage as I imagined what horrors he'd be facing. He was also at Rockland but in the men's prison across the road. We wouldn't be allowed to see each other, not even once we were on parole—which would be for the rest of our lives. I couldn't bear the idea of a life without Ryan, couldn't fathom how I was going to survive. Our only hope was to be found innocent. The lawyer said he was filing the documents so our case could get heard in the Court of Appeals. It could take three to six months before he even got a date for the hearing, but there might be a chance. I caught my breath for a second, swinging back from hate to hope.

The guard stopped in front of a cell, fit the lock into the key, and slid back the door with a loud clang.

"Here you go, Murphy. You're on the top bunk." I stepped inside, and he locked the door behind me with another loud clang.

I surveyed my cell. It was about nine-by-twelve, with a stainless steel toilet and a mirror over a small metal sink, everything in the open. One wall was covered with taped photos. On the bottom bunk a skinny woman with long straight black hair and arms covered in scars and tattoos was reading a book. I'd never seen so many tattoos on a woman. She was staring at me.

"My name's Pinky," she said.

"I'm Toni."

"You that kid on TV? The one who killed her sister?"

My face flushed, remembering the news trucks surrounding the courthouse, the cameras and microphones thrust in my face.

The words came unbidden out of my throat. "I'm innocent."

She laughed, a deep, rattling smoker's laugh full of phlegm. "Guess nobody told you we're all innocent in here."

I ignored Pinky, who was still laughing, as I made my bed. Then I climbed up to the top bunk, curled into a ball, my bag of toiletries tight against my stomach in case she tried to steal anything. I wanted to wash my face and brush my teeth but I was too tired, and too scared. I closed my eyes, started to drift off.

Pinky popped her head up and grabbed my arm. I tried to tug it back, but she was holding fast, her hands white claws with long nails. Her thin face looked like a skull in the dim light. I almost screamed.

"I wouldn't go around telling anyone that shit about you being innocent," she hissed. "They'll beat your ass."

She let go and disappeared down below. I stared up at the ceiling, my heart thudding, still feeling her fingers digging into my flesh. A few minutes later I heard her snoring. I pulled the thin blanket over my head, trying to drown out the sound, trying to drown out everything.

For the first few days, I stuck to myself and tried to learn about the terrifying new world I'd been thrust into. My mood swung between helpless rage, where I wanted to punch and kick something or someone, and depression. But mostly there was fear, whenever another inmate glanced at me, whenever I thought about how long I was going to have to stay in this place.

The prison was old, noisy, and housed about a hundred and eighty women of various security levels. The air was poorly ventilated, the corridors and stairwells dark and narrow. Everything felt cold to the touch: the walls, the bars on our cells, the floor. The prison was broken into four units. One wing was the minimum-security side, for women who were the lowest risk. Over on my side, there were two ranges. I had been placed on A Range, which was medium-security. Both ranges were long two-tiered banks of about sixty cells, but B Range was about half the size of A Range and was the maximum-security side. The other half of B was protective custody and the segregation unit.

I sat stunned, still trying to take everything in, while I was given an introduction class for general orientation, and a handbook with information on things like visiting, phone calls, and inmate accounts. I'd be going through an assessment over the next ninety days, where my institutional parole officer would look at my risk level and needs. Then they'd come up with a correctional plan. Everyone was polite, businesslike, and firm, and I tried to pay attention to what they were saying, but part of me kept screaming in my head, *No, this isn't for me. I don't belong here. I didn't do anything wrong. Nicole's killer is still out there!*

There weren't set visiting days, but I had to mail forms to anyone I wanted on my list. I also had to fill out a form to get a phone number approved. The cost of a call would be billed to the receiver—if I called collect. I was told it could be weeks before my phone number and visitor lists were approved. I could write people as much as I wanted, including Ryan, which was a relief, but all mail was inspected. I was allowed books, but a limited amount of paper, and each cell had a storage tote where prisoners could keep their belongings. There was a personal line each week for health and hygiene—anything else would have to be bought at the canteen. I was also allowed to purchase a fifteen-inch TV, a CD player, and a few clothing items like underwear and socks, or approved jeans. But I wasn't permitted to have more than fifteen hundred dollars' worth of personal effects in my cell. If I broke any rules I'd get a charge, which could be a fine or the loss of a privilege. If I did something really serious, I'd be sent to segregation. I wasn't allowed in anyone's cell, and I wasn't allowed physical contact with another inmate. At the time I didn't give a rat's ass about that part—there was no one I wanted to touch anyway. It would be years before I discovered that loss of physical contact was one of the hardest things to deal with.

For now, I struggled to adapt to the daily routine and all the rules. Guards shone their flashlights in the cells late at night and early morning, startling me awake after I'd finally fallen into a restless sleep, shivering under my thin blanket. They did hourly rounds and formal counts, the first at five in the morning. Then anyone who worked in the kitchens was sent down while the rest of us rushed for the showers. After breakfast, people left for work, went to programs, or hung out in their cells and the activity area. You got paid a little bit for working, five or seven dollars a day. The maximum-security-side prisoners had to remain locked in their cells unless they were working, but every hour they were given a chance to go to the activity area. After dinner we were allowed out in the yard if the weather was decent.

You were expected to work or participate in the programs, but I spent most of my time pacing my cell, sleeping, crying, or writing letters to Ryan—I was given a few pieces of paper and a pencil, which wasn't much more than a stub. We hadn't been able to have any contact for over a year, and then only at trial, so I was desperate to hear that he was okay. I didn't have stamps yet and was waiting for the canteen to open in a few days. I hoped my dad had been able to send money—everything seemed to take forever to process in prison.

After my arrest, I'd sworn to my parents that I was innocent, and I was pretty sure my dad still believed me, but my mom was a different story, especially since the trial. My dad was allowed to send some personal things, like CDs and some photos, but I'd been warned it would also take a while before the prison approved them. I'd asked for some of Ryan and our family, especially ones of Nicole. He'd paused on the phone when I asked for those, then agreed, his voice quiet. Mom had spent hours going through all our albums after the murder, crying, but I'd avoided even walking close to Nicole's photo in our house. And I'd hated seeing her yearbook photo on every news show, in every newspaper. But now, a year and a half later, I needed to see pictures of her, needed to remember everything about her, how she smiled, what she liked, what she didn't like, terrified that she'd slip from my memories, needing to keep her alive, somehow, in some way.

My institutional parole officer decided I should be in substance abuse programs because I'd been stoned the night Nicole was murdered, but I insisted I didn't have a drug problem and refused to attend. The parole officer was a small man, only a few inches taller than me, with tiny hands. I wondered if he liked the power he had over women in prison, if in the outside world they laughed at him.

"This is part of your assessment," he said. "If you don't participate in your correctional plan you won't be able to reduce your classification level. It could also affect your future parole eligibility."

"I'm innocent," I said. "My lawyer's filing an appeal—I'm getting out soon."

He made a note, his expression blank.

In the evenings I started to walk the track, around and around, passing the other women in their groups or the odd solitary woman running. Then one day I also broke into a run, zoning in on the feeling of my feet hitting the ground, each *thud, thud, thud* drowning out the constant thoughts in my head, the endless despair. I tried not to think about how much I missed Ryan and Nicole, tried not to think about my sister's empty room, all her belongings untouched. I'd never lost anyone I cared about before, not even a pet, and I was struggling to understand death, the permanence of it, the staggering thought that I would never see my sister again, never hear her voice. That she no longer existed. I wrestled with thoughts about heaven, about life after death, about where she might be now. I couldn't grasp that someone could just be *gone*. I'd also never experienced violence before and didn't understand how someone could have done those terrible things to my sister, couldn't stop thinking about how afraid she must have been, how much it must have hurt.

Each memory was a fierce blow, the grief wrapping so tight around me I couldn't breathe. And so I ran, over and over again.

My roommate and I didn't talk much. The morning after Pinky grabbed my arm, she gave me a brief rundown of the routine inside. Then her expression turned sly, her eyes narrowing.

"You got parents sending you money? I need a few things from the canteen, just until my old man sends money in a couple weeks."

"I can't buy you anything. Sorry."

We held eyes and I knew she was trying to intimidate me, but she was also nervous about it, her gaze darting around to see if anyone had heard us—no one was in the hall, and the women in the cell next to ours were loudly arguing. I had a feeling she'd timed it that way so she could save face if I turned her down.

"Don't matter none, if you're going to be like that." She turned back to her bed, muttering, "Just keep your shit tidy."

I didn't talk to any of the other inmates, just stayed to myself. I sat in a corner for all my meals and focused on my tray in the line for chow, but from the side I checked out the other women. They were mostly white, with some First Nations, and a few Asians. There were women who looked like men, short haircuts, broad bodies, a way of swaggering, sometimes grabbing at their crotches, which freaked me out. And some really hard-looking women who might have been bikers or druggies—those ones scared me the most. But the biggest surprise was how normal a lot of the women looked. A few of them were even kind of dowdy. Many were overweight, their skin sallow, their teeth stained. I saw plenty of tattoos, some really exotic and cool but others rough and faded. I didn't see many younger people, maybe a couple of women in their twenties.

None of them paid any attention to me until a big woman with gray hair pulled back into a long braid walked over to me one day. She held her head high, her shoulders squared, and walked like she was hoping someone would cause her a problem, but all the other women moved out of her way. She sat down beside me. "You in for murder, kid?"

My body tense, I studied her hands—each knuckle had a tattoo of an eye. Was she part of some gang? I glanced at her, then looked away. I remembered Pinky's warning but I couldn't stop myself from mumbling, "I didn't do it."

She gave me a poke in the ribs, a hard jab with her finger. My blood rushed to my face. I looked around for the guards, but they were talking to other inmates.

"Listen up, kid. I'm going to tell you how it is around here." I met her angry stare, noticed that she had dried saliva in the corners of her lips. "No one gives a shit what you did out there. You're in the joint now. Keep your cell clean and keep yourself clean. You need anything, you talk to me, not the guards. I run this place."

She got up and walked off. I stared at her broad back, looking away when she glanced over her shoulder. I pushed my tray to the side, having lost what was left of my appetite. No one on the outside had cared that I was innocent, and no one cared in here.

The woman next to me said, "You going to eat that?"

I'd barely had time to shake my head before she snatched my juice cup off my tray and speared my hamburger patty. I felt someone's gaze and looked up.

The woman with the gray hair was watching me.

# CHAPTER FOUR

## Woodbridge High, Campbell River

### January 1996

When Ryan dropped me off at home, it was late and I'd missed dinner. I came in the side door and noticed my dad tying some fishing flies in the garage. We used to go fishing all the time when I was little. We'd pack a lunch and spend the day out in the canoe. Now that I was spending most of my time with Ryan I didn't go with him as often, though I still liked fishing. Ryan and I had a few favorite spots on the river, but half the time we just ended up making out. Dad used to take me to the job site too, and I liked working alongside him. When I was five he bought me my own tool belt and I'd follow him around, hammering things.

All last summer I'd worked for him to pay off part of the car my parents had given me—a Honda my mom inherited when my grandparents died. It was a little junky, but once we fixed a few things and got some new tires, it should last me a couple of years. I was hoping we'd have it ready by spring so I could insure it and get a real job. Working with Dad was fun, and hard work—it had given me strong muscles in my arms and a flat, toned stomach, which Ryan loved—but I wanted to try something else, something that wasn't a family business.

Dad looked up when I came in the side door.

"Hi, honey. Where you been?"

"Over at Ryan's." My dad looked tired, his face pale, with bags under his eyes. He had a new subdivision contract and had been leaving early and coming home just before dinner. He had dark hair like me and Nicole—my mom was the only blonde—and olive skin that turned bronze if we were out in the sun for more than five minutes, so we looked more like him, in the face anyway. Mom was petite, with small hands and feet, narrow hips and shoulders, so we got our builds from her. She was tiny but she had muscles in her arms, and I was proud of having a hot, tough mom—you could see how toned her biceps were when she wore tank tops, and guys were always checking her out. Dad liked to tell people, "Pam's small and wiry, like a rat terrier," and she'd pretend to punch him.

Dad wasn't very tall either, maybe around five-nine, but he was stocky and had a good build from working hard, the backs of his neck and arms always tanned dark, his hands rough and his skin smelling like some kind of wood, cedar or fir, clean outdoor smells. Dad looked more like he should be a schoolteacher, though, with his kind face and glasses, than a guy who ran a construction company.

"Your mom's upset you didn't call." He was peering at me over his glasses now, admonishing.

"I told her yesterday I'd probably go to Ryan's after school."

"I think she'd appreciate an apology."

And I'd appreciate it if she got off my back once in a while, but that wasn't going to happen. My parents fought about me a lot. My mom thought my dad was too easy on me and that's why I got in trouble. The reason I got in trouble was because she was always so damn hard on me. When it starts feeling like you can't do anything right, there doesn't seem like there's any point. And it's not like I was really bad. I just didn't do things around the house as fast as she thought I should and I didn't spend hours doing homework, like my sister. I still got okay grades—I just didn't see the point in acing every test. Mom also didn't like how I dressed, with my rock band T-shirts, ripped jeans, and flannel shirts, or how I did my makeup, my eyes ringed in smoky shadow.

She'd say, "I know you're just trying to express yourself, Toni, but you might not realize the message it sends to people. If you dress like a hoodlum, that's how they'll treat you—like you're bad news. You used to dress so pretty."

Sometimes when Amy was over I'd see Mom eying up her army boots and her black nail polish. Later, she'd ask if I'd talked to Shauna lately, her voice kind of sad and hopeful. "Shauna's such a nice girl." Mom *really* didn't like me hanging out with Ryan, who she said was "heading for trouble."

When I'd tried to speak to my dad about how Mom was always on my case, he said, "She worries about you." No, she just hated that she couldn't control me, like she could control him and Nicole.

Dad was easygoing, which was kind of cool sometimes, like I could tell him stuff and I knew he wouldn't freak out, but he hated confrontation. If there was a fight between me and my mom, he left the room. Mom was scrappy and didn't take shit from anyone, which was embarrassing as hell when she was going off on a sales guy or a supplier. We'd always knocked heads, but it wasn't as bad when I was little. She could be a lot of fun and had this crazy imagination—she'd tell us stories for hours. And she came up with fun new things for us to do every weekend, maybe taking a day trip down to Victoria and checking out the undersea gardens, or hiking around one of the gulf islands. Sometimes the two of us would drive around and drop off flyers for Dad's business, then we'd get lunch and talk about all the houses we saw and who might live in them. I liked how excited she'd get about new ideas, how she'd ask for my opinion. She was also smart, and good to talk to if you had any problems, like she'd give advice—Dad would just tell you everything would be okay. She just didn't know when to stop.

She was so overprotective all the time, worried that something would go wrong and something bad would happen. She didn't trust me to figure stuff out on my own. Dad said it was because of her childhood—her mom was this super-anxious person, who was practically agoraphobic, and her dad was an alcoholic who'd disappear for days—and because she loved us so much. I tried to understand, but I hated having to answer a million questions, about my day, school, and friends, like she had to know every single thing that was happening in our lives, hated how she was always trying to guide me to do things her way.

Now that I was older, it had gotten worse. The more she tried to control me, the more it felt like tight bands were wrapping around me, sucking all the air out, sucking *me* out, which just made me want to do the complete opposite. But what bugged me most was that I could tell she didn't really like me anymore. It felt like she was always disappointed in me, and kind of embarrassed, but mostly angry, like it drove her nuts that she couldn't get me to be what she wanted. Sometimes I wondered if she even loved me anymore.

When I went in, Mom was doing some paperwork in the office. Dad was good with people and an awesome builder but he had no head for numbers, so Mom ran the business side of the company. She had her hair up in a loose ponytail, some of it coming undone. Without any makeup, she looked tired too, the dim glow of her desk light accentuating the hollows of her cheeks. She was wearing one of my dad's T-shirts and a pair of jeans. She could look pretty when we went out for dinner or something, but she also spent a lot of time wearing work boots and talking to the guys at the construction site. One of the reasons it bugged the hell out of me when she was riding my ass about my clothes.

I tried to pass by without saying anything, but she heard my footsteps and turned. "About time you got home. Thanks for the call." Her words were snarky, but she looked concerned, and I wondered if I was part of the reason she was tired, which made me feel bad. I wasn't sure which annoyed me more.

"I was at Ryan's. I told you that."

"You mentioned you might be going, but I'd appreciate it if you actually phoned home and kept us informed. I didn't know how much food to make."

"Okay, fine, whatever." I walked down the hall.

She followed me out of the office. "No, it's not *fine*. I'd like an apology."

I threw a "Sorry" over my shoulder, then mumbled under my breath, "that you're a control freak."

"What did you just say?" She pushed open my bedroom door as I was taking off my T-shirt.

"Hey, a little privacy, please?"

"As long as you live in my house, you obey *my* rules, Toni. And we've asked you time and time again to call if you're going to be late."

I felt another wave of anger. She was always calling it *her* house, like we didn't have a say in anything.

"I said I was sorry. Now can you leave it alone?"

"I don't know what to do about you, Toni." She crossed her arms over her chest. "Your attitude has gotten even worse since you've been seeing Ryan."

"You're just on my case because you don't like him."

It sucked that my parents couldn't see how good Ryan was, how good he was to me—he'd saved up to get me a necklace for my birthday, a black onyx star on this cool leather cord. They didn't see the sweet letters he'd write me, not trying to be all tough like some guys. There wasn't anything we couldn't talk about, embarrassing stories, our hopes and dreams. Ryan made me feel like I was *normal*, better than normal. My parents just saw that his father was an ex-con and that Ryan drove a big loud truck and listened to heavy metal music.

"Ryan's the only good thing in my life right now," I said.

She leaned against my doorframe, took a breath, preparing for a this-is-for-your-own-good lecture.

"That's the problem, Toni. He shouldn't be the only good thing. I know you have strong feelings for him—I'm just worried that you're forgetting everything else in your life. What about your other friends?"

"I still see my friends, but they have boyfriends too. Ryan and I like to do the same things. What's wrong with spending time with him? You just hate him."

Ryan rarely came by the house. Even though my mother was polite, I felt tense and uncomfortable—like she might count the silverware after he was gone. Dad and he talked about fishing and hunting, guy stuff. But one night after Ryan was over for dinner my dad came to my room and said, "Ryan seems like a nice boy, Toni, but you know his father's another story. They aren't the best people for you to be spending so much of your time with. Just think about it, will you?"

I was sure Mom had put him up to the conversation, one of those see-if-you-can-talk-sense-into-her things, but I felt betrayed. I'd thought my dad would see Ryan for who he really was. It was so unfair—Ryan wasn't anything like his father. I didn't speak to my dad for a week, and we never talked about Ryan again, not like that. He left it to Mom now.

"It's not about whether I like him," she said. "I just want you to have a future." She took a breath, paused for a moment. "Look, when I was your age I had fun too, dated the bad boys, but I got married young and never got an education." I knew my parents had gotten married when they were still in their twenties, but I didn't know it bothered my mom. She quickly added, "I don't regret getting married, but I wished I'd done a few things first, like go to college, so I could get a career of my own. You have lots of time to get serious with someone."

"Just as long as it's not someone like Ryan, right?"

"I'm saying you should keep your options open."

"I love *him*." I was near tears, which made me angrier. "Why can't you see that? Don't you want me to be happy?"

"You're *eighteen*."

"I still know what love is."

"So keep dating him, but at least try to get into college this fall, take some courses, see what you want to do, but don't give up on everything."

She was trying to sound like she was on my side, but I knew she just wanted me to go to college so I could forget about Ryan and meet some guy who had a better future, according to her bullshit standards anyway.

"I don't want to go to college—I'm not Nicole. I want to work for a while, save some money, then travel. I want to see the world."

"That's all fine, but you should have some sort of a plan."

"That *is* my plan. As soon as I graduate and have enough saved, I'm moving out."

"You're moving out?" Her face looked stunned.

"I thought you'd be happy about that."

"I hope you're not moving in with Ryan."

"You got it."

"How—" She stopped, her mouth still parted like she was so upset she couldn't find the words. "How are you guys going to afford your own place? You have no idea how to manage a budget. You have no money."

She was treating me like I was five, as though I had no clue about life.

"I've got enough to fix the car and get insurance soon. Mike from the Fish Shack said I can start waitressing on the weekends this spring, then in the summer I can go full-time."

"The *Fish* Shack? Toni . . ." She was already shaking her head. "You can't work there."

"Why not?"

"You really want to waitress? Do you have any idea how hard it is? And you hate taking orders from people. You'll work late all weekend, then you'll be tired all week at school. I'd rather you just kept working for your dad."

Where she could keep an eye on me, she meant. I was sick of her speaking for me, like she knew everything about me and what was best for me.

"Well, *I'd* rather work at the Fish Shack. I need more experience for a résumé, Mom—not just working for my father." I had her there, and I could see her mind working, trying to figure out her next argument. I quickly added, "Ryan already has a job at the outdoor store and he can start taking people out on some guided tours in the summer. His mom is putting aside some stuff for us too, like towels and linens and kitchen things. We don't need much to get started."

I smiled at her, feeling smug at how well we'd planned everything, and at her look of jealous annoyance when I'd mentioned Ryan's mom.

"So you've already told his mother? And she approves?"

"Yeah, she's happy for us. She likes me." I dug the knife in a little deeper and was rewarded by the telltale narrowing of my mom's eyes.

She tried a new tactic. "Even if you have a job, you can't just come and go as you please. As long as you're living here, you need to let us know where you are, and when you're coming home." She was grasping, still trying to find something to control.

"That's fine." I pushed past her and went to the bathroom. "Are we done? I'd like to have a shower now."

She shook her head. "There's no talking to you."

"I don't know why you even try." I closed the door.

"Don't use all the hot water!" she shouted.

When I got out of the shower, Nicole was studying in her room, books spread out on the bed. Our rooms were on the same side of the house, with a shared bathroom in the middle. My mom also had an office on the upper floor, but our parents' bedroom was on the lower floor, at the opposite end of the house. My bedroom walls were decorated with posters of rock stars: Nirvana, Soundgarden, Pearl Jam, Alice in Chains. My bedspread was dark purple, the walls the darkest gray my mom would let me paint them, and there were usually piles of clothes on the floor, jeans, some of Ryan's T-shirts I liked to wear, one of his jackets. I also had a collection of notes and letters from him, things he'd given me, little keepsakes like movie stubs or a decal from his motorbike. I kept those in an old tool kit my dad had given me with a padlock, the key around my neck.

Above my desk, a corkboard was covered with photos of Ryan and me. My favorite one, taken last summer at the lake, was on my night table. It was the two of us sitting on his tailgate and kissing. Sometimes when I couldn't sleep I'd rest the photo on my chest, feeling like Ryan was there with me. We'd never spent a whole night together and couldn't wait until we had our own place, where we could have the privacy and freedom to do whatever we wanted.

Nicole's room was tidy—no clothes on the floor—and painted in a light shade of buttercup-yellow, with sheer curtains and pretty pillows on her sage-green bedspread. Her room looked springtime fresh, which suited her sweet, cheerful personality. Right now she looked serious, though, chewing on the end of a pencil as she studied. She was probably trying to make sure she got an

A+ on her next test—I'd seen her cry when she got a B once. She never let that happen again. I got annoyed with her a lot, mainly because I wished she didn't need to be so perfect all the time. I also wished she had more backbone and stuck up for herself. It pissed me off seeing her give in to what Mom wanted, doing her chores right away, always telling her exactly where she was going and who she was with, then calling a million times, never late.

She was pretty, my sister, and looking at her now I could see that she'd become even prettier over the last couple of months. She'd lost that soft, baby roundness to her face and was getting cheekbones, which made her eyes look bigger—she'd gotten Mom's brown ones, I got Dad's green ones.

She was also starting to fill out in the top, like she might get bigger boobs than me, and her hips were definitely curvier. But she still dressed young and girly—lots of pink and peach shirts, nice jeans, never showing any skin, barely any makeup although she was allowed. The most I'd see her with was some lip gloss and a light coat of mascara. She had black hair like mine, but she usually wore hers in a ponytail and didn't tease it up with hair spray. We looked alike when she wore it down, similar features, hair, and small build, but up close we didn't at all. Nicole's expression was sweet, open and inviting. And me? Mom said I looked at the world like I was daring it to mess with me.

Nicole was a bookworm, always reading something, often swapping books with Mom. She tried to get me to read some of her books, V. C. Andrews, Anne Rice, or Jean M. Auel, saying, "Try it, Toni, you might like it," but reading just wasn't my thing. I never could focus long enough.

She put down her book and smiled. "How was your date?"

"We just hung out at Ryan's. It was okay."

I could tell she had a crush on Ryan. He didn't come over often, but when he did she found a reason to be around, getting something from the kitchen or the fridge. Ryan was always nice, asking about school or something, but I'd glare at her until she finally got the hint and left us alone.

"What are you reading?" I asked, still at Nicole's door. I felt bad that when she asked the night before if she could borrow some of my good conditioner I told her to buy her own. Normally I didn't mind sharing once in a while—I'd only said it because I was pissed at Mom. We'd just had another fight about my doing too much laundry and using all the detergent. Mom made me buy my own stuff, soap, shampoo, makeup if I wanted anything decent—she wasn't just controlling with my life, she ran the family finances with an iron fist.

Nicole looked up, surprised by my interest.

"It's a sci-fi book, about these kids who are super-smart and they have to save Earth from some aliens. It's called *Ender's Game*."

I glanced down the hall, my parents' voices carrying from downstairs. I could tell by Mom's tone that she was complaining about me again.

"I wish someone could save me from Mom," I said.

"Maybe just do what she wants once in a while, then you guys wouldn't fight so much. It's not that hard to make a phone call."

"Maybe she should let *me* do what I want once in a while."

"She's not going to, though. She's not like that, but you've almost graduated. Can't you try to get along until then?"

Nicole always seemed so wise, or at least mature for her age, and so reasonable, so unlike me.

"Probably not." I laughed.

"You're a nut bar." She shook her head. "She's only like that because she cares."

"No, she cares about *you*."

"She loves you too."

"Not the same way."

"I'm just easier." She shrugged, accepting her role in the family.

"Yeah, you are." It was hard not to like Nicole, and most people did, teachers, kids at school, my own damn boyfriend, which was one of the reasons I found myself picking on her sometimes. And she was so sweet—one of those people who always remembered birthdays and made personal cards. But, and it always made me feel bad thinking this, she was also kind of boring. She just never really did or said anything interesting. Not to me, anyway.

I'd noticed lately that she was changing, though. I heard her talking on the downstairs phone a few times when Mom was working, giggling and whispering, then she'd change the subject when I came into the room. I figured she was talking to her best friend, Darlene Haynes, another goody-goody. I doubted they were up to much of anything. What kind of secrets could my sister possibly have?

"You can use my conditioner if you want," I said.

"Really?" She jumped off the bed and ran to me, giving me a hug, enveloping me in her sweet lemony scent. "Thank you, thank you."

I hugged her back, wondering why she was so excited about some stupid conditioner. Since when did she care that much about how she looked?

The next week at school, Shauna kept hanging around in the hallway outside my locker or waiting in the parking lot with the other girls. If they saw me with Ryan, they'd walk away, but it was clear that they were trying to intimidate me. Ryan kept telling me, "Just ignore them," but I didn't know how much longer I'd be able to handle it.

That Friday night there was a party at one of Ryan's friends'—his parents were out of town. Ryan picked me up and we smoked a joint on the way over. My parents knew I smoked cigarettes and probably had their suspicions about pot. Mom had found cigarettes in my coat pocket once, and I'd endured a few lectures about that. I told them I didn't smoke a lot, which was true, but I didn't tell them I liked it because it was a ritual Ryan and I had together. I loved going to Tim Hortons with him, getting a coffee, then sitting at the beach and sharing a smoke. I'd started smoking pot the same year. I figured it was okay as long as I stayed away from the hard drugs. I liked how it made everything in life feel a little better, softer somehow, like shit just didn't matter as much. We weren't hurting anyone or doing really stupid crap. We were just having fun.

By the time we got to the party, things were well under way. The guys were standing around, smoking and drinking beer. The girls were hanging out on the couches or dancing in the living room, trying to look sexy for the boys.

I was feeling good, sitting on Ryan's lap in the corner, making out and grooving to the music, when I caught a flash of a face I didn't expect to see.

Nicole.

I sat up. "What the hell is she doing here?" I'd seen her at home earlier, getting ready to go out, but she'd told Mom she was going to the movies with Darlene, who picked her up in her car.

Ryan turned around, noticed Nicole. "Wow, she looks good."

I gave him a shove. "Hey!"

"Not like that," he said. "I'm just not used to seeing her dressed up and stuff." He gave me a kiss. "I've only got eyes for you, babe." I knew he hadn't really meant anything by his comment about Nicole, it was just an observation—and he had a point. She did look good, really good.

Her hair was loose and shiny black, and she'd used some rollers or something to style it, so it fell around her face and down her back in thick waves. She was wearing more makeup than normal, her eyes seeming exotic and mysterious and her lips shining with gloss. It even looked like she was wearing some foundation and blush, her skin smooth, and her cheekbones insanely high.

The real surprise was her clothes. She was wearing fitted jeans, faded and low-slung on her hips, with some cool brown belt I'd never seen before and a snug white T-shirt that rode up when she lifted her arms, revealing a bit of tanned skin around her waist. The shirt was V-neck, showing a hint of cleavage I didn't know my sister had, making me think she might even be wearing a push-up bra. She looked older—older than me. And super-hot.

I got off Ryan and made my way over to Nicole, who was swaying back and forth to the music, plastic cup in her hand. She was talking to Darlene and they were both looking over at a group of guys. One of them was kind of looking back at her. I tapped Nicole on the shoulder. She spun around. "Toni!"

She was flushed and her eyes were glassy. I lifted the drink out of her hand and took a sip that filled my mouth with a burst of sour peach. A wine cooler. I handed the drink back.

"What are you doing here?" I said.

"Just hanging out." She was nervous, her gaze flicking to Darlene, to the group of guys, back to me.

"I thought you were at the movies."

"And I thought you were at Ryan's."

It was the first time she'd shown some scrappiness, her chin jutting out and her eyes angry. I was surprised but also kind of impressed.

"Mom would flip out about you being here and drinking," I said.

She hesitated, then said, "Screw you, Toni. If you tell, I'm telling."

What the hell had gotten into my sister? I was pissed and wanted to put her in her place, but Mom would freak if she knew we were at someone's house when his parents were away. Did I want another fight with her over a stupid party?

"Fuck you." I grabbed Nicole's drink back and walked away.

She yelled, "You don't have to be such a bitch to me all the time!"

I went back to Ryan, still fuming.

"What's going on?" he said.

"I don't know why she's here—but she's up to something. She's acting totally weird."

"She's just trying to have fun, like we are."

"Maybe. . . ."

I watched my sister, who was now walking off with Darlene. It looked like they were going out the back door to the patio. Over her shoulder, she gave the group of guys another look. One of them broke off and also headed outside. I couldn't make out much about the dude, just that he was tall and wearing a hockey jersey. I had a feeling he was meeting up with Nicole, where I couldn't see them. Should I check on her? Was the guy drunk too? He looked older than her. Then I thought about my mom, how she was always checking up on me, acting like I wasn't smart enough to figure out shit on my own.

Nicole was sixteen now—she could look after herself.

Shauna and her girls showed up later, dressed to the nines, their hair and makeup perfect. They came over to talk to some of the people I was hanging with—Amy, her boyfriend, Warren, and a couple of his friends, one who was sort of going with Cathy. I snuggled against Ryan and kept talking to Amy like I didn't see Shauna there, but I could feel her watching me, checking out my clothes, my shoes, my hair, trying to mess with my head. I sat my drink down on the counter, then went to the bathroom and stared at myself in the mirror, put on a little lip gloss, fluffed up my hair. When I felt calmer, I went back out.

Shauna was standing close to one of the guys—an all-right-looking dude named Cameron, who was whispering in her ear while she smiled coyly. Good, maybe she'd be too distracted to give me a hard time.

I leaned back against Ryan, who smiled and said, "You okay?"

"Yup." I smiled back, reached for my beer, took a swallow—and my mouth filled with a foul taste. I spit it out, spraying a couple of the girls standing near me, who all jumped back, saying things like "Oh, my God!" "Gross!"

I wiped at my mouth, gagging and coughing.

"What happened?" Ryan said.

I choked out, "Something in my drink," and rushed to the bathroom again. I rinsed my mouth with water, but the taste lingered.

When I finally rejoined the group, I looked at my beer bottle and spotted the telltale signs of a cigarette butt—some tobacco was still floating on the surface and clinging to the sides. I said, "Someone put a cigarette butt in my beer!"

"That's messed up," Ryan said, looking at the bottle.

I glanced up. Shauna, Kim, and Rachel were laughing so hard they were almost bent over. Cathy was also smiling, but her cheeks were flushed and she didn't meet my eye.

"You think this is funny?" I held the bottle in my hand like I was going to throw it. Rage coursed through my veins.

Shauna laughed. "You should've seen your face."

"Did you do this?" I stepped forward. Behind me, Ryan grabbed my shirt.

She rolled her eyes. "Oh, my God. Talk about being paranoid. I wasn't even close to your stupid drink."

Had one of the other girls done it? Now I noticed that Amy was also hiding a laugh. "Sorry," she spluttered. "It was just so funny, your expression."

My face flushed with angry embarrassment—and hurt. My best friend was laughing at me. It was like ninth grade all over again.

Ryan's friend, Greg, patted my back. "You're supposed to smoke your smokes, not drink them."

Everyone started laughing again. I even heard Ryan chuckle behind me. I turned around, ready to spaz at him, but he whispered, "Just go with it."

Still angry, it took me a moment to catch on, then I realized what he meant. I started laughing, like swallowing a cigarette butt was the most hilarious thing in the world. The harder I laughed, the more everyone laughed with me. Shauna's face changed from malicious joy to anger to rage before she shut it down and pretended to go along with the others.

"Let's get out of here," she said to her girls when the laughter died down. "This party's getting boring."

At the door, she gave me a final look. I smiled and waved.

# CHAPTER FIVE

After the woman with the gray hair sat by me at lunch, Pinky, who'd been watching from where she worked in the kitchen, told me that her name was Janet.

"You don't want to mess with that bitch," she said. "Just listen to what she tells you but don't get too friendly."

I started observing Janet at lunch, careful never to look directly at her. Janet had a few girls she hung out with. One was really quiet—she watched everything with these intense blue eyes that reminded me of a wolf. She was short and stocky and they called her Yoda. There was also a younger girl, maybe in her twenties, who walked with all kinds of swagger, her eyes constantly flicking left and right, like she was itching for a fight. She talked really loud, using lots of hand gestures and swear words. Then there was Sugar, closer to Janet's age, who had big brown eyes and a soft, sweet voice, suiting her nickname. She was Janet's girlfriend, but I never saw them making out or anything.

Pinky said they weren't allowed to within sight of any guards, but gay women would sneak into the showers or each other's cells. Sugar and Janet were always breaking up because Janet would cheat on her, but then Sugar would forgive her. Janet also had a husband on the outside who sent her money.

When I'd been there a couple of weeks and was still waiting for my phone and visitor lists to be approved, Janet started sitting by me in the yard while I was cooling down after my run. She'd tell me how things were inside, who I should talk to, who I should avoid. I wanted to avoid everyone, especially her, but I was careful to stay neutral when she told me stuff, and didn't talk a lot. Sometimes I'd see her younger friend watching, the one who looked scrappy. Her nickname was Mouse, because she was always nibbling on crackers from the canteen. She'd run out and then have to trade cans of pop or packages of noodles for more. I could tell Mouse was jealous of the time Janet was spending with me and hoped she was too scared of Janet to do anything about it.

Janet and a few other women played cards every day in the activity area, which was where most the inmates hung out, but no one invited me to sit down. I still didn't have any friends inside—Pinky ignored me outside our cell—but I was fine with that. I didn't think of myself as one of them.

I started working in the kitchen, scrubbing pots and pans during the afternoon shift. To pass the rest of the time, I mostly slept or wrote long letters to Ryan. I cried so hard after reading his first letter that Pinky actually looked worried and asked me if I was okay. I rolled over and turned my back to her. I spent hours sleeping the next day, didn't even bother showering. On my second day of lying in bed, Pinky gave my arm a shake and said, "Better get your shit together or they'll throw you in the hole on suicide watch."

I dragged myself out of bed after that, but when I got a letter the next week I plummeted back into depression, thinking about

Nicole, what had happened to her, and about Ryan, wondering if we would ever see each other again. He was always so positive, writing about how we were going to be free soon, how we'd finally be together. His lawyer had hired a private detective and Ryan was sure he'd find who really killed Nicole. But it seemed like such a long time away, such a long shot, and I didn't know how I was going to make it.

I tried rereading Ryan's letters. I had to stay hopeful, had to focus on how much we loved each other. But my shock and disbelief were starting to fade, and I was spiraling more and more into the anger that had helped me get through my first day at Rockland. I woke up angry. I went to bed angry. When Pinky was down in the kitchen working, I'd wake up and start counting the days until we might hear about the appeal. I'd see each day stretching out in front of me like a long line of empty slots, and the despair and anger would build until I was sure I would crack.

My phone number list was finally approved, and I called home often, using the phone card I was given. Mom never answered. My dad's voice was the only link to the outside world, and I needed to hear that he still loved me, that he always would. He told me that Mom missed me, that she was out shopping or taking a nap, but I knew he was lying. She just couldn't bring herself to talk to me, couldn't stop hating me. She'd never said so, but I saw it in her eyes, the way the hope leaked out of them with each witness's testimony at the trial, until she could barely look at me. She just sat there, holding back sobs, Dad's arm around her back, rubbing her shoulders, his face bleak. She didn't even show up the last few days of trial. That's when I knew she had stopped believing in me.

My dad wrote me letters, telling me to be strong, hang in there, they'd see me soon. Mom never wrote, never even signed the letters. It was the first thing I did, turn to the last page and look for her signature, but it was never there. I still hoped that she'd look into her heart and see I couldn't have done it. Then, after I'd been at Rockland for a month, they both came for a scheduled visit.

Dad's face was flushed after he came through security but it paled when he saw me sitting in my prison clothes, the guard watching everyone in the room through a window. I hated thinking of my parents going through the metal detector, having their stuff X-rayed, putting it all in a locker. The room had about seven tables, four chairs around each one. A couple of families were at two of the other tables. We weren't allowed any physical contact, and I ached for a hug from my dad or to even hold his hand. They slid into the chairs across from me.

I tried to smile, fought to hold back tears thick in my throat. I didn't want to freak them out. I looked at my mom, searching her eyes, wondering if it was a good sign that she had come. Her face was even thinner than the last time I had seen her, giving her dark hollows beside her lips, which were pale. Only a faint trace of lip liner was left, as though she'd chewed off all the color. Her hair was pulled back tight, the ends ragged in her ponytail. She was also starting to show some gray at the roots, so she must not have been going to the salon anymore for her monthly touch-ups. The lines were deeper around her eyes, which had the same exhausted, desolate expression she'd worn since the murder.

"Are you okay, honey?" Dad's face was so kind, his voice so familiar. The voice I'd heard late at night when I battled measles or the flu, when I fell hard off my bike. But now there was this, and it couldn't be fixed.

"I'm all right," I said, doing my best to smile. "Three meals a day and I can sleep all I want. What's not to like?"

Dad tried to smile back, but Mom looked shocked for a second, anger flashing in her eyes: *How can you make jokes? After what you did?*

We retreated into silence. Dad glanced at Mom like he was waiting for her to say something, but her eyes were darting around to the other inmates and their families, her body stiff. Her hand fidgeted with her shirtsleeve, running the hem between her fingertips, twisting the buttons. For a moment she looked like she might rip one off, maybe run around the room screaming. I wished she would. Anything would be better than the contained agony she'd been walking around in. I wanted to reach out and grab her hand, hold her still, wanted to tell her a hundred times how sorry I was for bringing Nicole out with me that night. But I'd already said it before and she just stared at my mouth, watched my lips move. She couldn't hear the words, no matter how many times I said them.

"How are you, Mom?" I said.

She pulled her mouth back in a smile, but it was strained and made her lips look even paler—bloodless. "Good, busy, with your dad's work. We're finally getting some contracts."

I'd heard her hushed conversations in her office. *We aren't getting any calls. I don't know if we'll be able to keep the company, but we need the work, the lawyer bills, all the expenses.* And another part of me died with guilt. Dad had reassured me over and over again. *Don't worry about us, we'll be okay.* Now justice had been served in the eyes of everyone in town, and my parents were getting work again. Everyone was moving on, except me.

Dad started chatting about one of the new houses he was building while Mom fiddled with her shirt and nodded once in a while, agreeing or adding a bit of information. They could've been at a dinner party, making conversation with a stranger. I was just as bad. I told them my new roommate was okay and I was settling in. I had no intention of joining any of the programs but I mentioned a couple, wanting to make them think I was focused on the future. I was finally being the responsible daughter they'd wanted. I tried to sound upbeat and positive, anything to make my dad's shoulders ease down from where he was holding them around his neck—the way he'd been holding them for over a year.

Dad bought some chips and Cokes from the vending machine, and we shared them as we talked. Mom only nibbled on the corners and took tiny sips of her drink. The chips were dry in my own mouth, the carbonated liquid getting trapped in my throat, the sugar giving me a headache. I wished I had a cigarette.

They didn't stay long, only a couple of hours. Then Mom looked at her watch, said, "We should get going . . . the ferry traffic, and you have to do that estimate tonight." She glanced at Dad, and something was exchanged, some signal. She had come here for Dad, I saw it clearly now. He had made her come.

I met my dad's eyes. "I love you, guys. Thanks for visiting—I really miss you." The tears I'd been trying to hold back were now rolling down my face. I wiped them away quickly, before the other inmates saw me losing it.

Dad said, "We love you too," and turned away, blinking hard like he was trying hard not to cry too. Mom was silent beside him while he composed himself.

"We'll come back as soon as we can, hopefully in a couple of weeks," he said. "Hang in there and stay strong for us, okay?"

"I will." I glanced at Mom and she gave me a little smile, so forced it looked painful.

As they walked toward the exit Dad reached for Mom's hand, but she didn't hold it back, her hand limp in his. I remembered their raised voices behind closed doors after Nicole was murdered, how they'd retreat into silence whenever I entered the room. I'd thought my going away might help their marriage, but it seemed I was still the wedge driving them apart. I couldn't stand thinking I'd taken something else from them that night.

———

After I'd been at Rockland for almost two months, Janet sat down beside me outside. I'd gotten another letter from Ryan that day and hadn't felt like going for my run. I was just drawing circles in the dirt with my finger over and over.

"Pinky tells me you've got a boyfriend on the men's side," Janet said. "He was your codefendant?"

"Yeah." I kept drawing circles.

"Girl, you can do easy time, or you can do hard time. Those letters you're always writing, they just screw with your head."

"I need him."

"Things go a lot better in here if you don't have anything left to miss on the outside. This is your world now, your home."

My finger paused. "This isn't my home."

"Yeah, it is, kid. And you thinking you ain't one of us, pretending and hoping like the guards are going to open up your cell one day so you can bounce out of here, is just making shit harder for yourself. You're not going anywhere for a long time. And you're not doing him any favors either. Men, they like to fix shit. If you're sobbing to him, that's going to make him go insane."

"It's not like that with us."

"Just ask yourself if you feel better or worse after you get a letter from him." She stood up. "It's probably the same for him."

After she left, I thought about what she'd said, still tracing circles in the dirt. Was she right? Was I making things harder on Ryan? I thought of how tough the last year and a half had been, not seeing him, how much harder it got when I'd finally been able to see him in court, where we still couldn't be natural. Now we could only write. It was painful, being reminded of how much I loved and missed him, but I wasn't going to stop. I needed him to talk about our future, how things would be when we were found innocent, when Nicole's real killer was finally punished and she got some justice. I needed him to fill me with enough hope to carry me through the endless days. It was the only thing that kept me going. Our appeal date was only a month away. Thirty days. I could make it through another thirty days. I'd already made it through sixty.

I stared down at the unbroken circles in the dirt. *That's me and Ryan, unbroken.*

A few days later, my parents made it over again. I hadn't seen them in a month. I knew they'd already used up a lot of their savings on legal fees and couldn't afford to come every weekend—the ferry was expensive and it was an all-day trip, an hour-and-a-half drive from Campbell River to the ferry in Nanaimo, the hour-and-a-half crossing time, then Vancouver traffic all the way out to the prison. My mom seemed even tenser this visit, her hands tearing at her fingernails every time I mentioned the appeal or lawyer.

Finally she said, "If it doesn't go through, we can't take it to the Supreme Court. We can't keep paying for the lawyer."

My dad grabbed her hand, pulled it away and held it tight, so she couldn't pick at her nails. "Toni doesn't need to hear that right now."

"I think Toni does need to hear this." Mom's tone was bitter. "We're nearly broke. We've lost just about everything." The words hung in the air, tears forming in her eyes. She wasn't talking about money anymore.

I felt tears building behind my own eyes. "I'm sorry, Mom."

She stared down at my dad's hand holding hers and slumped back in her chair like all the energy had left her body. Dad stroked her hand with one thumb. I thought about how long it had been since I'd felt a soothing touch and shook off a stab of jealousy, ashamed.

"Don't worry, Toni," Dad said. "Everything's going to be fine."

Mom's head snapped in his direction so fast her ponytail swung. I remembered when we were growing up how much she hated it when he'd say, "It's fine, don't worry," or "Everything's going to be fine." She'd say, "You can't know that, Chris." And now I knew exactly what she was thinking.

*Nothing will ever be fine again.*

She stood up, her voice breaking as she said, "I can't do this." She hesitated, looking down at me like she wanted to say something else, but then she turned and rushed toward the exit, her hand over her mouth like she was holding back the words. Dad's face was red as he watched her leave, and he was breathing fast, his forehead shiny with sweat. I worried about his health. Mom wore her stress on the outside, but what had all of this been doing to my father?

He met my eyes. "Your mother . . . I should make sure she's okay. I'm sorry, honey. She's still struggling."

But she wasn't. She was done, and we both knew it.

As he got up and walked away, I heard a noise to my left and glanced at the other table. Mouse was sitting with her family, her mother beside her. They were talking and laughing. She looked at the exit, where you could still see my father leaving, my mother long gone, and Mouse gave me a slow, mean smile.

After that terrible visit, my father still sent letters each week but with no mention of a visit—just news about work, the house, friends, and only brief mentions of my mother, what she'd planted in the yard, how she was repainting the fence and had bought a new patio set. I tried to read between the lines, tried to tell myself she might still come around one day. I wondered sometimes now if my father also believed I was guilty but loved me all the same. I don't know which thought was more painful, and I knew I'd never be able to ask him.

I finally got the package from my dad with the photos I requested and Pinky grudgingly made room on the wall. Her side was mostly covered with photos of her kids—she had four, all in foster care. She cried sometimes because one of the foster parents wasn't sending letters or bringing the kid for visits. Every week she'd get letters from the other ones, or little handmade cards. I taped up all the photos of Nicole and Ryan, then lay on my bed and stared at them until I finally fell asleep, Nicole's sweet smile chasing me into my dreams.

A month later, I called my lawyer for news about my appeal, my hands shaking on the phone. His voice grim, he said, "I don't have good news."

I listened, my heart thudding loud in my head. The judges at the appeals court had decided that the original judge had made the right decision. The next step would be to take it to the Supreme Court, but it would be costly, and I could sense that he thought it would be futile. I also thought of what my mom had said and knew there was no way I could ask them to take this any further.

"What about legal aid?" I said.

"Without any new evidence or witnesses, you'd have a tough time finding anyone who's going to take this on."

"There has to be someone who can help." I felt panicky, my last chance slipping through my fingers.

"I've asked around, but no one was interested."

I sat silent, his words crashing down around me. *No one was interested.*

"I'm really sorry, Toni."

"There's *nothing* we can do?"

"Something may come to light in a few years." He was quiet for a beat. "But some people, they find it's easier to just do their time and learn to have some kind of life inside. You'll still be a young woman when you get out."

"But I didn't do it!" Anger was starting to choke my throat, making it hard to think, to speak. I looked around, took in my surroundings. This was all I was going to see for years, cement and metal. He was telling me to let go of hope. To give up. And he was right. There was nothing left.

"Try to focus on the future, take some courses," he said.

"My life is over." I hung up the phone.

My dad came for a visit a couple of days later, and he was alone. I noticed how gray his hair was getting, seemingly overnight. He had pouches under his eyes and he looked like he'd lost weight. I was just about to ask about Mom when he quickly said, "Your mom has a bad cold and couldn't make the trip, but she was sorry to hear about the verdict."

I nodded and forced a smile so he wouldn't think I was too upset. I knew I shouldn't be surprised that she hadn't come, but it still stung. She'd probably taken the court's decisions as another sign of my guilt—she'd been right about me all along. I had a feeling she'd have been more upset if I'd been freed and gone unpunished for Nicole's death. I wondered if they'd been fighting about me.

"Are you guys okay?" I said.

"We're fine. Everything's fine."

I wished he would just be real and tell me what was actually happening for them, but I knew he wouldn't. Just like I wasn't going to tell him what was really happening for me on the inside.

It had been like that for years with us, ever since my life started imploding in high school. Why would anything change now?

We talked for a while, but I couldn't get lost in the chatter. The stuff he was telling me about the outside, a new house they were building, things that were happening in town, either frustrated me or made me sad that I wasn't a part of them. I tried to disconnect from the pain he was stirring up, the noise in my head, but then I went to a hard place, an angry place where I wondered how he could talk about such trivial things when I'd lost what was probably my last chance at freedom, when Nicole's murderer was still out there. How could he move on like this? When I was in high school it felt like we weren't in the same world—now it felt like we weren't even in the same universe.

"I'll try to come back next month, okay, honey?" he said at the end of the visit. "Your grandma wants to come next time."

I thought of my grandma with her aching legs and varicose veins, traveling hours to see her granddaughter in jail. She was the only grandparent I had left—my dad's mother—and we'd been close when I was growing up. I'd spend weekends at her house, and she taught me how to make pierogies. She'd come to the trial, her head shaking at any negative testimony, her face determined and angry. She told me she knew I couldn't have done it and had written me a few times in prison. But I was scared to think that might have changed for her.

"You don't have to do that, Dad."

"What do you mean?"

"It's expensive and it's a long trip. You work hard all week—and Grandma, she'd be sore, sitting all day in a truck. I don't want to do that to her."

"Hey, don't worry about us, okay? We want to support you any way we can, and we miss you." I imagined him going home alone, Mom and him having dinner. Did they talk? Or did she give him the silent treatment for visiting me, for betraying Nicole?

"Dad, it means a lot that you've been coming, but it's really hard on me too—reminds me of everything, you know? And I get homesick. I can't do any visits for a while. We can write and stuff, but right now I need to get used to life in here, okay?"

"Okay." He nodded but he was blinking back tears. I was crying too.

"Don't cry, Dad. It will be better for us, I think—and for Mom."

He met my eyes and gave a sad smile. This time I didn't wait to watch him walk away. I got up first and went back to the guards, back to my cell, back to hell. I had done it. I'd pushed away the last family member who cared about me.

# CHAPTER SIX

## Woodbridge High, Campbell River

### January 1996

Monday after the party, I headed out to the parking lot at lunch to wait for Ryan. A car drove past me with some kids I knew from school. I was about to wave hello but only got my hand up partway when I noticed that they were all looking at me and laughing about something. What was their problem? I dropped my hand and kept walking to Ryan's truck, trying to convince myself that I was imagining things—they were probably laughing about something else. Then I noticed what someone had written in the mud on Ryan's tailgate:

*My girlfriend is a dirty slut. She gave Jason Leroy a blow job in ninth grade.*

I was frantically trying to wipe it off when Ryan came out. "Shit," he said when he saw it.
"It had to be Shauna." I studied his face, worried. It was bad

enough I'd fooled around with Jason, but he'd gotten into drugs the last two years and been suspended a couple of times, plus he hung out with the skankiest girls.

Ryan did look furious, but his anger wasn't aimed at me.

"If I catch her doing that again, she's going to have to deal with me."

"What are you going to do?" I felt relieved but was still shaken up by Shauna's crude message.

"I'll figure out some way to embarrass her. I know a few guys who've messed around with her." He looked at my face, saw how upset I was, and said, "Don't worry about it, babe. No one probably saw it."

He pulled me in for a hug. But I knew they *had* seen it. Over his shoulder I noticed some kids by their car looking at us and laughing. Ryan heard them and turned around, his shoulders squared.

"You got a problem, assholes?"

They shut up, one of the guys holding his hands out in a hey-we're-cool gesture. But it didn't matter what Ryan said or who he threatened, it was already all over school—kids whispered and giggled when I walked down the hallway to my afternoon class. I tried to look like I didn't care, but my cheeks were hot and I felt close to tears.

After school, Ryan and I got coffee at Tim Hortons and drove around on some back roads. We'd been silent for a while, just listening to the music, smoking cigarettes, both of us thinking, when he finally said, "Was it true?"

"Is what true?"

"About Jason. Did you, you know . . ."

My face burned. I'd hoped he wasn't going to ask. "He was different back then. And Shauna . . ." I told him the whole story, how she'd set me up, how Jason had pressured me. At the end, I said, "Are you pissed?"

"At you? Nah. It was a long time ago."

But his voice sounded kind of distant, and when I reached for his hand he didn't hold it as tight, and he didn't look over and smile like always. I stared out the window, blinked back tears. I couldn't wait to graduate, to leave this stupid school and Shauna far behind.

Ryan dropped me off. We kissed and he said, "I'll see you at school tomorrow," but I watched him driving off, feeling anxious when he burned rubber at the end of the road. I knew it was crazy, but I couldn't help worrying, for the first time ever, that he might break up with me, that this had changed things between us. My mom was serving dinner, but I said I wasn't feeling well, ignored her curious look, and went straight to my room. She'd be the last person I'd confide in about a problem with Ryan—hell, she'd probably throw a party and celebrate. Safe in my room, I put on some music and lay on my bed, my hand on my stomach, trying to hold in the sick feeling. I told myself it would be fine, Ryan would get over it. Then I got mad. If Ryan wanted to dump me over something I did three years ago, he was a jerk. It's not like he'd been a total saint before we met. Still . . . my gaze drifted over to my photo of us.

I couldn't imagine my life without him, couldn't imagine facing school or even walking down the hall if I didn't have Ryan. The thought was so awful, the pressure in my chest enormous. I went into the bathroom and turned on the shower, then stayed under the hot spray until I felt a little better, the terrifying emotions flowing out of me. It was going to be okay. It had to be okay.

An hour later I was on my bed writing Ryan a letter when I heard a soft knock at my window. It was Ryan. He was wearing a brown knit hat pulled low, almost to his eyes, and an older leather jacket, open over a gray sweater. His cheeks were ruddy from the cold. I motioned for him to stay there and checked that my door was locked. I could hear my parents talking downstairs and dishes clanging in the kitchen. I was pretty sure they wouldn't be able to hear anything, but my window could be loud, the wood tight so that it always squeaked when I slid it open. I turned up my music, then opened the window fast.

"What are you doing here? My parents are downstairs."

He must have climbed up to the roof from the tree behind my house. The tree Nicole and I had climbed down last summer, sneaking to the beach for a late-night swim, coming home cold and shivering but exhilarated by our bravery.

"I missed you." He smiled.

I didn't smile back, still upset about earlier. "You could've called."

His smiled dropped. "I had to see you. I'm sorry, baby. For how I was being after school. I don't like thinking about you with anyone else, and sometimes I forget it hasn't always just been you and me, you know?"

"It's the same for me when I see your ex."

He leaned into the window, grabbed some of my hair, and pulled me closer until we were eye to eye. "I never felt anything for her like I do for you. She was nothing. What we have is real and for-ever, okay?"

"Okay."

We kissed for a long time, him still sitting on my roof, the cool winter air wrapping around us and swirling into my bed-room, my hands on his warm back under his sweater. His hands on my face, my hair, our mouths desperate, needing to show each other how much we mattered, how this was all that mattered.

The next morning at school, Amy met me at my locker and said, "Oh, my God. I just heard. Are you and Ryan okay?" She'd been sick the day before and never saw what Shauna had done, but she'd already heard the rumors. When I told her what Shauna had written and how Ryan and I had made up last night, she gave me a big hug and told me not to worry about it, that Ryan was a good guy.

"And don't worry about Jason Leroy," she said. "I've messed around with a few losers myself." I laughed.

At lunchtime, Shauna drove by me and Ryan while we were making out in the parking lot. I peeked at her from the corner of my eye. Shauna's face fell when she saw us, and it was obvious she was trying not to stare, but she looked shocked. The other girls weren't smiling either. I kissed Ryan harder.

The next day at school Amy didn't come to my locker in the morning, which was unusual. We always walked to our first class together—Ryan's was in the other building. Thinking she might still be sick, I headed down to her locker, passing a few kids who gave me dirty looks in the hallway. One of the girls, Tricia, was someone Amy and I hung out with sometimes. She was a toughie like us, always wearing black and had lots of piercings. When she passed by, she gave me a shove with her shoulder.

I stopped. "Hey, what's wrong with you?"

She turned around and said, "I can't believe you did that to Amy."

"Did what?" I was getting a sick feeling.

"Like you don't know."

Then I saw Amy coming down the hall toward me, a few of our other friends behind her. Her face was angry but she also looked like she'd been crying. She stopped in front of me. "Thanks a lot, Toni."

"For what? What's going on?"

"I heard what you told Warren. He *broke up* with me."

"This is insane. I haven't talked to Warren—I don't even know what you're talking about."

The girls behind her were all shaking their heads and rolling their eyes. I heard one of them whisper, "What a lying cow."

"I know you called him last night and told him I cheated on

him at Christmas with Nathan." Amy looked around, saw how many people were watching. "Which is a total lie."

Amy *had* fooled around with Nathan, but I'd never said a word to anyone. Not many people knew, just Nathan and a few of his friends. One of them was Cameron, the guy Shauna was getting cozy with at the party. I had a feeling he'd told Shauna—and Shauna must have called Warren, pretending to be me. I remembered how good she was at mimicking people when we were younger, how she could copy the exact tone and pitch of their voice, how she even called home for me once and fooled my own mother.

"I never called Warren, Amy. It had to be Shauna—she was pissed that she didn't break me and Ryan up. Why would I do something like that?"

"Warren *swore* it was you." Amy's voice rose. Now kids were stopping in the hallway to listen.

I was too stunned to defend myself. I could only stand there and take it, my heart beating fast. But Amy was still going strong.

"Warren told me the other stuff you said, about how my parents were poor and he could do better than me. That I dressed like a homeless person."

"I would *never* say that." Amy bought all her clothes at the thrift store and tried to pretend it was cool, but I knew she'd rather have new stuff.

"God, you can't stop lying."

My shock and confusion were wearing off and now I was also pissed.

"You're nuts if you believe any of this crap. Think about it, Amy."

But Amy wasn't thinking anymore, didn't want to hear the truth. "You think your relationship with Ryan is soooo perfect, like no one else can have a boyfriend. He's the only thing you even talk about anymore."

Was *that* what this was really about? Amy was jealous?

"That's not true," I said. "I still call you to hang out."

"Yeah." She snorted. "When Ryan's busy. You're totally lame now."

"Screw you, Amy. You're the one who was always canceling our plans so you could follow Warren around—no wonder he broke up with you."

Amy's face was red, tears filling her eyes. "I *hate* you."

She spun around and walked off. Some kids followed, others stood around, waiting to see what I would do. I could barely move, still clutching my binder. My face was burning hot. *Ryan, I have to get to Ryan.*

I ran down the hall, away from everyone, and skipped my first class, hiding out by Ryan's truck, waiting for him to come out for a cigarette break.

"Toni, what happened?" he said as soon as he saw me. "Are you okay?"

"I hate this school and everyone in it." I wiped away angry tears.

He pulled me in for a hug. I hung on tight, my heart finally slowing as I felt his solid warmth, the strength in his body.

He murmured against my hair, "We're almost out of here."

I tried to focus on his words, but I kept hearing Amy say "I *hate* you." I'd never had anyone say that to me before. Had never felt like someone meant it.

The next few weeks at school, all through the rest of January and the first week of February, were brutal. Ryan and a few of his friends were the only people who would talk to me. Even the guys' girlfriends would give me the cold shoulder if the boys weren't around. I was doing terrible in my classes. My mom and I had a big fight one night, after she said, again, that I was spending too much time with Ryan, and she used my grades as proof. I told her she didn't know what she was talking about. She tried for the reasonable thing, sat on my bed and said, "Then talk to me and tell me what's going on. None of your friends call, your teachers say you're surly and difficult, you hide out in your room for hours . . ."

I was so embarrassed, hearing what my life had become, that I flipped out completely. "Maybe you're the problem. Did you ever think about that?" Then I stormed out of the house and walked down to the river. My dad came and got me an hour later.

"I don't know what's wrong," he said, "but I hope you know you can always talk to us—no matter what. If it's drugs—"

"Jesus Christ, Dad. You're as bad as Mom."

"We're worried about you."

"Well, don't be. I'm fine." But I wasn't, and he knew it. He rested his hand on my shoulder and didn't say anything else. I was disappointed by that in an odd way. Part of me wanted him to press, wanted him to force it out of me. But he'd given up, and so had I. When we got home, my mom was in her office. I closed my door and turned on my music. She knocked a little while later but I ignored her. I heard my dad say something to her, then they both walked away.

I'd tried to call Amy a couple of times, but her mom said she didn't want to speak to me—and the way her mom's voice sounded, stiff and cold, told me that Amy had confided in her. It made me feel even worse, thinking her mom believed I'd really said all those mean things. She'd always been so nice to me.

Nicole had heard what happened, but I was too upset to even talk to her. I also didn't want her telling Mom all about it because then she'd get involved and probably talk to our teachers or something stupid like that. I told Nicole some girls had been spreading lies, and acted like I didn't give a shit, blowing it off. But inside, I was a mess. I was barely eating and was losing weight.

Ryan was really upset with me about it, saying, "That's a stupid way to deal with it. You *have* to eat."

We got in a fight about it one night when I couldn't finish my hamburger, hadn't even touched my fries. I tried to explain that I just didn't have an appetite, food turned my stomach, but he kept pressuring me to take another bite. Finally I said, "Jesus, Ryan. Get off my back and stop treating me like a little kid!" I threw my food out and made him drop me off early. Then I tossed and turned for hours, feeling bad for how I'd snapped at him when I knew he was just worried about me. *I* was worried about me.

I closed my eyes and sent Ryan a mental message. It was something we'd started doing a couple of months ago. If something was bothering one of us, we'd close our eyes and mentally tell each other our problems. My fights with my mom. His fighting with his dad and worrying about his mom, who was working all the time, so tired she could barely drive home. The next day we'd check if the other person had sensed something and we always had, always knew when the other was upset.

Around one in the morning, Ryan came to my window, knocking softly. I opened it a crack, holding my breath against the noise.

"What are you doing here? My parents—"

"They're sound asleep. Your dad has his window open and I could hear them snoring."

"Nicole might hear you." She was a pretty solid sleeper, but you never knew.

"Stop worrying so much. Let's go for a drive."

"Now?"

"Yeah." He held up a joint with a smile.

If I got caught I'd be in big shit, but my life was already so screwed up it didn't seem to matter anymore.

Ryan and I drove around for an hour, smoking a joint, filling the truck with the sweet scent of marijuana while Pearl Jam wailed in the background. We didn't talk about anything serious, not until we parked up at the lake, overlooking the water. Then he turned to me.

"I'm sorry I was giving you a hard time," he said. "But it scares me that you're not taking care of yourself."

My face hot with shame, I stared out at the water. "I know. You don't have to be with me if you don't like it." It was a challenge, one I didn't really mean, and he knew it.

"Shut up. I'm not going anywhere. I know it's because things are so shitty at school right now, but you have to hang in there and push past it."

"Things are more than shitty. I don't have anybody."

"You have me."

I turned to him, tears dripping down my face.

"I miss Amy." Though I'd been spending more time the last year with Ryan, which had obviously annoyed Amy more than I realized, Amy was still my best girlfriend. I missed her sense of humor, missed talking about music, our boyfriends, helping each other with homework, gossiping, all of that.

"I shouldn't have said that stuff about her following Warren around," I said. "She was kind of right, I haven't been calling her as much. I feel really bad."

He wiped away one of my tears with his thumb. "I know, babe. But don't forget Amy's also pissed she got found out—it's not your fault she cheated on Warren. You guys might still work things out."

I took a breath, looked at him, and said, "Tell me again how good things are going to be soon."

We talked for a while about the apartment we were going to get, the stuff his mom had given us, how much money he'd saved, all the places we were going to travel. I closed my eyes and focused on his words, letting my head drop against the back of the seat, letting the marijuana take over. He was right, none of this shit counted in the big picture. School was over in a few months. I could make it until then. Screw Amy if she didn't want to be my friend anymore. If she was willing to believe Shauna, she was an idiot.

Ryan stretched out on the front seat with his head in my lap. He lifted up my shirt and rested his head on my belly for a moment, his cheek warm against my stomach, his breath sending shivers down my legs. He kissed my stomach.

I put my hand in his soft hair, running my fingers through the strands, tugging on a few. He whispered against my skin, "You'll always have me."

It was now the middle of February, and Ryan had taken me out for a nice dinner for Valentine's Day—at a fancy restaurant, where they brought warm bread to the table. I'd even managed to clean off most of my plate, happy that he loved the cologne I'd given him. At school, Amy and our friends still weren't talking to me, but a lot of the outright hostility in the halls—shoves, glares, hateful comments—had died down. Just being ignored was a blessing. Shauna still made snide remarks whenever I was around, but they didn't sting as much from her as ones from my own friends. Or at least the people I'd thought were my friends.

One lunch, I was playing floor hockey with some of the guys in the gym, while Ryan was off working on his truck, when Shauna decided to join the game. She was on the opposite team, of course. Rachel and Cathy were watching from the side. Kim was probably rehearsing—she was in the school play and I hadn't seen her with the girls as much recently. More often she was with one of the other girls who was playing the lead part, and I wondered if she was trying to break away from Shauna. Good luck with that.

At first the hockey game went okay. I was making some great passes, Shauna bringing out my competitive streak. Then she started getting closer and closer, crowding me. I tried to stay cool, to push back a little and not get cornered. But she kept coming at me, trying to slash me with her stick. Finally she hit me across the knuckles. It hurt, and I spun around and slashed her legs. She pushed into me with her shoulder. Now I was really pissed. I dropped my stick and used my whole body to slam into her, knocking her down. Then I jumped on top of her, straddling her torso, and started slapping her face. One of the girls, Rachel or Cathy, was screaming in my ear and pulling my hair. But I didn't stop, just slapped harder. The guys around us cheered. Finally, a teacher showed up and separated us. He hauled us off to the principal's office. The principal sat us in opposite rooms and called in our parents.

My mom and dad showed up. Dad looked like he'd just had a shower and I felt bad, knowing he'd had to leave the job site to come to the school. He gave my shoulder a squeeze, but Mom barely glanced at me. I tried to assess her mood. How angry was she? Her cheeks were flushed and her hair a little messy, like she'd brushed it fast. She'd been stressed out lately, buying some new properties to flip, and I remembered she had a meeting that afternoon with her Realtor. She was probably furious that my crap had interrupted her.

The principal said, "I'm sorry to have to call you in like this, but Toni was caught fighting on school grounds, so we're going to have to suspend her for a week."

"That's not fair," I said. "Shauna started it—she kept slashing at my hands!" I never did like this principal—and I knew he didn't like me. He was an older guy, gray hair, potbelly, and supposedly married to some rich chick—their kids were in private school, which I always thought ironic. Like our school wasn't good enough. We'd had a few run-ins before, mostly about my lipping off to teachers.

"We'll be talking to her father as well," he said, "but Shauna's saying you caused the fight and she was just defending herself.

There are some other girls backing up her story. They also say you've been threatening Shauna. "

"They're her *friends*. They're lying for her. This is such bullshit." I shouldn't have been surprised—it was the way it always was. Everyone believed Shauna, but it still amazed me how many times she got away with crap.

Mom turned to me. "Toni, watch your language." She faced the principal again. "I'm sorry it's come to this, but hopefully she'll learn her lesson." She shook her head and kept speaking as though I weren't there. "I can't control her anymore. We've talked and talked to her, but nothing is getting through."

My dad said, "Is there anyone other than this girl's friends who saw what happened? It would be good to have another side, seems a little biased . . ."

I smiled at him. *Thanks, Dad.*

The principal said, "The other students aren't sure what happened, but we're looking into Shauna's role in the fight."

I already knew how that would go, how everyone would cover for her or wouldn't want to get involved.

My dad looked angry but he didn't say anything else, just glanced at me, disappointed. He wasn't the only one.

Later, while I cleaned out my locker and my parents waited in their truck, I saw Shauna's father go in with her. Shauna saw me watching and gave me the finger. A couple of minutes later I heard laughter in the principal's office and remembered that Frank McKinney and the principal played on the same ball team.

I found out later that Shauna had only been suspended for two days.

That night I was sitting on my bed, flipping through a magazine and still fuming about what had happened at school, when my mom came to my room. She didn't knock, just pushed open the door and looked around.

"I want you to clean this up."

"I'll do it in a minute."

"I know you, Toni. You won't do it until I come in here and nag at you again. Put down your magazine and clean this room. It's disgusting."

Okay, so my room had gotten a little messy. When I got home from school, if I wasn't with Ryan, I just hid out in my room, napping or listening to music, dreaming about the day we would graduate—cleaning up seemed exhausting. It wasn't too bad, though, just a lot of clothes mostly and a couple of coffee mugs with moldy coffee on the bottom. I was still pissed that Mom had never even asked for my side of the fight. I'd tried to explain on the way home, but she said I had to find a way to control my temper, like it was all my fault.

"I'm reading this article, then I'll do it," I said.

She snatched the magazine out of my hands and flung it across the room. I stared at her. Mom could lose her temper sometimes, but she mostly just yelled and screamed.

"I said *now*." She spun around and slammed the door.

I waited until I heard her go downstairs, my heart pounding, then picked up the magazine. Screw her. I wasn't doing anything she said now. My jaw was tight with anger, the words blurring on the page in front of me.

Nicole knocked at the door, whispering, "Toni? You okay?" I let her in.

She leaned against the doorframe. "Why don't you just do what she says?"

I threw myself back down on the bed. "Because she's not being fair—she's just pissed at me about the fight."

After dinner, I'd told Nicole about the fight, so she knew it wasn't my fault. She'd been cool about it, giving me a hug and helping with the dishes.

Now she said, "She'll get over it."

"Maybe, but it's not going to be anytime soon."

"So what? If you just do what she wants, she'll leave you alone."

She was right, but that wasn't the point, and it annoyed the crap out of me that her answer to everything was to do whatever Mom wanted. What about what I wanted? Ever since we were kids, anytime I had a fight with Mom, Nicole would check afterward that I was okay, giving me a hug or trying to cheer me up somehow, but she always wanted me to smooth things over and be the one to apologize. I used to do it sometimes, thinking maybe Nicole was right, but I was sick of being the one to compromise when Mom never listened to me.

"I wish you would just leave *me* alone." I picked up my magazine.

She closed the door. A half hour later my mom opened it. When she saw that I was still reading, she yanked the magazine from my hands, grabbed the upper part of my arm—hard—and jerked me off the bed.

Too shocked to say anything, I pulled myself free but kept my arm held up as a shield. For a moment I thought she might slap me—her hand was raised, but then she dropped it and said, "I told you to clean this damn room."

My fear turning to anger, I yelled, "It's not even that dirty! You're just being a control freak."

She yelled back, "I'm sick and tired of your attitude, Toni!"

I held my arm, my eyes filling with tears that I blinked back. She was grabbing stuff off the floor and throwing it around. "You live like an animal." She picked up a pile of my clothes, threw it in my face. I flinched when a belt buckle hit my shoulder. She picked up some shoes, threw them at me while I cringed.

"Clean this up right now or you can *get the hell out of my house.*" She left, slamming the door so hard this time my mirror rattled on the wall.

Crying now, I picked up my laundry. *Soon Ryan and I can get out of here. Just a few more months. Then they can all kiss my ass.*

Mom came to my bedroom later that night. This time she knocked, but then she walked in before I could even answer.

"Can we talk?" she said.

I rolled over, facing the wall.

"I'm sorry I grabbed you," she said, "but you can't brush me off when I'm trying to speak to you—it's rude and you know it's going to cause a fight." I didn't say anything. She sighed and said, "You and I need to start getting along better. I'd like to try, but you need to work with me."

She was quiet, waiting for me to speak, but I just stared at the wall, tears trickling down my face. She left, closing the door behind her with a soft click that felt final, like I had just ended something, but I wasn't sure what.

The next week I was lying on Ryan's bed, going over my beefs with my family for the tenth time.

"Babe, you need to let it go," he said.

"You don't take crap from anybody."

"I take crap from my dad all the time."

"My mom's a total bitch."

"She's not that bad."

I rolled over, my mouth dropping open. "You're kidding me. She flipped out just because I didn't clean up my *room.*"

"No, she flipped out because you were ignoring her—you knew it would piss her off. That's why you did it. You were taking your anger out on her."

I rolled back over. He was right. I'd been angry at Shauna, and how no one believed that she caused the fight. I couldn't control any of that, so I did the one thing I could do, which was to make my mom mad. Watching her lose it had made me feel powerful. Still, I wasn't ready to admit that part of it was my fault.

"You shouldn't take her side—she hates that we're dating." I'd never really put that in words before, but Ryan had obviously sensed it for himself.

"I'm not taking anyone's side, you shit." He gave me a nudge. "Just telling it like it is. It would be great if she liked me more, but there's nothing I can do about it, so why waste the energy."

Ryan was the kind of guy who never worried about what other people thought of him. He was nice, but he sure as hell wasn't a people-pleaser. When his friends bummed too many rides, he'd ask for gas money. If they didn't have any cash, he didn't give them a ride, simple as that. He'd help friends out, sure, working on their trucks and stuff, but he expected the same in return and if it looked like someone was using him, he stopped hanging out with them.

"It still pisses me off," I said. "Mom's been in an even worse mood this week because the neighbors are away and my dad's going over there every day watering their plants and stuff. She thinks he's doing too much for them."

"Are these the neighbors who party all the time?"

"Yeah, they're always having people over." We lived outside of town, in a rural area within walking distance from a river. All the houses were newer—my dad had built a lot of them—with big pieces of property. Many of our neighbors had money, their driveways full of cars, boats, RVs. And the Andersons next door threw the biggest neighborhood parties. My parents would walk over with a bottle of wine, then stumble home hours later, laughing and joking with each other. I liked that even though they were really different, they were best friends.

Ryan looked up at the ceiling, like he was thinking. His arms were folded underneath his head, making his biceps flex in his T-shirt. Ryan had an endless supply of concert shirts, this one from Nirvana. But he'd never seen a real band play live. We always talked about going together once we had more money.

I rested my chin on his chest. "What?"

He gave me a lazy smile. "Bet they have lots of booze over there."

I smiled back. "Probably, yeah." I added, "My parents are going to my uncle's for the weekend. But I'm supposed to stick around the house and I can't have anyone over."

"Do you know where the key to the house is?"

"Hanging by our back door." I snapped my fingers. "And they wrote the alarm code down on a list of instructions they gave my dad—it's on top of the fridge."

"Want to have some fun Friday?" He grinned. "Both my parents are home, so we can't come over here, and Dad's been drinking more lately."

I'd noticed the fresh bruise on Ryan's arm. I kissed it now. He grabbed me hard, gave me another kiss. Then he said, "I think we both deserve some fun."

That Friday Nicole took off with the phone, whispering behind her bedroom door. She'd been acting funny since that party and I had a feeling she was seeing that guy, though he never showed up at the house. We were allowed to date at sixteen, so she must be hiding him for a reason. I still suspected he was older but didn't recognize him from my class. Was he older than me? Maybe graduated? Mom wouldn't like that. A half hour later I figured Nicole was finished, so I picked up the phone downstairs.

"Hey, I'm using the phone!" Nicole said.

"Sorry. I thought you were done. How much longer you going to be? I have to call Ryan."

"I'm not sure. We—"

"We're talking, okay?" A young male voice, kind of jerky. "Why don't you just wait your turn?"

Shocked, I said, "Who's this?"

"None of your business. Get your sister off the phone, Nic."

Now the guy was pissing me off. Why was he calling her Nic? And not telling me his name? What was up with that?

"Listen, you little shit—"

Nicole said, "I'll call you back," and hung up.

I ran up to her room and pushed open the door. "What's the matter with you? Who's that guy?"

"You had no right to talk to him like that." She was really upset, near tears. "Now he's going to be mad at me."

"Calm down. What's the big deal? He was being rude to *me*. I just have to call Ryan and then you can call this dude back." She still looked upset. "Who is this guy anyway? He sounds like an asshole."

She screamed, "Get out of my room!"

I screamed back, "No problem!" and slammed the door behind me. But I was surprised and shocked at my sister's behavior. What the hell was going on?

Ryan and I waited until it was dark. Nicole was still in her room. I knocked and said, "I'm going out," but she didn't respond. I grabbed the keys and the alarm code, then walked down through the backyard to where Ryan was waiting. He'd parked his truck in the shadows down the street. The neighbors' house was on an acre and set far back from the road—perfect. No one from the nearby houses could see what was going on, but just in case, we still used flashlights, laughing in the dark as we crept up on the house. I turned off the alarm.

Inside the house, we snuck around, breaking out in hysterical giggles as we bumped into each other. We lit some candles Ryan had brought and found the liquor cabinet, pulling out vodka, Southern Comfort, whiskey. Ryan found a suit jacket in the closet and put it on. I found some high heels and rolled up my jeans, strutting around while he whistled.

"We should put them back," I said. "I don't want to wreck anything."

He laughed but agreed. We were careful to smoke near the windows, balancing our drinks on our laps as we sat on the windowsill. Cold now, we found a blanket and turned on the gas fireplace. We cuddled, my head on his chest, the warmth from the fireplace making us sleepy. It was nice, pretending to be a real couple in a real house.

"Maybe we'll have a big house like this one day," I said.

"Yeah, that would show my dad—he's always telling me I'm a loser."

"That's bullshit and you know it. You're super-smart and amazing with mechanics—and the best fisherman I know."

I hated that his dad made him feel bad. I'd see how much he wanted his dad's approval, trying to get him to come watch his motocross races. But his dad would get drunk that day and never show. It made me even more disappointed that my parents weren't more accepting of Ryan—I could tell that he liked my dad. Sometimes, his voice all proud, Ryan would tell me how his mechanics teacher had said he'd done a good job on something, and I'd be happy for him but also sad, knowing his dad never said anything nice like that.

"You always make me feel better," Ryan said.

"It's not like I have some huge future prospects myself, you know. I'll probably be a waitress for the rest of my life."

"Now, that's bullshit. You're smart and can do lots of stuff too. You're a really great cook."

I smiled at him, flushing a little. I'd only made him a few things, like cupcakes or brownies, but he always loved them. My grandma had given me all kinds of recipes. Sometimes when it was just me and Dad, I'd cook us stuff and I really enjoyed it, especially when he'd say, "This is really good, honey," and ask for seconds. I didn't cook when Mom was home because she always had suggestions for how I could make it better.

I said, "Maybe I'll be a chef."

He rolled over, dragged a finger down my belly button.

"Oh, yeah? You gonna cook for me when we get our own place?"

"Sure, if you do the dishes."

We talked for a while longer, about how great it was going to be, how his uncle had an old couch for us, how we could stay up late and do whatever we wanted. We'd work for a year, then travel Europe for a year, maybe get jobs there. Ryan wanted to rent a motorbike so we could ride through Italy. We drank some more, giggling when some vodka sloshed onto the floor and our bodies.

Finally we made love, slow, not feeling rushed for a change, not worried about who might come home. We experimented, tried some new stuff we'd read about. I loved how brave I felt with Ryan, how comfortable, but mostly how beautiful he made me feel. When I straddled him, he caught his breath, reached up with his hand, and cupped my cheek. The glow from the fireplace made his skin turn to a dark tan. I moved slowly, gently, our gazes locked the whole time, then leaned down, pressed my mouth to his. We kissed hard and soft, until our bodies were sticky with sweat, until we both gasped, "I love you, I love you."

We fell asleep, my head on his shoulder, his hand playing in my hair, his chest rising and falling under my cheek. When we woke a few hours later, we cleaned the place, making sure we put the booze back in the right spot and hadn't tracked in any leaves or dirt. Ryan said he was okay to drive now, he'd lost his buzz, so he took off in his truck and I walked back to my house.

It was about four in the morning when I snuck in the front door, carefully putting the keys back in place, trying to be quiet. Upstairs, I startled Nicole in the hallway as she was coming out of the bathroom. She gave a little squeak, then, when she realized it was me, she said, "Are you just coming home?"

"Yeah."

She didn't say anything else, just kept her head down and walked to her room. Later, when I was climbing into my bed, I realized her face had been shiny, like she'd just washed it, and she'd smelled of soap. Her hair had also been brushed smooth, not messy like it was when she'd been sleeping. Had she just gotten home too? When I'd knocked earlier, before I left for the night, she hadn't answered. Had she even been here, or had she snuck out? And if so, who had she met up with? That boy on the phone? I wondered if I should talk to her and find out what was going on, but she'd been so defensive earlier I had a feeling she wouldn't tell me anything more now, and what was the point of another fight? She was home safe.

# CHAPTER SEVEN

## ROCKLAND PENITENTIARY, VANCOUVER

### JUNE 1998

I got a letter from Ryan a couple of days after my dad visited. His lawyer had also given him the news about the verdict, but his letter was still full of hope. His parents were out of money so his mom was trying to find a legal aid lawyer to take our case to the Supreme Court. The private detective hadn't turned up any new leads, but Ryan still thought something might break. The detective had told him about witnesses who came forward years later, cases where someone got arrested for a different crime and evidence linked them back to an unsolved murder, and Ryan was convinced the same thing would happen with our case. I'd speculated a lot about what had happened that night, whether it had been a drifter passing through, a random stranger, or someone we knew—someone *she* knew.

Those girls.

Shauna and her friends had lied at the trial, that I knew for sure, but I still didn't know *why*, didn't know if they'd really been there that night, or if it was all a lie. I'd also thought about the boy Nicole had been seeing, how she'd been acting that last while, like she was scared, and I wondered if he'd done it, if there was a link between them all. But the private investigator could never confirm Nicole had any boyfriends, secret or otherwise, and he couldn't find any holes in the girls' story. Still, I couldn't shake the feeling they were involved.

I'd also told the police about the boy after Nicole was murdered, and how Shauna and the girls had been harassing me all year, how they were lying about what they'd seen that night. I'd hoped for days that they would find the real killer. But then I realized that they weren't even looking, and they sure weren't looking now.

This time I didn't cry after reading Ryan's letter. I stared at the words. *Don't give up. It's just a matter of time.* I felt cold and hard. His hope made me angry. I was done falling apart each time something didn't come through for us, done being reminded over and over of how much I'd lost. Couldn't he see where we were now? That there was nothing left to hope for? No one was going to come forward with new evidence. The murderer wasn't going to be found.

I thought about what Janet had said, that you had to let go of the past, of anyone on the outside. I was in prison now and I was going to be there for a long, long time. Ryan and I would never be allowed to be together again. Even if we were freed one day, we weren't going to be the same people after years inside. I'd changed, and no doubt he was going to change. Too much had happened already. We didn't even have anything to write about anymore. All we had were memories, and those were going to fade. Eventually, so would our love. The idea that anything good between us might die, might turn dark and bitter, killed me more than anything.

This time I didn't write back. And when my father wrote a week later, I didn't answer that letter either. I took down all the photos taped on my wall, even the ones of Nicole, and put them in my storage box. I couldn't look at her face knowing that her killer, or killers, were still out there, couldn't stop thinking about what kind of life she might've had, a husband, career, children, how she could've done great things, but now she'd never even have justice. She'd be forgotten by everyone. And I had to forget everything and everyone on the outside or I'd go crazy, but that didn't mean I was going to accept my new life on the inside either.

Two weeks after I spoke to my lawyer, I was walking through the activity area when Janet looked up from a card game with some of the other women.

"Hey, kid, come join us."

"No, thanks," I said. "I don't like cards."

I felt them all staring at my back as I walked away. They were pissed—I hadn't seen anyone refuse Janet anything—but I wasn't scared. Instead I felt a shiver of excitement, a sense of pushing something to a head. I felt alive.

An hour later, when I was leaving the laundry room, I heard a noise to my left. Mouse and Yoda were standing in a dark corner of the hall, where there was no camera. Mouse had on her mean smile and was smacking her hands together. Yoda's face was blank, her ghostly blue eyes staring at me. They both rushed me at the same time. Yoda's hands ripped at my hair, grabbed at my face and skin, punching me in the head, as Mouse beat my body with a sock full of batteries.

I pushed back, hit any part of them I could reach, bit their shoulders, pulled their shirts over their heads. It felt good to be fighting, our grunts and curses filling the air. The pain of the batteries hitting against my flesh only enraged me more. But then Mouse got a couple of good blows across my head, and I felt blood trickling down my face. The world turned dark, my head ringing as I hung on to one of them, trying not to fall. Then a loud yell from another female voice: "Guard!"

The blows stopped. I slumped to the floor, spitting out blood. Before they ran off, Mouse said, "If Janet tells you to do something, you do it."

I was taken to the infirmary, patched up, then sent back to my cell, where I pulled my aching body up onto my bed and made a plan. The correctional officers had questioned me, but I said nothing. I hadn't needed Pinky to warn me that you never rat anyone out, not if you wanted to live. I didn't care about living at that point, but the last thing I wanted was for them to get locked up in the hole or moved to maximum. For one thing, I wouldn't be able to get revenge.

When I passed Janet in the activity room the next day, she told me again to join them. Again I refused.

Yoda and Mouse found me in the kitchen later, when I was washing some pots. The other inmates cleared out. But this time I fought back with my own homemade weapon—I'd learned how to extract one of the blades from my safety razor, then melt it onto a toothbrush handle, making a "slasher." My rage—at my family, at the system, especially at myself—boiled out. I sliced Mouse's face and Yoda's arm, and managed to break Mouse's nose before a bunch of guards finally pulled me off.

As they threw me to the floor and cuffed me, I was still screaming, "I'm in for fucking murder, you bitches! Don't ever fuck with me again!"

I spent twenty days in the hole. Twenty days staring at a wall, pacing and crying and trying not to think about Ryan. I'd stopped writing him but I couldn't stop caring about him yet. I couldn't believe that we were over, that I'd never be able to see him again in my life. It hurt so much, the pain welling up from deep inside my belly, making me sob in big heaving gasps of agony. I also thought about Nicole a lot, torturing myself with memories from when we were little and she used to follow me everywhere, begging me to "pway" with her.

Toward the end of my twenty days, I started getting spacey, losing track of time, and sometimes I'd imagine my sister was in there with me. I'd see shadows and try to reach out to touch her, but she always danced out of sight. I'd talk to her, and to Ryan, telling them how much I missed them. Then I'd just rock back and forth, my arms wrapped around my body, playing mental games to keep alert, like spelling things out loud or remembering lyrics to old songs, trying to hold myself together. But I feared that I was too broken now, that I was finally everything my mom always thought—a waste of a life.

Finally, I was released back into general population. I was treated different then, after that last fight. Mouse was sporting a red scar down her face and looked away when I stared at her. She was scared of me now. Even Janet gave me a wide berth from then on. It didn't make me feel happy like I'd thought. I felt *nothing*, not sympathy, pain, or remorse. I'd done it, I was finally dead inside.

I was given respect from most of the inmates, but I didn't give it to anyone else. I lipped off the guards, I still refused to attend any programs. I got in fights often with other inmates who looked at me too long or whispered when I walked past. I spent a lot of time in solitary. After three new inmates, trying to prove they were tough, attacked me in the shower, I waited until each of them were alone and returned the favor. But I also cut them and left jagged lines down the center of their chests. One day, a woman put a pillowcase over my head while I was napping in my cell and tried to beat the crap out of me. I managed to dislocate her shoulder. I became someone inmates either feared or wanted to challenge so they could prove themselves in there.

For the next three years, nothing changed. If I wasn't in the hole for fighting, I'd work in the kitchen, then run the track every night or work out in my cell. And if I wasn't working or exercising,

I slept. Once I stopped writing back, my dad's letters drifted off. He came over my first Christmas in the pen, but I'd gotten thrown in the hole the day before. Now he just sent money into my account every few months and new CDs, sometimes a card with a brief note. I wondered if those would also stop one day. My grandmother was the only family member who kept writing each month, the only one I answered sometimes.

Pinky was still my roommate and we existed fine with each other, never friends but never enemies. Other inmates who were also serving long sentences tried to talk to me sometimes, telling me I needed to chill out, I was making things harder on myself, but I ignored everyone. I had lots of sessions with my institutional parole officer and the prison psychiatrist. I did my best to piss them all off, and I succeeded every time. No one liked me.

Ryan still wrote, at first every week, then every month, and then months would go by and I'd think he'd finally given up, but he'd send another letter. I didn't read them, didn't even open them, though sometimes the urge was so strong I'd be physically sick, retching over our small metal toilet, Pinky watching and shaking her head. Sometimes I'd wake up from a dead sleep, Ryan's name on my lips, and know that he was thinking of me, calling for me. After every letter I'd retreat back into my cell to stare at the wall. I'd stop eating. They'd put me in a paper suit and back into solitary. I got thinner—and angrier. Some days I didn't even know myself anymore.

After I'd been at Rockland for five years, I was sitting in the hole one day, after spitting on a guard, when they sent the prison shrink to talk to me. He was a younger guy with an earnest face and big glasses. I got the feeling that he really cared about his job and wanted to help, but I'd spent most of our previous meetings trying to convince him that I was a waste of time—and doing a good job of it, I thought.

This time he said, "Toni, you've served a third of your sentence. You can get out of here and have a life, but you just keep making it harder on yourself. It's like you don't *want* to get out. Like you're scared of everything out there."

After he left I thought a lot about what he'd said. When I'd first come in, my sentence had seemed so long, but there was a light at the end of the tunnel now. The idea *was* terrifying and exhilarating. Did I even have a life to go back to? If I kept going the way I was, fighting the system every step of the way, I'd be nothing but a deadbeat or a druggie when I got out. I'd probably be back in a week—I'd seen it happen time and time again. I thought about what Janet had told me, about doing easy time and hard time. I'd assumed cutting my family and Ryan off would make things easier, but I'd never really accepted being in prison, never tried to fit in or make any kind of life on the inside. I'd seen other inmates laugh, love, learn, achieve things, but I'd closed myself off from any chance of any happiness.

It was like I'd thought finding some pleasure in prison would be giving in, or would be unfair to Nicole, but I hadn't proved anything to anybody except that maybe they were right about me all along—I was a bad kid. I was twenty-five and I'd done nothing to improve myself, nothing to give myself a fighting chance of succeeding in society when I did make it out. If anything, I'd made it harder to even get parole when I was eligible. And what if by some small miracle Ryan and I were proved innocent? What kind of future could we have if I kept screwing up? He'd finally stopped writing that year, but I couldn't help wondering if he still felt the same way about me. If maybe I'd been wrong and one day, somehow, we'd find our way back to each other.

I met with the shrink a lot after that and started listening to him, started answering his questions, even if I thought some of them were stupid. I told him I was innocent. I don't know if he believed me, but he said that it wasn't about my guilt or innocence, it was about my accepting that I was in prison and that I could try to make the most of it. I also started going to programs. At first I had a chip on my shoulder, the other inmates' problems weren't my problems. I didn't shoot drugs, I wasn't an addict, but when I listened closer I heard the stories underneath the words. How they hadn't belonged anywhere, how they didn't get along with their family, how they'd used drugs to get attention or forget their pain. I thought about all the times Ryan and I had gotten high just to deal with our family shit, how we thought there was nothing wrong with that. But if I hadn't been stoned out of my mind that night I might have been able to protect Nicole, might have heard her scream. I never wanted to do drugs or drink again. I even quit smoking.

I went to more programs, I followed the steps, and I read some self-help books. Then I started reading other books, novels I remembered Nicole talking about, some memoirs and biographies, anything written about survivors, people who had overcome adversity. Eventually I branched out into the classics, books I'd avoided in school: *Moby-Dick, Jane Eyre, Great Expectations, Of Mice and Men.* After years of being stagnant, my mind wanted to work, wanted to learn. There weren't many classes available unless I got moved down to minimum—I'd been placed in maximum because of my fighting—but I was trying to stay out of trouble. I told my institutional parole officer whatever he wanted to hear, about my remorse, that I wanted to make amends to all the people I'd hurt over the years, my family, the guards, others. I was more polite inside, respectful, and after another year I was moved back down to medium.

It wasn't a straight line. I still had the odd tussle with another inmate, but I was learning to walk away from fights more. In time, I finally opened up to the shrink about my guilt surrounding Nicole's murder, how even though I didn't kill her, I was the reason she was dead. And how sometimes I felt angry at her for not confiding in me about what was happening to her that last year, which might have had something to do with her death. He talked a lot about forgiveness, of myself and others, and said, "Punishing yourself isn't helping anyone, Toni."

But I wasn't ready to forgive myself, or Shauna and her crew for the things they'd said at our trial. I couldn't stop thinking they were involved somehow, that they knew what had really happened that night. And they were all still walking around free. The years had only intensified my hatred. I didn't tell my shrink that part, wanting him to report only good things to my parole officer.

Two years later, when I was twenty-eight, I was finally moved to minimum. I hadn't seen my dad or my mom in years, but they sent money on my birthday and Christmas. My dad would also still send cards once in a while. I would stare at the cards, wondering why they didn't even hurt anymore. They felt like part of another life, one that I would never belong to again.

One letter hit hard, though. Dad wrote to tell me that my grandma had died. I'll never forget her funny letters in her shaky handwriting where she'd bitch about her doctor, her friends, or her new boyfriend. They were some of the few bright spots in years of gray. I wasn't allowed to go to her funeral and I regretted not having written her more often, but I'd been too ashamed, feeling like I'd let her down so badly, ashamed of putting that return address on mail to her.

Now I didn't get letters from anyone, except once in a while a law student or a reporter wrote saying they wanted to work on my case. I never answered.

I couldn't really remember the outside as much, the scents and sounds of that world fading in my mind, and I didn't think about it as often. Or at least I didn't let myself go there in my mind. Sometimes the other girls and I would talk about what we'd eat when we got out of the joint, imagining burgers and fries and thick milkshakes, big steaks and baked potatoes, or maybe a strawberry cheesecake. But I always ended the game first. It hurt too much.

I had made some good friends, like Amber, Brenda, and Margaret. We didn't talk about our crimes. It wasn't something you ever asked about, but usually you'd hear something through the grapevine and you'd know what they were doing a "bid" for. Amber was in for manslaughter, and Brenda and Margaret were also in for murder. Margaret had been there the longest. She'd killed her husband and his friend after they raped her when they were all drunk one night—the jury decided the sex had been consensual and she'd shot them in a drunken rage.

I'd stopped telling anybody I was innocent, didn't talk about Nicole or my family. Most of the girls didn't have any family either and we became each other's support. Amber, a tiny blonde who could talk your ear off if you gave her half a chance, was obsessed with all things country and western. Only nineteen, she was our little sister. Brenda, a tough ex-druggie who dressed butch and had a shaved head, was our brother. She fell in love with a different woman every week, and provided us with lots of drama and excitement as we watched her try to juggle a couple of relationships at a time. Margaret was our mother.

Margaret was in her late fifties, with wild curly blond hair that stood out around her head like a halo. She was forever trying to calm it down, buying different potions, but within hours it would frizz up again. She ran the kitchen, and I worked as her prep cook. At first I thought she was a tough bitch, real cranky, and wasn't sure why everyone liked her, then I realized she had a lot of respect inside because she didn't take crap from anyone but she never had to raise her voice. She was like a bossy mama. She had this stare that made you want to apologize right away, and she treated everyone as if they were her kids—slapping them on the hand with a spatula if they stole a cookie, but adding a little extra to someone's plate if she knew that woman was having a bad day. She'd also get everyone to decorate their cells at Christmas or other holidays, and we'd hold contests—it was pretty amazing what a bunch of female inmates could come up with, just using colored paper and stuff. We'd also make each other home-made cards, and birthday cakes out of things we could get at the canteen. Christmas, we always exchanged presents, maybe an extra can of Coke or a few packages of noodles and chips. First time I made a Mother's Day card for Margaret, she cried and cried. Later she told me she had a few kids on the outside but she'd been into drugs when she was young and they didn't want anything to do with her anymore.

I told her about my family then, and what had happened that night. Margaret was cool, said I needed to forgive myself, but I told her I couldn't, not yet. I also told her about Shauna and her gang, and how my mom hated me. She said that after she went to prison her youngest son had been killed when he was a teen. He was drunk, in a car with a bunch of other kids who were also drunk, and they wrapped the car around a telephone pole. Her son was thrown out of the car and broke his neck. She blamed herself for a long time—if she'd been a better mother, her kid wouldn't have been out that night—and she blamed the driver of the car.

But then she said, "One day, I just saw all this hate I was carrying around with me, how it wasn't doing no good to nobody. People make mistakes, and the more they hurt inside, the more they hurt on the outside." She also said, "And your mom? Losing a child, it's the worst thing that can ever happen to a woman. It makes you crazy inside. She just can't let go of that grief yet. She's stuck."

I thought about that for a moment, remembering how the year after Nicole's murder my mom would make me go over everything that had happened that night again and again, every torturous detail, no matter how painful.

Margaret reached out and grabbed my hand. "She doesn't hate you, baby. It's just easier for her to be mad at you than herself. But you got to stop blaming *your*self for what went down."

After that, Margaret started giving me some books to read, stuff on living in the now by some dude named Eckhart Tolle and some other books on meditation, spiritual stuff like that. I was also taking some university correspondence classes and she'd ask me to read out sections to her, then we'd discuss different parts. When I got a good grade she'd prance around, telling everyone on our range how her "daughter" was so damn smart.

Margaret was really into yoga, which was pretty funny because she was a woman with an odd shape, big on top with broad shoulders and big breasts but skinny chicken legs. Still, she could bend herself into all kinds of positions and she got most of us to join her for sessions in the activity room. Amber and Brenda would grumble all the way through, but it was some of the most fun I had in there, watching those girls try to do warrior poses and downward dogs. I was the only one who stuck with Margaret and did a class with her every day. She had bad arthritis, with gnarled hands and feet, and she said yoga and meditation were pretty much the only things that helped with the pain.

One winter day she was rubbing her hands, in a foul mood. She'd even made Amber cry when we were all watching TV: "I can't stand all your chatter. Shut up or go back to your cell." Amber left, and a couple of minutes later Margaret said, "Shit. Now I'm going to have to give her some of my cookies."

I smiled at her. "Amber will get over it. But I can give you a foot rub if you want?" We weren't supposed to have any physical contact, but they were a little more relaxed in minimum and we had a guard, Theresa, who liked us, so she'd turn a blind eye.

After that, I'd come to Margaret's cell when she was having a bad day and give her a hand or foot rub. I even gave her a pedicure sometimes, then all the girls wanted them, so I got a reputation for being the beauty consultant, which I thought was pretty funny. I liked making them feel pretty. Margaret especially, the way she'd lean back in bliss, giving little sighs as I rubbed and molded her feet. She'd say, "Toni, you have hands of a miracle worker."

It was during the pedicures that we shared the most about our past lives. I talked about Ryan, told her all the things that I'd never shared with my mom. She'd get me to describe how he looked and say, "Oh, he sounds so cuuuute." I told her some of the fun stuff we used to do, and how we were always sneaking out to see each other. One day I told her about the time he'd climbed up the tree to my roof, just to say he was sorry for being jealous. It was nice, remembering, but then I saw his face so clearly, his smile, and I had to break off, the emotions still too raw.

Margaret waited for a bit. Then, her voice soft, she said, "Do you think you'll see each other when you get out?"

"I'd lose my parole."

"That's not what I asked." She gave a cheeky smile.

I thought about what she'd said. "Sometimes I wonder if he might try to find me, but it's been so long . . . I don't know if he feels the same way."

"Do you know if he's getting out at the same time?"

I shook my head. "No idea. We stopped writing years ago."

"I could put out some feelers for you."

For a moment I was tempted. But then I said, "I'm too scared to find out he's changed, that he's not the same guy anymore." I knew how much prison had changed me, and the men's side of Rockland was even worse. They'd been on lockdown many times over the years after a riot or a fight between inmates and guards, or because someone got caught sneaking in drugs, cell phones, or some other contraband. After prisons became nonsmoking in 2006, cigarettes had also become a hot commodity. If Ryan had survived prison, it was likely he'd turned into someone I wouldn't want to know.

I said, "We can never be together again, I know that, but I still have my memories—they're the only good thing I have left from that time. If I find out something awful about him, then it's like all the good will get erased."

Margaret sighed. "I understand. Some things are just better left alone." Then she told me about her husband, who was not a nice guy at all. She said, "I would have loved to have what you kids had, even if it was lost. You shared something special, something most people never find."

As the years passed and I got closer to my parole date, I worried about leaving Margaret in there, about who might take care of her. When I said as much, she brushed me off. "Don't you worry about me, girl. Just get your shit together and leave this place for the rest of us." On days when her arthritis was really bad, she told me that when she meditated she'd dream about being free, running on the beach, watching the birds, and never feeling pain again. She was tired of always aching. She said it was punishment for "loving the wrong men my whole damn life." She liked listening to me talk about Campbell River, the beaches and the ocean—she was from back east and had only been to the beach once in her life.

Sometimes she'd be melancholy, sipping her tea, her eyes blank, saying, "I'm going to die in this damn place. I know it." I'd get upset with her. And then she'd say, "Toni, honey, you got it all wrong. Death isn't the hard part, living is."

# CHAPTER EIGHT

## Woodbridge High, Campbell River

### February 1996

I was sure that Ryan and I had covered all our tracks after breaking into the Andersons' house, but a few days later I walked in after school to find both my parents sitting at the table. Their faces were serious, coffee cups on the table—half drunk, no steam, like they'd been waiting and talking for a while. Nicole was also sitting at the table, nervously scratching at her arm.

"What's wrong?" I said.

"We'd like to have a word with you," my dad said.

I sat down and glanced at Nicole, but she looked away. Not a good sign.

"Did you sneak into the Andersons' house?" Dad said.

"No." Crap. How much did they know? Had we left something behind?

"Don't lie," my mom said.

"I'm *not*. I wasn't there."

"Well, someone was," Dad said. "The Andersons' alarm shows

each time it's been disabled and which code was used. Someone used the one they'd created for me to enter their house late Friday night. Do you know anything about this?"

I shrugged, but my heart was racing. "Nicole was going over there to water plants, wasn't she using the code?"

"This was later—hours after she'd been there."

Mom chimed in, "Nicole said you were out with Ryan Friday night."

I glared at Nicole. *What else did you tell them?*

"Yeah, so what?"

"And you came home past four in the morning."

So Nicole *had* ratted me out. Two can play that game.

"Nicole was out late too. She had just gotten home when I did."

Mom looked shocked, and Nicole's face turned red.

Nicole stammered, "That's not true—I was just going to the bathroom."

Mom turned back to me. "It's bad enough that you're lying to us, Toni, but trying to point the finger at your sister is just low."

"I'm not pointing the finger at anyone. I'm saying I wasn't the only one out."

"This isn't about your sister." Mom looked flustered, like she was trying to regroup. "It's about you sneaking into our neighbors' house."

My dad said, "They trusted us, Toni."

Now I felt really bad. I hadn't wanted to get my dad in trouble. "Maybe their alarm is screwed up and it recorded the time wrong or something."

"Some of their alcohol was also missing." Dad's voice turned soft, doing the calm-and-reasonable thing. "We just want to know the truth."

I glanced over at Mom and knew there'd be hell to pay if she knew the truth. I kept with my story. "I *am* telling the truth."

Dad looked disappointed, my mom furious.

She said, "You're grounded."

"What? You can't do that!"

"For a month—that includes phone privileges. And you can't use the car or see Ryan after school. We want you home every night."

"You can't *ground* me—I'm eighteen." I was furious—I'd been a week away from getting the car on the road. "I'm supposed to start work at the Fish Shack the middle of March."

"You should have thought of that before." Then she took a breath, like she was bracing for something, and said, "If you don't abide by our rules, you'll have to find another place to live."

Blood rushed to my face. "You're kicking me out?" I knew it had to be some tough-love bullshit she'd read in one of the stupid books—I'd seen them in her office: *How to Talk to Your Teenage Daughter* and other crap like that. But it still shocked the hell out of me. I didn't think they'd ever go that far.

"We aren't kicking you out," Dad quickly said. "But your behavior is getting out of control. We don't know what else to do, Toni. Your mom's right. If you're not going to respect our rules, then you can't stay here."

He looked upset saying those last words, and I had a feeling it was more my mom's idea than his. I glanced back at her and she looked upset too, but more nervous or scared, her mouth tight and her eyes red-rimmed. She was probably freaked out that I might actually leave, and then she'd have no control over me.

I felt panicky, trying to figure out what I was going to do next. Where would I go? Ryan's place was no good. His mom was cool, but I was pretty sure she'd draw the line at my living there. Amy and the rest of my friends still weren't speaking to me. Maybe I could negotiate my way out of this.

"What if I did more chores around here and stayed home during the week?" Then I could still keep my job.

Dad looked at my mom.

"One month," she said, her voice firm. "It will give you time to realize that when you're with Ryan, you don't use your head. You have to learn there are consequences to your actions. "

What she meant was that she hoped it would make us break up.

"Now you're calling me stupid?" I said. "You didn't want me to work at the Fish Shack anyway. You're just trying to screw things up for me!"

"No one's calling you stupid," Dad said, "and no one is trying to screw anything up, but when you're with Ryan, you don't think things through."

That stung. "I think about things just fine."

"We just don't want to see you do something you might really regret. It will be good for you to have some time apart."

Near tears, I glanced across the table at Nicole, who was staring down at the floor.

"How come you're not asking Nicole why she's lying about where she was Friday night? Or about *her* boyfriend?"

Both my parents looked at Nicole.

Her face was flushed as she said, "I don't have a boyfriend."

"Right." I almost mentioned the party that Nicole had been at, but when I saw the look of fear on her face I dropped it. If my parents wanted to be blind, so be it, but I didn't need Nicole to retaliate and throw more fuel on the fire. I was already in enough trouble.

"We'll talk to Nicole in a minute," my dad said.

"Are we done?" I said.

"No. You'll also mow the Andersons' lawn every week for the next month."

"Are you *kidding* me? No way."

"You'll do it," my mom said, "or they're considering pressing criminal charges against you and Ryan."

That I hadn't expected. Ryan had already been in trouble for stealing gas last summer. McKinney wouldn't let him off so easy this time. I felt a jolt of fear. "That isn't fair."

"They're being more than fair," Mom said.

My dad said, "You can go to your room now."

I was still walking up the stairs when I heard them questioning Nicole.

"What's Toni talking about?" my mom asked. "Are you dating someone?"

"Mo-om. I'd tell you if I had a boyfriend." Nicole's voice was sweet.

"What did she mean about you getting home late?" my dad said.

"I don't know. Maybe she's confused. She saw me coming out of the bathroom, but I was here all night." Nicole even managed to sound like it really was a mystery. But I wasn't confused. I knew exactly what I'd seen.

I went to my bedroom and turned on my music, pulling my pillow over my head. How was I going to survive a whole month only being able to see Ryan at school?

Later, when my dad was making dinner and Mom was working in her office, I went into Nicole's bedroom. She was at her desk writing a note, which she quickly covered when I walked in.

"Thanks a lot," I said.

Her face was flushed and she looked guilty. "I'm sorry. I didn't want to lie."

I dropped down on her bed. "You mean you didn't want to lie about *me*, but you lied about your own shit."

"I don't know what you're talking about."

"I know you've been talking to some boy, and you were probably out with him Friday night. You can fool Mom but not me. Why are you hiding this guy?"

She stared at the note, like she was thinking, and for a minute I thought she might tell me the truth. But then she said, "It's none of your business, Toni."

"It's my business when you get me grounded. That was a shitty move."

"You got yourself grounded by going into the Andersons'. That was a *stupid* move."

I wondered if that's what this came down to. She was just smarter about her secrets. I also wondered if she could be in over her head this time, with this guy. But then I thought of other times, when we were kids, playing with Mom's things when we weren't supposed to, how Nicole always remembered to put Mom's things back perfectly while I invariably messed up and left something out. Nicole was too smart to screw up really bad or fall for some idiot. She'd be fine.

"Well, I've got an idea that might work for both of us," I said.

She snorted. "Your ideas just get you in trouble."

"Do you want to see your boyfriend or not?"

Her gaze flicked to the door, then back at me. "I don't have one." Sure she didn't.

"Okay, say you want to go out and see this boyfriend that you don't have, and I want to see my boyfriend. We can cover for each other."

"How so?"

"My window makes too much noise—let me go through yours."

"That sounds like you need my help, not the other way around."

"All I have to do is check on you one night and see that you're not here. Or follow you the nights you're supposed to be at Darlene's . . ."

She was glaring at me, but she knew I was right.

"Fine, but I'm not doing any other favors for you. And if you say anything to Mom, *ever*, I'll make sure she knows every single thing you're up to."

"Same here, darling sister."

———

And that's how I managed to see Ryan for the next month. We also skipped out of class so we could spend an hour with each other, and after school we lingered until the very last moment before I had to take the bus home. I missed driving home with Ryan, his hand on my leg, roaring down the road and watching him shift the gears, getting a thrill from how easily he handled the big truck. I especially hated standing in the bus line when Shauna drove by in her car, smirking. At least one night a week, usually on weekends, I'd sneak into Nicole's room and out her window, coming back a few hours later. She'd roll over and look at me, then go back to sleep, and once she whispered, "Be really quiet. I heard someone use the bathroom downstairs a few minutes ago."

Nicole was sneaking out herself, though not as much as me, and I still didn't know who she was seeing. But I could hear her footsteps sometimes on the roof outside my room. Once, when I crawled back through her window, she wasn't home yet, and I didn't hear her steps on the roof until an hour later. One day at school, I ran into her in the bathroom. She was putting on mascara in the mirror, and her eyes were red-rimmed, her face splotchy, like she'd been crying.

I waited until some other girls left the bathroom, then said, "What's wrong?"

"None of your business." She threw her mascara in her purse and pushed past me.

After that, I didn't ask again.

Mike at the Fish Shack had said that he'd hold the job for me until the end of March, and I was excited to start work the next weekend. I'd have to work hard that summer to make up the money I'd lost. Ryan was also trying to get some extra work lined up on the weekends, cutting firewood, cleaning people's yards, painting fences, stuff like that. I only had to deal with crap for another three months, then I'd graduate, and hopefully by the end of the summer Ryan and I could get our own place. Mom had been a little easier on me since I was home more, even took me with her a few times to get some supplies for Dad. It had been fun, but I had a feeling she'd be on my ass again as soon as I started work.

For the last month, I'd been staying clear of Shauna. We cast glares in each other's direction whenever our paths crossed, but generally we avoided each other. Her dad must have talked to her. Still, it seemed too good to be true, and I had the uneasy feeling she was just biding her time until I lowered my guard.

The Friday before I started my new job, I walked to the park across from school. I was going to cut through to the coffee shop on the other side, where Ryan would pick me up after he finished his shop project. I was making my way down a path, thinking how pretty it was in the park, when I noticed a movement out of my left eye, a flash of auburn hair. I paused. Someone was hiding behind a tree. Shauna? Then I remembered Ryan and me talking in the hall, the group of kids standing behind us, and Rachel hanging out with her boyfriend.

I glanced down the path behind me. Where were the other girls? I couldn't see them, but Shauna wouldn't face me alone—it wasn't her style.

Shauna stepped out from behind the tree. We stared at each other. Her eyes were narrowed, her face full of hate—and glee.

I took a breath, dropped my packsack, and stepped forward.

"If we're going to do this, let's go."

I saw her motion to someone, and the other girls came out from behind trees. They'd been waiting for me. Rachel was holding something, which she passed to Shauna, who stuffed it in her pocket. Sun glinted on metal for a second. A knife? Shit—that was a game-changer. I tried to think, but I was panicking now, my thoughts scattering in different directions. I had two options: try to fight my way out of it, or run like hell.

I clenched my fists, held them up in the fighter stance that Ryan had taught me, trying to remember some of the defense moves he'd also shown me.

Shauna started laughing. "You look like an angry little cat."

The girls also laughed.

I said, "And you look like a chickenshit who needs backup because you can't kick my ass on your own."

Shauna's smile dropped. "You bitch." She reached into her pocket. I held my breath, braced my body. Showtime.

Voices, coming up the trail behind us. My body filled with relief.

Shauna took her hand out of her pocket. I turned around. It was an older man and his wife, walking a little white poodle. They gave us suspicious looks.

I said, "Oh, my God, I love poodles! Can I pet him?" They told me all about Jinx as I started walking beside them, asking questions about the dog while we moved farther down the path. When I turned around again, the girls had left. But I kept close to the couple until I was safely at the coffee shop.

When Ryan picked me up, I told him what had happened.

"Shit, Toni, I don't like that at all." He reached under his seat and pulled out a switchblade. As he handed it to me, he said, "Carry this with you—always."

I wondered why he had a knife. He'd never shown it to me before.

"I could get in big trouble having this at school."

"Don't let anyone see it."

Later that night I was in my room, playing with the knife, running my fingers across the blade. I imagined Shauna coming at me and slashed at the air, pretending to stab her over and over.

My door whipped open. "Toni—" Nicole stopped and stared.

"Close the door!"

She closed it. "What do you have *that* for?" Her eyes were big and scared.

"Protection, okay?"

She took a step into the room, lowered her voice. "From who?"

Before I could answer, there was a knock on the door.

"Dinner's ready, girls."

I called out, "We'll be down in a second, Mom," and stuffed the knife under my pillow. I hissed to Nicole, "Don't you tell anyone."

"But why do you have it?"

She'd only freak out if I told her about Shauna. Then my parents would get involved, and then Shauna's dad. Plus, they'd take the knife away.

"It's Ryan's," I said. "He gave it to me for when I work late—in case someone's waiting in the parking lot or something one night."

"I guess that makes sense." She headed to the door, then turned back. "Just be careful, okay?"

That's why I had the knife.

I started work at the Fish Shack the next day. It was an old restaurant fixed up to look like the inside of a boat, with wood walls and lots of marine paraphernalia hanging around, nets on the ceiling, antique glass floats. It was down near the wharf and had a killer ocean view of the marina. Mike, my new boss, was really nice. He was a big friendly guy who always wore a baseball cap, backward, and Canucks team shirts. He knew lots of people in town and they'd come in to have coffee with him, his laugh booming out as he told story after story. I liked how it felt at the restaurant, kind of like a family. I got along with the other waitresses too. Most of them were older than me but they were cool, and we'd sit outside on our breaks having a smoke. I finally felt like I belonged somewhere. Sometimes I'd even go to the restaurant on the days I didn't work—I only worked weekends and Thursday nights for now. Ryan would come by and we'd order nachos or french fries. Later, the waitresses would tell me how cute and nice Ryan was and that I was a lucky girl.

Then Shauna and her crew started coming into the restaurant.

It was the middle of April, and I'd been there for two weeks. I was joking around with some customers when I heard the door jingle. I looked up, and dread wrapped tight around my chest, squeezing my breath out in a rush, when I saw Shauna, with Cathy, Kim, and Rachel. The Fish Shack wasn't their kind of place— they hung out at the trendy coffee shops or the burger place downtown. Only one reason they could be there. Shauna gave a friendly little wave of her fingers. The other girls were giggling, but trying to hold it in. I felt hot all over, like I might break into a sweat. While one of the waitresses greeted the girls, I finished taking my customers' orders, but my hand was shaking.

When I headed to the kitchen to put in the order, I heard Shauna say loudly, "We want to be in Toni's section. We're friends from school."

I considered asking the waitress to switch sections with me, but it wouldn't be professional, and I had some tables that looked like they were good tippers. I wasn't letting Shauna screw that up for me. I took a breath, and held my head high as I walked over to their table with some menus.

I stood in front of them and said in a cheerful voice, "Can I get you something to drink to start?"

Shauna smiled, her tongue flicking over her lips for a second, reminding me of a snake. A really poisonous one. "We'd like to hear the specials, please."

I described the chowder and sandwich of the day.

Shauna said, "I'm sorry, can you repeat that?"

I kept a pleasant smile on my face and recited the specials again.

This time, Rachel said, "Can you tell me how the soup is made? Like, what's in it, you know?"

The girls started laughing. I could feel my face getting hot.

Some of my other tables were glancing around, looking for me. Luckily, I'd been paying attention earlier when the chef was talking about the chowder, and I felt some satisfaction at the look on Shauna's face when I was able to answer Rachel's question. But then Cathy said, "What kind of sandwich did you say came with it? And what dressing comes on the salad? Can you list them all, please?"

They were grinning, their faces excited, enjoying their power over me. I wanted to walk away, but I gritted my teeth and calmly repeated that it was a shrimp and avocado sandwich and listed all the salad dressings.

"Now, can I get you some water or a drink to start?"

Shauna handed me the menu. "We've changed our minds—*nothing* looks appealing." She looked pointedly at me and my face burned hotter. "We just want coffees, please."

I nodded, my smile now so tight it hurt. "Four coffees coming up."

The entire time they were there, they only had coffee, ordering free refill after refill, sometimes complaining it wasn't hot enough, then saying the coffee was too hot. Next, they'd say that it was bitter and tasted old, they wanted a fresh pot. Whenever I had to pass them on the way to another table, they'd snicker and laugh or say "Oh, miss?" until I wanted to kill them.

Finally they left. The other waitress said, "What was up with that table? I thought they were your friends."

"We're not friends."

"Well, you did a good job of dealing with them." She leaned in. "I had a group of bitches like that when I was in school too. Just ignore them."

I tried, but they came in every weekend after that, sometimes two days in a row. Mostly they just ordered coffees, sometimes a plate of fries to share. And they'd do stupid stuff, like unscrewing the lids on the salt and pepper shakers so they'd spill when I picked them up. Most of the waitresses knew the girls were giving me a hard time and tried to seat them in another section, but sometimes the restaurant was full and there were no other options. If my side was full, I'd breathe a sigh of relief, but I knew they'd just come back another day.

. And then, on the first Saturday in May, Nicole came in with them.

I was shocked to see her there, let alone with them. Mike was running the front and he didn't know what was going on. I hadn't wanted to involve him, knowing he was friends with Shauna's father—Frank McKinney came in sometimes with other cops. Mike sat them in my section.

I went over to their table. "What are you doing here?" I asked Nicole.

Shauna said, "Hey, no one talks to my friends like that."

Still looking at Nicole, I said, "Since when are you friends?"

I'd never seen them hang out before—I'd never seen Shauna hang out with *anyone* younger before. Nicole looked up and I noticed she had on a lot of makeup—mascara, shadow, eyeliner, blush, and a bold pink lipstick. I hadn't seen her wearing that much since the party back in January. I also hadn't noticed her sneaking out for at least a couple of weeks, maybe a month, and I wondered if she broke up with that guy and was out looking for a new one. She'd done a good job with the makeup but it made her look older, and I felt a sudden stab of fear for my baby sister, who maybe didn't know how sexy she looked.

"I can be friends with whoever I want," Nicole said. The words were brave but she sounded tentative saying them, still not used to standing up to me. Shauna gave her a smile of approval, and Nicole sat straighter, smiled back.

I was going to say more but then I noticed Mike watching from the bar.

"Are you going to order anything?" I said.

Nicole ordered fries, and the other girls milkshakes. I could hear them giggling as I walked away.

"Doesn't she know how awful her hair looks?" Shauna said. "I mean, does she even brush it? Ugh."

I hated myself for doing it, but I went to the bathroom and stared at myself in the mirror and tried to smooth my hair down, fix my makeup, not sure why it mattered but feeling embarrassed just the same. When I came out again, Nicole was watching, but glanced away, smiling at something one of the girls said.

That night I confronted Nicole at home.

"Why are you hanging out with those skanks?"

"What do you care?"

"The only reason she's hanging out with you is to piss me off."

"Oh, get over yourself, Toni. She's fun—and she likes me. Just because you hate her doesn't mean I have to."

"You're not going to think it's so fun when she decides she doesn't like you anymore. Why aren't you hanging out with Darlene?"

I'd noticed that Darlene wasn't calling but hadn't given it much thought until now.

Nicole shrugged. "We're not friends anymore."

That was weird. They'd been friends since they were kids. "What happened?" Darlene was okay, a little quiet and boring and not as pretty as my sister, with a freckled face and an upturned nose, but she was still nice.

"I don't want to talk about it." Now she looked close to tears. "What does it matter to you anyway? You've never cared about any of my friends before."

"I'm just trying to help. Shauna will drop you soon, but not before she makes sure that no one else wants to talk to you."

"Shauna told me what happened between you guys when you used to be friends—you shouldn't have messed around with her boyfriend." Nicole frowned at me. "She was really hurt that you betrayed her like that."

"Is *that* what she told you? She's lying, Nicole." I sat on the bed beside her, held her gaze. "You have to listen to me. Brody and I were just talking one day and she flipped out—she turned into a super-bitch overnight and they made my life hell for a year. They're *still* making it hell."

Nicole looked doubtful. "But she's been really nice to me. All the kids in my class are jealous." She smiled, looking proud. I remembered being in Shauna's circle, feeling like I was on top of the world, powerful and cool. I also knew how much it hurt when she dropped me back to earth.

"Fine, figure it out for yourself. Just stay out of the restaurant."

She turned back to her homework. "Whatever."

# CHAPTER NINE

## Rockland Penitentiary, Vancouver

### March 2010

I had been in the joint for twelve years and would soon be allowed to have escorted temporary absences. I was scared and excited. Over the last year I'd been taking some life-skills classes, learning how to balance a checkbook, how to look for jobs, things like that. And Margaret had been teaching me stuff about grocery shopping, budgeting, finding apartments. But I was terrified I wouldn't be able to last on the outside, that I'd screw it up somehow. It was safe inside. I had friends, I knew the routine. Inside I had status. Outside I'd have the stigma of being an ex-convict, a murderer. I still remembered how brutal it had been while I was out on bail, the whispers and the shame.

Margaret and I talked a lot about it. "You're going to do fine," she said. "Damn right it's scary—a lot has changed in twelve years. But you just keep your head on straight and you'll make it through. You're a survivor."

She was right about a lot changing. Whenever we watched TV,

I studied the clothes and the gadgets. We weren't allowed Internet or cell phones inside, and I worried about finding a job when I got out. Who would hire me? Once I was on day parole and living at a halfway house, I planned on taking some computer classes, but I had a lot to catch up on. Now that I was getting closer to parole and had been showing good behavior, I was allowed to participate in a couple of work-release programs and had picked up a few skills. I was chosen to be part of the Puppy Program, training service dogs—which I loved, though it was hard to let them go. I swore one day I'd have a dog of my own.

I also worked a few hours every day at the prison mechanics shop, where I liked using my hands, the physicality of it. The smell of oil reminded me of Ryan, how he used to work on his truck or motorbikes. He'd also be nearing his parole date and I wondered how he was doing and whether he'd be released soon too. I worried that he might have screwed things up and added time to his sentence.

Sometimes we worked outside in groups, cleaning up parks and streets. It was nice, feeling the fresh air and sun on my face. I'd turn my back on the officers and the other girls and pretend that I was in a real job somewhere, or working in the yard of my very own house. However I imagined the outside world to be now, though, I knew it would probably still be completely overwhelming. An idea that became even more apparent when I had my first escorted temporary absence.

You're only allowed four hours on ETAs, so I went to the beach and sat staring at the waves, the correctional officer close behind, watching. I walked down to the shore and jammed my hands into the cold water, weeping because I'd forgotten what cold salt water felt like, smelled like. I threw my head back, inhaling the air, sucking it down in big gulps. I even licked my hand, my eyes closed as I pretended I was back in Campbell River. I felt happier than I had in years, but then we returned to Rockland and I saw those big iron gates and thought about how I wouldn't get another pass for months, and I cried.

The second time, I asked to go to a mall. I was excited at first, giddy and exuberant to be outside, with real people in the real world. I caught some stares and wondered if I looked weird or something, then I realized they were sensing my excitement, my joy. I felt a giggle welling up in my throat, the desire to shout, *I'm free!* But then the noises, the voices, the bright colors and lights, the scents of perfumes and food, people jostling me, crowding against me, became overwhelming. I had to leave.

For the rest of my time, I asked the officer to drive me around. I sat in the back of the car, looking out at the world, feeling safer with the glass and metal between us. I asked him to stop at a park near one of the high schools, where some kids were clustered. I studied the girls, their clothes and hair, their constant texting, remembered being young. It felt like a million years ago. Then I saw a young couple kissing on a bench, the boy brown-haired like Ryan, the girl with long black hair like me. I caught my breath at the stab of pain sharp under my ribs. The couple finally pulled apart. It wasn't Ryan and me. We didn't exist anymore, not like that. I asked the officer to take me back.

By my third ETA I was frustrated and impatient, angry with just four hours of freedom, wanting more. I was still on the out-side, looking in on the rest of the world. I wanted to be a *part* of it. This time I bought a hot chocolate and sat on a bench in the center of the mall, forcing myself to absorb the chaos. I had to freeze my legs in place and ignore the urge to run and run and run. Eventually my pulse settled, my body relaxed a little, and I started watching people. I thought about Christmas shopping with my parents, how Nicole and I would save up to buy the perfect shirt or pair of jeans, thinking we'd die without them. I saw some young girls in a store trying on dresses and wondered if they were getting ready for a prom. I watched them preen in front of the mirror and felt the old anger coming back again, the memory of the things that had been stolen from us.

I studied women who were about my age, their clothes and their mannerisms. If I hadn't gone to prison, would I be like them? Would I work in a bank or some business? Or would Ryan and I have gotten married, maybe even had kids? Would we have lasted? It was an impossible question. I thought of Nicole again. Would she have become a wife and mother? My mind drifted to Shauna and her friends. Where were they now? I imagined them all married, happy with families, and another hot stab of anger shot through me.

The officer came over. "Toni, time's up."

I threw my drink into the garbage, the taste now bitter in my mouth.

For the year after that, I was allowed unescorted temporary absences. I had to stay at the halfway house on the island and I was only allowed four a year, each one lasting seventy-two hours. It was all part of a gradual approach to integrating inmates back into society. The first UTA I had to stay inside, had to watch everyone come and go, hating the smell of fresh air on them. But after that I was allowed to wander around and get to know the city. I wasn't able to look for work yet, but I introduced myself at a few of the animal shelters and took a couple of brief courses at the employment office on basic computer skills and building a résumé. The Internet had been completely overwhelming at first, but then I found I loved zipping from Web page to Web page. I resisted Googling my own name, though, or anything to do with Ryan and my family.

Mostly I liked to walk around the parks along the ocean or sit on a bench and people-watch or read a book. I tried to take mental snapshots of everything so I could describe it to the girls when I got back to Rockland. I'd thought they might not want to hear it, but they said they loved my stories, so I made special note of different things I'd eaten, like a pumpkin scone with cream cheese icing, or weird people I saw. Margaret loved hearing about the food, Brenda liked hearing about hot chicks, and Amber wanted to know about boys. But I never looked at men, always too scared to see someone who reminded me of Ryan.

Finally, the middle of March, I was granted day parole. I was going to the halfway house. If I did well in the next year, I'd have another parole hearing and hopefully be granted full parole. The night before my release I was antsy, both excited to be leaving and terrified I'd mess it up somehow, and anxious about leaving Margaret and my friends. I didn't know what I was going to do without them. I could tell Margaret was also upset, because she'd been cranky the last couple of weeks before my hearing and snapped at me about stupid stuff. I'd been hurt when I saw her spending more time with the other girls and a new inmate who'd just joined our cell block. But then I remembered how I had to get angry and hard to let go of Ryan. Maybe it was the same for her.

I was in my cell, taking down the magazine photos I had on my wall—dogs I wanted one day, places I wanted to see, the ocean—when they all showed up wearing funny hats they'd made out of cardboard and carrying a cake they'd made from Twinkies. I burst into tears, and cried even harder when Margaret enveloped me in her arms and said, "I'm going to miss you, girl."

I gave Amber any treats I had left from the canteen, and Brenda and Margaret got my music collection. I also gave Margaret my TV and wrote each of them a letter. In the morning they stood on the range and waved me off as I followed the guard down the hall, carrying my few belongings. I didn't see Margaret at first and was hurt, then I noticed her downstairs by the doors. She held me for a long time.

"Stay safe out there, honey. And remember, you have to make it for all of us, okay? I don't want to see you back in here again."

We broke apart, tears in our eyes.

I said, "Don't worry. I'm not coming back."

# CHAPTER TEN

## WOODBRIDGE HIGH, CAMPBELL RIVER

### MAY 1996

Nicole was at the restaurant the next weekend, ordering count-less cups of coffee, sharing eye rolls with Shauna and the girls when I brought them over.

"No offense, Toni, but those jeans don't do a *thing* for you," Shauna said. "When you walk away, you look like a boy!" Nicole seemed embarrassed, her eyes shooting to my face. But then Shauna gave her a look and she laughed along with them. I was careful not to show that the words hurt, but I spent a lot of time in the kitchen trying to calm down. It hurt even more that my own sister was just sitting there, listening and not saying any-thing.

Ryan told me Shauna would get bored with Nicole soon, but Nicole started spending more time with them, going to movies, even having sleepovers at Shauna's on the weekend. When I heard Shauna's car pull up outside our house, music blasting, I'd dis-appear to my room, hating the sound of Shauna's voice as she politely talked to my mom in the kitchen. Once, Mom even came to my room and told me that Shauna had apologized for the fight that had happened at school and said there were no hard feelings on her part.

"I'm glad you girls worked things out," Mom said.

"We didn't work anything out, Mom. She's just saying that."

"Well, she's not upset with you. She's grown up to be a very nice girl."

The air left my lungs and I stared at my mom. "They're *awful* to me, at school, work, everywhere. They even messed up my friendship with Amy."

"I heard Amy was upset because you spend all your time with Ryan. You can't drop the rest of your life because of a boy."

"Who told you *that*?"

"It doesn't matter," she said quickly, and I wondered if it had been Nicole. If so, she had to have gotten it from Shauna.

"It *does* matter. They're lying. Shauna called Amy's boyfriend and told him that she cheated on him—but she pretended to be me, so Amy would blame me for it."

Mom paused, like she was thinking about what I'd said. I actually hoped for a minute that she'd see my side of things, might even be angry on my behalf.

"I can't keep up with everything that's going on with all you girls," she said with a sigh. "When Shauna's at our home, I'd like you to at least be polite—she's one of your sister's friends. Nicole says you've been really rude."

I was about to tell her how they'd been treating me at the restaurant, but the phone rang and my mom ran to get it. At dinner, I again thought about bringing it up, but then decided there was no point in saying anything else. No one, especially my mom, believed that Shauna was a bully and a liar.

Soon the girls started driving Nicole to school, and I left earlier so I didn't have to see them—sometimes I took my car, sometimes Ryan picked me up. I couldn't get away from them anywhere. At home Nicole and I avoided each other. Only speaking, and barely, when our parents were around. In the morning, Nicole would look normal—hardly any makeup, a T-shirt and loose jeans— then at school she'd morph into one of Shauna's girls, hair rippling down her back, tight jeans or skirts, full makeup, walking confi- dently down the hall—and never making eye contact with me.

She'd also started sneaking out again at night. I'd hear her win- dow opening and shutting, then in the morning she'd be in the kitchen, talking and laughing with my mom about something, cheerfully greeting me with a "Good morning, Toni!" And when I didn't respond, she sighed. Like I was the problem.

It got so bad at the restaurant I considered quitting my job, but no matter where I went, Shauna would find me. Plus, I liked working at the Fish Shack and I made really good tips. But every time Shauna and her gang showed up, I'd mess up an order or add something wrong on a bill. I was worried I might get fired.

One night when Nicole was out again with Shauna and the girls, I tried to talk to my dad about it while he was cooking some curry. The air smelled warm and spicy. I grabbed some plates and started to set the table.

"Where's Mom?" I didn't want her to know what was happen- ing. She'd turn it around somehow and make it my fault.

"She's meeting with the Realtor." My parents had gotten into buying and flipping houses. Mom loved real estate, poring over magazines, crunching numbers, talking to her agent on the phone, trying to get the best deal.

"Dad, I have to talk to you about something."

"Hmm?" He kept stirring the curry while reading a recipe.

"Those girls that Nicole's hanging out with are trouble—every time they come into the restaurant they totally mess with me. I don't know what to do."

He stopped stirring and faced me, his expression worried. "What are they doing?"

He listened as I talked, then shook his head sympathetically, but my face was hot. I wondered if he'd think I was a loser, which at the moment I kind of was.

"Sounds like they're being real jerks," he said. "How does Nicole react when this happens?"

"She just goes along with it. Did you know she's sneaking makeup to school? You should see what she's wearing too. Mom would freak."

"She's growing up, Toni. She's like you were at that age, starting to figure out who she is, but she's not partying and her grades are good." Unlike me.

I didn't want to tell him she was also sneaking out, partly from loyalty and partly because I didn't want to draw attention to myself. I was supposed to be home at a decent hour as long as I lived at home, so sometimes I came home from work on the weekend, then snuck back out again to see Ryan.

"It's horrible, Dad. I can't take it anymore."

He sat down at the table and thought for a moment, his hands fiddling with one of the napkins. "I'll talk to Nicole, okay?"

I let out my breath. "Thanks, Dad."

"Just try to remember that she's always looked up to you in a lot of ways. I think she admires how brave you are and wishes she was more like you."

That caught me off guard. I knew Nicole liked things peaceful at home, so I'd never considered there might be a part of her that wished she was more rebellious.

Dad continued, "She's probably flattered that older girls want to spend time with her, and maybe she's too intimidated to confront them about the way they're treating you. But she'll see them for who they really are soon enough."

Later, when I was lying on my bed, listening to music, I thought about what he'd said. I hoped he was right, but I worried about what might happen if Nicole tried to break away from that group. And what might happen if she didn't.

Dad talked to Nicole when she got home—Mom was still out. They came to my door afterward and Nicole said, "I'm really sorry that I've been bothering you at the restaurant. I won't do it again," while Dad stood beside her. Her words sounded sincere but her eyes were angry. She was pissed that I'd involved Dad.

"Maybe we should just keep this to ourselves," Dad said. "There's no reason to worry your mom." In other words, he didn't want to deal with Mom flipping out. Nicole and I agreed.

I hoped things would change after that, but Nicole was in the restaurant with the girls the very next weekend. She didn't laugh as loud at Shauna's jokes and barely looked at me, but she was still there, and in my mind that was enough. Then one day Mike saw me choking back tears in the kitchen—after Shauna had made a comment about my boobs being like fried eggs, while she poured ketchup all over her plate, making loud squirts with the bottle— and asked what was wrong. I tossed down the rag I'd been using to wipe the counter and told him what had been going on. He headed over to Shauna's table, motioning for me to follow. He placed both his hands on the table, his big body looming over them.

"You girls are going to have order meals if you want to keep coming in here. And Toni won't be serving you anymore. If you give *any* of my waitresses a hard time again, you won't be welcome back. Got it?"

Shauna's face turned red and angry. The other girls looked mortified. Mike stared hard at Shauna, his eyebrows raised. Shauna finally nodded. Nicole's eyes were big and scared. I thought Shauna would make some snarky comment after Mike walked off, but they left the restaurant right away. Mike told me that if they gave me any more trouble I should come see him immediately—he didn't care that Frank McKinney was Shauna's father. I loved him for believing me.

The girls stopped coming in after that. But Nicole was going to Shauna's house almost every weekend and a lot of nights during the week. One afternoon I came home and they were all in our living room. I stopped still, caught off guard. Shauna was sitting next to my mom, flipping through one of our photo albums while Mom pointed out a picture of us as babies.

"Oh, my God. How cute!" she said, then looked up at me. "Hi, Toni."

Rachel, Kim, and Cathy all looked up with smiles and said, "Hey, Toni," like we were best friends.

Nicole seemed worried, glancing around at all of us. I stared at them mutely for a few seconds, trying to convey my anger with my eyes: *What the hell are you doing in my house?* My mom shot me a dirty look, so I mumbled, "Hey."

Shauna said, "I was telling your mom how bad I still feel about what happened at school, and how glad I am that we got over it." She smiled at me.

So that's how she was going to play it.

"Yeah, me too." I smiled back. "Great to see you."

I grabbed something from the fridge, trying to look casual, though my heart was beating fast, then went up to my room. My bedroom door was open. Had they been in there? I quickly looked around. Some of my stuff seemed to have been moved. I didn't keep a journal and didn't notice anything missing, but I was sure they'd been in my room. What were they looking for? Did Nicole tell them about the knife? Luckily that was in my packsack.

I didn't know what they were looking for, or if they found it, but I hated thinking of them in my room, touching my things, laughing and giggling. I hated thinking about what they might be planning for me next.

Maybe that was the point. They wanted me to be scared, wanted me to know that no place, not even in my own home, was safe from them.

For the rest of May and into June, we settled into a grudging routine. They stayed away from the restaurant, and I stayed away from them at school. I tried to focus on graduation, getting our caps and gowns, rehearsing. Nicole was still spending all her free time with them and sneaking out at least once every weekend. Because she was careful not to alarm our parents, they never thought to check on her. I kept waiting for the fallout, for her to have some sort of fight with the girls, but they seemed to adore her, treating her like she was *their* little sister, walking with their arms around her, braiding her hair. She also seemed happy, happier than she'd been for a while. I noticed she'd started playing love songs over and over in her bedroom, sometimes softly singing along. I didn't see her with any boys at school or at any of the parties where I occasionally saw her when Shauna and the girls brought her. But I wondered if she'd started seeing that older boy again.

With both of us working, Ryan and I didn't have a lot of time together on the weekends anymore, but we'd leave notes for each other in our lockers, and we were counting the days until school was finished. Then we could work full-time and hopefully get a place together by the end of the summer. We were collecting things already, hitting flea markets and buying towels and dishes if Walmart had a sale. It made me feel grown up, shopping together, Ryan's arm slung around my shoulder as we pushed the cart through the aisles, comparing prices, talking about what we needed. I could see our lives unfolding, could feel how great it was going to be. We just had to get through the summer.

———

Finally it was the end of June and we graduated. Mom cried through the whole walk-up ceremony—I was pretty sure it was in relief. There was a dry grad the next weekend, like a prom, but I wasn't sure if we were going to that or up to the lake, where a lot of the kids would be partying. Ryan was pushing for the prom, then the party—he said he wanted to slow-dance with me and see me in a dress for once. But I was worried about what Shauna and her friends might do—a big school dance would be the perfect place to humiliate me one last time.

The week before we graduated, Amy had called me at home one night. I was surprised when my dad handed me the phone and said who was on the other end. I took the phone to the living room and said a cautious, "Hello?"

"Hi, Toni. How've you been?" She sounded nervous.

"I'm okay." Why was she calling? Was it a setup? I waited for the telltale laughter in the background.

"I just wanted to say I'm sorry for how I treated you. Fiona, she's mad at Shauna right now because Shauna's been flirting with Max." Fiona was another girl we used to hang out with, until she got a new car, better clothes, and started hanging out with the popular kids. Fiona and Max had been going together since the ninth grade. "So Fiona told me that Shauna told *her* that she was the one who really called Warren."

"I tried to tell you that it wasn't true."

"I know." Now she sounded embarrassed. "He was just so convincing."

"I was your friend—you should have believed me."

"The way Warren said it, it sounded so real. And then all that other stuff he told me you'd said about my family and all . . . It just made me so upset I couldn't even think straight. I'm sorry I said those things about you and Ryan."

I was quiet. I could imagine how convincing Shauna had been, but it still hurt—and I didn't know if I could trust Amy anymore.

"Some of the stuff you said, that was harsh," I said.

"I'm *really* sorry." Her voice was thick, her nose stuffy, like she might be crying. "But you also said some mean things."

"I know. I'm sorry too."

"Can we be friends again? And go to the dry grad together? I'm dating Chad now, and he hangs out with Ryan sometimes at the pit."

"I don't know. A lot has changed." I wanted to forgive her, but I felt tears come to my own eyes when I remembered how devastated I'd been when she dumped me, how humiliated I felt standing in the hall while she called me a liar.

She sighed. "Okay, I understand. Just think about it, please. I *really* miss you."

I talked things over with Ryan, and he thought I should forgive Amy. Part of me still wanted to be angry, another part wanted to show Shauna she hadn't taken everything away from me—and I had missed Amy a lot. I called her and we got together a couple of times, but it was different, and I wasn't sure if we'd ever be close again. I was cautious now, scared to reveal anything personal to her. I did tell her Nicole and I hadn't been getting along, and she also thought it was weird that Shauna would even want to hang out with someone younger.

"I mean, your sister's really cool and popular and pretty, but Shauna doesn't usually like anyone who could be competition. I wonder what will happen after they graduate. I heard that all of Nicole's old friends are pissed at her."

"Yeah, me too." Ryan had told me the rumors. I felt a pang for my sister, who was so caught up in Shauna's world she wasn't seeing how many bridges she'd burned or what Shauna and her crew might do to her one day—how brutal they could be when they decided someone had wronged them. Then I remembered her looking away when the girls said mean things to me at the restaurant. She was one of them now, and there was nothing I could do about it.

In the end, I decided to go to the dry grad with Amy and her new boyfriend. Ryan really wanted to go, and in a way, so did I. Ryan told me it would be stupid to miss out on something just because of Shauna. When he looked at me with his brown eyes all hopeful, sliding his hand up my shirt, talking about how we could bring a blanket out to the lake for later, I had to say yes.

I found a dress at a consignment store, a simple sheath in a deep red, kind of 1950s old Hollywood glamour. I also found some long gloves and a beaded clutch purse. I felt good when I brought it all home, but the night of the grad I started second-guessing everything. Maybe my outfit wasn't glamorous, just weird and old-fashioned. I regretted not taking Amy up on her offer to get ready together but I'd thought it might be too distracting, and there was a part of me that was still holding back a little from her.

Nicole came to the bathroom door when I was staring at myself in the mirror. "Wow. You look so pretty—that dress makes your body look amazing."

I thought she was being sarcastic and spun around to tell her off, but she looked sincere, had this proud sort of smile on her face. I muttered, "Thanks," and turned back to the mirror, holding my hair up, trying to decide what to do with it.

"Do you need help? I can do your makeup," Nicole said.

I wanted to tell her to screw off after how she'd been treating me for months, but she sounded like she meant the offer—and she was really good at makeup. I wanted to look different that night, classier, so I said, "Okay. Thanks."

Nicole put my hair in a loose chignon and did some cool things to my eyes with pencil, shadow, and mascara. When she was done, she said I looked like a dark-haired Marilyn Monroe, and I felt beautiful. I couldn't wait to see Ryan's face. While Nicole was working on me, we laughed and joked for the first time in a long time. It was so nice I almost forgot everything we'd gone through, until my mom called out, "Phone, Nicole. It's Shauna." And she ran downstairs, after giving me a guilty look. I felt sick, wondering if they'd planned something for that night. Was that why Nicole had helped me? Just so Shauna could humiliate me later? I stared at myself in the mirror, at the girl I barely recognized. For a moment I was tempted to take all the makeup off and let my hair just go loose, but then the doorbell rang.

Ryan looked handsome in his tuxedo as he made small talk with my mom and dad, and confident, like he'd worn one all his life. The expression on his face as I walked toward him—stunned, proud, awestruck—made me glad I hadn't undone all of Nicole's work. He gestured down at himself, his eyebrows raised. I gave a thumbs-up and he laughed. In the other room, I could see Nicole still talking on the phone. She smiled, but there was something in her face now that I didn't like, a nervous guilt. Dad took our photos, Mom calling out, "Come on, Nicole. I want one of you girls together."

Finally Nicole put down the phone and we got a picture together, but her body language was different now, tense, almost like she thought being nice to me was the betrayal.

At the dry grad Shauna stayed to one side of the gym with her girls and I stayed on the other with Ryan, Amy, and her boyfriend. I tried to relax and have a good time, but I was tense, waiting for something to happen. I was even nervous about being there with Amy. Though she was being like always, and if anything a little nicer, still trying to make up for our fight, I couldn't help wondering if it was all an act. Shauna looked really pretty in a tight white satin dress with her hair curled, and seemed to be enjoying her date, who was the captain of the hockey team. Cathy and Rachel were also beautifully dressed, though I noticed Shauna had made sure her dress was the tightest, and each had dates—other players on the team. Kim had brought one of the guys who was part of the drama club.

Whenever Ryan and I danced, we stayed out of Shauna's sight. I buried my face in his neck and tried to let myself get carried away by the music and the feel of his body against mine, but I kept taking little peeks, trying to see what Shauna was doing. Once, she danced by me and mouthed, *I'm going to get you, skank.*

Ryan told me to brush it off and spun me away, but the night was ruined for me after that. What had she planned? How was she going to get me this time? Was there something else she knew about me, some other lie she could make up?

Finally, the teachers announced the night was over. I watched Shauna and her friends filter out, still shocked that they hadn't done anything. I half expected them to have written something on Ryan's truck, but nothing seemed to be wrong with it.

"I told you they weren't going to do anything," Ryan said.

"There's still the party."

"Nothing will happen."

I appreciated that he was trying to make me feel better but I couldn't help thinking, *You can't keep me safe forever. Not from her.*

In the front seat of the truck we changed into jeans and tank tops and I let my hair down, then we headed out to the lake. I tried to get into things at the party, tried to enjoy the roaring fire, getting high with our friends, drinking beer after beer, but I had a hard time catching a buzz, my fear pulling me down, making me edgy and tense. I could tell Ryan was getting annoyed, he kept telling me to relax. But I couldn't because Shauna had also come out there with the girls and their dates. This time, though, Shauna didn't even glance in my direction as she laughed with her friends and danced to the stereo someone had set on the hood of a truck. But I couldn't forget she was there, couldn't stop wondering what she had planned, couldn't stop waiting for the hammer to fall.

Around two in the morning, parents were picking kids up, and some of them, who were supposedly sober, were driving off. Finally Shauna and her date, and Rachel and her date, got in a car. They were leaving. I took what felt like my first breath of the night. But then I saw the window rolling down as they drove past Ryan and me. I flinched, waiting for something to be thrown at me. Ryan tried to pull me behind him. Shauna, her head out the back window, said, "Hope you had a nice night, loser." Then she collapsed back inside, everyone laughing.

Ryan threw his bottle at the back tire rim and the glass exploded. The car stopped, like the driver might get out and fight, but Ryan picked up another bottle as if he were going to throw it, and the car took off. Ryan gave me a hug.

"I'm sorry, baby. At least she didn't screw up our whole night."

But then I realized she had—or actually I had. Just like she wanted.

Ryan drove up to the highest cliff at the lake and we sat in the truck, looking out over the water, smoking another joint. We had music playing softly, our hands entwined, my head on Ryan's shoulder. We could see headlights from other trucks and cars in the distance, the glow of campfires.

Ryan said, "Do you want to join them again?"

"Not really, but we can if you want to."

He pulled me closer and whispered in my ear, "You're the only person I want to be with."

I closed my eyes, smelling his cologne, feeling the heat of his body, the solidness of his shoulder under my cheek, and let the music wash away Shauna and Nicole and my parents and everything that had happened that year. We had graduated. It was over. Shauna was over.

# CHAPTER ELEVEN

## ECHO BEACH HALFWAY HOUSE, VICTORIA

### MARCH 2012

The halfway house was on a quiet tree-lined street two blocks from the ocean. Whenever there was a crime in the neighborhood, the police came knocking on our door first. The house was old and drafty but big enough—three stories high—to house twenty-five parolees. The staff had offices on the main floor, and we had to sign in and out at the front desk. The kitchen was also on the main floor and we were responsible for our own food. Everyone had a set of dishes and cutlery, and a small cupboard. Until I found a job I'd get a minimum allowance of $77 per week. Once I was working, I'd have to pay a small rent.

I'd arrived in the afternoon, feeling exhausted and messy. The first thing I did was take a shower. It had been years since I'd had one to myself, since I could actually lock the door and blast the hot water. I didn't have to watch everyone around me, my body tense. Even now, I still caught my breath when I heard a movement out in the hall. I paused, listened. It was nothing, just someone walking to her room. I lathered my body again and again, face up to the water, eyes closed, glorying in the moment, the strong water pressure that hadn't turned to a freezing cold trickle after five minutes. Last year, when I was still on temporary absences, I'd never been able to relax long enough to have a shower, just took sponge baths in the sink—I could hear easier without the water running.

My skin, pale from lack of sun, was getting red and splotchy, so I turned off the shower now and stepped out, taking my time as I toweled dry, savoring even this moment: a decent towel, peace and quiet, a feeling of what it might be like once I had full parole and a place of my own. I thought about what to do that day. I had to start looking for work soon—that's where most of the other parolees were, the house was empty—and there were some programs in the community I needed to attend. But for now I thought I might go to the beach, or maybe a coffee shop.

I'd found one on my last UTA, had stood in line and stared at the people ordering their lattes, mochas, and cappuccinos with such ease while I studied the chalkboard and all its offerings in a panic. I settled on a black coffee, only to be thrown again when the clerk asked which size: tall, grande, venti. I muttered, "Large," but then, feeling trapped by a man standing too close behind me, pushed my way out of the line, stumbled to the bathroom, and hid in a stall until my heart rate settled down. I left without getting my coffee. Today I wanted to try again, wanted to order one of the drinks with the whipped cream on top.

Back in my room, I walked around, still in my towel, and put away my things. The rooms were just large enough for two single beds, with bedding in a pale blue and beige checked pattern that looked like it had been washed a thousand times, and two chests of drawers. In a corner of the room there were lockers for our personal stuff. My new roommate was out, probably working. We hadn't met yet and I was nervous—a bad roommate could make your life hell. I tried to focus on the goal: one more year and I could apply for full parole. I just had to stay out of trouble.

I had pulled on a pair of jeans and was standing in my prison-issue sports bra—I was going to have to go shopping for clothes soon—when my door was flung open. Instinctively, I grabbed one of my shoes from the floor in case I needed a weapon. A woman came rushing into the room, heading toward the dresser on the other side. She looked about my age but was probably a few years younger. Bleach-blond hair, too much makeup, scarred skin, like she'd been a druggie. She glanced at me, her eyes surprised, then started frantically searching through her top drawer. She kept looking back at the open doorway, saying, "Shit, shit, shit."

"Are you okay?" I said.

She glanced at me again and looked like she was about to say something, then I heard heavy footsteps in the hall outside our room. The woman froze, her hand still in the drawer. We both turned toward the door.

A large woman was standing in the hallway, her face angry and mean. Wide-shouldered, with huge breasts that hung low under her black T-shirt, salt-and-pepper hair in a crew cut, a jagged pale pink scar running down the side of her head, almost to her ear. She was wearing men's jeans with a wallet chain, and tattoos covered most of her throat, forming a collar. My body tense, I studied the tattoos up and down her meaty arms—prison style. Was she from Rockland?

One of the tattoos was a name, HELEN, with a knife through the H and a rose wrapped around the handle. Her eyes flicked to me. Now I remembered. Helen Rosanboch. She'd been at Rockland last year, but we'd been housed in different cell blocks, so we hadn't had much contact. She had a violent reputation, and I'd heard she was a doper. But she got along well with the guards, knew how to play the game, and had friends on the inside. I didn't know why Helen was at my door, but it couldn't be for anything good. I gripped the shoe tighter.

"Where's my fucking money?" she said to the blond woman.

So that was it. A beef over a bad debt.

"I've got some—and I'll get the rest by the end of the week." The woman's voice was scared, her body almost cringing into the corner.

Helen took a few steps into the room. "We had a deal, Angie." Helen glanced at me again. This time it was a challenge, daring me to interfere.

I turned back to my suitcase, but I could still see them both from the corner of my eye. I dropped the shoe onto the bed, where I could reach it. I was worried about a fight starting in our room. It was the last thing I needed.

Angie said, "I'll get it—real soon, okay?" She grabbed a sock from the drawer, pulled out a handful of crumpled bills.

"You've been holding out on me?" Helen came all the way into the room, snatched the money from Angie's hands, and started unfolding the bills. She mouthed the numbers as she counted, then tucked them into her bra.

"No! I was just waiting until I had it all. Can you give me a break, Helen? Just a few more days. You know my kids—"

"I don't give a fuck about your kids. I've got kids too. What about my fucking kids, Angie?" Helen's voice was enraged, her face beet-red. She gave Angie a shove. She fell against the side of the dresser, slid down to the floor with a thump. Helen leaned over her. "You think you can play me like that?"

Angie was cowering, one arm over her face. "I'm not. I swear!"

I turned back toward them, my pulse racing. Should I do something?

"I told you—you don't pay me back on time, I'll fuck you up."

Helen smacked Angie hard in the face, bouncing the back of Angie's head against the side of the dresser with a hard crack. Angie let out a gasp.

I stepped forward. "Hey, that's enough."

"Stay out of this," Helen said over her shoulder, giving Angie another slap. Angie was trying to curl into a ball, her arms covering her face and head.

"Stop, please. I'm sorry." Angie's muffled voice sounded terrified.

I glanced at the door. Where the hell was the house staff? Couldn't anyone hear this? No cameras in the room either. Shit, I really didn't want to get involved but I couldn't stand by while this woman got her ass kicked.

Helen bent over and grabbed the top of Angie's hair, lifting her off the floor. Angie cried out and scrabbled at Helen's hand. Helen spun her around, threw her facedown onto the bed. Her knee in the middle of her back, she pressed Angie's face into the pillow. Angie was crying hard now, making muffled pleas.

"Come on, Helen. Cool it," I said.

She turned, her knee still on Angie's back. "What did you just say?"

I had to be smart now, had to try to head this off without a fight. "If you fuck her up, she's not going to be able to pay you back, right?" I smiled, trying to show we were all good, I was on her side. But I sat on the edge of my bed and gripped my shoe as if I were loosening the laces to put it on. If she rushed me, I could rear up and smash my head into the bottom of her chin.

"This isn't your problem," Helen said.

I loosened a lace. "When it's in my room, you make it my problem."

Helen's hand lifted from the back of Angie's head. Angie turned her face to the side, gasped for air. Her eyes met mine.

"You want to take me on?" Helen said.

"I just want to unpack my shit and have a nice day." I kept my voice calm. "First day out of the joint, you know how it is." I gave her another easy smile.

Helen got off Angie. Took a step toward me. Her face was calculating, like she was trying to figure me out. Close up she was even taller and bigger than I'd thought, and I had a feeling that if I tried to jam my head into her chin, I'd be blocked before I made it halfway up her body. I got to my feet so I'd have a better chance of fighting. The shoe was still in my hand.

She walked over, until we were barely a foot apart. Her gaze roved over my body, my small breasts, my tattoos. It wasn't sexual—it was intimidation.

"I remember you." She smiled, and it wasn't friendly. "You hung with Margaret and her girls, thinking your shit don't stink, thinking you're all that. Here I run the house, and my bitches don't run around causing problems. Got it?"

"Got it." I was trying to keep my cool, but her trash talk about my girls, disrespecting Margaret, pissed me off. She was so close I could smell her—onions and something muskier, sweat covered by perfume.

Her lips curled. "What, you don't like me talking about your bitches? One of them your girlfriend or something?" She lingered on the word *girlfriend*, trying to make it sound dirty.

A voice in the back of my head was saying, *Toni, let it go, she's not worth it.* But something about the way she was standing there, so confident, like she could get away with anything, made me want to take her down a peg.

"You need to back the fuck off," I said.

The second the words were out of my mouth and the mean smile spread across her face, I regretted saying anything. I'd just given her exactly what she wanted—an opening. I felt her step closer and braced. Was she going for it?

"I don't like your attitude," she said.

"That makes two of us."

"You fucking stupid?" Helen said. She gave me a hard push.

I stumbled back a few paces, almost hitting the edge of my bed. "Touch me again and I'll break your hand."

She rushed me, trying to grab me in a bear hug. I put my hands up to my forehead, my arms tight to my body, then pushed out fast with all my strength, breaking her hold. I reached up and clapped the shoe hard against her ear. Her eyes were stunned, but she shook off the pain like a dog shaking off water and punched me hard in the gut, making me double over. She came in for another blow. I jabbed my elbows into her lower ribs, forcing her breath out in a whoosh, then kneed her hard in the inner leg, then the outer leg, then her groin. Quick hard blows. She grunted but she was still coming at me, her face red and sweaty, striking me in the kidneys, ribs, thighs, anywhere it wouldn't make a mark. I reached up and dug my fingers deep into the notch below her trachea, into the tender spot. She gasped and fell to her knees. I pressed down harder.

A noise behind me, the door opening, another woman's voice.

"What the hell are you doing?"

It startled me, and my hand loosened for a moment. Helen reared up, slammed her shoulder into my gut, grabbed me around my knees, and knocked me onto my back. I hit the floor with a thud. She flipped me onto my stomach and sprawled her massive body over me, pinning my arm behind my back.

I squirmed, gasped for air, tried to kick up at her, but she had to weigh well over two hundred pounds.

"Better make it fast," the woman said. "Harley's coming up the stairs."

Harley was one of the staff. I hoped to hell Helen wasn't as stupid as she was mean. She leaned close, her breath hot in my ear. "Stay out of my way."

Finally the weight left my back. I stayed still, trying to catch my breath, slowly moved my aching arm forward, groaned into the floor.

Helen's voice said, "One week, Angie." Heavy footsteps walked out of the room. The other woman followed.

I rolled onto my side, then eased up into a sitting position. I winced as I held my side and tried to flex my arm. I glanced at my roommate. She was gingerly rubbing the back of her head where she'd hit the dresser.

"Why did you do that?" she said.

"She had it coming." I stood up slowly, sucked in my breath from the pain in my side.

She glanced at the door, like she was expecting Helen to burst in. "Now she's pissed at you too. She's going to make your life hell."

I crawled onto my bed, nursing my wounds, my roommate's warning resonating. I'd been so close to finally getting my life back. Now Helen was going to screw up everything. Why did I let her get to me like that? She was nothing.

I got up early the next morning and showered while my roommate and most of the other residents were still sleeping. The faint smell of coffee lingered in the kitchen, and I assumed some of the house residents were off to their jobs. One older woman with short dark hair and a scar that dragged down the side of her mouth sat in the corner, eating her breakfast. She gave me a nod and a "Good morning." But she looked down again, making it clear that she didn't want a conversation. Maybe she'd already heard about my run-in with Helen.

I could deal with loneliness—I'd gone through it before—but it still stung. I thought about my girls on the inside with a pang, remembering how close we'd all been. I hoped the shit with Helen would settle down and I'd make some new friends at the house eventually. I hadn't reported the assault—nothing would get me beaten up faster. Plus, there's always an assumption by officers that you must have done something to incite the problem. They might pull me out of the halfway house until things calmed down, which was the last thing I wanted. I just had to deal with it.

At Rockland, I'd spoken to the counselor about job opportunities once I was on day parole and I had a résumé made up. The counselors at the halfway house also provided guidance, and there were some house sessions once or twice a week on living skills. That morning I was going to the labor office to see what was posted, then I planned to drop off some résumés around town. I had a meeting with my community parole officer that afternoon to check in. That evening I was going to attend a Narcotics Anonymous meeting in town—the halfway house staff had already given me a list of the local chapters, and there were also meetings in the evening once a week at the house. I still didn't believe I'd had a substance abuse problem, but that didn't mean crap. I was high at the time of my sister's murder, so one of my conditions of parole was that I had to stay away from drugs and alcohol. No problem there. I never wanted to feel again like I did the night Nicole was killed, never wanted to be that oblivious.

There were other challenges—how to figure out a bus schedule, how to get my driver's license reinstated, how to apply for ID so I could open a bank account. But I decided to take it slow, one thing at a time. I took my envelope of résumés, dressed in my best jeans and shirt, and headed out. First, I was going to the thrift store so I could buy some clothes for job interviews. I walked along the road, breathing in the fresh air, noticing the shadows the big oak trees made on the streets, the tidy homes with their flower-filled yards. Despite the fight with Helen the night before, I was thrilled to be on parole.

We hadn't gone down to Victoria often when I was growing up because it was almost a two-and-a-half-hour drive. Sometimes, though, our mom would take us to the museum or Fisherman's

Wharf, and we loved shopping in the city. Campbell River only had one old mall with a few small stores, but Victoria had three big malls and lots of boutiques downtown. Victoria was the oldest city on the island and also surrounded by the ocean, but it had a much different feel than Campbell River. There were Parliament buildings, quaint Victorian-style homes, horse-drawn carriages, the inner harbor, and lots of tourists snapping photos of the float planes and street artists. On the boardwalk, I stopped and admired a few sketches, wishing I could buy one, but clothes were more important right now.

I found a few items at the thrift store, a pair of black pants, some shoes, a plain white blouse, a small fitted blazer. It looked like something I'd seen women wearing on TV. I wished I could show it to Margaret. We used to watch *Dancing with the Stars* at Rockland, oohing and ahhing over the skimpy costumes. Margaret would get a crush on a contestant each season, getting upset if they didn't win. We'd make ourselves snacks—you get creative with food from the canteen—then plop ourselves down on the old couch. Trash-talking with the other inmates was the best part, especially when Margaret would tell them to "shut your holes." I liked watching the dancing, but none of the guys did it for me. I wasn't like Margaret, who loved all of them—she even wrote fan letters. The only one I had a soft spot for was a moto-cross racer who competed one year. He'd reminded me of Ryan. Sometimes, when he was dancing, I'd blur my vision, and imagine it *was* Ryan, but then I'd want to cry, so I stopped doing that. It was easier not to remember, not to think about it.

But I found my mind drifting to him now. Was he at the men's halfway house? Did he ever think about me anymore?

I changed into my new clothes, then spent the afternoon walking around and delivering résumés, with no luck. I also found a bus schedule and figured out how to get to the animal shelter. When I told the staff I was available for walking the dogs, they said I could come by any weekend. I spent some time in the back, poking my fingers through the kennel bars and rubbing muzzles and talking to the dogs, saying things like "Hey, I've been locked up too." The chain-link fences, the noise, the shelter uniforms reminded me of Rockland, but there was a kind of comfort in that familiarity. The outside world was now the scarier place.

When I got back to the halfway house it smelled like burned meat and onions. Helen was in the kitchen, frying some hamburger patties and talking to a couple of women sitting at the table. I was starving but didn't want to make my dinner with her in there, so I kept walking. She grabbed my arm when I passed the kitchen door.

"Hey, Murphy, one of my forks is missing. You take my fork?"

I gave her a dirty look. "No, and get your hand off me."

Nervous snickers from the table while Helen's fingers dug into my arm, pressing on the tendons. I tried not to flinch. She moved closer.

"You better hope it's not in your room or you're in deep shit, you hear?"

I couldn't figure out why she was making such a big deal about a fork. At the most I might get a warning from the staff for accidentally taking someone's belongings. What was her problem? Was she just trying to start another fight?

Her fingers dug in harder. "I said, *you hear?*"

"I heard."

In our room, Angie was on her bed, playing music on an iPod. The night before we'd talked a little after Helen left. She was twenty-six and had been in for drugs and prostitution but said she was clean now, trying to get her life together so she could get her kids back. She'd borrowed money from Helen so she could get her youngest a birthday present.

I crouched to look under my bed, lifted up the mattress, felt along the edges for any cuts or tears.

"What are you doing?" Angie turned off her music.

"Helen's missing a fork."

"And you think it's in here?" She sounded confused.

"Something's in here. Harley will be up any second."

"Oh, shit." Angie stood up. "If he finds drugs in here, we're screwed."

We ransacked the room, trying to work fast and quiet. We checked our pillowcases, drawers, the tops of the sills, light fixtures. Every time we heard a step outside or a noise in the hall, we froze and stared at the door, only letting out our breath when the person moved on. Finally we heard the knock.

I tried to look calm as I opened the door. "What's up, Harley?"

"Sorry, girls, going to have to do a room check," he said. "Stand out in the hallway, please."

Angie and I watched from the doorway. Harley was a big guy with yellowed teeth and a two-pack-a-day smoking habit. He had small, mean eyes, and was supposed to be a real hard-ass if you messed up. I hadn't had any trouble from him yet, and didn't want any now. Each time he lifted a book or checked the pockets on our clothes or reached into our shoes, I held my breath. Finally he stopped in the middle of the room, slowly looking around, his face thoughtful.

Then I saw the smudge of dirt on the windowsill, near the potted fern. I stared at the spot, tried to remember if the dirt had been there before. I checked Harley's face. Had he noticed? He started walking toward the window. My body felt hot all over. I glanced at Angie. Her cheeks were also flushed, her eyes shiny like she might cry. Harley was reaching out toward the plant.

I rested my head against the doorframe, closed my eyes, felt like crying too. I was screwed. Two days out and I was going back to Rockland.

"Your window's leaking," Harley said. "I'll have someone look at it."

I opened my eyes. Holy shit, he hadn't noticed the dirt.

At the doorway he gave us both a hard look. "I don't know what you two did with the stuff, but we'll be watching you."

When we heard his boots going down the stairs, I walked over and felt around in the plant. My fingers touched something round and soft. I pulled out a small bag of marijuana. We both stared at it.

"Shit, she *really* has it in for us," Angie said.

I hid the drugs in my shampoo bottle. When the kitchen cleared out and I heard voices in the backyard, where Angie said Helen and the girls liked to smoke, I went down and made myself some soup. Then I walked to an NA meeting, dropped the marijuana in a Dumpster on the way. I was feeling good when I got home later. Though I wasn't an addict, I'd come to enjoy the support of twelve-step programs and had made some friends that way in Rockland, plus I'd learned some stuff. I was hoping the same thing would happen on the outside.

I was getting ready for bed when Helen came into my room.

"I know you got my fork, Murphy." She looked around, her eyes stopping at the plant. I'd drawn a smiley face on a piece of paper and balanced it on the leaves.

She turned to Angie. "You think you're funny?"

I stepped in front of her. "Fucking hilarious."

She glared down at me. "Give me my shit back."

"You fuck with either of us again, Harley's going to be searching *your* room. And I'll make sure he finds something interesting."

She grabbed the front of my shirt and brought her face down

close to mine. I met her eyes, tried not to recoil from the sour smell of her breath.

"You're screwing with the wrong person," she said.

"I'm just getting started."

She let go. At the door she turned and said, "I won't forget this."

# CHAPTER TWELVE

## CAMPBELL RIVER

### JULY 1996

After graduation, I started working full-time at the Fish Shack. I didn't see Nicole much because she was usually at the beach with Shauna and the girls. Sometimes, when I was leaving the house for work, they were outside waiting for her. They'd laugh and call out taunts when I walked to my car, but only when my parents weren't home—sometimes they were hanging around the kitchen, using our phone and drinking all our pop, their high-pitched voices setting my teeth on edge. It was easier to ignore them now, though, easier to just smile and walk away. School was over and Ryan and I were starting our new lives. Soon we'd get out of Campbell River and I'd never have to see those bitches again.

We'd been getting some hang-ups at my house, never when my parents were home, only when it was me and Nicole. She'd look nervous when she saw me answering the phone, and I wondered if it was that boy calling again. If it was one of the girls, they'd say something mean, and they called often. Nicole spent even more time over at Shauna's now, staying overnight a lot of weekends.

One night, I heard the doorbell ring and answered it. Frank McKinney was dropping Nicole off, one arm holding her up. She could barely stand, her eyes glassy, her clothes messed up, the smell of beer rolling off her.

"Can I talk to your parents, Toni?" he said.

I called for them, and they came to the door. I pretended to leave but stood just out of sight at the top of the stairs so I could hear what was going on. McKinney was apologizing to my parents, saying he'd come home from work and found that the girls had all been drinking. They'd gotten into some of his beer.

"I've already spoken with Shauna, and it won't happen again."

My mom sounded really upset when she said, "Please go to your room, Nicole, and we'll talk about this in a minute."

Nicole stumbled past me at the top of the stairs, her face angry and embarrassed, then disappeared into her room.

Downstairs, Mom said, "I'm so sorry she acted like that in your home."

"It's normal for kids to experiment at this age." McKinney's voice was calm. "You don't want to come down too hard on them or they'll just start hiding it."

My mom nodded, her gaze intense on McKinney's face, as though he held all the answers. "Daughters, they can be so challenging sometimes."

"They sure are." He leaned against the side of the doorjamb, one hand resting on his utility belt, his head cocked as he smiled down at my mom. "But you've got a good one there. I don't think you need to worry about her."

"Usually she's so responsible. I just don't know what got into her. . . ." My mom looked up and saw me at the top of the stairs. "You don't need to be here right now, Toni."

As I walked away, I heard her say, "What did I just say about challenges?"

After McKinney left, I heard my parents talking to Nicole in her bedroom. They didn't sound that angry, though, more surprised and embarrassed that a policeman had driven their daughter home. Nicole apologized and said, "I won't do it again. I just wanted to try a few sips and I didn't realize how much I'd had until I started feeling weird." My parents went on for a while about responsible drinking, and Nicole agreed with everything they said, her voice contrite.

When I opened the bathroom door an hour later, I caught her staring at herself in the mirror, wearing just her bra and panties, her eyes soft and dreamy, her hand pressed to her lips like she was savoring something.

"Jesus, Toni, can't you knock?" she said when she saw me, then shut the door quickly.

I wondered if there'd been a boy over at Shauna's, but Nicole never really talked about guys in general. She didn't even have posters up of rock stars or actors—if anything, she talked more about women she admired. Part of me wondered if she was messing around with one of the girls—if that was the big secret. I'd heard rumors that the girls fooled around with each other sometimes, usually just to tease boys. But I remembered Shauna teaching me how to kiss, her soft, cherry-flavored lips pressed against mine. Though Kim was the more obvious choice, I'd never noticed her and Nicole being overly affectionate. I considered snooping through Nicole's room, then remembered how much I'd hated it when Mom did that to me once. And since the night when Nicole helped me get ready for grad, we'd just been doing our own thing and getting along okay. It made me uneasy, but if I started to pry that would just create another war.

After the night Nicole came home drunk, she started sneaking out more and staying out later—I wouldn't hear her footsteps on the roof sometimes until three or four. One morning, around seven, I knocked on her door to ask if she'd seen a pair of my sunglasses. She was usually up by then, so when she didn't answer I got suspicious and opened her door a crack. Her bed was empty, but a few pillows were stuffed under the blankets to look like a sleeping body. I was standing there, trying to figure out what to do, when my mom called up the stairs.

"Did you still want a ride to the beach, Nicole?"

I hesitated, then yelled down, "She's sleeping."

I held my breath, half expecting Mom to come upstairs, but she muttered something about teenagers and left the house. Dad was already at work. When Nicole crept in through the back door a half hour later, I was waiting in the kitchen.

She stopped when she saw me, her eyes widening. I could see her mind working, thinking up lies, wondering if I knew she was only just coming home.

"Why are you sitting there?" she said.

"Where have you been?"

"I went for a walk."

"Seriously? You can do better than that. You're still wearing makeup from last night." It was faded and smudged, but she was definitely wearing eyeliner, and her clothes, a short jeans skirt and white tank top, weren't walking clothes.

She dropped the act. "Does Mom know?"

"No, I told her you were sleeping."

She looked relieved. "Thanks."

"Yeah, well, I shouldn't do anything nice for you. Not after how you treat me. What were you doing all night?"

"None of your business," she said, and tried to walk past me.

I stepped in front of her. "It is my business when you're staying out this late and I'm lying for you. I don't want to tell Mom and Dad, but if something bad happened to you . . ."

"Nothing's going to happen to me."

We held gazes, her eyes big and innocent. I considered dropping it, but I still had that uneasy feeling. "You've been acting weird—for, like, months."

"Everything's fine, I'm just—" She stopped herself.

"You're just what?"

"I'm having fun, okay? You sneak out all the time."

"I'm older than you. And fun can lead to trouble sometimes."

She rolled her eyes. "Puh-lease. You're starting to sound like Mom."

My face flushed. "I'm not *anything* like her."

Nicole pushed past me. "Then don't act like her." At the stairs she looked back at me, softened her voice. "Don't worry about me, Toni. Really, I'm fine."

The next weekend, Nicole said she was going camping with Shauna and the girls. Rachel's parents were taking them all and picking her up while both my parents were at work. Nicole had her gear down by the front door and was sitting in the living room, waiting for them, while I made myself a coffee in the kitchen.

"I thought you were supposed to be at the restaurant," she said.

I glanced at her, saw how nervous she looked. Something was up. I had been about to tell her I was leaving in five minutes, but I decided to say, "I don't have to be in for another hour."

She blinked in surprise, stood up and looked out the window, then back at me. Her panic was obvious.

"What's going on, Nicole?"

She tried to look casual, hooking her fingers in the belt loops of her jeans shorts. "Nothing. Rachel's parents are late."

I sat on the couch. "Maybe I'll wait with you."

"Fine," she said. But I could tell she was freaking out, a fine sheen of sweat making her face glow. She glanced at the phone.

"Do you need to make a call?" I said.

She glared at me, but I could see her thinking. "Maybe I'll call and make sure things are okay." She walked over to the phone, dialed a number.

"Hi, it's me. I just wondered if your mom was coming soon?" She paused for a moment, then said, "Okay, I'm just hanging out with my sister. . . . No, she doesn't have to be at work for an hour. . . . See you then." She hung up the phone and walked back to the living room. "They're running a little behind."

"Who are you *really* meeting?"

"I've already told you, Rachel's parents are picking me up."

I took my coffee to the kitchen and picked up the phone. "Then I guess if I hit redial I'll hear one of them answer, right?"

Before I could do anything, she ran over and shoved me hard, pushing me into the edge of the counter. I was so surprised that I dropped the phone. We both reached for it at the same time, struggling as we scrambled on the floor. She was stronger than I remembered, but I was finally able to straddle her.

I held the phone up in the air, started fumbling for the button.

"Toni—please!"

Nicole's face was so desperate and panicked that I hesitated, the phone still in my hand. I really wanted to know who she'd called, but then I noticed the diamond flower pendant sitting in the hollow of her throat. I'd never seen her wear it before. It must have slid up from under her shirt during our fight.

"What's going on with you?" I said.

She started to cry. "It's a secret, okay?"

"Are you sneaking off to see that boy from the party?" I pointed to the necklace. "Did he give you that?"

She nodded, tears rolling down from the sides of her eyes. "He's in college, okay? Mom and Dad wouldn't approve of him. We want to spend the whole weekend together. You understand, right? It's like you and Ryan."

I sat back on my heels, still straddling her. "I don't lie about him being my boyfriend." I narrowed my eyes, thinking. "What else is wrong with him?"

She hesitated, then said, "He works for Dad."

Holy shit. Mom and Dad would be so pissed if they knew she was messing around with one of their employees. I tried to think which one it might be, but Dad had a lot of young guys working for him on a few different job sites.

I handed her the phone, then stood up and glanced at the clock. "Is that the time? Oops, I think I screwed up. I do have to leave for work now."

She jumped up off the floor, her hands on her hips. "You bag. You were just messing with me!"

"It's not fun, is it?" I grabbed my purse and keys, then paused at the door, looking back at her. "Are you okay, going off with this guy? Some of Dad's workers, they're pretty sketchy."

She nodded. "It's totally safe—we just want to be alone." Her face was pleading. "Don't tell Mom and Dad. I love him, and they'll make us break up."

I thought of my own relationship with Ryan, how I thought I'd die when they grounded me for that month and I couldn't see him as much.

"I won't."

Later, at the restaurant, I wondered if I should have found out where they were going. What if this guy did something to her? Should I tell my parents what she was really doing? They'd flip, and I'd have hated it if she ratted me out. Despite how shitty she'd been that summer, Nicole was still my sister.


A few days later I was at the beach with Amy, relaxing and enjoying the sun, talking about our guys. Ryan and I had looked at some apartments, feeling very mature as we discussed pros and cons of the various buildings and locations. Amy was jealous because her boyfriend didn't want to move in together yet. Amy and I had been getting closer as I slowly let down my guard, and it almost felt like old times that day. Eating chips, reading magazines, laughing.

Then Shauna, Cathy, and Nicole showed up.

I don't know where Rachel and Kim were, but they both had summer jobs. Kim was now living full-time with Rachel. She'd gotten kicked out of her home in July, but no one was really sure what had happened. I had a feeling it had something to do with her being gay—her mother was supposedly a religious fanatic.

Amy and I were sitting on our blankets and talking as they walked by.

"Hi, Amy," Shauna said.

Amy said, "Hi," and Shauna moved on.

I shot Amy a glare and she gave me an apologetic look, whispering, "It was just reflex." It bugged me that she was still so nervous about Shauna—that we were both nervous.

The girls spread out their towels a few feet away from ours.

I said to Amy, "We should just get out of here."

We both stood and started gathering our things. I was wearing a new black tankini—which Ryan loved—and I was feeling pretty good until I overheard Shauna say, "She still doesn't have *any* boobs. Poor Ryan!"

Cathy started laughing and said, "Maybe she's saving up for a boob job!"

I glanced over, ready to tell them off, but was distracted when I saw Cathy pouring a wine cooler into her plastic cup. Now I realized that all of the girls had the plastic cups, in bright colors, straws poking out from the top. Nicole's face also had a telltale shine and she fumbled as she reached for her suntan lotion.

I turned to Amy. "Screw them—they're all drunk. Let's stay for a bit."

"You sure?" She glanced over at the girls, looking freaked out—which made me angrier. Why should we be so damn scared of them?

"Yeah, I'm not running away from her." Truth is, I kind of wanted to keep an eye on Nicole. I didn't like that she was drunk like that, especially out in public. And it was only noon. When had they started drinking?

We sat back down. A couple of times I went to the water for a swim, but it took all my strength to walk with confidence, hearing the whispers and giggles from where the girls were sitting. I noticed that Nicole was quiet, though, almost seemed depressed. She'd laugh, but it sounded fake, and a couple of times I saw Cathy and Shauna roll their eyes at her. Were they starting to pick on her?

I went for another swim, and when I got back to my towel, Amy's face was tense. "I want to leave. They're saying awful stuff about us. "

"Okay." I started gathering up my things, shaking out my towel. I was tired of them glaring at me anyway. We could just go to another beach. If Nicole did something stupid, that was her problem. But I still glanced over at her, checking to see if she was drunker, and noticed she was staring at the parking lot, her eyes narrowed like she was trying to see something better.

Shauna turned too. "Shit, what's my dad doing here?"

Now I saw the black pickup parked slightly around the corner. Nicole was covering her drink. "Should we hide the—"

"I'll handle this." Shauna left her drink out in the open and said to Nicole and Cathy, "Stay here and don't say a word."

She walked to the parking lot, spoke to her dad through the window for a moment. He drove off and she walked back to the girls.

"He was just seeing if we wanted a ride home, but I told him we're okay." She noticed me watching. "What are you staring at?"

She was so confident, so sure that she could get away with

whatever she wanted. She wasn't even worried that her dad had almost caught them drinking. What else were they getting away with? What else were they getting *Nicole* into?

I turned back around, but not before I caught Nicole's eye. She looked down at her drink and took a long swallow.

A couple of weeks later, near the middle of August, Nicole started acting weird at home. She spent hours in her bedroom listening to music and only left the house when Mom and Dad dragged her out. When Mom called her down for dinner, she'd say she wasn't hungry. During the day she just lay on the couch watching TV, flipping through the channels. Some days she didn't even shower.

"Why aren't you going to Shauna's anymore?" I asked her one day when she was on the couch again. I was hoping they'd had a fight. I'd seen a car like Shauna's drive by one night, turn around, then drive by again.

"She's away with her family." Guess it wasn't Shauna. It had been a white car, though, I was sure of that. Maybe that guy she was seeing?

"What about Cathy and the other girls?"

"They're all busy. They've got jobs and stuff."

"So what's wrong with you? You've been moping around."

"I'm just bored." But she looked like she might cry.

"Did you break up with that guy?"

She threw down the remote. "Why can't you just mind your own business?" Then she ran up to her room, slamming the door behind her.

The next night when I came home after work, Mom was waiting up, sitting at the kitchen table. Dad was sitting beside her. Their faces were serious.

"What's going on?" I said.

"The Percocet from when your father had his surgery is miss-ing from our medicine cabinet," Mom said, her voice cold and hard. "There was nearly a full bottle left." I remembered that Dad had been given painkillers after his shoulder surgery last year but hadn't thought about them since. I didn't even know he had some left.

Now I was pissed. "Are you accusing me of stealing it?"

"It didn't walk out of the house on its own."

"I don't do drugs like that, Mom."

"We know you smoke pot."

"So what? Most people on the island smoke weed." *And I could use some right now.*

Dad said, "Ryan's father has been arrested for dealing prescrip-tion drugs in the past, so we wondered if Ryan might have—"

"He didn't *steal* them—I can't believe you're saying this!" My face was hot, and I was near tears. "He's never done anything wrong."

"I doubt you snuck into the Andersons' house all by yourself that night," Mom said. "You've lied to us before."

I sat in frustrated silence, angry at myself for breaking into the neighbors' house, for giving them something they could use against me. I was even angrier when I thought about who probably took the pills.

"Nicole's been partying with Shauna every weekend this sum-mer. I even saw her drinking at the beach. Why don't you ask *her* about your pills?"

My parents shot looks at each other, and my dad said, "Maybe we should ask Nicole to join us."

He went to get her while I stared at the table, refusing to meet my mother's eyes. Nicole came downstairs. Her eyes flicked to me, then to Mom. She was wearing pajamas—frilled cotton shorts and a pale pink tank top with a kitten on it. She looked even younger than sixteen. I was suddenly aware of my tight black tank top, my dark makeup, seeing myself through my parents' eyes, their troublemaker daughter. But I wondered if they'd taken a good look at Nicole lately. She'd lost more weight, her collarbone showing, and her hair was limp, like she hadn't washed it for a couple of days. She sat down at the table, arms wrapped tight around her body.

"What's wrong?" she said.

"We just want to talk to you for a moment," Mom said. She told her about the pills being missing, then gently said, "Are you okay? Is there anything you want to tell us? I know sometimes you have bad cramps—"

"Oh, sure," I said, "you accuse me of stealing your pills, but—"

"Give it a rest, Toni. We're talking to Nicole."

I sat there, shaking my head at the bullshit and glaring at Nicole. She'd better tell the damn truth or I was going to kick her ass.

"I didn't take them," she said, "but I saw Toni in your room yesterday."

"You little bitch!" The words exploded out of me. "I'm going *to kill you.*"

My dad said, "Toni, that's enough!"

"I didn't take them. She's lying." I turned to Nicole. "Tell them the truth—you know I didn't touch them."

She just stared at the table as she mumbled, "I didn't take them either."

I said, "I'm going to get you for this."

"Don't you threaten your sister!" Mom said.

"She's lying her ass off—and you don't even care." My voice turned mean and mocking. "You think she's soooo perfect. Why don't you ask Rachel's parents if Nicole really went camping with them last month? She's got an older boyfriend—he works for Dad. She snuck off with him."

Nicole gasped, tears coming to her eyes. "That's not true. I was with Rachel and the girls all weekend—we went to Big Bear Ridge. You can call her mom. She'll tell you." She shook her head, crying now. "I don't have a boyfriend. I don't know why she's telling these lies about me."

Mom was also shaking her head as she looked back at me. "I'm sick of your hateful attitude, Toni. We've done everything we can to get through to you, but nothing works. We didn't want it to come to this, but you're turning into a liar and a thief—and you've left us no choice. It's time you moved out."

I stared at her in surprise and hurt, the words ringing in my head.

"Fine," I said, choking back tears. "We were going to move out in a couple of weeks anyway. We found a place, but we can't get in until the end of the month." I wished I could leave now, but Ryan's dad had been on a bender all week—Ryan had been staying at a friend's. And Amy was on a family vacation.

"You can stay until then." Mom looked sad but resigned, like the fight had gone out of her. "I'm very disappointed in you, Toni. I sincerely hope you start getting your life together soon, before you waste it all away."

My dad also gave me a sad smile. "If you need any help moving, you kids let me know."

I looked at him through my blurred tears. "I didn't do it, Dad."

"I'd like to believe you, Toni, but you make it hard to trust you."

"Dad—" I wanted to defend myself, wanted to make that disappointed look leave his face, but I couldn't get any words past the tight lump in my throat.

He turned to Nicole. "Is there anything you want to tell us? Your sister said she saw you drinking at the beach."

She hesitated. I thought she might confess, her body stretching forward for a moment, like she was reaching out, but then she slumped back in her chair.

"She's just making that up because she was mad that I was hanging out with Shauna. I don't drink."

My dad looked doubtful. "You've been moping around the

house the last couple of weeks. If there's anything you want to talk about . . ."

"I'm fine." Now she sounded annoyed, but she quickly added, "I'm just bored. Everyone is away. Can I go to bed now? I'm really tired." She gave a big yawn.

I could tell my dad knew she was lying about something and wanted to ask more, but my mom reached out and touched Nicole's shoulder. "I think we could all use some sleep," she said. "Let's go to bed."

They left the room, left me sitting at the table, crying and hating my sister. She'd lied, and I was going to get her back for it.

# CHAPTER THIRTEEN

## Echo Beach Halfway House, Victoria

### January 2013

After I threatened to plant something in Helen's room, she backed off and we stayed out of each other's way for almost a year. I still didn't like her, and I was damn sure she didn't like me, but as long as she left me alone, I didn't care. Angie, my roommate, moved on and I got a new one named Joanne, who was all right. She kept her side clean but was hyper and talkative. Younger than me, with brown straggly hair, squinty eyes that needed glasses, and a big mouth—she was always talking while eating, which drove me nuts. She'd done time for drug dealing, and I had a feeling she might still be doing a little dealing on the side. Sometimes when I was walking home I'd see her and Helen talking to a shady-looking character in the park down the street, their bodies hunched over and secretive. I was careful to never show any facial expression that would reveal I noticed or gave a shit. And I didn't. If they wanted to screw up their parole, that was their business. I had different plans for my life. I just had to stay the course.

I had a decent job at a local restaurant. I'd started scrubbing pots in the kitchen, moved up to prep cook, and was now allowed to take on some shifts at the grill. It was hot, greasy work, and I came home stinking of fried food, but I didn't care. I was happy to be finally socking away some money. When I wasn't working I was meeting with my community parole officer, going to my programs, where I made a few friends, and helping out at the animal shelter, walking dogs. I wasn't settled enough to get a dog of my own, but it was one of the first things I wanted to do when I got my own place in Campbell River. I'd decided to move back there when I was granted full parole.

I knew it was crazy—that's where all the shit had gone down, where people still hated me, including my own mother. Still, I had to go back, had to prove I wasn't the bad person they thought. I don't know if I wanted, needed, to prove that to myself or to everyone else in town. But I had to go there and at least try.

When I'd gotten day parole I'd written my dad, told him I was in Victoria. My parents would've already known that I was eligible for parole because, as victims of my "crime," they would have been allowed to come to the parole hearing, but they never showed. He wrote back, saying that he was happy I was out and doing well. He made no mention of a visit and neither did I.

I didn't know where Ryan was or whether he was on parole but I figured he'd probably stay in Vancouver. Knowing he could also be out made it more tempting to try to communicate in some way, but we still wouldn't be allowed to see each other. My parole officer had made that condition very clear, which made me think Ryan might also be out on day parole. Sometimes I'd wake up abruptly in the middle of the night, feeling like I'd heard a tap on the window, half expecting Ryan to be out on the roof, but of course he was never there.

It was now the end of January, and I was going before the

Parole Board in the middle of March. I needed to show that I had work lined up for when I was on full parole and a place to live after I left the halfway house. I'd written a long letter to Mike, my old boss in Campbell River. I told him I was working at a restaurant in Victoria, attending programs, and trying to get my life together. I asked if there was any chance I could work for him again, explaining how hard it was for ex-convicts. I included a résumé detailing all the jobs I'd had in prison and a nice letter from my current boss, who said I was a hard worker. I knew it was a long shot, so I was surprised when I got a letter from Mike a week later saying he could use another cook starting that March, which was when he knew I'd hopefully be granted full parole. He also told me a friend of his had an old boat in the marina that I could live on and rent for cheap. I was excited and relieved. If everything continued to go well, I could have full parole soon and be back in Campbell River, building a real life.

One day, around the second week of February, I was cutting through the park when I noticed a blond woman standing by one of the trees. She had an old denim jacket pulled tight around her and she was dancing on the spot, like she was trying to keep warm, but her movements were jerky, agitated. She was watching the path ahead of us and didn't notice me coming from behind. She was close to where I often saw addicts huddled in the bushes, so I had a feeling she was waiting for her dealer. Finally she heard my steps and turned around. I could see now that she was clearly an addict, her face thin and skeleton-like, her overbleached long hair dry and brittle-looking, her eyes dull. I was about to give her a wide berth when she whispered to me—softly, almost hesitantly—"Toni?"

I stopped in my tracks, took another hard look at the woman. She did look familiar, but I couldn't place her. Did I know her from Rockland?

She laughed nervously. "Wow, never thought I'd run into you again."

It was the laugh that did it. That deep, raucous laugh that all the boys in high school had liked. The drug addict was Cathy Schaeffer.

Painful memories assailed me in quick snapshots: Cathy and the other girls laughing at me at school, hounding me at the restaurant with Nicole, sitting close together at my trial, whispering. Finally I got a grip: this was serious, my being with her. I quickly glanced around and made sure no one was coming down the path. It wouldn't look good if I was caught talking to one of the key witnesses from my trial—being seen with a drug addict was bad enough.

I was about to keep walking when she said, "Are you out? Like, are you free now?"

I wanted to move past her, forget I ever saw her, but there was something in her voice, a nervousness mixed with shame that stopped my feet. I met her gaze, noticing her large, dark pupils, the sores on her face and hands, and wondered what had happened to the fun-loving wild party girl from high school. I could see faint traces of her former beauty—the high cheekbones, the wide curving mouth, the deep-set eyes, all eroded by years of substance abuse.

"I'm on parole," I said.

"That's good, right? Are you going back to Campbell River?" That nervous voice again, almost pleading, like she wanted me to forget all the damage her lies had done to my life. I stared at her. Did she know what had really happened that night? Had she helped kill my sister? Did she know who had? My silence was making her more agitated. She was bouncing on her feet, pulling her coat tighter, licking her lips like they were suddenly dry.

"Yeah, probably," I muttered, my own throat dry.

"I still live there—I'm just down for the weekend," she said. "Shauna's still there too . . . with her husband." I didn't know if she was just making conversation or warning me, but I felt my guts twist at the name. I didn't know much about the girls' lives since the trial, was surprised that Shauna was even still married. She'd hooked up with an older man that September, not long after Nicole's murder, and was already married with a child by the time she testified at our trial.

Cathy continued, speaking fast, either from nerves or drugs. "Rachel's got a family now too, couple of boys. She works at the hospital. Kim left right after your trial. We don't talk anymore. . . ."

"Good for her." I heard the anger in my voice, the bitter rage.

Cathy heard it too, stopped bouncing for a moment, her eyes registering danger. She took a step back. I felt my hands curl at my sides, fought the urge to attack her, to push her to the ground, and almost took a step forward, but then she said one word, one word that stopped the breath in my throat.

"Sorry."

We stood still, locked in the moment. A gust of wind blew one of her hairs across her face; a car alarm was going off somewhere. My heart was racing, my mind wheeling with questions. What did she mean? Was she about to confess to something? I tried to make myself calm down, take a breath. Think.

Speaking slowly, I said, "What are you sorry for, Cathy?"

"I'm just . . ." But she hesitated too long, like she was now thinking about what she'd been going to say. "I'm just sorry, you know, about the trial and stuff, how we were . . . in high school. . . ."

Her voice faded as she began to space out, her face pale, coming down from her high. She stumbled to a park bench, looked desperately down the path. Her dealer was going to show any minute. I started walking away.

"See ya, Toni," Cathy mumbled, like we were just two old friends who'd bumped into each other.

I ran the last mile to the halfway house—fast, trying to outrun my thoughts, my memories, and the fear that was still there. Those girls.

———

A week later I was starting to get over my encounter with Cathy and the painful memories it stirred up, but I was having second thoughts about moving back to Campbell River now that I knew Shauna was still there. In the end I decided to stick with my game plan and focus on the future, which was almost in my grasp.

Then Helen came to find me.

I was eating cereal in the kitchen one morning when she plopped her heavy body on the seat across from me, the chair creaking under her weight as she leaned forward. "You been talking to Harley about me?"

I looked up, confused—and noticed Joanne hanging out in the hallway, like she was keeping a lookout. This wasn't good.

I finished my mouthful of cereal. "Now, why would I do that?"

"Someone told him I've been dealing drugs—they searched my room."

And she thought it was me because of my threat. They obviously hadn't found anything or she'd have been sent back to Rockland. But she was still pissed. I glanced around the room and noticed one of the other parolees sneaking out of the kitchen. She met my eyes, looked away. Her name was Dawn and she also walked through the park on her way home from work. Did she rat Helen out?

"I haven't told anyone anything," I said, "because I don't *know* anything. I just served years for a murder beef. You think I'm stupid enough to cause a problem over you when I'm this close to my parole?"

I brought up the murder because I wanted to remind Helen I was someone she should be scared of, but she didn't look the least bit intimidated.

"I warned you not to screw with me, Murphy."

She got up and walked out.

———————

Later, I searched my room—if the staff hadn't found anything in Helen's room, she had to have stashed it somewhere else. I'd have to check every day. I did a cursory inspection of Joanne's side, not wanting to move her shit around too much. I didn't see any drugs, but they had to be somewhere. When Joanne came back from her job I ignored her as I got ready for bed. I hadn't had a problem with her hanging out with Helen before, but as far as I was concerned she'd crossed a line. Joanne was ignoring me too, which was just fine by me. I wanted to kick her ass but I had too much to lose—my hearing was in a month.

It stayed like that for the next week: Joanne and I ignoring each other, Helen watching me. There was a coffee shop I liked to visit, just to sit or read, but now I'd see Helen and Joanne there in my usual spot, so I'd have to get my coffee to go. I was barely eating and exhausted from waking up and glancing over at Joanne if she so much as turned over, waiting for her to attack me. I thought about Shauna and the girls, remembering the constant feeling that something bad was going to happen. I tried to tell myself that shit was different now, I was an adult, but I felt just as helpless and full of rage as I had in high school.

Helen started bumping into me in the halls, a push here, a little shove there. Some of the other girls I'd gotten friendly with started ignoring me. No one wanted to get involved. I couldn't go to any of the staff because essentially nothing had happened yet—and even if it had, I couldn't say anything, not without risking my parole. All Helen had to do was plant something in my room again and I'd be screwed. I had to hang tight, but it was getting harder and harder not to fight back. It wouldn't take long before she upped the ante, before the pushes and shoves wouldn't be enough for her. I didn't want to point the finger at Dawn because she had kids, but it wouldn't matter anyway. The only thing that would make a bully like Helen feel better was to seriously hurt me. She was going to try something, I just didn't know when.

A week later, I had the afternoon off. It was sunny, though still cool, only the first days of March. I grabbed one of my thick hoodies, a book, and a coffee, and walked to a park near the house, which overlooked the ocean. It was my favorite place to unwind. Sometimes I didn't even read, I'd just sit and stare out at the water, at the vast space. Often my mind would drift to the girls back in Rockland and I'd hope they were okay. I usually chose a bench that was in the open so I could see anyone coming or going. That day, though, an older couple were in my usual spot so I had to pick another one that was set back in the trees more. I still felt safe because Helen and Joanne were working.

I'd just turned a page in my book, eager to get to the next scene, when I felt a movement behind me. Before I could react, an arm went around my throat and I was being hauled over the back of the bench. The book went flying. I kicked and struggled. The hard metal of the bench dug into my back as I was scraped along it and thrown to the ground, my teeth biting into my tongue. I had just enough time to register that it was Helen, Joanne standing behind her, when they started coming at my face. I blocked the punches, twisting and rolling, felt a jolt of agony as Helen connected with my arm. Shit. They were wearing brass knuckles. This time they were trying to leave marks. I curled into a ball, protecting my face and head, and took hit after hit, to my kidneys, my back, my legs and arms.

Then a muffled voice. Joanne's. The blows finally stopped, footsteps running away, loud breathing fading off. Now another voice. "Oh, my God, are you okay?" Gentle hands on my arm.

I took my hands away from my face and opened my eyes, tried to catch my breath. I slowly uncurled my body, groaning.

A woman in a jogging suit said, "Do you want me to call an ambulance?"

I shook my head. "I'm okay." She looked worried, her hand on her cell.

I got to my feet and leaned against the bench, gripping the back as spots swam before my eyes. My knees almost buckled, but I held tight.

I forced a smile. "I'm fine, really. I'll call the police myself."

Once the woman had jogged off, I limped to the bathroom in the park and tried to clean up as best I could. Bruises were already starting to show on my body, but my face at least was untouched. When I walked in the door of the halfway house, I held my body stiff, every breath sending a stab of pain through me, but trying not to show that I was badly hurt. Helen was at the front desk, talking to one of the staff members. She looked surprised for a moment and nervous, her gaze shifting from me to the staff member and back to me, like she was waiting for me to say something.

"How you doing, Murphy?" she said as I signed in.

"Great." I nodded, smiled. "Never felt better."

Now her eyes flashed anger, but she couldn't do anything. I finished signing in and headed upstairs without giving her another glance.

Joanne was in our room. I walked over and grabbed the front of her shirt, pulling it up tight around her throat so she was forced to gasp for breath. My body was in agony, but I gritted my teeth. Her gaze flicked to the door, her mouth open as though she was going to call for help. I slapped my hand across her lips. I leaned closer until I could see every red vein in her eyes, smell stale cigarettes and something chemical drifting off her skin, made more pungent by her fear.

I said, "You touch me again, you do one fucking thing to me, and I'll kill you, understand?"

She nodded frantically. I released her and she dropped back down onto the bed, rubbing at her throat. I stood in front of her.

"Keep the fuck away from me or I'll gut you like a pig."

She met my eyes, looking even more terrified than when I'd been gripping her. She knew I wasn't making idle threats. I went to my bed, this time sleeping solid.

After that, Joanne stayed out of my way. Helen was still watching me, and I didn't doubt that if she had a chance she'd try to finish what she'd started. But I didn't plan on giving her an opportunity. I stopped going to the park and the shelter, only walking to work or my programs, and always with other people, never alone. When I was at the halfway house I avoided any of the common areas and stayed in sight of the staff at all times unless it was bedtime or I had to shower. Even then I made sure I came out holding something, like a mirror in my hands that I could smash and use as a weapon. My teeth ached from clenching my jaw tight, all my muscles at the ready. I lost some weight, only eating when I was working at the restaurant, and my breath constantly felt like it was stopped in my throat, but the days passed without any more incidents.

Finally, I was driven back to Rockland and had my parole hearing. I'd been nervous, damp circles of sweat under my dress shirt, and I'd hated having to express remorse for murdering my sister when I knew I was innocent, but it had to be done. To make my words resonate and ring true, I focused on my real regret about that night, how much I wished Ryan and I had made different decisions, how I'd do anything to take it all back. It was easier then, to express my shame, easier to share how much I wanted to do the right thing for the rest of my life.

I was granted full parole and would be allowed to live in Campbell River. I was going home, to a place where no one would be welcoming me.

While I was packing my belongings at the halfway house, Helen came to my door.

"Got a going-away present for you, Murphy." She threw a plastic bag at my bed and it came to rest by my suitcase. The bag had opened slightly when it fell and its gruesome contents spilled partway out onto my bed. A dead rat.

I remembered Harley setting traps under the house a couple of days ago, how Helen had smirked when I walked by. I glanced at her now.

"You better hope you never see me again, bitch," Helen said.

I turned back to my suitcase and kept packing. She stood there for a moment, watching me. I wanted to tell her off. But I kept my mouth shut until she finally walked away. She didn't matter anymore. I was finally free.

# CHAPTER FOURTEEN

## Campbell River

## August 1996

After Nicole lied about my stealing the pills, we didn't speak for a couple of days. We didn't even look at each other when we passed in the hall, and I waited until she was out of the bathroom before I left my room. Once, I heard her stop in front of my door and thought she was going to knock, but then she kept walking. The phone rang late one night and I thought it was Ryan, but when I went downstairs Nicole was just hanging up, her face pale and tears in her eyes. She brushed past me and ran upstairs, slamming her door.

The next day, I told Ryan about the call. "I think some guy's messing with her head. She's acting so weird. I still don't know why she lied about the pills."

"You don't think she'd do anything with them, do you? Like hurt herself?"

I paused, fear running through my body, then thought it through.

"No, not Nicole. She's always too worried about my parents' feelings and stuff. Shauna used to take her grandmother's pills sometimes for parties, so we could experiment. She probably talked Nicole into doing the same thing."

"Well, it's pretty shitty that she blamed you."

"Yeah." I still wasn't over it. It was bad enough that she'd been treating me like crap all year, but for her to outright accuse me? I could still see the looks on my parents' faces, the disappointment and shame that I was their daughter. The way they'd been treating me since was even worse, the stiff politeness, like they were just trying to keep things calm until they were finally rid of me.

That Friday evening, the second-to-last weekend of August, they went out to a late dinner with friends, then they planned on going to an outdoor concert down at the harbor. I was packing some of my books, getting ready to move out, when Nicole showed up at my bedroom door. I didn't even look at her.

"Toni, can I talk to you?"

"I don't have anything to say to you." I still didn't turn around.

"I'm sorry—for what I did." Her voice was small and timid.

Now I faced her. She was nervous, fiddling with the strap on her tank top, her shoulders burned. I'd seen her in the backyard the day before, lying on one of the chairs, not reading or anything, just staring at the fence.

I wasn't letting her off that easy.

"Sorry for what? Treating me like shit for most of the year, or blaming me for what you did and lying about it?"

She burst into tears, her shoulders shaking as she covered her face with her hands. I didn't know what to say. I was used to fighting, had wanted to swear and yell and scream at her. Her reaction caught me off guard.

I sat on my bed, waited for her to calm down. Finally, she took a few breaths and wiped her face with her hand.

"I know I've been awful. I can't believe what I've done." Her horrified expression made me think she was talking about more than just how she'd treated me.

"What's been going on with you?" I said. "You've been a super-bitch."

"I . . . I can't tell you."

I shook my head, angry, and made to get up again.

She held out a hand in a plea. "I *want* to tell you, I do, but I can't. I'm sorry, Toni. I just can't."

"So why are you here?"

"I needed you to know how sorry I am for how terrible I made you feel. It makes me feel sick." She grabbed her stomach. "I'll tell Mom and Dad I stole the pills. I just couldn't sleep—and I thought they'd help. I'll even tell them how mean I've been to you."

She sounded sincere, and she did look really upset, so I had a feeling she meant it, but she still wasn't telling me everything.

"Why aren't you sleeping?" I said.

"I just . . . I have a lot on my mind."

I gave her a look, but it was obvious she wasn't going to share anything else. "I'm moving out anyway," I said.

"You're really going?" She looked like she was going to cry again.

"Why do you even give a shit? You've spent months treating me like dirt."

"I told you, I'm sorry for all that. You're my sister, and it's weird thinking that you won't be here anymore. School's starting soon, and it will just be me for two more years, and—" Her voice broke, and she took a shuddering breath.

"I thought you'd like that."

"No." She shook her head but didn't say anything more.

"Okay, well, thanks for the apology." I got up and started packing again.

She stood there for a moment, then slowly walked over and sat on my bed, her body tense, like she was waiting for me to kick her out. Annoyed about how she kept stonewalling me whenever I asked about what was happening in her life, I was tempted. But I also wanted to see if she revealed anything else on her own.

"Are you working tonight?" she said.

"No, I'm going to the lake with Ryan." I wondered why she was asking, suspicious that she was going to tell Shauna or something.

"Can I come with you? It's just if you're leaving soon we might not be able to do stuff like this anymore. "

I turned around. "You've got to be kidding me. Now you want to be *friends*? I don't think so. "

"Toni . . ." Her voice was raw and thick. "I know I messed up. Those girls, they're so popular. They made me feel like I was cool too, like I was above everyone else, which is wrong. I know I hurt you, I hurt a lot of people." She stood up and started walking to the door. "I understand if you hate me."

I stared at her back, thinking. She'd talked about her friendship with the girls in the past tense, and maybe she was seeing things differently now that she hadn't been hanging around with them so much, but I had my doubts. I remembered that expression: *Keep your friends close, and your enemies closer.* Something was up with her, and I wanted to know what.

"I guess you can come out—if Ryan's okay with it."

She turned around, her face hopeful and almost relieved. "Yeah?"

"Yeah." But as the word left my mouth, I wondered if I'd just made a big mistake.

We drove down to the lake that night, Ryan's hand on the wheel of his pickup truck, his other on my bare leg, my arm bumping up against his tanned one, and Nicole sitting on my right side. Her hair tickled my face as it blew back from the open window, the summer air still hot and smelling of pine. We were both wearing cutoffs and tank tops, the faint scent of coconut suntan lotion lingering on our sticky skin. Nicole stared at the dark road ahead, her face serious. I still couldn't understand why she wanted to come out with us and didn't trust her. Ryan and I would rather have been alone, but we figured there'd be some other people she knew at the lake and she could hang out with them for a while.

Ryan was smoking a cigarette, an open bottle of beer between his legs. We weren't worried about the cops, not on the back road leading out to the lake in the middle of nowhere. Sometimes they'd block the main road, but once you were past a certain point, you were good to go. When we reached the lake, Ryan turned down the music and drove slow, checking who else was out there. It was after ten o'clock by then, and there were only a couple of trucks at the south end of the lake, a fire blazing and some kids from high school with their music blasting. We gave them the nod and they raised their beers in a greeting. I was disappointed that there weren't any kids Nicole knew—we'd be stuck with her all night now. Ryan gunned the truck, making it go sideways on the rough road. I laughed, but Nicole was still quiet. I elbowed her in the ribs. "Jesus Christ, lighten up." She attempted a smile, but it was fake. I wished I hadn't let her come.

We found a spot at the north end of the lake and sat for a moment, listening to music, Ryan's headlights shining out on the dark water. He rolled a joint, took a long inhale, and passed it to me. I took a drag, coughed a couple of times, then offered it to Nicole. She shook her head.

I narrowed my eyes. "Why did you even come out with us?"

"I told you. I wanted to spend some time with you before you moved, and I needed to get out of the house." Nicole's eyes flicked to mine, then around the dark woods, her body tense. I remembered how she was acting the night of the prom, like she knew Shauna was up to something.

"Is Shauna going to jump me tonight?" I said. "Did you set me up?"

She looked startled. "No—of course not! The woods are just freaky." She'd always been creeped out by the woods at night. Hated camping when we were kids. I relaxed a bit, handed her one of the beers I had at my feet. She opened it, took a small sip, looked around at the woods again.

I glanced at Ryan and he motioned to the door with his head. I knew what he was thinking—we hadn't been alone for days.

"Ryan and I are going for a walk," I said.

"You're leaving me here?" Her voice was shocked, her brown eyes big. "I thought we were hanging out together."

"We will—in a little bit."

Ryan turned off the headlights but left the radio playing, then jumped out. I followed. He grabbed the blanket from behind the seat and a mickey of Southern Comfort. I laughed, excited to be with him, giddy from the beer and pot.

We shut the door. Ryan leaned through the open window and said, "We won't be long."

"Okay." Nicole nodded but she still looked scared.

I felt a twinge of guilt. "If you're that freaked out—"

"No, I'll be fine. Have fun." She gave me a smile.

I grabbed Ryan's hand. "Let's go."

We headed into the woods, Ryan leading. I turned back for a moment and saw my sister locking the doors and rolling up the windows.

I shook my head. What a chickenshit.


Ryan and I found a spot farther down a couple of trails and be-hind one of the rock bluffs. He spread out the blanket in a patch of moonlight and built a fire. I lay on my back, my hands behind my head, looking up at the stars, wishing my life always felt this free, just Ryan and me and no one else's bullshit.

Ryan rolled another joint. He took a drag, blew it into my mouth. We laughed, then necked for a while, until my body felt loose and easy, my legs wrapping around him, feeling the zipper of his jeans scraping against me. He peeled off my shirt, unhooked my bra, my skin goose bumps in the cool air. We made out, took sips of the Southern Comfort until my lips were on fire, tasting the sweetness in his mouth, my head spinning, delightfully stoned. We stripped naked, had sex. I licked his neck, tasting the salt, his boy smell, clean hair, work-sweaty skin. Over the sound of his moans in my ear, I thought I heard a noise in the distance and paused, wondering if it was Nicole, then shook off the thought when I didn't hear anything else. We were too far away.

Afterward we cuddled, using our clothes as blankets, finishing the last of the booze and a roach that Ryan handed me. Sleepy from the sex and the drugs and the warm fire, I closed my eyes, hearing Ryan already snoring beside me.

I woke suddenly, scared at the sudden blackness, my body freezing cold. The fire had died down but the moon gave off enough light for me to see one of Ryan's arms up over his face, some scratches on his wrist. I tried to peer at my watch in the dark. Found Ryan's lighter, flicked it on. One in the morning.

"Shit. Ryan, wake up."

He opened his eyes and looked around, disoriented.

I was already standing, struggling to pull on my clothes. "Get *up*. My mom's going to kill me." I'd left a hastily scrawled note at home saying we'd gone to the lake and we'd be home by midnight, Nicole's curfew.

We ran back through the trail, the branches slapping and scraping at our skin, searching for the main path. I fell, cutting my knee and my hand. Ryan helped me up. We finally stumbled into the clearing. The music was off. The truck quiet. I couldn't see Nicole. Was she lying down?

Ryan opened the truck door, turned back to me, his face confused. "She's not here."

"Are you serious?" We didn't have time for this crap.

He shone his lighter. The truck was empty.

I called out, "Nicole, hey, where are you?"

Silence.

Ryan raised his voice. "Nicole, we're sorry, come on out."

We heard a crack in the bush. Held our breath. Ryan turned the lighter off, letting our eyes adjust to the dark. We stared at that spot, the shadows. Was she playing a game now? Turning the tables? I felt myself starting to get mad.

"Maybe she's looking for us," Ryan said. "I'll turn on the truck. If she hears the engine she might come back."

"Okay." I stood outside, looking into the dark trees while he flashed the engine. It started up with a roar. We waited a couple of moments. No sign of her. My anger had all turned to fear that something had happened to my sister. Had she gone hunting for us in the dark and gotten lost? We had to find her.

"Where could she have gone?" I said. "Should we just drive around? Look for her?"

"I don't know." He also looked worried. "She might have gone to hang out with those people partying at the end of the lake. Hop in and we'll check down there."

If she was with those other kids, I was going to kick her ass for freaking me out like this. I came around the front of the truck, blinded for a moment as Ryan turned on the headlights. Then he let out a yell.

I spun around, my heart jamming up into my chest at his fear.

He'd jumped out of the truck, was running toward the lake. Then I saw what he'd seen.

My sister's body, floating at the shore, lit up by the truck's headlights.

We both rushed into the water. I was yelling, "Nicole, Nicole!" I could hear Ryan breathing hard.

She was naked, her skin freezing. We pulled her to shore and crouched over her. I lifted her hair back, to see the side of her face, and realized that part of her skull was smashed in, her hair coming loose in my hands. I looked down at the dark blood covering my hand, the clump of hair, then back at my sister's face, barely recognizable. I screamed, a high-pitched wail that echoed over the lake.

Ryan was feeling her neck for a pulse. He reached over, grabbed my shoulder. "Stop, Toni. She's dead. We've gotta get help."

Dead. The word stole the breath from my lungs. I focused in on his face, my teeth chattering, gasping for air.

He said, "You have to calm down." But his face was white and terrified, his voice also high and strangled.

"She can't be dead." I said it as a plea, begging.

He stood up. "Let's go." He grabbed my arm, tried to pull me up.

I leaned over my sister, pressed my face to her cold chest as I sobbed, "No, no. Oh, God, I'm so sorry." I clutched one of her hands, noticed that a fingernail was torn off. "Nicole, wake up, please wake up." I pulled at her hand uselessly, trying to tug her back into this world.

Ryan knelt beside me. He was also crying. His voice cracking as he said, "We've got to go, Toni."

"I can't leave her. I can't."

"We don't know who hurt her—they could still be out here."

I shook my head. "I'm not going."

He lifted me up under my arms while I fought, biting and kicking. He dragged me to the truck, threw me inside. He backed out in a spray of gravel, shooting down the road. I barely registered that the other partiers were gone, the broad expanse of dark highway, the yellow line, the smell of stale pot and booze and lake water and fear rolling off of us. Ryan turned on the heat but I couldn't stop shaking, couldn't stop crying.

Then we were at the police station. The harsh neon lights blinding. An officer was walking to his patrol car. Ryan and I got out. I collapsed onto the pavement, screaming that my sister needed help. Ryan was trying to explain what happened, but the cop was staring at his truck. I looked back and saw the bloody hand print smeared down the side. Like someone had been trying to get back in.

# CHAPTER FIFTEEN

## CAMPBELL RIVER

### MAY 2013

I woke late, unsure of what to do with my day off. I'd told Mike I'd work an extra shift if he needed me—it was starting to get busy now that it was the middle of May and the tourists were coming—but he gave me hell, told me I needed a life. We both knew that since I left the halfway house, the restaurant was my life. I'd be forever grateful to him for giving me my job back. Sure, I had to work in the kitchen now, not up front where the diners could whisper and speculate about the woman who had killed her sister. But I preferred the noise of the kitchen anyway. Besides, a job was a job and when you have a record like mine, work was pretty hard to come by.

Captain, my gray-brindle pit bull, was still in my bed. The lazy-ass would sleep all morning if I let him, but I didn't care. He was the best thing that had happened to me in a long time. Since I moved back I'd been helping at the shelter, walking the dogs. The shelter staff was glad for the assistance—they didn't give a crap about my past. The manager, Stephanie, was a tough broad, somewhere in her late forties, lots of tattoos and piercings. We hit it off right away. She didn't ask any questions; we just talked about the dogs. One day this sad-looking pit bull came in. He'd been beaten up and dragged behind a truck. They weren't sure what to do with him, figured he'd have a hard time getting adopted because of his scars and mangled ears from a home cropping job—if I ever found out who did it, I'd return the favor. I took him home that day. He loves living on the boat. It's just an old sailboat, not seaworthy anymore, but it was the first time I had a place of my own and I'd slowly been buying things for it, new curtains, covers for the cushions, a small microwave.

I took Captain off the boat and up the wharf for his morning constitutional. On the way we greeted a few people who were down on the docks, preparing for the day. They were used to me by now, but I was sure they had their suspicions and probably talked about me when I wasn't around. After Captain was finished, I brewed some coffee and cleaned the boat, which didn't take long. I sat on my upper deck for a bit, enjoying the sway of the boat, watching the gulls circle overhead, Captain sprawled out on the warm surface. I still couldn't get used to how incredible the salt air smelled. It had been the first thing I noticed when the bus, which I'd taken up from Victoria, pulled into town. I wanted to run from window to window and suck it all in.

It had taken me a while to get used to this kind of outdoor space, to the freedom, and it still made me twitchy sometimes. I was glad for the hustle and bustle of the marina. In prison, you're used to constant noise around you all the time, and even in the halfway house you heard people talking, eating, working, the staff doing counts, my roommate breathing or rolling over in her sleep. My first night on the boat I thought I might go insane from the quiet. At least the smallness of the boat helped me feel safe. I was used to living in tight quarters.

I decided to take Captain for a walk on the beach—I walked

miles every day now, sometimes I felt I could just keep walking—then head into town. I needed some new clothes, though I hated shopping. I got confused by all the options, so I lived in jeans, hiking boots, and white T-shirts, flannel shirts, or hoodies if it was cold. I still didn't like drawing attention to myself.

When I got back to the boat, it was dusk. I parked my beater truck—a good deal I found online for eight hundred bucks, using a lot of my savings and the mechanic skills I'd picked up in the joint. I also bought a secondhand laptop when I was at the halfway house, and I had Wi-Fi at the marina. I was walking down to the wharf when Captain stopped, his body alert as he stared at one of the other vehicles, a low growl starting up in his throat. I paused, my own body tense.

A man got out of a truck, leaned against the side.

"Hey, Toni." He smiled, the left side of his mouth lifting up as he took off his baseball cap.

It was Ryan.

I sucked in my breath. Was it really *him*? I stared at his face, his eyes, trying to take it all in, but my heart was beating so fast I couldn't think straight. I looked around. Was anyone watching? The parking lot was quiet. I looked back at Ryan, who was staring at me, his head tilted to the side, the smile gone and his face now serious. Why was he here? I gripped Captain's leash, pulling him closer. I'd figured Ryan would stick around Vancouver, not be stupid like me and move back to Campbell River. I felt his gaze lingering on different parts of my face. The last time I'd seen him was at court as I was dragged away by the sheriff, and now we were facing each other in a parking lot with twenty feet and fifteen years between us.

He was thirty-five now, and still good-looking but in a harder way, a dangerous way. His hair was still dark brown, no gray, but his face was lined, one cheek scarred. He was wearing faded jeans and a form-fitting white long-sleeved shirt, pulled up to his elbows. He was bigger and looked like he worked out a lot, with broad shoulders and bulging biceps. His forearms were covered in tattoos.

"You look good," he said. "Little different, but you haven't changed much. I like your hair."

I used to be able to read his face so easily, but now I had no idea what he was feeling, if he was also trying to adjust to seeing me as an adult. I looked better than when I was first released. I'd gained a little weight now that I was eating healthier, just enough to give me a few curves. Assholes still seemed to think I was cute, but one look from me and they got the idea. I had no idea what Ryan had been expecting, though. The last time he'd seen me I was twenty years old.

"What are you doing here?" I said.

"We need to talk." His face was still serious, remote. The look prisoners get after years in the joint, where survival depends on hiding your thoughts.

"You know we can't talk to each other."

He met my eyes, his sad for a moment, finally revealing a hint of what might be going on inside. "You stopped writing."

He said it casually, but I noticed how he shifted into a tough-guy stance, his legs spread, his thumbs hooked into his belt loops, exactly how he'd stand in school when he was trying to hide that he was upset or hurt about something.

I struggled to think of a way to explain myself, still shocked that he was standing in front of me.

"It was the only way I could survive. I had to move on and try to forget everything—and everyone. It was just . . . easier."

Now his face showed his old anger, the expression he'd get when someone would say "I know your father, kid," and turn him down for something.

"It wasn't easier for me," he said.

I tried to find some anger in myself, some sort of defense, but I just felt sad, remembering how hard it had been to ignore his letters, feeling like I was abandoning him. "After we were convicted, I lost my mind. I shut down, shut everyone out. I went kind of crazy in there for a few years."

He looked away, out at the water. "Yeah, I get that. I did too."

I wondered what he'd gone through, but I didn't ask, didn't know if I could bear to hear about his pain, not without breaking down over everything we'd lost.

"There's nothing we can do about it now," I said.

"What if there is?"

There was something in his voice, a resolute sound, like he was about to make some sort of declaration that I wasn't ready to hear. I glanced around. The parking lot was still empty. "What are you talking about?"

Now he looked excited, hopeful. It made me even more nervous. Hope was a dangerous thing.

"Remember Cathy?"

"Of course." Since I'd run into her in Victoria, I'd seen her a few times outside one of the bars at the waterfront when I was driving home late. She was always smoking and hanging on to some guy. I'd overheard Mike talking about her at the restaurant once—she'd worked there briefly before her addiction became a problem. He also knew her mother, who was raising Cathy's kids now.

"I've heard from some people that she's been crying at parties lately about that night, saying she knows what really happened—that we were innocent. I'm sure now that Shauna and the girls did it."

Ryan was watching me, his eyes steady, waiting for my reaction. But I was so surprised and shocked by what he'd said I didn't know how to react. My head was spinning, memories from that last year, the trial, all rushing back.

I finally found my voice. "I saw her in Victoria a few months ago." I told him about my run-in with Cathy.

"That might've been the trigger. It was easier to forget when we were out of sight, but then she saw you and now the guilt's getting to her."

I thought about Cathy's nervous apology, her pale face. All these years I'd wondered. All these years I'd had a feeling they were involved. Was I right?

"She was acting really weird—and they were awful in school. But do you think they could have actually *killed* Nicole? It was so violent. . . ." I remembered Nicole's cold hand inside mine, her nail ripped off. She must've fought so hard.

"It *had* to be them," Ryan said. "They didn't lie at our trial for fun."

"If Cathy really is blabbing, don't you think the police would've pulled her in for questioning?"

"Even if someone reported it to the cops, they're not going to follow up. They don't want anyone to find out that they got the wrong people."

"How do you know she wasn't just stoned and talking smack?"

"Her brother, he's also a crackhead, he told an old buddy of mine his sister confessed to him that she knew what really happened to Nicole, but she wouldn't say anything else—she was too scared. Why would she say crap like that if she wasn't involved? I think she's been itching to tell people for a long time but it just comes out when she's high. She's agreed to meet me this week."

"Shit, Ryan."

Was it true? They really did it? But why would they have gone after Nicole? It was me they hated. I wanted to search out Cathy myself and force her to tell me what she knew, but I pulled myself back from the ledge. Nothing was going to change the facts. We would never get those years back, would never be able to prove anything she said anyway. The system had already failed us once.

"You better be careful," I said. "If Suzanne finds out, she could suspend your parole." I knew Ryan and I would have the same parole officer—she was the only one in the north end—and talking to a witness from our case was bad news. You could get accused of intimidation. It didn't take much to get sent back.

"Cathy won't tell anyone. She's too scared of Shauna."

I imagined the girls that night, maybe hunting for me and seeing Nicole alone in the truck. I saw Nicole's face, felt a jolt of anger at the brutality of the attack, and tried to shake it off. I had to think this through, had to be careful. We still didn't know for sure what Cathy knew—if anything. But Ryan was right about one thing. If Cathy wasn't involved, why would she be admitting that the girls lied back then? It might be to get attention—I saw that a lot in the joint. But revealing that you knew the truth about an old murder was a dangerous game. One I couldn't get involved in—not if I wanted to stay out of prison.

"Even if it's true, even if she does know something, no one would believe it. There's no point to any of this. Just stay away from them, Ryan. Cathy's proved she talks about shit she's not supposed to when she's high. You're out on parole now. Don't fuck everything up for yourself."

"Don't you want the real murderers to pay? They killed your *sister*—and took years of our lives. They took everything."

He held my gaze and I saw the words he wasn't saying: *They took you.* The moment swelled between us, the emotions raw. I remembered the kids we were, how I would have gone over to him and thrown my arms around him, how he would smell and taste, but now I knew nothing about him. He was a stranger.

Captain whined at the end of the leash, breaking the moment as he tried to pull me toward the docks.

"Of course I want the right person to be punished." I wanted it so bad I couldn't even think about it. And beneath that was another need. I wanted to sit and talk to Ryan. I wanted to go for a drive with him, wanted to get a coffee and share everything that had happened to him over the years. I wanted to know him again, but I couldn't. We couldn't. "But I'm not screwing up my life now. Do what you have to do, but leave me out of it."

"Toni—"

Before he could say anything else, before I started to cry, I turned and pulled on Captain's leash. "Let's go."

It wasn't until later that I realized Ryan never said the real murderers should be caught—he asked if I wanted them to pay for it.

# CHAPTER SIXTEEN

## CAMPBELL RIVER

### AUGUST 1996

After Ryan and I showed up at the police station, blood on the truck, an officer put us in a room. Frank McKinney and Constable Doug Hicks came in. I'd cried when I saw McKinney, choking out between sobs that "something horrible happened to Nicole." His face was stunned and serious while I tried to tell him our story, stumbling and incoherent at times. Ryan had to step in and finish my sentences. When they said they needed to talk to us alone, I grabbed Ryan's arm, saying, "No, I need him here with me," but they said it would help them sort things out faster. Someone brought me a blanket and a warm cup of coffee. McKinney gave my shoulder a squeeze and said, "I know you're upset, but try to walk us through the night, Toni. Take it one step at a time. You drove out to the lake?"

I told them again what had happened, what we found when we got back to the truck, begging, "Please, you have to go, help her.

We can't leave her there." I still couldn't fathom that she was dead, that she was far beyond any help.

The other officer, Hicks, said, "We've sent someone out there, but we might need your help locating her. Do you think you could go back to the lake with us, Toni?" I didn't like the way he said my name, the familiarity, like we were friends. He didn't know me. I turned to McKinney, spoke only to him.

"I'll go if you need me to, but . . ." The idea of going back there was terrifying, yet I couldn't stand thinking about her still there alone. I said, "What about my parents? Who's going to tell them?" The thoughts going through my mind were overwhelming. My teeth wouldn't stop chattering, my body shaking. My mom. My dad. I wanted them there with me, but I was scared of how much pain they were going to feel when they found out what had happened.

"We'll have someone talk to them soon," Hicks said. "We just need to confirm some things first." They asked questions like "Did you see anyone else at the lake?" "How long did you leave her alone?" "How much had you been drinking?" "How much drugs had you taken?" "Have you had blackouts before?"

I didn't know why any of it mattered. I just wanted them to help Nicole. They stopped the interview and left for a while. When they came back they said that they needed us to go up there with them, they couldn't find Nicole. They got Ryan, who was also pale and shaking, his eyes bloodshot like he'd been crying. We drove up to the lake in the back of McKinney's car, huddled together, not talking, just gripping hands. The lines on the road blurred. I went in and out of shock, sometimes almost numb, then all of a sudden gasping with sobs. Once, I met McKinney's gaze in the rearview mirror. I remembered then how Nicole was his daughter's friend, how he'd have seen her often at his house. I wondered if he was glad his daughter was safe at home, not dead at the lake.

When we got near the lake I saw other vehicles, a coroner, and more cop cars. I couldn't speak anymore, my body shuddering with violent shivers, and Ryan had to point out where we'd been parked. One of the car's headlights shone for a moment on the water, and I saw Nicole's body, still on the shore.

I started screaming, again and again.

After that all I remember is Ryan trying to calm me down, Hicks saying, "Get them out of here." The rest is still hazy, scraps of voices and lights flashing and uniforms. McKinney stayed at the scene and another officer drove us back to the station, where we were separated and questioned again. By then someone had told my parents and they'd been brought to the morgue to identify her body. Ryan gave the police consent to search his truck, which was then seized. Ryan's parents showed up and took him home. He gave me a hug before they left, looking worried as he whispered in my ear, "Be careful what you say." Then he was gone. I was kept in a room with a female officer who kept asking me questions about my job and school, but I couldn't focus on anything she was saying. I just wanted to go home, wanted my parents.

A couple of hours later, the female officer drove me home. Another female officer was sitting in the living room with my parents. She stood when we entered. Frank McKinney was there too, sitting beside my mom on the couch. My dad rushed over, grabbed me in his arms, and held me tight. I broke down sobbing and felt his body shaking against mine. Over his shoulder I could see my mom on the couch, her face white. There were makeup streaks down her cheeks, the skin red and splotchy, and agony in her eyes.

"Mom . . ." I wanted to run to her, want to throw myself in her arms.

She screamed at me, her mouth wide and anguished, "Why did you take her out there? *Why?*" Then she started sobbing, her hands over her face.

"Mom, I'm sorry. . . ." I took a step toward her, but McKinney motioned for me to stop and put his arm around her back.

Mom took her hands away from her face, looked at him helplessly. "Frank, *why*? Why would someone do this to my baby?"

"I don't know, Pam. I really don't." His voice was thick. "But we're going to do whatever we can to find them. Someone will pay for this." Now his voice sounded rough and angry, his expression almost violent. I was assured, felt safer. *Yes, they're going to find who did this.*

I didn't know yet what Ryan had realized, that they were already considering us as suspects, already watching our reactions, our words. We were the ones who were going to pay.

In the week after Nicole's murder, Dad spent most of his days and evenings out in the garage or sitting in the living room, his face unshaven, dark shadows under eyes that stared at nothing even if the TV was on, the hiss of another beer opening the only sign that he was awake. He also spent a lot of time staring out the windows, first at the camera trucks and reporters, once even going outside and yelling at everyone to "get the hell off my lawn," and then, when they faded off, just out at the dark night, like he was waiting for Nicole to come home. Mom wandered around dazed and pale, her hair a mess, looking at me like she didn't know who I was or how I got in her house. I'd hear her talking on the phone with friends, crying and whispering, "I don't know why they took her out there that night. I don't understand what happened. "

I knew what she was really saying: *It's Toni's fault that Nicole's dead.*

She was right. It *was* my fault. If I hadn't brought Nicole out with us, she'd still be alive. I replayed that night over and over again. Trying to make sense of it, but there was no sense to anything anymore. My sister was dead.

I'd go into her bedroom sometimes when my parents were sleeping—the doctor had given my mom pills and she went to bed early. Dad usually stumbled to bed around one or two in the morning, or I'd find him on the couch. I heard him crying down there one night, and it had killed me, listening to him sob like a little boy.

I had my own rituals. I'd lie on Nicole's bed, holding her pillow, which still smelled of her lemony clean scent. Then I'd take her clothes out, even the dirty stuff still in the hamper, and press my face into them, smelling her skin, her body scent, teen girl. I could hear her laughing in my head, excited about going out or talking with a friend on the phone, then I'd see her face, scared when we left her alone in the truck. And I'd see what she looked like later, when we found her, and the breath would stop in my throat.

I had nightmares constantly. I'd wake abruptly, my heart pounding in the dark. Once, I'd heard crying in her room and for a terrifying moment thought it was Nicole's ghost, then heard my father's deep voice and realized it was my mom weeping and my dad trying to comfort her. I cried alone in my bed and thought about Ryan. We hadn't been able to see each other much since that night but we tried to talk on the phone every day. He'd ask how I was, and I'd start to cry while he tried to comfort me. I could hear it in his voice too, the fear, and the same confusion I felt, the guilt.

My mom came into my room sometimes, asking me again to go through everything that had happened that night. I'd tell her how Nicole came to my room, how she apologized, how she asked to come out with me and Ryan. Mom would stop me at different places, asking me to repeat something, wanting every detail. "What was she wearing? How did she stand when she said that?" When I told her Nicole had said something was going on that she couldn't tell me about, Mom fixated on it, trying to get me to think of anything I'd missed. I would always hesitate when I got to the part at the lake, hating the look on my mom's face when I told her how we left Nicole alone, and I'd cry when I got to the part where we'd made out in the bushes and slept while she was being killed. By the time I told her, sobbing, how we'd seen Nicole's body in the headlights, she'd usually be rocking back and forth and moaning. Once, I reached out and rested my hand on her shoulder, but she stood up and left the room. I didn't try to touch her again.

We had a memorial service for Nicole. Most of our school came, and we had to rent a big hall. Friends and teachers all talked about what a wonderful girl she had been. Some of her friends had made slide shows with photos of her. Shauna and her girls were there but they didn't speak. I saw them, all dressed in black, as we passed by to sit at the front of the room with the rest of my family. Shauna's and Rachel's faces were cold as they stared at me, Kim's was streaked with tears, and Cathy just looked out of it. Afterward my mom and dad walked around thanking people for coming, but Mom sounded like a robot, her responses mechanical and stilted. Close friends and family were invited to come with us when we put Nicole's ashes in the river near our place, then back to our house for food and drinks. The girls came to the river, standing together in a huddle, then drove off in Shauna's car. At the house, my mom reached for wineglass after wineglass. When my dad tried to take one away from her, she glared at him and jerked it back, sloshing some out. That night, after I'd helped clean up with some of the other women, I passed by their room and saw my dad trying, tenderly, to button up her pajamas, her head hanging down like a broken doll's. I turned away.

I stayed at home those days, not even sneaking out once to see Ryan, afraid to do anything to upset my parents. I cleaned the house, cooked our meals, finally being the daughter my mother had always wanted. I kept telling myself the police were going to find Nicole's killer soon, but it had already been two weeks since she'd been murdered, and on the phone one night, Ryan, his voice scared, said, "They're going to arrest us, Toni."

"Why would you say something like that?" Fear flooded my body. Was he right? Did they think we did it? My dad had been on the phone with them every day and they said they were following up on leads, but they never told us if they had any suspects. Was that because we were their only ones?

"Because it's the truth." His voice was urgent. "With my record—and us getting in trouble together before—it doesn't look good. We were the last people to be with her, Toni. There's no one else they can blame."

"You don't know what you're talking about." I hung up on him for the first time ever. Then sat in the dark, my heart thudding.

The police arrived the next afternoon, on a Friday. There were two of them, older men in uniforms, one tall with gray hair, the other shorter with salt-and-pepper hair and a big mustache, both with serious faces when my father opened the door. I'd been doing the dishes in the kitchen when I saw the patrol car pull up. I set down the towel, moving toward my dad. Had they found the murderer?

The gray-haired officer said, "I'm Constable Brown. We're here to see your daughter."

"What's going on?" I said.

The shorter officer introduced himself as Constable Ruttan. "We're here to advise you, Toni Murphy, that you are under arrest for the murder of your sister, Nicole Murphy. Please turn around and put your hands behind your back."

I was stunned, unable to speak or move.

Dad reached for my arm, pulling me behind me. "Do you have a warrant for this? Where are you taking her?"

"Sir, please move away." The gray-haired officer stepped closer, his face stern.

Dad didn't budge, his voice rising. "We want to talk to our lawyer."

The officer rested his hand on my dad's shoulder, trying to guide him to the side, using his body to separate him from me. "Sir, I know this is upsetting, but we need you to stay calm." Dad was grabbing for me, trying to hang on.

The other officer was behind me. Cold metal cuffs snapped around my wrists. I pleaded with the officer. "This is a mistake. I didn't *do* anything."

Dad yelled, "Get your hands off my daughter!"

The other officer was blocking him, forcibly holding him in place. "Sir, if you don't calm down we're going to have to arrest you as well." My dad's face was flushed, his face furious. But he let go, held his hands up.

The officer turned to me. "I need you to listen to me. It is my duty to inform you that you have the right to retain and instruct counsel in private, without delay. You may call any lawyer you want. There is a twenty-four-hour telephone service available which provides a legal aid duty lawyer who can give you legal advice in private. This advice is given without charge and the lawyer can explain the legal aid plan to you. If you wish to contact a legal aid duty lawyer, I can provide you with a telephone number. Do you understand?"

My mom was rushing toward us, almost running down the stairs.

"What's going on?"

"They're arresting Toni," Dad said, as I started to cry. "They think she killed Nicole."

She stopped in front of us, her eyes huge as she turned to the officers. "Why are you doing this to my family? I want to talk to Frank McKinney."

"Ma'am, please remain calm," the officer said, then repeated to me, "Do you understand what I have told you?"

"Yes, but you have the wrong person. I didn't—"

He said, "Do you want to call a lawyer?"

I looked at my father. "Dad—"

"We'll call someone right away. Just listen to the officers, Toni, and do what they say. Don't say anything to anybody until you speak to our lawyer." I'd never heard him sound so scared. My heart was pounding.

The officer said, "I want you to know, Toni Murphy, that you are not obligated to say anything, but anything you do say may be given in evidence. Do you understand?"

I stammered, "Yes, I guess . . ." Then they were leading me out to the patrol car. Neighbors were watching from their houses. A car slowed down as it drove past. I recognized a girl from my school in the backseat. She was staring, her mouth open.

Outside near the car, the gray-haired officer said, "Do you have any sharps or weapons on you?"

"What? No."

He said matter-of-factly, "We're just going to search you." They patted me down. Behind me, I could hear my mom crying. I couldn't think, didn't understand what was happening. Where was Ryan? Were they arresting him too?

"It will be okay," my dad shouted as the officer put me in the back of the cruiser, his hands on top of my head, guiding me in. The door slammed shut. Dad ran over, touched his hands to the window, his face covered in tears. I was crying too, hard gasping breaths, screaming, "Dad!"

The officer said, "Sir, I need you to move away from the vehicle." Dad stepped back. My mom ran out to stand by his side, grabbing at his arm, her face scared. As the officers drove away, I could see Dad mouthing, *It will be okay.*

But it wasn't okay. At the station they removed my handcuffs and took my photo, asked for my name and birth date and medical history, then took my fingerprints. I tried to follow everything they were saying, but I was frantic with fear. I kept trying to ask them why they arrested me but no one would explain anything. A female guard took me to a search room where I was only allowed to keep my underwear and pants and shirt. I was told that the rest—jewelry, shoes, my bra—would be put in a locker. Then I was taken to a jail cell, bare except for a stainless steel sink and toilet and bed. They gave me a pad and blankets for the bed. After a couple of hours they brought me to a room where I met with my lawyer. He had a big belly and bushy eyebrows, looked like a dark-haired Santa. I could see a bit of ketchup on his tie. He told me his name, Angus Reed, and I recognized him as a well-known criminal attorney in town.

"I don't want you to tell me anything yet," he said. "The rooms are wired. Don't talk to any cell mates, don't say anything to anyone. Okay?"

I nodded, my heart hammering in my ears, his serious voice scaring me even more, making it clear the severity of the situation that I was in.

"My job is to help you from now on," he said. "I don't care what you've done or what you've said. Be polite to the police but don't tell them anything, don't describe anything, don't point to anything. They're going to try to talk to you again, they *will* lie, and they'll do whatever they can to trip you up. I want you to keep saying, 'On the advice of my lawyer I wish to remain silent,' okay?"

I nodded again. "Ryan—"

"He's probably been arrested too. It's Friday, so they're going to keep you in here until Monday, when you can be brought before the provincial judge. They want to wear you down. Again, don't speak to them about *anything*. Don't ask about Ryan, don't say anything about him. You understand?"

"Yes." But I didn't understand why I was there or what was going to happen. I just wanted to go home.

They moved me that night to a different jail cell, where I could hear drunks screaming and yelling in other cells. I was cold and scared. I couldn't sleep and sat huddled on the bed, the thin blanket wrapped around me. My mind was spinning, thinking about everything the police had said. It didn't seem possible that I'd been arrested, that we might go to prison for murder. I got up a couple of times to use the toilet, first trying to clean the seat off with the rough toilet paper. Then I got back on my bed, staring at the walls and the ceiling, worrying about Ryan, wondering how far away his cell was in the station. I told myself the real murderer would be found and we'd be cleared. Everything was going to be okay. Still, I couldn't stop thinking about all those stories you'd hear about people being falsely convicted and imprisoned for years. I prayed that it wouldn't happen to us.

The next day an officer brought me to an interview room. Doug Hicks, the constable I'd met the first night, was waiting for me. I'd seen him around town before. Unlike Frank McKinney, who would let you off with a warning, he seemed to enjoy arresting kids. He was younger than McKinney, maybe late twenties, blond with pale eyelashes and light blue eyes, ruddy cheeks that always looked windburned, and walked like he thought he was tough shit, his shoulders back and chest out. When I'd seen him around before, I just thought he was a jerk, but now I was terrified of him, scared he might twist things and mess me up. I held on to what my lawyer had told me—I didn't have to tell them anything. I looked around the room, remembering what else he'd told me, that everything was wired.

In a calm voice, Hicks started off by asking me again to go

through the events of that night, but this time I said, "On the advice of my lawyer, I wish to remain silent."

He looked annoyed, his cheeks flushing redder, but said, "You don't have to tell us anything, but it would help us clear things up a lot faster if we heard your side of it again. We might even be able to let you go."

Now I knew he was bullshitting. They wouldn't have arrested me in the first place if a simple explanation from me would get me out of this mess.

He waited for a moment, but when it was obvious I wasn't going to say anything, he said, "We've been talking to Ryan."

Ryan. He *was* there. I felt my heart stop, my breath catch in my throat. What had he been saying? What had he told them?

"He says it was you, Toni. You wanted your sister gone and it was your plan to kill her at the lake."

What the hell? I knew I shouldn't talk, but I couldn't help it. "Ryan would *never* say that—because it's not true. And he loves me."

"Does he? Strange things happen after people have been arrested for murder, they get a lot more honest. And according to Ryan, this was all your idea. But if you want to tell me your side of it, I'm more than happy to listen."

I looked him straight in the eye. "On the advice of my lawyer, I wish to remain silent."

He didn't show any reaction, just glanced down at a file in front of him.

"We heard you've been carrying a knife around with you."

I jerked back in my seat. How did he know about that? Nicole must have told someone, but who? Shauna? My face felt hot, and I fought the urge to explain how the girls had been harassing me. He was trying to trip me up, messing with my head. A knife didn't mean anything—Nicole wasn't even killed with a knife.

"And we know your sister had been making your life hell, coming into your work, flirting with your boyfriend at parties . . ."

My heart was beating harder and harder with each word out of his mouth. Who had been telling them this stuff? What was he talking about, flirting with my boyfriend? I wanted to ask questions, wanted to explain and defend, but I kept my mouth shut.

Hicks continued, "We also know that you lied to your parents recently and snuck into your neighbors' house and stole some alcohol. But that's not the only thing you've stolen recently. You also took your father's pills."

This time I couldn't stay quiet. "I didn't do that. It was Nicole." Had my parents told them I stole pills? I felt sick with fear now, with betrayal.

He leaned forward, excited that he'd provoked me. "You were angry with her for telling on you, weren't you? You wanted to teach her a lesson."

I was shaking my head. "No, no, no."

He leaned back, stared at me, assessing, waiting. The pressure built. He was going to hit me with something else, something big. I could feel it.

"There are witnesses," he said, "who saw you arguing with your sister the night she was murdered."

The room closed in on me and I gasped for breath. "No, that's not true!"

"We've got four girls who saw you at the lake with Ryan, fighting with Nicole before she was murdered. We know you did it, Toni."

Four girls. It had to be Shauna and her friends. Why would they lie about something like that? My head was spinning, trying to understand what this meant.

This time I broke.

"They're making it up. They hate me—they've made my life hell for the last year. Nicole was hanging out with them all the time, and she was sneaking out to see some guy, but I don't know his name. They might know who really—"

"We also have DNA, yours and Ryan's. You both had scratches

on your arms and hands. There was no one else's DNA or blood at the scene, not on Nicole's body, not on the truck. You were the only people there."

I tried to stay calm, but I had to fight to hold back tears. I knew we hadn't killed her. Someone else *had* to have been there. I wanted to talk to my dad and to my lawyer. I wanted someone to explain all this. What was going to happen to us?

I met Hicks's eyes. "On the advice of my lawyer, I wish to remain silent."

He tried a few other tactics, telling me that Ryan was in the other room right now, spilling everything. That he didn't believe I'd delivered the killing blows—I wasn't strong enough—but I had to tell them what really happened. That he knew I wanted to come clean, wanted to spare my family the hardship of going through a lengthy trial. He went on and on. It was hot in the room, and I was thirsty and exhausted. His voice began to lull me, and I started to think maybe he was right, maybe it would be easier for everyone if I just confessed, but I snapped myself out of it. I didn't kill my sister, and he was lying about Ryan.

"On the advice of my lawyer, I wish to remain silent."

He gave me a cold smile and stood up. "I know you did it, Toni. You and your boyfriend are going away for a very long time."

I stared at the table in front of me. He was wrong. He had to be wrong.

# CHAPTER SEVENTEEN

## CAMPBELL RIVER

### MAY 2013

The day after Ryan surprised me at the marina, I had a meeting with my parole officer. Her office was in Courtenay, about a half hour from Campbell River, so she either came up for a "walk and talk" or we got coffee at a restaurant. Suzanne was all right. I liked her a lot, which was amazing considering my general dislike of authority figures. She was an older woman, somewhere in her fifties, and heavy—she was always sucking back iced mochas, sugar candies, chocolates, told me I was too skinny. She liked Captain and let me bring him on our walks, sneaking him cookies, talking to him in funny voices, rubbing his big block head.

Suzanne was pretty tough on me at first, though, said she wanted me to do well, that none of her parolees had been sent back and she planned on keeping it that way. But I could tell that it was more than that. She genuinely gave a shit, made sure I was following my programs. She knew how hard it was for former inmates to transition, how institutionalized we could get. We'd started off with weekly meetings and phone check-ins. Now we were meeting twice a month, and eventually, if all went well, we'd be down to once a month.

That day we went through the usual questions. At the end she said, "Anything you want to talk about?"

"Nope. I'm good."

She stared at me for a moment. I held my breath. She knew something. Had she heard that Ryan had come to the marina? Had someone seen us?

"I just want to remind you of your parole conditions and that you need to avoid known offenders."

Okay. So she didn't know he'd already seen me, but she knew Ryan was around and she was testing me. I decided to cut through the bullshit.

"If you're talking about Ryan, I don't want anything to do with him."

She studied my face, her friendly expression now all business. She'd been doing this job for years. She could sniff out a lie in a heartbeat. But I'd also spent years in the system. I knew how to keep my feelings locked in.

She nodded, satisfied, but added, "Be careful."

"Of course."

It was the first time I'd kept something from her. It made me nervous, but I didn't want her to start keeping a closer eye on me. Just in case Ryan came back. Just in case he did have something I wanted to hear.


I was getting groceries on the way home when I saw my parents in the store. I stopped, my hands gripping the cart, and watched them making their way through the produce section. I hadn't seen either of them for years, not even a photo. My father looked a little stooped in the shoulders and his brown hair was almost all gray now, but he was still tanned. I'd seen his truck around town a few times since I'd been on parole, so I knew he was still working, but I suspected he was managing the guys more than he was swinging a hammer. A couple of times I'd fought the urge to visit him at one of the job sites with his construction signs. It looked like Mom was dyeing her hair now, a soft brown she'd pulled back in a loose ponytail. She was still in shape, small like me, like Nicole had been—too small to fight off her attacker— but she looked healthy, not gaunt like the last time I'd seen her. She was wearing a scoop-necked pale blue shirt with jeans and white flip-flops. If I blurred my eyes for a moment, I could almost see Nicole.

My father was making his way around to a barrel of potatoes, motioning to Mom, who was putting some apples in a bag. I imagined them having some friends over for dinner, maybe clients. Or was it just the two of them? Sitting silent over their dinner, thinking about their daughters. My father looked up and caught my eye. I'd let myself muse too long. I was stuck. My mom had been saying something to him, but when he didn't answer she followed the direction of his gaze. She startled, her cheeks flushing when she recognized me. Her eyes shot around, checking to see if anyone was watching, then she stared back at me. She didn't look happy. I should have walked away, but Dad was wheeling the cart over now. Mom hesitated, then he glanced back at her and she followed, slowly, still carrying the bag of apples.

"Toni, how are you?" Dad said when he was closer. He gave me a tentative smile. His hand lifted slightly off the cart for a moment like he wanted to reach out, wanted to touch me, but then it dropped down.

"I'm good. Things are really good." I wanted to say, *I saw Ryan. He thinks he can prove we're innocent. Would you believe him? Would you still hate me?*

"I heard you were working at the restaurant," Dad said.

"Yeah, Mike's been great. I've got a boat too. Down at the marina."

Mom didn't know where to look. She was glancing at me, then at Dad, then around to the other shoppers.

I turned to her now. "Mom, you're looking well."

She startled again, then spoke hesitantly, like she was trying to think of something to say. "You . . . you too. You look good." Her gaze flicked to my fauxhawk, the tattoos. And I was the one who was supposed to be the liar.

We were all quiet. I hated the heavy tension in the air, the moment stretching out like a live wire that I wanted to snap, even if it burned.

"It would be great to see you guys sometime." My face felt hot. "I have a dog, and I help out at the shelter." I knew I was almost babbling, my voice breathy from nerves, sensed that my dad knew how uncomfortable I was, that he wanted to make it better but didn't know how. I kept talking, my gaze flitting to my mother, trying to think of something that might make her look at me, *really* look at me. "And I go to programs, for substance abuse." She finally held my gaze, but I couldn't tell what she was thinking. I said, "I'm not the same person. I've changed."

My mom set down the apples she'd been holding in the cart with a thump. She stared down at them for a moment while Dad and I watched her. I knew she was going to say something, and so did Dad. He reached out to her. "Pam . . ."

She shook her head. "No." She held her hand out in the air just in front of him, as if pushing him away. "I'm not doing this. I'm not pretending everything's okay now." She looked back at me. "I wish you well, Toni, I really do. But I can't do *this*. I can't see you or speak to you." She rested her hand on her heart, her voice breaking as she said, "I can't forget—what you did." Then she shook her head again, quick movements that looked painful as she blinked back tears.

Tears were flooding my own eyes, my throat tight with words

that I couldn't get out, could never say. *I didn't do it. Why won't you believe me? I just want you to love me. That's all I've ever wanted.*

Mom turned to Dad and said, "I'm going to get milk," then quickly walked away. I saw her hand wipe across her face, erasing the tears, erasing me. Dad and I watched her for a moment, then he turned back to face me.

"Toni, I'm sorry, she just . . . can't."

"Yeah. That's obvious." My hurt turned to anger, my voice bitter. "She still hates me."

"No." He smiled sadly, studied his hands on the cart, then reached out and held my hand for a moment, gave it a squeeze. I almost pulled away, surprised by the unexpected human contact. "She hates what happened, and you remind her too much . . ." He didn't have to say the rest. I reminded her of Nicole, I reminded her of everything that had happened that night.

I looked at my father's hand on mine, saw the age there, in his skin, wondered how much time we had left, if I'd ever be able to put things right.

"I miss you, Dad. I'd like to see you, now that I'm out. Can we . . ."

I held my breath, scared that he'd say no like my mom or that he wouldn't want to see me because of her. He looked in the direction she'd gone, and I felt the tears build in my throat again as I waited for the rejection.

He turned back to me. "I'd love to have a coffee with you. Why don't you come by the job site sometime? You don't have my cell . . ." He grabbed his wallet out of his pocket, pulled out a business card, and handed it to me.

"Thanks." I stared at the card, the numbers blurring in front of my eyes. I hadn't even known my own father's cell number until now. I wondered if I should give him my number, if he would call, but he was glancing back toward where my mom had headed. I caught a glimpse of her hair, moving down another aisle.

"I better go," he said.

I nodded, tried for a smile, but had to stare back down at that card so I didn't cry at the look of sadness in his face.

"It's been really hard on her lately with the anniversary coming up," he said softly. "Maybe try again in a few months."

It was hard on me too. That summer it had been seventeen years since my sister was murdered, seventeen years since someone stole all our lives, and I knew that my mom wasn't going to change her mind about anything in a few months. But I was silent as my father walked away. I grabbed Captain a big bone from the meat section and waited until I got home to cry.

The night after I saw my parents in the store, I pulled into the marina parking lot after a late shift at the restaurant, Captain on the seat behind me. Mike let Captain hang out with his dog in the backyard of his house, which was across the street from the restaurant. I went over on my breaks and visited him, though I could tell it annoyed Mike's wife, Patty, who didn't really like me. I figured it was just because of my past and in time she'd trust me.

I was tired and looking forward to a shower, so I wasn't paying attention when I parked the truck. I was about to get out when I saw something move behind the Dumpster. I stared at the spot. What the hell? Then I caught a glimpse of a baseball cap. It was Ryan again.

I let Captain out. He ran over to the Dumpster, body tense, hackles up, and a low growl leaking from his throat. I knew he wouldn't do anything, not unless someone was attacking me, but I called out, "Captain. It's okay."

Ryan crouched down and turned his body to the side, not making eye contact as he let Captain sniff him, then he slowly tossed out a couple of dog cookies, which Captain gobbled up. Ryan glanced up at me and said, "He's a beauty," then started scratching Captain, who was leaning against him with one of his big pittie smiles, tongue lolling, trying to get more cookies.

I looked around the parking lot, the marina. It was after midnight, no one in sight, but I still wasn't comfortable talking to Ryan in the open.

"What are you doing here, Ryan?" I was angry, but mostly at my body's reaction to seeing him. I'd been happy for a moment, excited even, before I remembered that speaking to him could cost me my freedom. He looked good, though, in a faded black denim shirt open over a fitted gray T-shirt, a silver chain at his neck. His baseball cap low, almost hiding his eyes.

"I met with Cathy," he said. "She's definitely covering up something. The whole time we were talking she was looking over her shoulder."

"She was probably afraid you were going to slit her throat and steal all her drugs or something."

"Funny." He smiled at my gallows humor. We did always have that in common, the ability to make fun of our fucked-up families and fucked-up lives, but then everything got too fucked up. I hated him for reminding me, hated how much I wanted to smile back, wanted to make him laugh deep from his gut, like when we were kids and he'd throw his head back, one hand over his heart, his whole body getting into it. That was one of the things I'd loved about him, how physical he was, how loose and relaxed and easy he was with his body.

He took a step forward now, leaned against the side of the Dumpster, rubbed at his unshaven chin. His shirt rode up a bit, showing a black belt through his jeans, his waist still slim. I remembered wrapping my arms around him, the feel of my hands tucked into his back jeans pockets, him lifting his shirt up so our bare stomachs could touch. My face flushed and I stared down at Captain.

"It was more than that," he said. "Every time I mentioned Shauna, that's when she got nervous."

I didn't want to get pulled into this, didn't want to know anything more about their lives now. Three of them still lived in town. That's all I needed to know. But, despite myself, I said, "Are they still friends?"

"Not sure what you'd call it. Sounds like Shauna goes over sometimes and cleans up Cathy's house—tries to get her to clean up too. Brings food, toys to the mother's house for the kids, stuff like that."

"What is Shauna doing these days? Cathy said she was married. . . . Is it the same guy?" I hated how much I wanted to hear that she was fat and on her third marriage, preferably miserable.

"Yeah, that older dude. He owns a big trucking company and they have a fancy house, cars, but apparently he's not around much. Cathy was kind of rambling."

"About what?"

"She was hinting that she knew some other things about Shauna—basically saying Shauna isn't all that shit-hot. I get the feeling she might kind of resent how Shauna's been taking care of her."

"She likes it but she resents needing it."

He looked up at me from underneath the brim of his baseball cap.

"Yeah, exactly. I knew you'd get it."

I fought the sensation of our old connection rebuilding, the similar way our minds worked. "So what does that have to do with anything?"

"I told her I had some information about that night, just messing with her. I said there was another witness, someone who saw Shauna's car tearing away. Told her if she knew something, she better spill it before the others did. She got real scared—and twitchy, like she was jonesing. I knew I couldn't get much more out of her then, but she agreed to meet with me tomorrow night."

I felt disappointed, but what had I expected? A confession and years of bullshit suddenly wiped clean? We'd need a lot more than that, details, hard facts.

"Doesn't sound like she's going to make it easy," I said.

"That's why I want you to come with me when I talk to her."

"No, no way." I took a step back, about to turn away.

"Just listen." He held out a hand in a plea, his eyes asking me to wait, the same look he'd get when we were kids and he was trying to get me to stay with him a moment longer. I felt another tug inside, tried to ignore the old memories piling up, tried to remind myself how dangerous this all was.

"If she saw you, and you were talking about Nicole," Ryan said, "it would mess her up a little more. She saw you once and look what happened. She's not a bad person. She was screwed up when we were kids, she's still screwed up, but I get the feeling somewhere in there she wants to make things right."

"All she wants is another hit. Did you give her money?"

He looked embarrassed, his cheeks flushing as he glanced away, watching Captain, who was sniffing around in the grass near the edges of the parking lot.

"You did," I said, "and now she's stretching it out. Telling you nothing about nothing."

He shook his head. "She knows something. You can see it in her eyes. It's been eating at her." He sounded angry. "We could've been out a long time ago."

"But it didn't happen, and the only thing that's going to happen now, if I go anywhere with you, is both of us getting sent back to prison."

"Shit, they're just waiting for their chance. I've seen Hicks watching my house."

That was alarming. Doug Hicks was a sergeant now. I'd never forget the interrogation, the things he said, his voice droning on and on. *We know you did it, Toni. You might as well tell us now, so the*

*courts will go easier on you. You know what will happen to you in prison?*
I didn't know. But I sure found out.

"Then what the hell are you doing here?" I looked around the parking lot again.

"Relax. I've got my own watch going on. He's with his family tonight."

"Don't you have a job?"

"I'm doing some labor stuff, trying to get onto one of the tugboats." He was holding his chin high, the way he used to when he was self-conscious, like he wished he had something better to impress me with. I'd never cared what he did, always loved that he worked with his hands, that he was strong. Loved knowing he could fix anything, even me. But not anymore.

"Focus on that," I said. "Forget Cathy."

"Not going to happen, Toni. I'm going to break her, but it'll happen quicker if you're there. I'm sure of it."

"That's not going to happen either."

"Why are you giving up so easily?"

"I'm not giving up. It's just . . ." I searched for words to explain what I was feeling. I wanted to prove our innocence badly, especially after seeing my parents in the store, but I was terrified of losing the little bit of freedom I'd finally gotten back. The thought of going to prison again made my chest tight, panic racing down my legs. *No, never again.*

"I just can't. I can't do *this*." I stopped, thinking of my mother again, how she'd said almost those exact words to me.

"You are giving up, Toni. Just like you gave up on us." His gaze was holding steady on mine, waiting for an answer.

"I didn't give *up* on us. We were in prison—our relationship was over."

"It wasn't for me."

He was still holding my gaze. I couldn't look away, couldn't break eye contact. I didn't know what to say, just shook my head, at the words all jumbling in my head, the frustrated thoughts and anger at how our lives had gone, at the things he was making me feel and say and think. I said, "My parents, my mom, she's not speaking to me. But my dad, we might meet for coffee. I don't want to mess that up. I don't want them to see me go back . . ."

"How's that really going to be, Toni? You and your dad sitting there, you knowing he's still not sure if you're guilty, him thinking about Nicole the whole time." I sucked in my breath, my eyes stinging. Ryan was right. It would be agonizing, like the prison visits all over again. I'd been stupid, thinking things would be different because I was on parole.

Ryan was still talking. "My dad's dead. I never got to show him I wasn't a fuckup, that I didn't murder your sister, but my mom's still alive. And you can still prove it to your parents. I know we can do it."

I was tempted. Then I thought of Suzanne, her warning. It was a long shot that we'd get Cathy to confess to anything, and we'd likely get caught doing it. I'd be back in Rockland, where Helen's friends were no doubt waiting for me.

I shook my head, tears building behind my eyes. "I can't do it. Just stay away from me."

For the second time I left Ryan standing alone in the parking lot.

That weekend Mike hired a new waitress. I was peeling carrots in the kitchen when she came back to introduce herself. She looked about sixteen and was stick-thin and pale. Her long straight hair was dyed jet-black and she had blunt bangs, ending just above her dark-rimmed eyes. Her hands were covered in silver rings, skulls and crosses. She also had a heavy chain around her neck with a cross and was wearing black leggings and a tunic. Great, another Goth teenager thinking she's badass just because she dressed in black.

"Hi, I'm Ashley." She stuck out her hand.

I shook it. "Welcome on board."

I thought that would be the last of it and turned back to my work, but she lingered, looking around the kitchen, fiddling with some spices. What was she doing? Then I caught her sneaking sideways glances at me. She knew who I was.

I set down the grater and put my hands on my hips. "Can I help you?"

"Sorry." Her cheeks flushed. "It's just . . . I saw a TV show about your case. It was for this journalism class I was taking last summer."

So that was it. I was angry, but part of me also admired her guts. Not many people had the balls to just straight-out say crap like that. Usually they pretended like they didn't know, but I could always tell what they were thinking

"I don't like to talk about that." I could be just as blunt.

"That's okay. I mean, I can understand why you wouldn't. You're trying to move on with your life." She grabbed a carrot and started grating. "I wanted to work here because I need money—I'm saving for film school. My mom doesn't know I've got a job yet. She doesn't like me doing anything I really want to do."

Her bitter tone made it clear that she resented the hell out of her mother. But I couldn't figure out why she was telling me all this. I stared at her, waiting.

She looked at me from the side. "I also wanted to meet you."

What was the deal? Was she one of those kids who got off on crime? Thought it was cool or something?

"Why would you want to meet me?"

She stopped grating and faced me, her eyes intense. "I want to film you."

Didn't see that one coming. "What the hell for?"

"For a documentary. I want to tell your side of it. What happened back then, what your life is like now, why you came back here, stuff like that."

"Kid, you're insane if you think I'm going to let you film me."

"Really?" She looked disappointed. "I thought you'd want people to understand you more, see your side of things, you know?"

"People are never going to understand me."

"You've always said you're innocent. The documentary could get you exposure, and some new witnesses or evidence might turn up. I'm really good at investigating stuff. I've been part of the Vancouver Film Festival every year."

We held eyes. Was she making it up? Saying she wanted to help just so she could film me, then screw me over somehow like all the reporters had? She seemed serious, but it could be part of her angle. Either way, I didn't want anything to do with her, and I sure as hell wasn't going to be her little project.

I turned back to the carrots. "It's too late to help me now—I already went to prison. Mike probably needs you up front and I've gotta get this finished."

"Just think about it, okay?" She handed me the grater.

"There's nothing to think about."

She leaned forward, her face serious. "I've read the interviews with you, all the newspaper articles, everything you said, and Ryan, how in love you two were. I got it, you know? You were just angry, at your sister, your parents, but that didn't mean you killed her."

I didn't know if I was messing with her or wanted to hear what she'd say, but I asked her, "So who do you think did it, Ashley?"

She glanced down, fiddled with one of the carrots for a moment. "I don't know, but the police, they only looked at you two. I watch those cold case shows. I know how it goes when the police focus on someone right away."

"Some of those cops are still pretty well known in town."

She hesitated, a flash of fear in her eyes. "When you're searching for the truth, you have to be willing to look at everything."

I wanted to slap her down for her naïveté, her youthful ideals, but mentally I said, *Be nice, Toni. She's just sixteen.*

"Thanks for wanting to help, but I'm not going to make a documentary. It's over and I'm trying to move on."

"But it can't ever really be over, can it? What happened to you?"

Okay, now she had it coming. "You know what makes it worse? Thinking about it makes it worse. Talking about it makes it worse. Having teenagers who don't know shit about the real world asking questions about it, *that* makes it worse."

"I totally get that." She nodded, still trying to find a way around me, to speak my language and connect. This kid didn't give up. "All I'm trying to say is, I don't think you got a fair chance. And I can help you."

"Life isn't fair. You'll figure that out in a hurry."

"Maybe just read this when you get a chance." She reached down into the side of her combat boots and pulled out some papers she had stuffed in there.

"What's this?"

"It's an essay. I wrote it last semester. Just read it, please." She walked out, the door swinging shut behind her.

I glanced down at the essay. It was titled "That Night."

When I got home after work, I took the papers out of my bag. I was tempted for a moment to burn them or chuck them out. What did I care what this girl wrote about me? But I was curious. Sure, I'd had letters from people over the years who said they believed in my innocence, but they were all fruit loops or fame junkies or kids in law school who wanted to prove themselves—until they found someone else who had a more interesting story, until they decided that maybe I *was* guilty.

I sat at my little table and stared at the essay, then thought, *Fuck it,* and started reading. It was well written, a thoughtful look at the whole case. She'd talked to some of my old teachers and friends, waitresses at the restaurant, even Nicole's friends, including Darlene Haynes. And my friend Amy, who told her how Shauna and her friends had bullied me. It was unnerving, how adult Ashley came across, how in many ways she *did* seem to get it, that I was just an angry teenager who fought with my sister but it didn't mean I killed her. She'd even talked to Ryan's father. She'd tried to talk to mine but my mom closed the door in her face.

Ashley also wrote about the trial, how the most damaging testimony had come from Shauna and the other girls—my known enemies. They were popular, and I was the underdog. She referenced some psychobabble about teen girls turning on each other, the viciousness and pack mentality that can arise, how gossip can become truth in people's minds. She cited some cases where it had been proven later that people gave false testimony against someone they didn't like, and questioned if Shauna and her friends had lied. At the bottom, she also speculated about the real murderer, and whether Ryan and I could be innocent. She finished by saying, "Whoever the murderer is, wherever he is, he didn't just end one life that night—he ended three."

The next day at work I left the essay in Ashley's bag with a note stuck to it: *Good writing, but I can't do the documentary. Sorry.*

# CHAPTER EIGHTEEN

## CAMPBELL RIVER

### SEPTEMBER 1996

The police tried to talk to me a couple of times over that weekend. They'd bring me out of my cell, then sit me in that same room, the heat jacked up, offering me water or a cigarette, trying to be my friend. I'd take both, puffing on the smoke, which only made me more anxious. I never saw Frank McKinney again, but before I was arrested my mother had left him several messages that he didn't return. Mom would pace in the kitchen, the phone tight in her hand, saying, "Frank, I just need to know that you'll find whoever did this."

Hicks was the one who interviewed me. He'd tell me again about all the evidence they had stacked against us and how much easier things would go for me if I just cooperated with them. I kept my mouth shut. I thought about Ryan and how he was faring. It was taking all my strength not to defend myself, not to tell Hicks to fuck off, but I had a feeling Ryan would handle the interrogations okay. He was used to people and teachers giving him a hard time.

Finally it was Monday and I was brought before the provincial judge. My lawyer said Ryan was probably coming in after us. My parents were in the courthouse, my dad in a suit and my mom in dress pants and a blouse, her hair pulled back. They both looked nervous, their faces strained. I thought I'd find out about bail that day, but now my lawyer explained what he hadn't wanted to tell me on Friday. This was just to set a bail hearing with a Supreme Court judge. That would take another couple of weeks. Meanwhile I'd be in custody at the pretrial center over in Vancouver, in the women's unit. I was going to jail. I listened to the judge asking my lawyer questions, talking about things like disclosure, but I couldn't grasp anything, couldn't stop thinking about jail. What would happen there? Would I get beaten up? What about Ryan? Would he be hurt?

I'd been transported by sheriffs that morning to the courthouse, and they took me now in one of their vans to the airport. I watched the world go by, already feeling separate, removed from the people going about their day, on their way to work or home, carrying on with their lives.

*I'm going to jail. I'm going to jail, to jail, to jail.*

The pretrial center was a terrifying place, concrete and institutional. Because of my age, I was held in protective custody, placed in a cell with heavy metal doors and a small window. I sat on my bed and cried so hard I threw up. They brought food later, dry tasteless stuff that I couldn't eat. The next days were a blur. I sat scared in my cell most of the time, sometimes venturing out to the TV room but leaving when the news came on because I'd see an anchorman talking about me with photos of my dead sister up on the screen, or a shot of my parents' anguished faces as they left the courtroom, or my high school photo. The other women in protective custody gave me curious looks, but no one talked to me. They just whispered in their little groups.

Two weeks later I was brought before the Supreme Court judge. My lawyer, Angus, argued that I wasn't a flight risk, pointing to my parents, saying I didn't have the means to run away, didn't have a record. Though Angus was heavy, moved awkwardly, and sometimes seemed to drift off midsentence, he spoke so passionately and eloquently on my behalf I began to hope that maybe everything would be okay, that maybe we could win at trial.

I was granted bail, but I had to stay in the holding cell at the courthouse for a couple more days until my parents were approved as guarantors. Then I was brought before the judge again and had to agree to all the conditions. I'd have to meet with a bail supervisor weekly, continue to live at my parents', not drink or do any drugs, have a curfew, hand over my passport, not leave the jurisdiction of the court—but the worst was that I wasn't allowed to have any contact "directly or indirectly with co-accused except through legal counsel." I started to cry when Angus explained later that it meant I couldn't communicate with Ryan until we went to trial, cried even harder when he said it could take a couple of years to get a date. My only hope was that something would happen in the meantime. There would be a break in the case and we'd go free.

"Angus is the best," my father said on the tense ride home from the bail hearing. "The best lawyer on the island." He was saying it forcefully, like he was trying to convince himself. My mom glanced over, watching his face, then gazed back out the window. I couldn't tell what she was thinking. I saw her trace a small symbol in the condensation in the window and remembered how she and Nicole used to play tic-tac-toe on the windows when we went on road trips.

That night they came into my room after dinner. My dad was pale, and my mom looked like she'd been crying. Dad sat on my bed, Mom at my desk.

"Why do the police think you did it, Toni?" Her voice was anguished. "What did *you do?*"

"Nothing! Shauna and her friends, they lied and said they saw us fighting with Nicole. But it's not true. I didn't even *see* them out there."

My dad was staring at me, like he was trying to look into my soul.

I met his eyes. "Dad, I swear we did *not* do this. I could never hurt Nicole like that. The way she died . . ." I was crying now, hating the look in their faces, the fear, wondering if their daughter was a killer. "The girls are lying. They *hate* me—I told you they were coming into the restaurant all the time."

I could see him thinking it through, remembering. He sat back, looking relieved. "Then it will get cleared up. Angus, he'll be able to sort this out."

Mom said, "But the police, they must have more reasons to think Toni . . . to think . . ." She started to cry, her hands shaking as she tried to wipe away the tears.

"No, I mean, they said other stuff, like about scratches and DNA, but that's just because we were in the bushes and we touched Nicole, to help her, but we didn't do anything to her." I was babbling, talking desperately, my voice pleading through my own sobs. "*Please*, Mom, you have to believe me."

My dad reached over and grabbed my hand. "We believe you, honey." He looked at my mom. "It's going to be okay, Pam. She didn't do anything wrong."

She nodded but she was staring at my outstretched arm, her face haunted, almost scared, and I knew she was remembering the scratches from that night.

I said, "Mom, you believe me, right?"

She met my eyes, blinked a couple of times. "Your father's right. It's going to be okay. If you didn't do anything, there's nothing to be worried about." She stood up. "I have to go to bed."

The next months passed by slowly. I thought of Ryan all the time and wrote him epic letters that I couldn't send or pass to him. Amy came by to see me a couple of times, then stopped. Her mom didn't want her coming over, said that Amy associating with me was making them look bad. Amy said, "I'm really sorry, Toni. I totally don't think you and Ryan did it, but . . ." I told her I understood, but I felt marooned at home, with parents who were still struggling with their own grief, missing my sister, missing my boyfriend. I'd lost my job—not being able to work nights made it impossible. Mike had told me I shouldn't worry about it. "When you're cleared, you can come back, okay?" I loved that he said it, but as far as I knew the police weren't pursuing any leads.

Three months after our bail hearing there was a preliminary hearing, then a month later the judge decided there was enough evidence for a trial and gave us a date for the end of February 1998, over a year away. It felt like an eternity. I met with my lawyer often, and I knew Ryan was meeting with his. My parents had put up sureties of a hundred thousand so I could get bail and said Ryan's family had been able to do it too—their house had almost been paid for—which made me feel bad when I thought of his mom always working late at the hospital. I overheard my parents fighting about money, but they'd stop talking when I entered the room. I started working with my dad again, and that was the only time I felt somewhat normal, taking my anger out with the tools. But then I'd see Dad space out in the middle of a project, his face suddenly stricken, like he'd been stabbed, and I knew he was thinking about Nicole, and that his only living child had been arrested for her murder.

The worst was when I'd catch Mom or Dad watching me. I'd see a hint of something in their faces, like they were gauging me, and I'd know that they were wondering if I *had* done it. One night, late, Mom stumbled away to their room smelling like wine and Dad stayed in the living room. I sat by him on the couch. He glanced over, gave me a tired smile.

I took a breath, then said, "You still believe me, right, Dad?"

He looked confused for a moment, then held my hand and gave it a squeeze. "Of course. I know you'd never want to hurt Nicole." It bothered me that he'd said I wouldn't *want* to hurt her, not that I *wouldn't* hurt her, but I was scared to ask anything more and dropped the subject. At our trial, he'd see.

The trial lasted two weeks. I was allowed to sit with Ryan in the prison docket and we held hands, tight. I wanted to cry when we were first seated together, our eyes roaming each other's faces, searching out the other's emotions, saying everything without words. *I still love you, I miss you, I'm scared.* And the trial was terrifying. I felt helpless, listening to people talk about us, analyzing all of our actions. We were only going before a judge, not a jury—our lawyers didn't feel we were sympathetic enough for a jury. Angus had tried to get me not to look so angry, made me practice smoothing my face into a neutral mask, showed me how to sit and talk, polite and sweet, told me what clothes to wear, but he said I still looked pissed off at the world, a girl with a bad attitude. And I saw it now on Ryan's face. Before, he'd looked like he could brush off anything, nothing would get him down, but already his jaw was tighter, his neck corded from clenching. I grabbed his hand, and noticed some small circular red scars. I stared at him, horrified. Ryan quickly turned his hand around, hiding it from view, but I knew what I'd seen. Cigarette burns. I wondered if he'd done them himself, or if his father had been taking his anger out on him for the last year and a half. I didn't even know if Ryan had been working anywhere or what he'd been doing.

I listened to experts explain about DNA, listened to Doug Hicks and Frank McKinney talk about the night we'd stumbled into the police station. McKinney didn't look at me once while he was speaking, his voice calm and controlled, sounding like a cop. He only got emotional a couple of times when he described how Nicole had become friends with his daughter, how she'd been at his home often and he knew she was having problems with her sister. Something Shauna was more than happy to back up when it came her time to testify.

Shauna looked beautiful that day. Her auburn hair gleamed against her chic black suit, and her eyes had never looked bluer than when they spilled tears down her face as she talked about Nicole, how close they were, close enough for Nicole to share about the knife I'd been carrying. A knife Shauna said I'd threatened Nicole with on many occasions. The lies went on and on.

Rachel also testified, backing up Shauna's version of everything, tossing her hair with every declaration. "I mean, like, we knew Toni hated Nicole, but we never knew she'd do *that*, you know?" And Cathy cried so hard that the lawyers had a hard time getting anything out of her. She just sobbed into her Kleenex, saying over and over again, "I can't believe she's dead."

Kim stumbled over her words when she verified what the other girls had said, that they were out at the lake that night and "clearly" saw me fighting with Nicole, saw Ryan trying to pull us apart. "I keep thinking about that moment," Kim said, her eyes dead and flat. "If we'd gone to help her . . . but we didn't want to interfere. We were all scared of Toni, especially because we knew she carried a knife and she'd already attacked Shauna at school a couple of times. . . ."

Though Nicole had died of blunt force trauma, presumably from the tire iron still missing from Ryan's truck, the prosecutor said my carrying a knife showed intent long before the murder, and much was made of the violence of her death. How that kind of rage had to be personal. Her clothes had also never been found and it was assumed we had disposed of them on the way to the station.

Ryan and I had the chance to speak for ourselves, and I tried to explain away each piece of evidence, but the prosecutor kept tripping me up, until all I could do was turn to the judge and say, "Please, Your Honor. You *have* to believe me. I didn't kill my sister—I loved her."

Ryan looked stiff and uncomfortable in his suit on the stand. His face flushed red when the prosecutor kept cutting him off every time he tried to defend me or my actions. Like me, he tried to explain that Shauna and the girls were lying, but the prosecutor said, "What possible motive could those four girls, exemplary students with no criminal records, have for lying about something so serious? One of them is a policeman's daughter!"

The last day of trial the lawyers made their final summations. I held my breath, listening to them plead our case, studying the judge's face, trying to read what he was thinking. Our lives were going to be decided by one man. My lawyer had told me that this judge had three daughters of his own. I hoped that meant he understood sisters fight, but that didn't mean they would kill each other. At the end of summations, the judge said he needed a few days to deliberate.

Finally, we were brought before the judge again. Both my parents were in the courthouse that day. My mom had left the room a couple of times the first week when the coroner testified or whenever there were photos of Nicole's body. Then she stopped coming altogether when the evidence against me mounted higher and higher. I'd seen her face when Shauna and the girls testified, seen the shock as she looked from them to me and back again. At home she couldn't meet my eyes.

Ryan and I held hands as the judge said, "The issue in this case is who killed Nicole Murphy . . ." He droned on while I tried to focus, but my breath was coming fast, my body breaking out in a cold sweat. Then the words: "I have no doubt that you, Toni Murphy, caused the death of Nicole Murphy. You had motive, you showed stealth, and you intended it. . . ." I let out a gasp, saw Ryan's body jerk with the blow.

From the corner of my eye, I saw my dad put his face in his

hands, his shoulders shaking. The judge was saying stuff about Ryan now but I couldn't hear anything, just the words, *No, no, no, no,* chanting in my head. I glanced at Ryan. His face was pale as he stared at the judge. He looked at me, his eyes stunned. I reached for him and we hugged, me crying, his body stiff with shock. Then my dad was there, hugging me hard, and Ryan's mother, sobbing, her arms trying to circle around both of us. The sheriff put handcuffs on us. I saw my mom, still sitting at one of the benches, her hands over her mouth, her eyes horrified.

"Ryan . . ." My voice sounded helpless. Our eyes met, and I saw the same panicky despair in his face. The finality of the moment hit me, the handcuffs wrapped around my wrists, the sheriff gripping my arms as he led me out of the room, his clipped orders, my last glance at Ryan. He looked at me over his mother's shoulders as she sobbed and sobbed. He mouthed, *I love you.*

# CHAPTER NINETEEN

## CAMPBELL RIVER

### JUNE 2013

Ashley stayed away from me after I told her I wouldn't film a documentary, or at least she stayed away from the subject. She was only working weekends until she finished school, so I didn't run into her a lot, but whenever she came into the kitchen she was friendly. And when she saw me with Captain one night, she asked if she could pet him and brought him cookies the next day. I knew she was trying to gain my trust and I kept my distance.

One evening on my break, after she'd been there for a couple of weeks, I went outside to the back alley, which overlooked the docks—my hiding place from the busy kitchen. I sat on a milk crate, caught my breath in the cool air, wiping the sweat off the back of my neck.

Ashley followed me outside. "That pasta special you made was really good."

"Thanks." I scuffed my feet against the pavement, avoided her gaze.

"My mom freaked out that I was working here," she said.

"I'm sure."

"She doesn't like me working late at night. She thinks some-one will attack me in the parking lot or something stupid. I told her I was staying, though."

I flashed back to a fight with my own mother. *The Fish Shack, Toni?*

When I didn't say anything, Ashley continued, "She always has to know what I'm doing every second." Her voice turned bitter. "She's always checking my Facebook and I can't have a pass-word on my cell or my e-mails or anything. That's why I want to go away to school. Working here, it's kind of the first step."

I had no idea why this kid was telling me all this, but I was struck by how much it reminded me of my own mother and how she had wanted to control everything. I felt a pang, thinking that maybe I should have listened more.

"Sounds like it's between the two of you," I said.

"Yeah, I know. I just thought you'd get it."

It seemed like Ashley had created this whole character for me, based on things she'd read. She probably imagined it would be like the movies: we become buddies, she solves my case, and everyone lives happily ever after. I didn't want to be an asshole, but I didn't want to feed into her fantasy either. I stared down at my feet, making it clear that I didn't want to talk about this any-more.

She glanced at her watch. "Time for me to get back to work, I guess."

The next day we were slammed at the restaurant. Later, after most of the kitchen staff had left and I was cleaning the grill, Ashley came to talk to me.

"Wow, that was crazy busy!" She leaned against the counter,

stole a french fry out of the deep fryer. "Least I made good tips. I wasn't sure I'd like waitressing, but it's fun. Did you like waitressing when you worked here before?"

"For the most part." Except when Shauna and her crew gave me a hard time.

"That's cool."

What part of it was cool? Was she imagining herself walking in my shoes? Re-creating my life? I sure as hell hoped not. My hands were slippery and I dropped the grill brush, which slid partway under the stove. I squatted down and reached for it. As I stood back up, I noticed Ashley staring at my biceps.

"Did you get those in prison?" she asked.

"The tattoos?"

She nodded. "What do they mean?"

I paused, caught off guard by the question. She was the first person to ever ask. I studied the brush in my hand, wondered how much I should share.

"Each bar is for every year I was locked up," I said finally.

"I'd love to get a tattoo but my mom would kill me. She already thinks I'm too . . ." She made quotation marks in the air. "Hard-looking."

"What does that mean?"

"I'm not pretty enough—and she hates how I dress. She tells me I look like a pathetic vampire and she's embarrassed by me." She shrugged. "It wouldn't matter what I wore. She just wishes I looked more like her, but I look like my dad."

I was shocked at her candor, the lack of hurt in her voice, like she was talking about the weather. This was obviously something she'd come to terms with a long time ago. Again I was struck by how adult she seemed.

"My mom didn't like how I dressed either," I said. "She thought I was trying too hard to look tough. Maybe she was right."

"Was it a way for you to get back at her?"

I wasn't sure if she was still trying to get information for her documentary, but I got the feeling she was asking more for personal reasons.

"I don't know, maybe. She didn't like my dating Ryan."

Now Ashley looked angry. "My mom can be a bitch about that too. I was supposed to have a date with this guy I like, but my mom *hates* him because he's a mechanic and he's gotten in trouble before, so we had this big fight. She wouldn't listen to anything when I tried to tell her about him, just said she was looking out for me." She laughed. "It's not about me."

I didn't want to get drawn into her life, her problems, but I was curious. "What's your dad think?"

"He's always working, so he just lets my mom do whatever she wants." The bitter tone again.

I felt bad for the kid, but it was none of my business. The whole family sounded screwed up—and her mom sounded like a bully, who probably had no idea how her daughter really felt about her. I started scrubbing the grill again, but Ashley wasn't ready to end the conversation.

"What did your dad think of Ryan? Did he like him?"

"I think so. He was just scared about how reckless we . . ." I realized I was about to slip, about to let this kid into my world, into my memories where it was Ryan and me sitting in his truck, sharing a joint, him saying, "Don't worry about your parents. They'll see it's real when we've been married for twenty years." And me thinking I was so tough, such a rebel, I didn't need them. I had no idea.

Patty popped her head into the kitchen, saw us talking, and gave me a dirty look.

I said to Ashley, "I really need to finish up here."

Ashley looked disappointed, seeing that a door had closed.

The next weekend she followed me out back again when I was on my break. I sat on one of the milk crates and tried to ignore her, focusing on my iced tea, the boats tied up at the dock, their lights glowing on the dark ocean.

"So I went on a date with the guy from my school," she said. "His name is Aiden."

I squinted up at her. "I thought you weren't supposed to be seeing him."

"I snuck out. We went to a party but I was nervous that my mom would find out and couldn't really relax and have fun." She looked angry. "I can't wait until I'm away at school and can do whatever I want."

I nodded, understanding. But I also wondered about this boy. Maybe he wasn't any good for her. Maybe her mom was right. I thought back to my days with Ryan, trying to see it from my mother's eyes. I probably would've worried too. Then I remembered Nicole at that party, sneaking out the back to meet up with a boy. I wondered where he was now, if he ever thought about her. After she died, I'd tried to find the necklace he'd given her, but it wasn't in her room.

"Was it like that for you?" she said. "When you just wanted to be with Ryan and your parents didn't like him? I mean, you knew he was a good person, just because he got in a little trouble didn't make him a bad guy."

"Sometimes it *does* mean that, though. You have to be careful. When we were kids, it was different. Drugs are different now, everything's changed."

"I heard Ryan's back in Campbell River."

Who told her that? I took a sip of my drink, letting the ice bump against my teeth. Ignored her implied question.

"Have you seen him?" Her tone was more tentative now, curious but sensing that she was crossing a line.

"I'm not allowed to associate with him."

"God, that must be hard." Her face was awash in tragedy. "You guys were so in love."

"We were kids. We didn't know what love was."

She looked angry. "You don't mean that. That's something my mom would say. She hates my boyfriends, always says they're going to just leave me one day, but not every guy is like that. She just doesn't want me to leave *her*."

"I've gotta finish cleaning up the kitchen." I walked back inside. She followed.

"I'll help."

"It's not your job."

"I want to." She paused. "I'm sorry if I upset you, I just think it's so sad that you guys can never see each other again after everything you went through."

I was starting to get the feeling the kid liked to torture herself with painful thoughts. I said, "It was sad, but you get through stuff. You have to."

"I guess . . ." She was fiddling with the sponge, her face still troubled.

I handed her a pot. "Here, clean this."

We worked in silence for a while, the music keeping us company. I noticed her energy seemed to pick up, her shoulders lifting as she worked, one foot tapping to the music. I guess hard work helped her too. While I mopped the floor she started chatting about different documentaries she'd seen, techniques she was trying, how she'd won a grant from the National Film Board of Canada for her last movie. She obviously read a lot—speaking passionately about the Canadian art world and well-known female Canadian filmmakers like Sarah Polley and Deepa Mehta. She also knew a lot about cameras and had some nice equipment her grandfather had bought her, but her mom didn't know because it was expensive.

She was going on about her favorite teacher, who also ran a camera shop in town, when I saw a shadow at the open back door. I glanced up just as I heard a female voice say, "So this is where you are."

Ashley spun around. "Mom!"

The woman seemed familiar, like I should know her. And then I realized I did—it was Shauna McKinney.

She was a little fleshier under her chin and around her waist but still attractive. She was wearing shorts, and her legs were muscled like a runner's. Her auburn hair was shorter now, falling to her shoulders in a sleek bob. She was wearing a yellow shirt, her arms crossed in front of her, a large brown leather handbag hanging off her shoulder and keys in her hand, which she was jittering angrily. She studied me while I studied her, neither of us saying a word.

Ashley finally broke the silence. "I was coming home soon." She sounded really pissed that her mom had shown up at the restaurant. Not that I gave a shit—I was pissed that Ashley had never mentioned who her mother was.

"I thought you were a waitress," Shauna said, still staring at me. "Why are you in the kitchen? I've been worried—you didn't answer your cell."

Ashley set down the sponge, stepped away from the sink. "Sorry. It was busy tonight and I was just helping Toni out."

What the hell? She was blaming me? I turned back, gave her a look.

She flushed, then added, "I wanted to stay and help. She didn't ask."

"It's time to go. Your dad's home tonight and he wants to see you."

"Megan's picking me up."

"Call and tell her you have a ride. I'll meet you in the parking lot."

Making it perfectly clear that she had no intention of letting her daughter linger for one more minute. Ashley looked furious and embarrassed as she glanced back at me, but she left the kitchen. I kept mopping, not looking at Shauna, gripping the handle hard as I remembered her at the trial. *Nicole was always talking about how mean Toni was to her. Toni hated her, everyone knew it. . . .*

"Stay away from my daughter," she said now.

I stopped and leaned on the mop. "Pretty hard to do when she got a job where I work. I didn't know she was your kid."

"Then I guess you're going to have to find a new place to work."

She was right. I hadn't realized until that moment what this meant. I'd probably have to find another job. What was I going to do now?

"I don't want a convict getting cozy with my daughter."

"I wasn't getting cozy with anyone."

"Keep it that way."

She left, but the faint scent of her perfume lingered. Something fruity, tangerine, reminding me of high school. Nothing had changed.

That night Ryan was waiting at the marina again. He came out from the shadows when he saw me pull in. This time he was wearing a black knitted hat pulled down tight, his hair winging out from below, and a brown T-shirt with a faded emblem from some band on the front. It reminded me of something he'd wear in high school but looked different on his man's body. At eighteen he'd played at looking tough, now he was the real deal.

I slammed my truck door, barely looking at him as I unloaded Captain from the front and grabbed the small bag of groceries I'd picked up on the way home. He was closer this time, standing near the front of my truck. It made me nervous, having him so close, being able to see the tattoos on his forearms, wondering what each one meant, who did them for him, whether he had more on the rest of his body, whether any of them reminded him of me.

"You can't keep coming here. You're going to get me sent back."

He stepped into the shadows again, careful to keep his face out of the light as he glanced around. "I'm not the problem."

Fear shot through my body. "What's going on?"

"Cathy's missing."

I relaxed slightly. "She's a crackhead. She's probably stoned somewhere or hiding out because she didn't want to talk to you."

"But she did talk to me, Toni." His eyes and face were serious, tired-looking. "She was high, but she kept saying she was sorry and crying. I asked what she was sorry for and she kind of danced around it at first, but then she admitted that they lied at the trial. She got really nervous and said, 'We were just pissed off at Nicole.'"

"Pissed off at *Nicole*, not me?"

"That's what she said."

"Maybe she was just fucked up and didn't know what she was saying." But I thought back to how strange Nicole had been acting the week before she died. *Had* she been fighting with the girls? "We already knew they lied at the trial—that's not new information."

"She knew exactly what she was saying. She kept going on about how I couldn't tell anyone we were talking, that if Shauna found out . . . she wouldn't say what she was afraid of, but she was definitely scared. She started coming down from her buzz and said she had to meet her dealer. We were going to get together last night, but she never showed. I got a friend to go over to her apartment but her roommate said she never came home the other night—all her shit's still there."

My stomach began to curl inside itself. "She's a druggie, she could be anywhere."

He shook his head. "Something happened to her, Toni. Something bad."

"Maybe Shauna got her out of town, put her up somewhere."

"She could still talk—there's only one way to shut someone up for good."

"It's a big leap to murder."

"Not for someone who's already done it once. I've talked to a couple of my old buddies and they said Shauna and her crew changed after that night—you never saw them anywhere; they never hung out with anyone except each other."

"They were always tight."

"It was different. Cathy was the only one who went to any parties, and she started getting into heavy drugs. Then Kim left right after our trial . . ."

"Nothing weird about that. Her mom was a nut job—she probably couldn't wait to get out of town."

"Yeah, but *this* is the weird thing. I heard she just moved back."

"So what?"

"To help her mom, who's dying or something."

"That doesn't mean anything, Ryan." I heard the anger in my voice and wondered why I was feeling so agitated, like I wanted to tell him to shut up.

Ryan looked pissed too. "Why are you being so stubborn? You're shooting down everything I say."

"I'm just playing devil's advocate."

"You're scared because you know I'm on to something and you don't want to deal with it. You know I'm right."

That stung, but I wondered if he *was* right. If the possibility that the girls had killed Nicole—and now Cathy—was so enraging, I didn't want to believe it, because then I'd have to get involved, and risk everything that I'd worked so hard to get back, not least my freedom. Still angry, I didn't answer.

Ryan continued, "From what I hear, Kim hasn't set foot back in Campbell River since the trial. She's got a dance studio and a girlfriend. You think she's going to just leave all that behind to help her mom, who kicked her out when she was a teenager? She has an older sister who still lives in town. Why isn't *she* looking after the mom?"

"So why do you think Kim's back, then?"

"Shauna had to have called her. They must've caught wind that Cathy was talking to me and decided to get rid of her. Now Shauna's making sure she's got all the players back in town, so she can keep an eye on them and fuck us over."

"What does she care? Even if they did it, they already got us sent to jail."

"Yeah, but now she has to make sure the truth never comes out. If Cathy's dead, who do you think the police are going to look at first, Toni?"

I knew exactly who would get blamed for it.

"What night did she disappear?"

"Wednesday, I think, but I'm not sure. It could've been earlier."

I tried to calculate, think back, panic digging into my blood. "I was at the restaurant that night. I stayed late, cleaning up the kitchen. "

"That's good. And if it did happen in the last couple of days, I was at my mom's every night—I've been staying there, fixing the house up for her. But we'll still get questioned, and you know the second there's any kind of trouble, especially a murder, our parole's going to be suspended while they investigate."

And I'd get sent back to Rockland. How many friends did Helen have on the inside? How long before one of them got to me? What about Captain? Even if our alibis checked out, it could take months to get your parole reinstated.

"This is bullshit, Ryan."

"Damn right. That's why I wanted to give you the heads-up. Those girls don't want us out. As long as we're alive, we're a threat."

"If what you're saying is true and Cathy's gone, we're fucked, Ryan. She was the only person who might've been willing to talk about what really happened that night. The other girls are never going to admit they lied."

"I just have to keep digging. Put enough pressure on them, something will blow."

A door slammed. Someone had pulled into the parking lot. Ryan ducked behind a car. I pretended to get some stuff out of my truck.

"Good evening," I said to the old man as he went down to his boat. He gave me a smile, but my heart was still tapping in my chest.

When he was gone, I whispered over my shoulder, "You better get out of here." There was no response. I turned around. Ryan had already left.

# CHAPTER TWENTY

## CAMPBELL RIVER

### JUNE 2013

I sat up for hours, drinking hot chocolate, looking around at my boat, thinking how much I'd already come to love it. Captain's big head was on my lap as he snored. If Ryan was right and I lost my parole, even temporarily, would Captain have to go back to the shelter? The girls there were nice, maybe one would adopt him, but most of them already had several pets. Could I convince my dad to look after him for a couple of months? I hated how it was going to look to my parents if I was questioned in another murder, how it would look to anyone in town—instantly guilty. I would never be free of this, or of Shauna. I thought about asking Suzanne for a transfer to another city, but that could take at least thirty days. And if Cathy was dead, my leaving town wasn't going to make me look any less guilty. I thought about my mom and dad again, and about how sure Ryan was that he could get to the truth. I decided to hang tight for a little while longer.

The next morning I tried to convince myself that Cathy was

going to show up—alive. Meanwhile I had to deal with the immediate problem. I called Suzanne and told her what had happened at the restaurant with Shauna.

"You can't keep working there," she said.

"I'm really happy, though—and doing well. I don't have to talk to the kid. I'll just tell her to stay away from me." I knew it was useless, but I couldn't help myself, hating the pleading tone in my voice.

"You can be happy working somewhere else, but that's not a good situation for you to be in—especially if her mother's going to be coming by. You don't need the stress, Toni. You've got to focus on getting your life back."

That's what I'd been trying to do. I remembered Shauna coming into the restaurant years before, how she'd made my life a living hell. And here it was happening again. I bit my lip against the anger, stuffed it down low.

I said, "Mike has another location, downtown." It wasn't on the water or as nice a restaurant, but it was a job. "What if I asked him for a transfer?"

She paused, and I held my breath, my fingers crossed. She said, "We can try that, but if you run into her again, we'll have to find you something else."

I let out my breath. "Thanks, Suzanne."

I was about to hang up when she said, "Toni, if you see Shauna McKinney again, turn around and walk in the other direction."

After I got off the phone with Suzanne, I called Mike at the restaurant and explained the problem.

"Damn, Toni. I'm sorry. I had no idea she was Shauna's daughter."

"Yeah, she didn't tell me either, but I was wondering if you could transfer her down to the other restaurant." If one of us had to go, I'd rather it be her.

"I would, but I need the extra hands at the waterfront location."

"Do you have room for *me* at the downtown spot?" *Please, please.*

He thought for a moment, then said, "Yeah, but not cooking— I've got a good guy there, and he doesn't want to work uptown. You'd be a prep cook."

It was better than nothing. "I'll take it."

For the next couple of days I settled into the downtown location, getting to know the staff, ignoring curious stares and whispers. I hated that I was back prepping salads, scrubbing potatoes, and cleaning up after the cook, but I tried to focus on the fact that I still had a job. That was what mattered.

I'd been there for a week when Mike came by after the night shift with his wife and asked me to meet him out front when I was finished cleaning up. He seemed kind of serious, so I was worried but didn't think it could be anything too major. Maybe they needed to cut my hours or something.

I walked over to their table, a flutter of nerves kicking up in my stomach when I saw him and Patty exchange a look. What was going on? When I reached the table, she got up and mumbled something about leaving us to it. The place was empty and dark, the chairs all upside down on top of the other tables.

I sat across from Mike. "What's up?"

"This is a tough one, Toni." He took a breath. "Patty double-checked the count from last night at the waterfront location before she went to the bank this morning, and the safe was missing some money."

Now I knew what this was about, and it wasn't good. Not by a long shot. My hands started to shake under the table. "And you're asking if I did it?"

"I know you were upset about having to change locations . . ."

My voice hard, I said, "I didn't do it, Mike. I worked here until midnight, then I went home. Why would I steal from you?"

"Someone called this morning. They left a message saying they saw a truck there late, after everyone else had left, and someone wearing a hoodie was loitering around the back door. They were concerned."

"That's total bullshit. Who's the witness?" Suddenly a name came to my head. "Was it Shauna McKinney?"

"They didn't leave a name, and we couldn't tell if it was male or female."

I remembered Shauna's talent for altering her voice and was willing to bet it was her, but there was no way to prove it.

"Why aren't you questioning anyone else that worked that night? I couldn't have gotten into the restaurant—I don't even have a key."

"One of the waitresses lost her set a couple days ago. . . . And you're the only one of my employees who has a record."

"That doesn't mean I'm a thief—" My voice broke. He looked at me, his face flushing like he was embarrassed. I took a breath, tried again. "Mike, you know I love this job, this place. I wouldn't screw you over like this. For what?"

He stared down at his coffee. "We had to talk to the police and make a report. They'll probably want to speak to you."

"You know this puts me at risk of losing my parole. Why would I do something so stupid when I *just* got full parole?"

He finally met my eyes again. "It's not only me, Toni. It's Patty. She's never been comfortable with you working here. But now, with Ryan back . . . She's worried that maybe he needed the money, so you helped him out."

"Come on. Give me more credit than that."

"The thing is, Toni, trouble seems to follow you, and we don't want any more problems."

I didn't have an answer to that. It was the truth. Since I first started working for him as a kid, there was always some drama around me.

"You're a good worker," Mike said. "One of the best I've had. I hate to do this."

He was going to fire me. I distanced myself, accepted the hit that was coming. "Just say it, Mike."

"We've got to let you go."

I nodded once, twice, taking in the words. "That it?"

"Your last check, I'll drop it off." So I wasn't even allowed back on the premises. He added, "Patty . . . she also called your parole officer."

"Mike, you know my parole officer can send me back to prison if she believes one second of this bullshit."

"I'm sorry." I could see that he was, but it didn't mean anything now. He was letting me down. I fought tears as I stood up. I wanted to leave with my head high, but I couldn't resist a parting shot when I walked by Patty at the door, her face scared like she thought I might hurt her.

"You're wrong about me," I said. "I'm going to *prove* you wrong."

I grabbed Captain from Mike's yard, taking a moment to give the other dog a good-bye kiss. Captain was thrilled to see me, but I was fighting tears. Who had taken the money? Was it Ashley? I was sure Shauna had set me up somehow. I just prayed that Suzanne wouldn't believe Patty and that they didn't have any evidence other than the asshole witness, but this all felt too familiar. The crazy-making feeling of knowing you're innocent with no way to prove it, the awful shamed feeling that you've done something horrible even when you know you haven't, and the terrifying feeling that your life has slid totally out of your control.

I made it back to my boat, sat down at my table, still jittery and on edge. I tried to focus on practical matters. Would I be able to get another job? Who would hire an ex-con who just got fired for theft? The best thing to do would be to face it head-on. After a sleepless night, I called Suzanne first thing in the morning.

"I didn't steal the money, Suzanne."

"I'm listening."

"There's no way I'd risk losing a job I like over a few bucks."

"It was almost a thousand dollars."

"That's still not worth the risk."

"It might be if you wanted to help someone else." It was back to Ryan again. I was so angry I couldn't speak. She continued, "Maybe he's in trouble or something, but do yourself a favor and tell the truth. Don't cover for him again."

I caught the slip. "I've never covered for him, *ever*, because he's never done anything wrong."

"I could suspend your parole right now," she said, her tone firm, angry herself now. "You're hanging by a thread, Toni. If the police find one scrap of evidence that you're responsible for that theft, you're out of here."

"I'd like to say they won't find anything, because I didn't *do* anything, but that didn't help me the first time around. Someone wants me gone, Suzanne. They're setting me up to look bad."

She was quiet for a moment, then said, "That may be, but you need to come in for a disciplinary hearing so we can sort this out."

I closed my eyes. Damn. "When do you want me there?"


The police called next and I had to go into the station. The officer was decent, polite, but I was on guard as I walked him through my actions the night of the theft. At the end, I said, "Look, I know there's been a witness, but it's just someone out to get me.

A lot of people in this town hate me for what they think I did to my sister. But you won't find one camera in that complex that saw me, one other person, or one fingerprint on that safe. I finished my shift downtown and went home. There's no way I'd lose my job over a thousand bucks."

All the officer said was, "We'll be in touch if we have more questions."

Outside the station, I saw Frank McKinney getting out of his patrol car. He stopped when he noticed me. I was frozen, suspended in time, remembering how I'd liked him as a kid, his eyes watching me in the rearview mirror the night we drove to the lake, how he wouldn't look at me at the trial. Another person who thought I was a murderer, who was disappointed in me. He looked different, still handsome but worn down somehow. His mustache was mostly dark, with just some streaks of silver, but his hair was almost fully gray. He wasn't that old, only his early fifties, but his face was heavily lined now.

He walked toward me, said, "Toni."

"McKinney," using only his last name, unwilling to put him above me.

"I heard you were out on parole." He glanced at the station behind me, no doubt wondering what I was doing there.

"Yeah, and I'm trying to keep it that way but your daughter's making it difficult for me." I held my breath, pissed at myself for letting my anger show.

He looked at me. "What's going on?"

"Ask her. And while you do that, tell her I'm not going anywhere."

I walked away, my back stiff and my face hot. I sat in my truck for a moment, trying to calm down. I glanced over. He was standing on the front step of the station, watching me. *Toni, that was really stupid. Way to draw attention to yourself.* I pulled slowly out of the parking lot, praying I hadn't just started a shitstorm.

In the morning I met with Suzanne and her supervisor. I went over everything again, careful to keep a polite tone though I was angry I was even in this situation. "I have no priors for theft and I had a good prison record. There's no evidence I did this—just a witness who wouldn't give a name, and if it's who I think it is, she hates me and wanted me to get fired. I think I've proved that I'm trying to get my life back together and complying with all the conditions of my parole."

Suzanne made some notes, then held my gaze, her eyes revealing nothing as she said, "You can go now, Toni. We'll be in touch if we need anything else."

I drove back to Campbell River wondering if this was it for me, if I was going back to prison. For a moment I was tempted to pull a runner, flee for the border or up north, get lost in the woods where no one could find me. But then I thought of Captain, waiting for me to come home. I had to suck it up and wait.

I was on the boat, trying to come up with a list of places where I could apply for work, assuming I wasn't going back to prison, when Suzanne called.

"We're not going to suspend your parole right now, but if anything else happens . . ."

My body filled with relief. "Nothing will happen—I swear."

"And you need to find a job where you aren't near any cash."

"Seriously? That means I can't work in any restaurants."

"There are lots of other jobs."

I gritted my teeth. *Just agree, don't argue.* "Okay, I'll get on that right away. Thanks, Suzanne."

"Stay out of trouble—and stay away from anyone who's going to get you in trouble."

Easier said than done.

———

I was upset that I couldn't work as a cook but tried to think positive. When this shit blew over and I proved myself again, I could be back working a grill. Then I thought of Cathy. Had she been found yet or were my days numbered? I turned my mind away from the terrifying thoughts. I had to focus on finding a job. I looked online for some sort of manual labor. If I didn't get a job soon my savings were going to disappear, plus I didn't have the luxury of goofing around—one of the conditions of parole is that you have to show you're trying to get a job. I tweaked my résumé and decided to go into town and get some printed off. It was getting warm now that it was the middle of June, so I left Captain on the boat.

The rest of the afternoon I dropped résumés off around town, but no one seemed to be hiring. Later, back on the boat, I wondered if Ryan had gotten a job. I wondered what he was doing in general. I remembered, when we were kids, if one of us was having a shitty time we'd go to the lake or the pier or anywhere and just feel better because we were with each other. I didn't think I'd ever have that feeling with anyone again. I reached over and scratched Captain—not human, anyway. I also wondered who Ryan had been talking to. Was he getting closer to the truth? Was that why Shauna got me fired? She obviously didn't like me working with her daughter and one way of solving that was to get rid of me, but I was sure she had a bigger motive. I thought of Ryan's words: *She's got all the players back in town, so she can keep an eye on them and fuck us over.*

I hoped she'd be satisfied that I lost my job and leave me alone now. But if the past had proven anything, Shauna didn't give up that easily.

# CHAPTER TWENTY-ONE

## CAMPBELL RIVER

### JUNE 2013

That night I was lying on my bed, Captain's big head weighing down my arm. I didn't want to disturb him, so I was using my other hand to turn the pages of my book. I heard some soft footsteps coming down the dock. I set the book down, listened. Captain's head also lifted, his ears alert. The footsteps stopped near my boat. I sat up and reached for the baseball bat I kept near the door. Captain rolled over in bed, his body tense, a low growl in his throat, then a woof. I silenced him with a look. He paused, his mouth still open in an O, ready to bark.

I heard a light knock. Captain barked louder now. I let him for a moment, so whoever was on the other side got the idea there was a big dog in there. Then I silenced him: "Captain, enough." He stopped, his eyes intent on my face. I tiptoed through my galley kitchen. The curtains were closed, so I couldn't see who was outside. Captain followed, his toenails tapping on the wood floor.

"Who is it?" I said at the door.

"Ashley."

What the hell? I opened the door. Ashley was standing on the dock, a hoodie pulled over her head. She was chewing on her lower lip, her face tense and pinched. I glanced up and down the wharf, making sure she wasn't with anyone. Captain jammed his head through the door, sniffing at the air, breathing it in with big chuffs. He recognized Ashley's scent and started a full-body wiggle, his tail slapping against the table.

"What are you doing here?" I said.

"I need to talk to you."

I opened the door and motioned for her to come in. "Watch your head."

She ducked down and entered the boat, looking around curiously, then sat at my little table. "This is cute."

"It's a boat."

"It's a cute boat."

I grabbed a sweatshirt off a hook by the door, pulled it over my tank top, and sat down across from her. Captain had his head resting on her knee, eyes closed, and she was scratching behind his ears.

"I heard you got fired." Her tone was a little higher-pitched than normal, anxious, her eyes roaming my face, checking to see how I was feeling.

"I'm sure you've heard a lot of stuff."

"I know you didn't do it." She said it emphatically. Was she just trying to show loyalty or did she know something? If she was working late that night . . .

"What's going on, Ashley?"

She stared down at Captain for a moment, then back at me. "Jeremy was finished in the kitchen, and Hannah wanted to meet her boyfriend, so he said he'd give her a ride. They left and I was still doing the count. I was going to call Aiden to pick me up, but then my mom came by. . . ."

Shauna had been in the restaurant that night? I sat up straight, my spine stiff.

"She said she was worried because I hadn't made it home yet. I told her she shouldn't be there, but she said she wasn't letting me be in that building by myself at night, it wasn't safe. She sat up at the bar while I finished counting out the till. Normally I take the money bag straight to the back, but we were talking, so I got distracted and I left the bag on the counter until I'd finished mopping the floor behind the bar. Then I went into the back and dumped the water out."

She held my gaze, making sure I got what she was saying. I did—loud and clear. Shauna had been in front of the till with the money. Alone.

"When I came back, I put the bag in the safe. I was tired and wanted to go home, so I didn't notice the cash was gone. I just locked it up. When we left the restaurant I double-checked that I had my keys—I told Mom another waitress had lost hers recently."

So Shauna knew that there was a loose set floating around out there, a set that someone might now think had been stolen.

"A witness left a message that someone who looked like me was loitering outside the restaurant late that night."

"I don't know who called. . . ." But she also thought it was her mother. I could see it on her face. The fear, that she was being disloyal, like she was walking the edge, breaking some secret code. "I told Mike and the police that I didn't think you did it, that I didn't see your truck outside or anything."

"Why are you telling me this, Ashley?" I was surprised she was ratting her mother out, even if she was dancing around it, and wondered at her motive. She'd clear my name of the theft if I let her film me? Something else? She had an agenda, I was sure of it.

"It's not right that you got fired. I feel really bad." She did look upset, near tears. And her face was blotchy, like she might have been crying before. "I had a huge fight with my mom tonight because I said I was going to tell Mike she was at the restaurant. She said she couldn't believe what I was insinuating, that if I didn't trust her then maybe she shouldn't help me pay for the Vancouver Film Festival this year. And there's more. . . ."

"More about what?"

She dropped her voice, her eyes big. "I heard her talking on the phone. She sounded really angry about someone, which isn't unusual—she's always complaining about something—but she was saying they had to make sure the person they were talking about couldn't cause them any more problems."

"That could have been about anything." But I felt my pulse speed up, my nerves alert and on edge. The same feeling I'd get when I was inside, right before a big fight broke out.

"I know, but she was acting weird. She didn't know I was watching but she was still quiet and looking around, not saying names. And she's been snapping at me over nothing. She and my dad had a screaming fight."

I was silent, thinking over everything. My fear was obviously accurate. Shauna might have more planned for me than a simple theft. I flashed back to high school, how Shauna had wanted to destroy my life, how she had succeeded.

As though Ashley had read my mind, she said, "Why does she hate you so much?"

Her face was serious and scared. I sensed she wasn't sure if she really wanted to know, like she was aware she was opening a door that she might not be able to close. But she couldn't stop herself, had already gone too far. I felt the same way. I wanted to tell her to leave, but she was a key. I might not know which lock she fit yet but I wasn't ready to let go of her either. We held gazes, the only sounds now the ticking of my clock and Captain's breathing.

I decided to follow Ashley's lead and shoot straight from the hip. "It started in ninth grade. She liked some guy, and when he talked to me one day she flipped out. She made my life hell, spread lies, and made sure I had no friends. She forgot about me until high school, when she got a crush on Ryan and he picked me instead. After that, she made it her mission to destroy my life."

Ashley was nodding. "My mom comes across tough, but she's actually really insecure. She wants—needs—everyone to like her, and she's super-competitive. Like she wants all my friends to think she's the coolest mom. It's probably because my grandpa was always busy when she was a kid, and now he spends more time with me. But I don't care—she shouldn't take it out on me."

A surprisingly insightful comment, but I didn't see how it was going to help my situation any. I felt tired, worn-out. I thought things had changed, had actually dared to believe I could finally have a normal life. Now the noose was closing around my neck again, and Shauna was holding the end of the rope.

"I'm going to do it," Ashley said. "I'm going to tell Mike that Mom was at the restaurant." She was scared to death, you could see it in her face, but she also had a fervent energy, high on the idea of doing the right thing.

I thought over her statement, feeling relief at first: Mike might let me come back; Suzanne would see that I was telling the truth. Then I wondered what Shauna's next step would be. If she was gunning for me, it might be better to let her think she'd won. She might back off for a bit, give Ryan a chance to find out more about that night at the lake.

"Don't," I said. "I don't want you to get in shit with your mom, and Mike will be pissed that you let her in. You need the money for school."

She looked shocked. "You got *fired*."

"Patty wanted me out of there anyway. She was just waiting for an excuse."

"But it's not fair."

I remembered being shocked when I was arrested for Nicole's murder, thinking how unfair that was, how unfair everything felt when I was a teenager. But it's an imperfect system and I learned that most things in life weren't fair.

"Fair or not, it's the way it is. Look, if the shit really hits the fan and it looks like I might get sent back to prison over this, then I might ask you to step up, okay? Meanwhile, let's just see how everything unfolds."

She nodded, pleased that we were in this together, our little secret. I'd known she'd like that. But I still wondered at her motives. Was she really doing the right thing or just trying to get back at her mother for something?

There was another knock on the door.

Both Ashley and I jerked back. Captain started barking, his hackles up.

I motioned for Ashley to stay still, called out, "Who's there?"

"It's Shauna. Open the door, please. I know my daughter's in there."

Ashley's eyes widened. We stood up at the same time. I held Captain back by his collar as I opened the door. Then we stepped out and I closed the door behind us, blocking Captain, who'd started growling the minute he glimpsed Shauna.

"I thought we had an agreement, Toni." Her voice was icy calm, polite. "You were going to stay away from my daughter."

"Your daughter's leaving. I suggest you do the same."

"Come on, Mom, let's get out of here." Ashley tugged on her mother's arm. Shauna ignored her, her face still composed.

"Toni and I need to talk about a couple of things," she said. "Get in my car. I'll be up in a minute." But Ashley wasn't backing down that easily.

"I'm sixteen—you can't order me around like that."

"Unfortunately for you, you're still a minor and living under my roof." Shauna's voice was level, but I could tell by her stiff shoulders, her tight grip on her keys, that she was fighting to keep her cool.

"That doesn't mean you own me." Ashley's face was now red.

"I saw your car in the parking lot. You only have your learner's. What were you thinking?"

I hadn't thought about how Ashley had gotten to the marina. Now I saw real concern under Shauna's anger.

"I'm going to have to take away your keys for this stunt," she said.

"I'm sick of you running my life and all your stupid threats," Ashley said, her faced twisted in rage. "I know what you did to Toni—"

"Just go, Ashley. I'm fine." The last thing I wanted was her to accuse her mom of the theft and get herself—and me—in more shit.

Shauna turned around, her face livid, but her voice was still calm as she said, "Thank you, Toni, but I can handle my own daughter."

Ashley was still standing on the dock, watching us.

"She came to my boat, *Shauna*. I didn't show up at your house. Maybe you need to get better control of her."

Inside, Captain was going nuts, sounded like he was taking the wall apart. Shauna got a calculating look, then her expression changed to fake concern.

"Toni, I'm worried about you. Rescue dogs like that have been known to snap. Are you sure you're safe? Are you sure *he's* safe?"

I caught my breath as I registered the threat underneath her words. "What the fuck are you getting at, Shauna? You think you can just threaten me like this?"

"I'm giving you some friendly advice. You've always taken on the hardest cases, rescuing damaged creatures no one else wants. . . ." She paused, letting it sink in, waiting for me to get what she was really saying. And I did.

She was talking about Ryan. The wharf tilted as a tugboat cruised by, sending waves in our direction. I focused on it for a moment, gathering my thoughts, trying to find my balance. I couldn't let her throw me.

"But there's a reason no one wants them," she said, "why someone else let them go. You just never know when they might turn on their owner."

Now I was really pissed. "If you have something to say, Shauna, then—"

"If I were you, I'd stay away from Ryan Walker," she said. "He's no good for you, Toni. Look what happened last time."

I tried to hide my panic, tried to keep my face neutral. Did she know? Had someone seen us talking one night? Was she threatening to turn us in?

"You need to stay the fuck away from *me*, Shauna. You come here again, I'm calling the cops."

"No, you won't." She turned to her daughter. "Come on, Ashley."

They left. At the top of the dock Ashley turned back, tried to mouth, *I'm sorry*, but her mother grabbed her arm.

I went inside and held Captain, my body shaking. I kept hearing Shauna's words over and over again in my head.

*Look what happened last time. . . .*

# CHAPTER TWENTY-TWO

## CAMPBELL RIVER

### JUNE 2013

For the next couple of days, I got up early every morning before the heat of the day and drove around handing out résumés, Captain riding shotgun. I was nervous about leaving him alone in case Shauna tried anything. So far I didn't have any leads for a job, but I talked to one of the women at the shelter who said she knew someone who might dog-sit Captain during the day once I found something. Stephanie, the shelter manager, and I had coffee one day after I walked the dogs. She said the shelter might be hiring in a few months, but that wouldn't help me at the moment. She was cool, though, and I enjoyed the visit. It was nice being with someone who wasn't freaked out about my past.

I came home and spent some more time online checking for new postings, but still no luck. Exhausted by defeat, I went to bed and pulled out my book. I'd developed a taste for Steinbeck in prison and was reading *East of Eden* for the third time. I drifted off and woke hours later to someone knocking on my door. It was Nate, the guy who'd rented me the boat.

"Hey, Nate. What's up?"

"Sorry, Toni, but you can't live here anymore. You need to leave right away."

"You can't just kick me out. There are tenancy laws and stuff."

"We never had a real rental agreement—it was just verbal. And I got a report that Captain's been harassing people."

"Who would—" I stopped. It had to be Shauna. "That's not true. He's a good dog—ask any of the people down here. Someone's just out to get me."

"I also heard what happened at the restaurant. Some of the other people living at the marina, they've got expensive equipment on the boats. They don't want to take a chance, and I don't want my customers leaving."

So that's what it was really about. He didn't give a shit about my dog. No one wanted a thief living near them.

"I'll be out in the morning."


I packed my few belongings and left that night, while it was dark. I didn't want to face everyone going down to their boat in the morning, didn't want to see the judgment in their eyes. I now had no job, no home, and barely any money. What the hell was I going to do? A hotel would eat up my savings in no time.

Then I remembered that there was a campsite down in Miracle Beach, fifteen minutes south of town, with older cabins for rent. It wasn't the best time of year—heading into peak season—but they might have something and it was cheaper than a hotel. I pulled up at the campsite, relieved to see that it didn't look too busy. Tourist season had been slow this year, and this wasn't exactly a top-rated campground. The pool was drained, the bottom covered by dirt and leaves, and the playground had seen better days, half of the swings missing. A lot of the RVs were also in rough shape. They probably belonged to people who lived there year-round—pad fees were cheaper than apartment rents.

The man in the office didn't ask many questions, just eyed my dog and asked if he was friendly, then told me one of the older cabins in the back was empty. I could have it for cheap. I knew that probably meant it was a piece of shit, and I was right. The bed sagged in the middle, everything smelled old and musty, including the orange curtains on the windows and matching bedspread. But it was stocked with pots, pans, dishes, and I could get new bedding the next day. Captain and I snuggled on the bed that night, both of us waking up at every sound.

In the morning I called Suzanne and told her where I was staying, and that I was still looking for work. I plugged in my laptop and searched my e-mails, hoping I might have heard back about a job, but nothing yet. I left Captain in the cabin and headed out to print off more copies of my résumé and buy towels—the ones in the cabin were so threadbare and small they couldn't dry a frog.

I dropped off a few more résumés, stopping at the shelter to tell Stephanie what had happened in case she got a false report about Captain, then took a couple of dogs for a walk. Next I hit Walmart, buying a foam mattress, some bedding, towels, and cleaning supplies. I wasn't hungry but I made myself eat a salad for dinner while Captain inhaled a bowl of kibble, then I took him for a long walk along the ocean. I already missed living on the water, feeling the gentle rock of the waves.

I remembered how Ryan and I would send each other thoughts when we'd had a bad day or fought with our parents. I sat on a log and closed my eyes, mentally telling him about losing my job, the boat, and now living at a shitty campsite. I imagined myself saying, *It's going to get better, right?* And him saying back in his teenage voice, *Of course, babe. We've still got each other.* I opened my eyes, sad now, thinking how innocent we were back then. We thought that our relationship was all that mattered, all we needed, and that it meant we could survive anything. We didn't know they'd take that from us too.

I was getting ready for bed, brushing my teeth, when I heard a soft rap at the door. Captain jumped up and ran to the door, gave a warning bark.

"Who's there?" I said.

"Ryan."

How the hell had he found me? I opened the door, holding Captain back and forgetting for a moment that I was in shorts and a tank top.

"What are you doing here?" I glanced around, made sure no one was in sight.

"I heard you lost your job and your boat. We need to talk."

"How did you know I was here?"

"One of my buddies knows Stephanie, the shelter manager—he does her tattoos. She was talking to him about you today, said you were looking for work and staying at one of the campsites. I drove around today, checking them out and looking for your truck. I saw you walking on the beach earlier. . . ."

I remembered the thoughts I'd sent him on that walk. He'd felt it. I knew it. Our eyes locked. I looked away first. "Hang on a minute."

I shut the door, pulled on a hoodie and some jeans. One of the things I liked about the cabin was that it was set in the far back of the campsite, surrounded by a dense wall of trees. No one could see it, but I could still hear campers talking in the distance, their laughter carrying in the breeze along with the smoky smell of their fires, and I didn't feel comfortable talking to Ryan outside.

I opened the door and made a motion. "Come in."

Ryan sat at the table, looked around. "Not bad."

"It's a shithole." I sat down across from him. This was the closest I'd been to him in years and it made me uneasy, self-conscious, aware of my messy hair, my unmade bed, my clothes draped over a chair. We'd never been alone in my bedroom at home, and now he was in my space. He was a stranger but he was also so familiar to me, the way he moved, his voice. He looked good, his hair damp, like he'd washed it before he came over, but he hadn't shaved and had a dark shadow covering his face. I remembered how when we were teens he barely had to shave. He was wearing faded jeans and a fitted white shirt under a black sweatshirt, unzipped. One of his tattoos peeked out at his wrist. An eagle claw.

"We've seen worse," he said.

"Yeah." I didn't want to think about that, what he may have gone through, didn't want to talk about prison. "Where's your truck?"

"Down on the back road, hidden in the bushes. I hiked in. I got some work on one of the tugboats with an old buddy of my dad's. He also has a sailboat down in the marina and he heard you got evicted."

"So what did you want to talk about?" I said.

"You smell like the ocean."

That caught me off guard. A warm heat spread through my stomach. I flushed, angry at my reaction. "That's what you came here to tell me?"

Our eyes met again. This time he looked away, saying, "I'm sorry about you losing your job and everything."

"I didn't lose everything. Not yet." I glanced at Captain, who was staring out the window, his ears twitching at a sound here and there, bunnies and mice scurrying in the night. I turned back to Ryan.

"I'm pretty sure Shauna set it up. She's pissed that her daughter is crushing on me." I told him what had been going on, about the confrontation with Shauna, how she'd warned me to stay away from him.

"I'm positive it was those bitches who killed Nicole," he said. I was caught by the deep anger in his voice, the hatred in his eyes. I felt the same way, but it concerned me, the rage barely contained. What would it take for him to explode? He took a deep breath, like he was trying to calm himself.

"They found Cathy today. She's dead."

"Shit." I sat up straight, thoughts crashing into each other. I glanced at the door, half expecting the cops to break it down and start screaming orders at us.

"Yeah, that guy who works on the tugs with me, he was down at the pier when they brought up her body and he overheard the cops talking. They said it was a known drug user, Cathy Schaeffer."

"Did she OD?"

"Don't know yet, but it sounds like they had a lot of cops down there. My gut tells me it was murder and we're going to be hearing about it."

"There has to be a lot of people she's pissed off." I could hear the panic in my voice.

"Probably, but we're the only ones with a murder conviction."

He was right. We were screwed. I sat back in my chair, the hard edges digging into my calves and thighs. *I'm not going back. No way. I can't go back.*

"Even before this, Hicks has been following me everywhere," Ryan said. "The fucker even walked in when I was taking a leak at the gas station. He asked if I liked hanging out in men's rooms, said he sure hoped so because I was going back to prison soon. He's been pushing me, trying to get me to snap."

"Why does he care?"

"He's never liked me. He hated my dad too. And I tell you, Toni, I wasn't scared of him before, but I am now. I've got a bad feeling we're going back in."

I had a bad feeling too. "I made an enemy at the halfway house—she's got friends on the inside, and they'll be waiting for me." I told him about Helen.

He was quiet, thinking, his face worried. He fingered a scar on his arm, the ridges still red like it was fresh.

"That's fucked up. Will you be all right? Do you have friends inside too?"

"I've got some girls. But you know all it takes is someone to get you alone for a minute."

"If Suzanne suspends us, she might keep us in for the full thirty. We could be in for even longer if she doesn't cancel it. You'll have to watch your back every second." Ryan was right. Suzanne had the authority to suspend us for thirty days while the police investigated, and if she still thought we were a risk, she could refer us to the Parole Board for a post-suspension hearing. That could take another ninety days.

"What about you?" I said. "Will you be okay?"

"I'll be fine." But he fingered the scar again, and I wondered if he also had enemies inside. For a second it was like we were kids again and he was showing me another bruise or cut that his dad had given him. I almost reached out to touch the scar, then curled my hand under the table, digging my fingers into my leg.

Ryan said, "The cops are going to tell you stuff about me, trying to turn us against each other like they did the first time." We'd never spoken about our interviews, the lies the cops had told, but obviously they'd tried to screw with his head as well. It made me feel good, knowing that neither of us had thrown the other to the wolves. We'd stayed loyal. "It looks bad that I was talking to Cathy, but I didn't hurt her. I wanted her alive."

"I know." And I did—though I couldn't stop thinking about the anger in his face, the rage, how prison changes a person. How it changed me.

"I want to clear our names," he said. "It's not enough that we're out. I want to be free, no bullshit parole conditions." He paused, looking at my face. He was gauging my reaction, testing me. "I want it how it used to be."

The words hung in the air, an invisible cord that pulled me

closer. I caught my breath. I knew what he really meant. I felt myself on the edge, wanted to give over to it, wanted to get up and walk around the table and sit in his lap like when we were kids. But something held me back. Fear held me back.

"A lot's changed over the years, Ryan. We grew up."

"Haven't you heard?" A bitter smile. "No one grows up in prison."

I had heard that. I'd heard it a lot, but it wasn't true for me. I felt like I'd aged a thousand years. My skin weighed me down. I imagined it sliding onto the table, puddling on the floor, wanted to climb back into it like a sleeping bag.

Ryan's voice pulled me out of my thoughts. "What if we *could* go back in time?"

"If we could go back in time I never would've gone to the lake that night. If we hadn't taken Nicole, she'd still be alive." It was the hard, painful truth that I lived with every damn day and that beat in me like another heart.

Ryan nodded and sighed, his shoulders slumping as he sat back in his chair. After a moment, he said, "I've been talking to some people we went to school with and found someone else who was at the lake that night, at that party we saw down below. Her name's Allison—she was a year younger than us. She said she told the cops back then that she saw a white car like Shauna's tear out of there that night, just after eleven. I asked which cop and she said it was Hicks. He told her she wasn't a reliable witness because she was drunk. Then he kept asking her stuff until she said she wasn't sure what she saw."

I remembered the girls' testimony at the trial, how they said they'd been at the lake earlier, saw me fighting with Nicole around ten, not long after we got there, then they left before ten-thirty. The police figured Nicole had been murdered around eleven. So if Allison saw a white car later, that backed up the girls being involved.

Ryan was still talking. "I figure because Shauna's dad's a cop, they didn't even consider that she and her friends could've been involved."

If the girls had been hunting for me, or saw Ryan's truck and decided to screw with us but mistook Nicole for me in the dark . . . We did look alike. Or maybe something had happened between all of them during those final weeks of summer. I had a flash of an image, the white car slowing down outside the house a few days before Nicole was killed. She'd said Shauna was away. Was that a lie?

"She's willing to give another statement, but it's not enough," Ryan said. "Hicks was right—if she was drinking, she's not a reliable witness. They'll just say she got the time wrong." He thumped his fist on the table. "I've got to find someone else willing to talk before Shauna kills any other witnesses."

Or we got sent back to prison.

"Maybe we should talk to Suzanne about getting a transfer out of Campbell River," I said. "We shouldn't have come back here."

"I'm not going anywhere. This is no kind of life, being on parole. We still don't have any freedom. I want to clear my name, I want my mom to be able to hold her head up high in this town, and I want Shauna to feel the pressure. If she did it, she's never going to feel safe as long as we're on the outside." He looked at me steadily. "It doesn't matter where we move. We're a threat as long as we're alive—especially now that she knows we're not just going to go away quietly."

He was right. We might be out of prison but we'd never be truly free unless we were cleared. I'd never be able to look into my parents' eyes and see they finally believed I didn't do this terrible thing to my sister.

"So what's your plan?" I said.

"I'm going to keep talking to people, see what I can stir up. Something's going to break, but it might just take some time." He looked up and around, like he was sensing danger in the air. "I should go, just in case anybody's watching."

"I'll go out the front with Captain, like I'm taking him for a pee. The back bedroom window's open."

I thought about all the nights Ryan and I had climbed out of windows to see each other. I knew he was thinking about that too because he gave me a rueful smile and said, "We thought we had it so hard, hey?"

This time the memories overtook me, and I reached out and touched his hand, then rested my palm on top of his for a moment, feeling his warmth, the substance. I thought about how many nights I'd lie awake in my cell, holding my own hand, imagining it was his. He flinched, stared down at our hands, his face a mixture of wonder and fear and sorrow. The moment built in my throat, until it scared me. I took my hand away and stood up. "I better get Captain outside."

He nodded and got up. I put on Captain's leash while Ryan moved toward the back of the cabin. At the last second he turned around.

"If we get questioned and our parole is suspended, stay alive, okay? Because when we get out again—and we will—we're going to kick some ass."

I tried to smile, but I couldn't help thinking that this could be the last time I'd ever see him. I remembered a similar moment, all those years ago when I was being led away from him after the trial, how it felt like something was being ripped out of my body. He saw it in my eyes, my doubt and fear, and closed his own eyes for a moment, blocking it out, like he couldn't bear to face that pain either. He turned quickly and climbed out the window, not looking back this time.

I took Captain out the front, thinking of Ryan making his way through the dark woods, then I thought about Cathy and breathed in the night air, wondering how much longer I'd be out. How much longer I'd be alive.

# CHAPTER TWENTY-THREE

## CAMPBELL RIVER

### JUNE 2013

The next morning the police called. They had some questions and wanted me to come into the station that afternoon. I had a suspicion that shit was going down and made a difficult call to my dad. I tried his cell first, but he didn't answer, so I had to phone the house. My mother answered.

"Hi, it's Toni. Can I talk to Dad, please?" She was quiet so long I worried that she might hang up on me. I held my breath, waiting for the click.

"Just a minute." Sounds of a phone being passed. Urgent, angry whispers.

My dad finally got on the phone. "Toni? Are you okay?"

"Yeah, for now. I lost my job. There was a theft—but I didn't do it." There was no sense covering it up. If they hadn't already heard the rumors, they would eventually. Dad was silent and I wondered if he was remembering when I was a teen, how we'd broken into the neighbors', the stolen bottle of Percocet.

I said, "Someone is setting me up, and they might try to cause me more trouble. I just . . . I just want you to know that whatever you hear, it's not true. When I was a kid, I didn't give you any reason to trust me, but I'm not a bad person, Dad. I'm trying to do everything right. . . ." I was surprised to feel tears running down my face. I brushed them away. Captain watched me from the bed, his head on his paws, his brown eyes sad and worried.

"I know you're trying to turn your life around," Dad said. But his voice was quiet, muffled, like he was trying not to be overheard.

I pushed past the hurt. I had to focus on the goal. "If my parole gets suspended, can you take my dog? It would just be until I got out again."

"I'm sure we can—" I heard Mom say something in the background. Dad answered, but it was muted, like he was covering part of the phone. More arguing.

Mom got back on the line. "I'm sorry, but we have a cat now. Your dog is going to have to go somewhere else. We can't take him."

"You mean you won't." I hated the bitter tone in my voice, the disappointment.

She didn't answer.

"Thanks." I hung up the phone.

Later, I called Stephanie at the shelter and told her there was a chance I might lose my parole even though I hadn't done anything wrong. I had to stop a couple of times to fight back tears, feeling ashamed, wondering if she'd also heard about the theft at the restaurant, and struggling with an overwhelming sadness that I might have to let Captain go. Thankfully, Stephanie didn't ask any questions.

"He can live at the shelter until we find a home," she said, "but he'd have to go up for adoption."

I didn't want him living at the shelter, or with anyone else, but it was the best I could hope for. "Thanks, Stephanie."

I climbed into bed, pulled Captain's head against my chest, trying not to think of him back in that cage, how I'd promised to take care of him forever.

At the station, they took me into the same interview room that they questioned me in after Nicole died. I flashed back to waiting huddled under a blanket, terrified, and wondered now if their choosing this room was deliberate. Sure enough, here came Doug Hicks walking into the room. He'd aged, had to be in his early forties by now, but was in good shape. His white-blond hair and pale eyelashes still creeped me out, and he still looked like a man who thought knocking some heads together was fun times and scaring the hell out of teenagers was just part of the job. When his ice-blue eyes met mine, I felt instant fear and dread. I could already see he'd made up his mind. He hadn't believed me then and he wasn't going to believe me now.

He pulled the chair close, leaned on the table. "It seems we have a problem, Toni. I'm hoping you can answer a few questions so we can eliminate you as a suspect, but you're free to go at any time, okay?"

I was silent, waiting. I knew the drill. I wasn't under arrest, yet, so he had to make sure he let me know I wasn't being detained.

"You've probably heard that Cathy Schaeffer's body was found yesterday," he said. "It appears she was murdered."

I knew that had to be the case or they wouldn't have called me in, but the news still hit hard. I thought about Cathy crying at my trial, the lies falling out of her mouth. I'd hated her, but I hadn't wanted her dead. "Sorry to hear that."

"Are you?"

"Of course."

He narrowed his eyes, stared at me hard. In prison you learn never to make eye contact with the guards, and it took all my strength now not to look away.

"I thought you might be happy she's dead—after how she testified at your trial. That had to have really pissed you off."

I kept my mouth shut.

He leaned so close I could smell his lunch on his skin, something Italian, basil and tomato sauce. I focused on that, not the fear.

"The way she died, the blows, it looks a lot like your sister's murder," he said. "Seems the weapon might have been a tire iron again."

I tasted acid in my mouth, my stomach contents threatening to rise. I tried to block the memory of Nicole's body when we'd found her, how her skull had been crushed, her face mangled, but I couldn't help the flashes that slapped into me, the image of a tire iron smashing down, Nicole trying to cover her head, cowering in terror. I didn't want Hicks to know he was getting a reaction out of me, but I felt hot all over and beads of sweat were forming on my forehead. He was studying my face, his gaze lingering on the pulse beating frantically in my neck.

"Where were you last Wednesday night?" he said.

"Working late at the restaurant." I let out my breath a little. I was relieved to hear it was that day. The night before that I'd been home alone, no alibi.

"What time did you get off?"

"It was midnight by the time I finished cleaning up."

His face was speculative and I wondered what time they figured she had died, or if they knew.

"You go anywhere after?"

I thought back. "I stopped at the gas station for some dog cookies."

"Got the receipt?"

"I'm not sure, maybe." I sure as hell hoped so.

"You remember the clerk?"

"It was a young guy, blond hair, goatee." We'd talked briefly about our dogs. I prayed he would remember me.

Hicks leaned back in his chair. Giving me that same look he had when I was eighteen, like he knew I was no good and was just trying to find out how deep the rot went. "Don't suppose you know where Ryan was that night?"

I had to be careful now, not show even a flicker of fear in my eyes.

"No idea."

"You see him since he's been out?"

"We aren't allowed any contact."

"That's not what I asked." Bastard was as smart as I remembered.

"No. I haven't seen him."

"I heard he's pretty pissed off about the girls testifying at the trial."

"I wouldn't know how he feels."

"So how do you feel about it?"

I couldn't help myself. "They were lying."

"That's what you said back then too."

"Because it's the truth."

"So you must be pissed off at them."

I recited what I'd learned to say in my parole hearings. "I've learned from my past mistakes and just want to become a productive member of society."

He gave me a look that made it clear he knew I was really telling him to fuck off. I came close to saying it out loud, rolled the words around on my tongue, savored them. Then I thought of Captain and swallowed them whole.

"I've thought about your case, what happened that night," he said. "Ryan, he was bad news, but up until you hooked up with him you were a pretty good kid. I'd hate to think of the same thing happening again."

"It won't."

"Just in case you *have* seen your old friend, you should probably know that when he was inside, he got himself quite the reputation as a fighter with a violent temper, beat up some guards, spent a lot of time in segregation."

I was surprised, remembering how Ryan had always tried to walk away from fights unless he was pushed to the limit, and wondered just how bad things had been for him in prison. It filled me with rage, thinking of him in segregation, knowing what it was like for me, neither of us deserving it. I kept my mouth shut.

"I've been talking to a few people you two used to pal around with," Hicks said. "One of the guys said Ryan used to talk about Nicole, how sexy and hot she was." He shook his head. "Apparently he used to have a fantasy about getting the two of you together for some action." I knew he was just trying to get a rise out of me, but his lies were hard to listen to. Jesus, my sister was *dead*.

He leaned even closer, his leg brushing mine, his body language intimate, like we were close friends. I stared at the wall, refusing to look at him.

"That night, you say you were passed out the whole time, but how do you know your boy Ryan *stayed* passed out? How do you know he didn't wake up and decide to try his luck with Nicole? He had some scratches on his arms."

I flashed briefly to the image of Ryan's wrist over his face when we woke up that night, the bloody scratches. Was that what he was talking about?

"He got those from the bushes. He wouldn't *touch* my sister."

But Hicks wasn't done. "Are you sure? Did you know he took

Nicole into a bedroom at a party that summer? They didn't come out for an hour."

My head jerked back. I tried to recover quickly, but Hicks had picked up on my surprise.

"You didn't know."

"Because it's bullshit."

"There are witnesses."

I laughed. "Right, probably the same ones who lied at our trial."

He was shaking his head. "A few people saw them go off. Nicole was extremely drunk by all counts, who knows what happened?"

I stared at him, thinking back to that summer. What party? Was it when I was working at the restaurant? Was Hicks just making this up?

He continued, "See, Ryan was just starting to get in trouble, stealing gas, talking you into breaking into your neighbors' place. His dad, he was a real bad character. I know he used to rough Ryan up, and Ryan had a lot of anger in him. Stuff like that, it comes out eventually. We have a dead girl seventeen years ago, now we have another one. So I ask myself, what do these two girls have in common? Ryan Walker. Maybe you protected him back then, but now? I don't think you want to go back to prison. So if you know something else, something about your boy, you might want to start talking now."

I kept my voice calm and controlled, but my blood was pumping hard in my ears, threatening to drown out common sense, making me want to slam his head into the table.

"I don't know anything about Ryan now, but I do know he's not stupid enough to kill a witness and make it look exactly the same as Nicole's murder. Cathy was a crackhead. Wouldn't it make more sense to get her to OD? We were problem kids, no doubt about it, but you can't say we were stupid, and we never hurt anyone who didn't mess with us first."

"That's my point, Toni."

I could have kicked myself for saying so much, but I couldn't stop now.

"And my point is that we aren't killers. You guys fucked up back then. The killer is still out there and someone wants to make sure we look guilty as shit again, to get us out of the way. So while you're messing around with us and your bullshit questions, that person is laughing at how fucking stupid the cops are."

His face flushed red. He sat back up, finally giving me some space.

"I'm trying to help you out here, Toni. Give you a chance to come clean. There's already the theft hanging over you, now this. It doesn't look good."

"I didn't do the theft—and I didn't do this. You aren't trying to help me. You know that by even talking to me you've probably just fucked up my parole."

"If we find out you had something to do with Cathy's death, parole is the least of your problems."

"I'm not saying anything else. You cops only see what you want and hear what you want. And as far as I'm concerned, you're deaf and blind. If you're going to ask anything more, I want my lawyer or you better arrest me."

He nodded, acknowledging that he'd pushed me as far as I was going to go. He stood up. "Thanks for coming in today, Toni. We'll be in touch."

He walked me out of the station and down to my truck, watched me drive off. My heart rate didn't settle until I got back to the campsite, then it jacked up again when I remembered I had to call Suzanne right away.

She answered on the first ring. "Hello?"

"Hi, Suzanne, it's Toni. I just wanted to let you know the cops pulled me in for questioning."

"What for?"

"Cathy Schaeffer, her body was found. She was murdered. They think she was hit with a tire iron." Deafening silence on the other end of the phone. "I have an alibi for the night they asked about—I was working until late, then I stopped at a store on my way home and talked to the clerk. When they check into it, they'll see I couldn't have been involved."

"This isn't good, Toni."

"I know it doesn't *look* good, but I didn't do anything wrong. Someone is trying to screw with us."

"Us?"

Shit. I almost let that slip. I had to be careful how I talked about Ryan.

"The cop was asking a bunch of questions about Ryan, too—but I haven't seen or spoken with him." And I was praying *his* alibi would also hold up.

"I'm going to have to talk to my supervisor and we'll probably want you to come in for a review." A review. I didn't like the sound of that.

"Give it to me straight, Suzanne. Are you suspending me?"

"Just come in and we'll talk." She was walking the line, trying not to spook me, which meant I was probably screwed.

I clenched my fist, fighting the urge to throw the phone across the room. *Stay cool, Toni. Don't make things worse.* "When do you want me?"

"I'll get back to you."

She hung up.


Too upset to hang around the cabin, I went to get some milk at the store and saw the newspaper right away. I stood frozen, staring at the headline: "Local Woman's Body Found." I kept my face down, bought the paper, then sat in my truck and read every terrible word. They mentioned Nicole's murder, me and

Ryan being on parole, the upcoming anniversary of Nicole's death, Cathy's having been a star witness at the trial. Every sentence insinuated that Cathy's death was no coincidence. I thought of my parents and how this was going to rip everything open for them again. They were probably already getting calls. I stayed awake for hours that night, Captain beside me, trying to come up with a plan, going over everything that Hicks had said. I still couldn't think what party Ryan and Nicole would have been at together. It had to be a lie.

There was a knock on the window at one in the morning. Captain and I both startled, Captain barking. I pulled back the curtains. It was Ryan. I slid the window open.

"What the hell are you doing here? You know—"

"I need to talk to you."

"You could've phoned."

"I wanted to see your face. Did they question you today?"

"Yeah, you?"

"Yeah. I've got an alibi. I was home with my mom all that night, repainting her kitchen. They were still giving me a hard time, saying she was lying to protect me, but her boyfriend stopped by and saw me there. "

I was relieved for him but still angry at the situation we were in, that he had put me in. "I was working, then stopped at a store on the way home, but I don't know what time she was killed. I called Suzanne. They want me in for a review."

"I got a call too. It's going to be more than a review, Toni. They just say that shit so you don't pull a runner. As soon as you show up, the cuffs are on."

I'd already figured that out for myself. "You shouldn't be here. I told the cops I hadn't seen you, but they're probably keeping an eye on us."

He was studying my face. I glanced down, fiddled with my blanket, but he'd caught on that something had changed.

"What else did Hicks say?"

I looked back at him. "That you got in trouble in prison and that he'd heard you had the hots for Nicole."

"That's a fucking lie—like I'd screw around with your little sister. You know you were the only thing I gave a shit about."

"I know. He was just messing with me. He also said something about you two going off to a bedroom at a party, but I know it was bullshit."

This time, though, Ryan's face flushed.

"What the hell, Ryan?"

He met my eyes, his jaw tight. "You were working late one night, so I stopped at a party. I didn't know Nicole was there with the girls. She was super-hammered and falling all over herself. She told me she was going to be sick, so I took her to one of the bedrooms. She was puking in the en suite, and embarrassed, so we stayed in there until she sobered up a little. I tried to talk to her about drinking, said she had to take it easy. . . ."

"Why didn't you tell me?" I felt unsettled and confused, shocked that he'd never told me. I thought we had no secrets.

"She begged me not to say anything, and you guys were already fighting so much that summer. I didn't want to cause more problems or stress you out."

"You should've said something." My face was hot with anger and hurt.

"You're right. I screwed up."

I couldn't look at him, afraid I'd cry. Our relationship had been the only thing I could count on back then, the only thing I knew was true. Now I didn't know what to think. I stared down at the table.

He grabbed my hand. "Hey, I'm telling the truth, okay?"

I thought about Shauna's insinuations the night she came to my boat. She must've known about the party, but was there something else? I remembered how Nicole would always hang out when Ryan was over, how he said she looked good at that party we were at together, how he always stuck up for her.

I pulled my hand away. "What else are you keeping from me?"

Now he looked angry. "Look, I know you're pissed, but it was just a stupid lie—I was a kid, I thought I was protecting you. You were all I cared about."

I held his gaze, until I saw the truth in his face and felt relief, then guilt and shame. Why had I let Shauna and Hicks mess with my head? "I believe you, okay? But you *have* to get out of here, Ryan. It's too risky."

"I know." He sighed. "I just wanted to warn you that we're going back in. I can feel it, so take care of whatever you've got to take care of."

He reached in, grabbed the back of my hair, and pulled me in for a kiss. His mouth was hard against mine, his unshaven chin rough. I tasted his scent, his skin, his open warm mouth, his tongue pushing into my mouth, familiar but stronger now, a man's kiss. I opened my mouth wider, my tongue tangling with his for a moment, and moaned deep in the back of my throat. The sound startled me, snapped me out of it. I pushed him away, saying, "What the hell did you do that for?" Captain stood up on the bed, hackles raised and a low growl coming from his chest. I gave him a signal to stand down.

Ryan's face was agonized, his breath ragged, but there was also relief in his eyes. "I had to see if it was still there." Then he disappeared into the dark.

The next morning I took Captain for a long walk, trying not to think about the kiss, telling myself that it didn't mean anything, it *couldn't* mean anything. But the truth was that it had meant way too much. I'd felt something in those few moments that I hadn't felt in years—excitement, happiness, and fear of feeling that good again. But it didn't matter if there was something still between us—what could we do about it? Nothing at the moment, that was for sure. I couldn't let it mess with my head, not now. I had bigger shit to worry about.

I packed Captain's bed, bowl, leashes, all his toys, and drove to the shelter. It killed me to see how excited he was, thinking we were going somewhere fun, his head hanging out the window. When we got to the shelter, he was still wagging his tail, looking for his friends in the backyard, which made me feel a little better about what I had to do. Stephanie came out of her office when she heard me talking to the other girls.

"Hey, Toni." She knelt down to give Captain a kiss, which he returned enthusiastically.

Some of the other staff were watching us, so I said, "Can I talk to you alone in your office for a moment?" No one had mentioned the newspaper article, and they'd been polite, but I was sure they'd all seen it.

"Sure thing."

We went in and she lifted a small white dog off my chair, then sat down on the other side of her desk, the dog in her lap.

"What's up?" Her face was neutral, but when I glanced to the side of her desk, I noticed a corner of the newspaper sticking out, like she'd quickly tried to cover it when she heard me out front. A wave of disappointment and sadness crashed over me. I'd liked Stephanie a lot, had even imagined we could be friends one day, but now I was sure she'd want nothing to do with me. I just hoped she'd still help me out.

"It looks like I was right and my parole's going to be suspended." I felt close to tears. "The cops questioned me about something recently, and that's all it takes. I have an alibi, a *solid* one, and I didn't do anything wrong," I stressed, holding her eyes. "But until I get cleared, I'll probably be sent back."

"So you need to surrender Captain?"

I nodded, struggling to get the words out. "I could be gone for a couple of months." Tears were running down my face now.

She leaned forward. "Look, if you surrender him, he probably won't get adopted for a while, and I can try to make it that way."

I tried to smile through my tears. "That's what I was hoping, but I just hate that he's going to think I'm abandoning him."

"He'll be upset at first but he's got lots of friends here and he'll get walks every day. He'll be safe. And when you get out, if he's still here you can adopt him again, okay? If he goes anywhere, I'll make sure it's a great home."

I took a breath, tried to think of what was best for Captain. "What do I have to sign?"

After I was done with the paperwork, I handed over Captain's leash and asked Stephanie to take him to the back before I brought his stuff in. While he played with the other dogs I carried his bed and toys inside. I also gave Stephanie my laptop and asked her to look after it for me, explaining that I didn't have anyone else I trusted. She said she'd take it to her house. Then she let me go in the backyard to watch Captain play for a while. I stood in a patch of sunlight and tried to hold on to that image: Captain having fun, running around and chasing the other dogs. While he was distracted, I slipped out.

In the parking lot, I looked back. Captain was standing at the chain-link fence now, barking and howling, racing up and down, having caught on that I was leaving him. I turned my back, walking fast until I got to my truck, then drove away. I cried for a few miles, hard, painful sobs that shook my whole body, then I shut down. I told myself to toughen up—he'd get over me and find a better home.

I wiped at my face, took some deep shuddering breaths. He would be okay.

# CHAPTER TWENTY-FOUR

## ROCKLAND PENITENTIARY, VANCOUVER

### JUNE 2013

I went back to the campground and packed my stuff, putting it in cardboard boxes that I'd found in the Dumpster. I worked systematically, not allowing myself to feel anything, or think about Captain, even when I stumbled over one of his bones. I used all the skills I'd learned in prison, concentrating on the task, tuning everything else out, disconnecting from my emotions. An hour later I got a text from Suzanne: *Please come in for a talk this afternoon at 2:00.*

I spoke to the campsite guy, paid my bill, and asked if he could store a few things there for me. He said, "Yeah, for a price." So I paid a small amount and hoofed everything down to his storage room. I drove to Courtenay, my window rolled all the way down, the music hard and loud, making the dashboard vibrate while I tried to suck up every last bit of fresh air and freedom.

At Suzanne's office I was buzzed in, then the door automatically locked behind me with a solid click that was familiar and terrifying. There were already two police officers standing in the office. They read me the parole suspension warrant, then asked me to turn around and put my hands behind my back. The cuffs circled my wrists, tight and cold. I'd been prepared, but my legs were wobbly with fear, my brain crowded with memories of my first arrest, going to Rockland, where I had no say over my life, and now it was all happening again.

Suzanne was watching. Her face was expressionless but for a second I thought I saw something in her eyes, a slight hesitation.

I said, "Suzanne, I didn't do anything—I have an alibi."

"It's just a time-out, Toni, until the police finish their investigation and can clear you. It's an issue of public safety."

"What about *my* safety? There are people inside who are going to try to kick my ass."

"Who?"

"You know I can't tell you." The second I started naming names, I was asking for a worse beat-down.

"Then I can't help you."

I already knew that. No one could help me now.

I was put into the back of the police car, my hands still in cuffs behind me, uncomfortable. I stared out the window, already feeling separate, removed from the world I'd just become a part of again. We stopped at a light and I looked over at the ocean, remembered walking on a beach with Captain just the day before.

They booked me in at the station, then flew me over to Rockland, where I went through the intake process again. I was trying not to worry about what might happen once I was put in general population. I told myself the odds of Helen being aware that I was back in the joint were slim. She'd also be out on parole by now and she had better things to worry about than old enemies. I also had a lot of friends inside, and if some of her friends tried to mess with me, they'd have problems.

I was given a single cell in my old block. At least I wouldn't have to deal with a roommate. It was late by then, and everyone was already sleeping, so I made my bed and climbed in, exhausted. In the morning, Margaret was the first person I saw in the cafeteria. She gave me a smile, happy to see me, but her eyes told me she was sad I was back inside. When the officer was looking the other way, we gave each other a quick hug.

"Heard you were back in here, girl," she said as we pulled apart. "I hoped it wasn't true, but then I saw the news last night. . . ."

I had a feeling it wouldn't take long for the media to find out that I'd lost my parole, but it made me sick and embarrassed, thinking of my parents and Mike and everyone else who'd seen the story, the whole town likely gossiping that Ryan and I had killed Cathy in some sort of revenge thing.

"It's total bullshit," I said.

We sat in the corner and I told Margaret what was going on and what had happened at the halfway house with Helen.

"I'm hoping I don't run into any of her friends," I said.

"I'll keep an eye out for you." When Brenda and Amber joined us in the cafeteria I filled them in and they also swore they had my back.

The first week wasn't too bad. Once I'd gotten over the initial shock, I settled into the prison rhythm again, clinging to the belief that I was going to get out of there soon. I'd called Angus Reed, who was still practicing in town though he was in his late sixties now, and he made a few calls. He said the police were being quiet but it didn't seem like they had any real evidence on me or Ryan. Suzanne came to Rockland for a post-suspension interview, getting my side of everything that had happened, so she could see where my head was at. She asked me a lot of questions about Shauna and the girls. I told her about Shauna coming to the boat, but never shared that I'd seen Cathy in the park. Suzanne told me she'd be in touch. I had a feeling she was going to keep me in for the full thirty days even if the police cleared me, so she could let things cool down. I just hoped that she canceled the suspension herself and didn't refer me to the Parole Board or I'd be trapped for months.

It was good to see Margaret again and I realized how much I'd missed the old broad—how much I'd missed having friends. She made me give her a pedicure and foot rub the first day I was back, saying she hadn't found anyone else decent—but I wished we could spend time together on the outside, like real people. I talked to her about Ryan and Captain, how I hoped they were okay.

"You'll get out soon, girl," she said, groaning when I hit a sore spot. She stared down at her feet, looked at her gnarled hands. "I don't know how many more years I can last in here. It's no kind of life, my body always hurting."

"I'm sorry, Margaret." I felt like an asshole. At least I had a chance of getting out soon. Margaret had to wait another ten years before she was eligible.

"Nothing for you to be sorry about." She wiggled her foot. "Now get back to work."

Margaret and I played cards every day, and I started running the track again, trying to pass the time. The first week Suzanne called with a few more questions, asking me again about Shauna. I could tell that she was trying to assess my anger. It was hard to keep my frustration contained, especially when she wouldn't give me any firm answers about my suspension status, but I kept my mouth shut.

So far I hadn't had any issues with other inmates, other than one run-in with a new inmate who thought she could get me to buy stuff for her in the canteen, but I set her straight in a hurry. I just had to hang in there for a little while longer.

Then one day, when Margaret and I were playing cards on the range, an inmate named Josie, who I didn't know very well, ran up to Margaret and whispered in her ear, glancing at me, her face nervous.

"What's going on?" I set my cards down.

Margaret motioned for Josie to leave us alone, then turned to me. "Helen's parole got suspended—for dealing. She's back in."

"Shit. That's not good."

"It gets worse, Toni. She's been telling everyone you ratted her out when you were both at the halfway house."

"That's bullshit. I never said crap about her."

"Don't matter. You know as well as me there's no trial in here, just guilty as charged."

"So what are people saying?"

"Everyone's pissed at you—you got more than a few enemies now."

That day out in the exercise yard, I felt the tension in the air. I tried to focus on running the track, but it was hard to get a good pace going when I had to keep an eye on the other inmates, making sure no one tried anything. Amber and Brenda were both nearby, walking around the track in case I needed them. There were a few women standing around in clusters, watching me. Many of them I knew, and I hadn't had a problem with them before, but that didn't mean anything. Once you get labeled as a rat by another inmate, you've got trouble. I hadn't seen Helen yet but I knew that was a matter of time. Some of the guards were keeping an eye on me and the other girls, so they'd probably heard rumors, but I wasn't sure they'd break anything up if someone started to give me a hard time. Some of them liked to get shit rolling, so we'd get thrown in segregation.

Later, in the range, I sat down beside Margaret at one of the tables, where she was playing a game with a few women. The other cardplayers got up and walked away, giving me dirty looks.

I said, "Shit, I'm sorry, Margaret."

"Don't be. I was losing." She smiled, and I had to laugh, though it came out sounding nervous and stressed. She said, "Come on. Let's play a game."

Margaret had just dealt me a hand when I saw her look up, her body tense and her face serious. Helen dropped down beside me, real close.

"Hey, bitch, I missed your skinny ass."

"Can't say the same." My gaze flicked to one of the guards, who was talking to another officer, neither of them aware of what was going on.

Helen leaned closer, sniffed at the air. "Something stinks. Smells like a rat to me."

"I never ratted you out, so you need to let go of this beef with me. If I were going to say something, I'd have done it when I first got to the house."

Margaret said, "Why don't you just back off, Helen?"

Helen said, "This isn't your problem."

"You mess with my girl here and you make it my problem."

Brenda and Amber materialized behind Margaret, glaring at Helen.

"You better leave our girl alone," Brenda said.

"It's okay," I said. "Helen and I were just working shit out. Right, Helen?" Brenda could hold her own, and Margaret had status—I'd be surprised if Helen tried anything with her—but Amber was young and small, and I worried about her.

"We haven't worked anything out," Helen said. "I know it was you. And I'm going to fuck you up good. And if any of your friends get in the way . . ." She took a moment to stare at Brenda and Amber, lingering on Amber, with a vicious smile. "I'll fuck them up too." And with that she walked away.

I casually laid my cards on the table, trying to look calm, and said, "Full house."

After that, I told Brenda and Amber to stay out of Helen's way.

I didn't want them to get hurt. They got mad and said they weren't going to leave me unprotected, but I tried to keep to myself and avoid them so they wouldn't get caught in the crossfire. I worked in the kitchen, did my chores, stayed in my cell, and kept one eye on the door. Most of the other inmates were ignoring me too, which was fine, and I only saw my girls at meals, where we'd all eat tense, watching Helen and her friends watching us. I was careful when I walked around the grounds, remembering the danger spots, the hidden corners. The next couple of weeks ticked by as the tension grew thicker in the air with each passing day.

Finally, she got me.

I was in the kitchen, preparing dinner, when I noticed the other inmates who were working leave in a hurry. I turned around—and a tray full of spaghetti was whipped into my face. I was trying to clear the stinging sauce out of my eyes when a sock full of batteries started hitting me in the stomach, legs, back. I rushed my opponent, dropped my head low, and hit a belly, hearing a satisfying grunt. I could see clear enough now to realize it was Helen. We slammed into kitchen equipment, knocking pots and pans to the floor. I grabbed one and hit her hard across the head, the sound ringing through the air. It didn't slow her down. She punched me in the breast. Blinding pain shot through my body, bringing me to my knees. I thought I was about to pass out when I finally heard someone yell "Guard!" Helen took off. I pulled myself up. Tried to suck in my breath.

The guard looked at me, at the mess around me.

"Everything okay, Murphy?"

It took me a minute before I could say anything. "Yeah, just slipped on the wet floor and knocked some stuff down." He grunted, looked around again, then walked off. He had to have realized there'd been a fight, but he didn't want to deal with the paperwork and he knew I wasn't going to give him any details.

I limped back to my cell, where Margaret found me later.

"You okay, honey?"

I rolled over in bed, groaning. "I'll be all right."

"Brought you some tea bags." She tossed them at me. I knew how much she treasured her tea—it was something we all gave her on holidays.

"Hey, you don't have to do that."

"Of course I do." Her face was angry. "You're my daughter, and Helen just messed with the wrong family. She's going to pay for this."

I sat up. "Margaret, don't do anything, okay? I can handle it."

She looked conflicted, then said, "Fine. But we're not leaving you alone anymore."


For the next few days I kept out of everyone's way. I could have asked to be put in segregation, for protection, but I hated it in there—locked up twenty-three hours a day without any windows, and only one hour in the yard. I just made sure I wasn't alone and kept Brenda with me whenever I had to leave my cell—I knew she could fight like hell—and Margaret and Amber when Brenda had to work. We had to keep my ass covered until my suspension was canceled. I saw Helen a lot, when I was running the track or in the range, and she always gave me shitty looks, but she didn't try anything as long as I was with the girls.

Finally, when I'd been inside for almost a month, Suzanne came for another interview. Our alibis had checked out but she wanted to assess my motivation to come back to the community and whether I'd follow my conditions. I told her all I wanted to do was live a productive life and stay out of trouble. She canceled the suspension and I'd be released the next day. Walking out of that room was the first time I'd taken a full breath in weeks. Margaret and the girls were happy for me. It had been hard on all of us, especially Margaret, whose arthritis had flared up from the tension. That night I avoided the cafeteria, the showers, and the yard. I packed my stuff and stayed in my cell. The only people I spoke to were Margaret and the girls, who made sure no one came near me.

I'd heard from Ryan earlier that week, a "kite" sent through other inmates. He must have found out that Suzanne was interviewing me. All the note said was, *Are you in?* I knew he wanted to know if I was committed to trying to clear our names. I'd been thinking about nothing else for the last month.

I didn't want to live the rest of my life wondering if Shauna was going to get me sent back to prison at any moment. And Ryan was right, being on parole wasn't a real life, everyone still thinking I was guilty. Like how I was fired for the theft, people were always going to see me as an ex-con. The second I was out of there, I was going to do what I should have done when Ryan first showed up. I was going to find out what had really happened that night, even if it meant putting my life on the line. I sent him a letter back saying, *Hell, yeah.*

I was walking downstairs in the morning with my girls when I saw Helen in the middle of the range, waiting for us. As we moved past her, Brenda and Margaret forming a barrier around me, Helen called out, "See you soon, Murphy."

I turned back to look at her, but she'd already disappeared into the crowd.

# CHAPTER TWENTY-FIVE

## CAMPBELL RIVER

## JULY 2013

A couple of days after my parole was reinstated I was back at the campsite and trying to settle in, but I'd barely unpacked and had only bought a few groceries. When I had my first meeting with Suzanne, I told her I was going to start looking for a job right away and was careful not to show any anger about what had happened. But I was still pissed off, and she was smart enough to know it.

Just before she drove off, she said, "Remember, stay away from Ryan Walker and anyone else involved in your case."

I said, "Of course." But I had no intention of following any of my parole conditions this time. I had checked for a few jobs online, but I was going through the motions. Ryan was going to contact me soon. I was sure of it. Meanwhile, I'd been thinking about our next steps and how we could finally get to the truth.

I also thought about Captain often and hoped he was okay, but

I couldn't get him out yet, not until I knew I was safe. I called the shelter once. Stéphanie got on the line.

"Hi, it's Toni. Is Captain all right?"

"Are you coming to get him?" she said.

I wanted to cry in relief. He was still there.

"I can't just yet. I have to take care of some things. Can you give me a little more time?" I closed my eyes, praying.

She paused and I wondered if she was going to tell me to fuck off, that I couldn't have him back. The moment stretched out.

"Give me a call when you're ready."

"Thanks, Stephanie. I really appreciate it. I'll be there soon. I promise."

I hung up the phone, hoping I hadn't just made a promise I couldn't keep.


The night after my meeting with Suzanne, I was ready to put things in motion with or without Ryan, but I decided to give him one more day. Around midnight he finally knocked at my back window. When I let him in, he looked around.

"Where's Captain?"

"Still at the shelter."

He met my gaze, and I didn't need to say anything else.

He paced around my kitchen. I noticed he had a fading bruise on his cheek and wondered if he'd gotten it in prison, remembered Hicks's warning about Ryan's reputation. Tonight he was agitated, angry. He looked like how I felt.

He said, "I'm not going back."

"I'm not either." I was still sitting on the bed, the covers pulled around me. He was looking at my face, a hard searching look.

"Are you in this for real? Whatever it takes?"

"Whatever it takes."

He took a breath and let it out, his body finally calming. "I've been thinking about this. Cathy had a lot of friends, maybe one of them—"

"We need to talk to her dealer."

We drove around town, stopping at a few known crack houses. We always parked the truck out of sight and made sure to keep our heads down when we entered the buildings—I wore one of Ryan's baseball caps and an old work coat. If anyone recognized us and reported it, Suzanne would suspend our parole instantly. At first no one would talk to us, but finally Ryan recognized a guy who used to hang out with Cathy. He told us that Cathy's dealer, a guy named Boomer, lived in an old white house near the train station. We cruised up and down his street, unsure which house was his. I was getting worried, then we saw some shady characters leaving one of them. Ryan gave the door a hard rap. A skinny man wearing jeans that were sliding off his hips opened the door.

"You Boomer?" Ryan said.

"Who's asking?"

"We want to buy some weed."

Boomer ushered us in after glancing down the street. Inside the house, he sat on the couch, pulled out a bag and a scale, and said, "How much you want?"

Ryan asked for a gram, but Boomer just stared at us.

"Who the fuck are you?" he said. "No one asks for dope like that unless they're in high school."

"I've been in prison—I'm out of touch. You got any or what?"

"You cops?"

Ryan laughed. "Right."

"We need to talk to you," I said. "About Cathy Schaeffer."

"What about her?" His gaze flicked to the door, like he was wondering if someone was going to burst in.

"We know she was with you before she died," I said.

The guy stood up. "Get the hell out of my house."

Ryan said, "I'm not leaving until you tell us what we need to know."

Boomer reared back and threw his beer bottle. It shattered against the wall behind Ryan.

Ryan rushed the man, grabbed him around the neck, then backed him against the wall. "Listen, asshole, I'm not fucking around here, got it?"

The guy was nodding, his eyes panicked, his face red. I stepped closer to Ryan, saw how angry he was. He wasn't letting go.

Shit, he was going to kill him. "Hey, Ryan. Take it easy."

Ryan slowly released Boomer, who slumped to the floor, rubbing his throat. "You're nuts, man," he croaked out.

Ryan crouched in front of him. "You're right. I am, so you better start talking."

"Shit, dude—all I know is she showed up here with a bunch of money and bought a shitload of dope. Cathy was fucking happy, man, like she'd won the lottery." He looked upset. "She said she was going down to the pier. I didn't know what was going to happen to her."

"Do you know where she got the money?" I said.

"No idea."

It had to have been Shauna.

"Anything else?" Ryan said.

"That's all I know, man."

Ryan reached out and grabbed the guy by the back of his long hair, pulling it tight. "You better not be bullshitting me, or I'm coming back."

"I don't know anything else—I fucking swear."

I touched Ryan's shoulder, said, "Let's get out of here."

We drove away, fast, then parked down a side road to talk. My heart was beating hard from the adrenaline rush. Ryan's eyes were intense as he stared out the window, and he kept running his hands through his hair.

"What happened in there?" I said. "You lost control."

He looked at me, surprised. "I knew exactly what I was doing."

"You looked like you were going to kill him."

"What are you saying, Toni?"

"Nothing." I stared out the window.

He paused for a moment, then said, "We both did shit to survive inside, we had to. There were times when I wondered if I'd ever be human again, but I do still have control. I wanted to scare the shit out of him and it worked."

When we were kids and he got in fights, I'd seen that he was capable of violence and could kick some ass, but I'd never gotten the sense that he would let things go too far. Tonight, I wasn't so sure. I thought again of Hicks's warning.

"It scared me too."

"No, I think you recognized it. You've got the same anger in you, Toni. You're just not letting yours out again yet. But you will."

I had been violent in prison too, and whenever I thought about Shauna and her friends my body would get tight and agitated and I had to fight the powerful urge to make them suffer. I always stuffed it down, but was that self-control or fear of what might happen if I released all that rage? Maybe Ryan was right, but I wasn't ready to say it out loud.

Instead, I said, "The next step should be to talk to Kim—she broke away from Shauna before, so she might be willing to do it again. But I'll go alone. She might open up if it's just me."

"Okay. What's the plan?"

"I'm not sure yet. I need to think about it." What I wasn't sure of was how much I wanted to reveal to Ryan. He'd changed, we both had, but I didn't know yet what that meant, just that something was telling me to be careful. I looked at him now, his face blurred in the dim light, and saw the shadow of the boy he used to be. He looked sad, and I wondered if he sensed my distrust, or was just seeing the same thing as me, who we were once.

"Do you have a cell?" he said.

"Yeah, but the cops can trace that shit."

"I'll call from a pay phone for now if I have to reach you, but get one of those pay-as-you-go phones and I'll get one too."

I gave him my cell number and he gave me his. We agreed to buy new phones as soon as possible.

"How are you going to find Kim?" he said.

"I think her mom still lives at the same place." She'd had a party there once when we were in high school, before she started hanging out with Shauna.

"Be careful," he said. "These girls are scared, they're not going down without a fight."

"Neither am I. They've fucked with us long enough. "

He smiled, hearing the old tough-Toni talk, but there was also recognition in his eyes. He knew this time I meant it. We held gazes for a little while longer, the energy in the truck changing as I became more physically aware of his presence. His hands on the wheel, his arms hard, his jeans tight on his thighs, the dim light making hollows and shadows on his face, his chin still unshaven. I wanted to feel it again, scraping against mine. I remembered how we used to make out for hours as teens, our hands greedy for each other, then later how sometimes we'd have sex in his truck, my hands and feet pushing against the dash or the window, anything to get him closer, deeper. My face flushed warm, and I looked away. I could feel him studying my profile. I glanced back at him.

"I haven't been with anyone since you," he said.

I caught my breath, holding his words close to me for a moment, savoring what they meant, then whispered, "Me neither."

There was something else in his face now, relief, as though maybe he hadn't been sure of my feelings. He hesitated for a second, then shifted his weight and leaned forward, bringing his face close, at an angle. There was a questioning look in his eyes. I could have pulled away, could have gotten out of the truck, but my body leaned toward his. Our mouths touched, soft at first, testing, like we were trying to remember what we liked, then we grew more confident and the kiss deepened. I gave over to it this time, and Ryan cupped the back of my head, pressed his body closer. I lifted my arm, wrapped it around his back, kneading the hard muscles along his shoulder blade. He groaned into my mouth, "Toni." And I felt an answering ache in my body, a desire to be even closer, skin against skin.

His hand caressed my lower back, the cool summer air making me shiver as he lifted my shirt slightly, his hand now coming around to the side of my ribs, stroking up toward my breast, his thumb grazing the underside. My body broke out in goose bumps.

I shifted my weight, pushed him back against the seat, and straddled him, grinding my hips forward, pressing against him. He moaned again into my mouth, his warm hands around my waist. Then he slid them up and covered my breasts. I caught my breath, grabbed the back of his hair, tilting his head back, getting rough with my kissing, feeling angry all of a sudden, a violent urge in my body. He reached up and grabbed some of my hair, pulling my head to the side, kissing my neck and my ear, whispering, "God, I've missed you."

I covered his mouth again with mine, shushing the sentiments, the affection, but the words echoed, and I thought about all the years we'd been apart, and then there were tears all of a sudden because I remembered the last time we'd been together, in the woods, while Nicole was being murdered. I couldn't stop the tears now and had to pull away, covering my face with my hands.

"Hey, hey, what's wrong?" Ryan tugged my hands away, but I couldn't look at him.

"I was thinking about the last time . . ." I couldn't get the rest of the words out.

He gently cupped the back of my head and pushed my face toward his shoulder. I gave in to the sobs, in to the comfort of leaning against another body, solid and real. No one had held me for seventeen years. One of his hands was resting on the back of my neck, the other arm wrapped around my back, holding me close, safe and secure. Finally my sobs eased, and now embarrassment settled in. I lifted myself off his lap, and his arms let go, but slowly, reluctantly. I sat on the passenger side and wiped my face on my sleeves. We were both quiet for a moment, staring out at the dark night.

"I don't want it to be like this," he said, "in a truck like we're still teenagers hiding out from our parents."

I turned to face him, not sure what he was getting at.

He said, "When this is over, I want to take you out for real, on a date."

"I don't know, Ryan, so much has happened. Maybe we can't get past it."

"We can, and we will."

I remembered how much hope he'd had when we first went to prison, how none of those hopes had ever come true for us. I wondered if anything would be different this time. And just like back then, I was scared to let myself go there in my mind. I needed to focus on the moment.

I looked out the window again, turning away from him, trying to shut myself down. "I should get back."

He was silent for a few beats, and I thought he might say something else, but then he flashed up the truck. Neither of us said a word until we got back to the woods behind my cabin. I didn't meet his eyes until I climbed out of the truck.

"We're not finished," he said. "If we are, we'll find out on our own, but I don't want us to be finished because of *them*." His voice turned hard and angry. "They aren't going to take anything from me again."

I watched him drive away, hating the way his voice had just sounded. It made me think of the look on his face when he was gripping that drug dealer's throat. Like he wanted to keep squeezing.

# CHAPTER TWENTY-SIX

## Campbell River

### July 2013

The next day I bought a disposable phone and drove by Kim's old house, then parked on the side of the road while I tried to figure out if her mom still owned the place. I noticed that the front yard was overgrown, the grass and weeds more than a foot high. Nothing looked like it had been watered or pruned for years. The house was also run-down, the siding stained and the windows filthy. But I could see a statue of Jesus on the sill and remembered that Kim's mom was a religious fanatic. She'd also been tidy, from what I remembered, so she must've been sick for some time. There was a car in the driveway, probably hers. I ducked low when I saw someone come out the door. I peeked through my steering wheel.

Kim still had long hair and a dancer's body, lithe and trim in her capris and fitted tank top that showed the sinewy muscles in her shoulders as she reached down for the newspaper that was on the doorstep. I thought about her other life, with her dance studio, her partner. Did they have children? Were they married? I remembered Kim at the trial, the empty look in her eyes. Was it guilt?

After she went inside, I considered going up to the door, but decided it would be better to wait until there were no possible witnesses. Her mom probably went to bed early, and if she was on pain meds she'd be a heavy sleeper.

Around nine-thirty I made my way back to Kim's, keeping an eye on the road behind me. I didn't see any cops, but they could be using ghost cars. I made lots of turns and stopped at a few stores, gathering receipts—I'd been doing that lately, in case they tried to pin anything on me again.

When I got to Kim's I parked down the road, taking another look around before walking down her driveway and under the carport. From inside I could hear faint sounds from a TV. I peeked through the side window. Kim was curled up on the couch, with a book opened in her lap and a healthy glass of wine in front of her. She rubbed her forehead, yawned. There was no sign of her mother.

I went to the door and knocked softly. Silence, then unsteady, cautious steps toward the door.

A tentative whisper. "Who's there?"

She didn't sound surprised. Maybe she'd had other late-night visitors.

"An old friend. I have some information you might be interested in, something about Shauna."

I thought for sure she'd ask for my name, but she opened the door behind the screen. Her eyes widened when she saw it was me. Her expression of horror would've been humorous if I'd been in a laughing mood. She looked like she didn't know whether to run or slam the door. She said, "I can call the police."

"And tell them what? I haven't done anything."

"You're trespassing—and you're not supposed to be talking to me. It's harassment."

"So tell me you want me to leave. But I think you'll want to hear what I have to say."

She paused as she thought it over. Then she said, "My mom's sleeping," and glanced over her shoulder.

"We can meet in your backyard." Now she looked up and down the street. I added, "No one followed me. I made sure."

"I'll grab a sweater and meet you at the bottom of the garden."

I let myself into her backyard, careful not to let the garden gate squeak. Inside, I could see Kim moving slowly through the house. She didn't reach for the phone. If she was genuinely afraid of me, a convicted killer, she'd have called the police. But she felt safe—probably because she knew I hadn't killed my sister. She also didn't call Shauna or anyone else, which meant she wanted to hear what I had to say.

She came out a side door, walking down the edge of the garden and keeping to the shadows. When she reached me she studied my arms, her eyes big as she stared at my tattoos.

She took a pack of cigarettes out of her pocket and held them out.

"No, thanks," I said. When had she started smoking?

She lit up, her fingers shaking slightly, her face lit with a ghostly glow for a moment. "I can't smoke in the house, my mom's on oxygen."

"I heard you were back to help her."

She nodded, took a deep drag on her cigarette, and held the smoke down a long time before she exhaled.

"Your mom's been sick for a while. Why are you back now?" She turned to look at me, hostility in her eyes.

"You said you had information."

"And you want to hear it, because you know Shauna's a problem."

"I don't have any problems with Shauna, but when someone shows up at my door saying they know something about a good friend of mine, I want to know what's going on."

"I heard you guys haven't been in touch for years."

"People lose touch, doesn't mean they stop being friends." She took a drag, sucked hard on the cigarette, and blew the smoke out in a rush. "What's this all about? If you don't explain why you're here, I'm going back inside."

"Shauna's getting rid of you next."

Her body jerked back, her face flooding with fear as her mouth opened wide. I waited for her to speak.

"What . . . what are you talking about?"

"Shauna killed Cathy."

"This is ridiculous. I'm leaving." But she didn't make a move.

"You know it's true. Whether she's admitted it or not, she did it."

Kim's eyes narrowed, smoke drifting around us. "From what I heard, the cops suspect you and Ryan. They just didn't have enough to charge you."

"Lots of people like to say we did things we didn't." I changed the confrontational tone of my voice, tried to soften my words. "I don't know why you lied at the trial, Kim, but I've spent most of my life in prison—for a crime you *know* I didn't commit. How have you been able to live with yourself?"

She was silent, her face frozen, but I could sense that every word had hit her like a blow. And I had more for her.

"I don't know what happened the night Nicole was murdered—but you do. And so did Cathy. She was talking to people, the story was coming out, and now she's dead. If you thought I killed her, you wouldn't be standing here."

"You don't know it was Shauna."

"But *you* know, and she's going to make sure anyone who knows what happened to Nicole can't talk. Maybe your mom's oxygen tank blows up, or maybe you have a car accident. There are a lot of ways someone can disappear."

"Shauna wouldn't kill Cathy or me." She caught herself and added, "She wouldn't kill anyone."

"You can keep telling yourself that, but you know what she's capable of doing. The only thing that's going to save you is if you go to the police first."

The reality of my words was sinking in, her face pale in the dim light, the cigarette in her hand burned down to the filter. She was either going to accept the truth and start considering her options, or run away from it.

"Get off my property." She pointed a shaking hand toward the driveway. I had my answer.

"You're a fool if you think you can trust Shauna," I said. "Nicole was your friend—and look what happened to her."

Her face almost buckled for a moment, then she collected herself.

"Nicole got me kicked out of my house. And if you don't get out of here in five seconds, I'm calling the police."

I turned and walked away. When I got in my truck I drove by her place fast, so she could see me leaving, but then I circled back and parked on a side street where I could watch her house. I waited, thinking about the conversation. Her guilt was obvious. I also thought about her saying that Nicole had gotten her kicked out. What was she talking about?

An hour later she left the house, glancing around before she climbed into her mother's car. I followed at a distance.

I tailed her to a subdivision and noticed her car slowing down, her brake lights flashing like she was going to stop soon. I didn't want to get too close, so I parked on the side of the road and hoofed it up the hill. I spotted her car in front of a big house with elaborate landscaping that had to cost a fortune. It also looked like there was a pool in the backyard and that the property overlooked the ocean. It had to be Shauna's place. Then I realized Kim was still sitting in her car—at the last second I caught the glow of her face, lit by a cell phone. I ducked behind some bushes, close enough to see the car. She was texting someone. A moment later, Shauna came out of the house and got into the passenger seat. Kim rolled down the window, lit another cigarette.

They talked for a while. I couldn't see much, just Kim's profile, puffs of smoke. After about ten minutes Shauna got out of the car and leaned through the window, said something. She walked away, but Kim stayed in her car for a couple more minutes, blowing smoke out the window as she stared back at the house. Finally she drove off.

I got back in my truck. Partway down the road, I recognized a girl standing in the shadows on the shoulder. Ashley. How long had she been watching? When she saw me slowing down, she tried to turn her face away. I stopped beside her and rolled down the window.

"What are you doing, Ashley?"

"Same thing as you." She pointed toward the house. "Watching my mom talk to Kim. I was just coming home when I saw her get in the car, and thought it was weird."

Now I noticed the video camera in her hand. The red light on.

"What the hell, Ashley? Are you recording me?"

"I was recording *them*." She flicked the light off. "I didn't see your truck until later."

"I'd feel a lot better if you gave me the memory card."

"It's on the hard drive—I can't take it out. And I have other stuff on here."

This wasn't good, but I didn't want to piss the kid off. She could really screw things up for me and Ryan. "If that got in the wrong hands and my truck was seen near your mom's place, I'm going back to prison. Do you understand?"

"I won't show it to anyone."

"Ashley, this is my *life* on the line."

She looked up the road toward her house, gnawing her lip. Finally she did something on the camera, showing me the delete button as she pressed it.

"It's gone, but I'm just trying to help you."

"This has nothing to do with you."

"Yes, it does, she's my mother." She looked angry, but not at me.

This time I looked back at the house, wondered what it must be like to grow up with a mother like Shauna. I still didn't know if Ashley was just trying to get at the truth or get back at her mom for something.

"If you want to help me, just stay out of it. I don't want anyone else caught up in this mess."

An outside light went on at the house beside us, casting light onto the road. I put my truck in gear and tore off, watching Ashley in my rearview mirror as she walked toward her house, head down, like she was deep in thought.

The next day I drove to the hospital early, hoping to catch Rachel coming in from the parking lot, or leaving—I didn't want to go to her house because I knew she had a family. I had a feeling it was going to be a long wait and brought some snacks and water, but after a few hours in my truck I'd gone through all my supplies. I was hungry and desperate for a pee when I finally saw Rachel leave with a group of nurses around lunchtime. Shit. I'd been hoping she'd be alone. I decided to wait and see what happened.

The group sat at a picnic table under a maple tree, laughing as they ate their sandwiches and salads. I thought of my girls back at Rockland and wondered if I'd ever find that camaraderie again with people on the outside. I'd come close, at the restaurant and the shelter, but that had been ripped away from me too. I felt another hot jolt of anger, reminding me that I had to settle this once and for all.

After they were finished, the other nurses went inside, leaving Rachel while she flipped open her cell phone, texting someone.

I got out of my truck and headed in her direction. Intent on her phone, she didn't notice me.

"Hi, Rachel."

She glanced up, a confused smile on her face that vanished as soon as she recognized me. She stood up, grabbing at her things. "Get away from me."

"I have some information you need."

"There's nothing I need from you." She was looking around like she was about to scream for help. I worried about staff security. I had to get her attention.

"It's about Shauna, what she's going to do to you."

"Shauna's not going to do anything." But she still didn't walk away. Same as with Kim, there was something in her that wanted to hear what I had to say.

"You have a family now—kids."

"How do you know about my family?" Anger and fear mixed on her face.

"It's a small town. And I know you're a good mother. You don't want your kids to suffer. But if you keep on with what you guys are doing, you're going to get caught. You know Shauna killed Cathy."

"That's ridiculous." She tossed her head, reminding me of her teenage self. How much she'd wanted Shauna's approval, how she'd do anything for her. "You and Ryan killed her—and they'll prove it soon."

I felt a moment of fear, wondering if she'd heard something. Did the cops have new evidence? I had to continue with the plan.

"She was starting to talk about what really happened that night, how you girls killed Nicole. She was going to help us prove we were innocent. Why would we kill her?"

Rachel was breathing hard, her face flushed and panicked.

I gave it another push. "She was talking to *a lot* of people. It's just a matter of time before some of them start coming forward.

Then the police are going to take a look at you girls for Cathy's death. I wouldn't be surprised if Shauna even points the finger at you. She covered up one murder by blaming it on someone else. What's to stop her from turning on you guys now?"

"We didn't do anything." Her voice was desperate.

"But you did, you *know* you did. And you know that Shauna killed Cathy. Whether she's admitted it or not, you *know*. And you can be sure that she'll cover her own ass if the shit hits the fan. But who's protecting you?"

"If I were you, I'd be worried about yourself." Now she wa angry, fear making her attack. "This is harassment."

"Here's the difference between me and you, Rachel. I hav nothing left to lose. But you do."

She sucked in her breath, her eyes wide and scared, and for second she looked like she might cry. I stepped closer.

"There's already another witness who can place Shauna's out at the lake at midnight. If I were you, I'd go to the police n and tell my side *before* Shauna points the finger. Maybe you w only a witness to Nicole's death, maybe you don't know for s what she did to Cathy, but you know she was involved. If you now, you might be able to get a plea bargain and be out in tim see your kids grow up. But if you wait, she's going to sink yo

Her face was pale with fear, but she grabbed her things said, "I'm not going to prison, because I didn't do anything.

She spun around and hurried back to the hospital.


I was almost back at the campsite when I noticed the cop ca ing me. My heart started going crazy in my chest. Had Ra Kim called the cops? If they had, I was fucked. I check speed, dropped it down, hoping the cop just happened to the road at the same time. But then he turned on his

coming up fast behind me. I pulled over and watched in my side mirror as a man got out and sauntered toward my truck. Shit. It was Doug Hicks.

I rolled down my window and waited, heart still pounding.

"Good afternoon, Toni."

"Afternoon, Officer."

"Where you coming from?"

"Just visiting an old friend. Was I speeding?"

"That friend wouldn't be Ryan Walker, would it?"

So maybe he didn't know about my visits to Kim and Rachel.

"Nope. It's against the conditions of my parole to speak with him."

He glanced up the highway, back down again. My nerves were tight with tension, my mouth filling with saliva. What exactly was going on here?

He leaned closer. "I've been talking to a few people."

"Yeah?" I worked hard to keep my expression flat.

"Maybe you're right. Maybe we should have another look at your sister's murder. Problem is, if your boy Ryan's also talking to people, things get messed up in witnesses' minds. They might remember things differently. That makes it hard for us to get to the bottom of what really happened."

I stared at him. "Are you saying you believe us now?" There had to be a catch.

"I'm saying we can't reopen the case or take another look at any of the evidence if you guys are running around stirring up trouble."

So that was the deal. We back off and he might reopen our case. I hated the position he was putting me in, the hope that his words were kicking up. I didn't want to screw up anything if he was serious. Then I realized that he was probably bullshitting. There was no gain in this for him, no reason he'd want to take another look at a case that could make him and the other cops who were involved look like idiots. It was just another game.

"I don't know what Ryan Walker's doing, and I don't care," I said. "I'm staying out of trouble and trying to find a job, *sir.*"

Hicks said, "I know you don't like me, Toni. But right now I'm the only person who can help you stay out of prison."

"It seems more like you want to get me sent back."

"I want you to stay away from Ryan. He's trouble and always was. Everything I told you before was true. I think you were a good kid who just got hooked up with the wrong guy. I'd hate to see you go down that path again."

His arrogance was pissing me off—his certainty that he knew all about Ryan.

"Is that all? Are you going to write me a ticket?"

"I'm not messing around, Toni. If you want us to reopen the case, stay away from Ryan." He rapped on the top of the roof, making me flinch. "You're a young woman, got a lot of life left. Let's keep you on the outside."

I watched him walk back to his car, my blood still pulsing hard and my chest tight. After he pulled back into the traffic I eased out myself, my body vibrating with nerves. What the hell was I going to do? *Was* he just bullshitting me about opening up the case again? Trying to get me to stop Ryan from talking to people because the cops didn't want the real shit to come out? But what if he'd been telling the truth? I didn't know who to trust anymore.

# CHAPTER TWENTY-SEVEN

## CAMPBELL RIVER

### JULY 2013

An hour later, back at the campground, I was still trying to recover from my run-in with Doug Hicks when my cell rang. I didn't recognize the number, so I answered with a cautious, "Hello?"

"Toni, hey." It was Ryan.

"I'll call you back." I knew the cops probably couldn't tap my phone without some sort of warrant, but I was still freaked. I grabbed my disposable phone and dialed the number that had shown up on my call display.

When he answered, I said, "Doug Hicks stopped me today when I was coming back from talking with Rachel. He's watching me."

"Shit. Did Rachel or Kim call the cops on you?"

"That's the thing. I don't think they did, so it's weird."

"Then what did Hicks want?"

I told him what Hicks had said, finished with, "If he's right, we could screw things up."

"Come on, you don't really believe him?" Ryan was pissed off. "There's no way he's looking into the case again. Why would he want everyone to know he screwed up and sent the wrong people away? He's trying to stop us from finding out the truth, not help us. What are you thinking? You just want to believe him."

I'd had similar thoughts, but Ryan's angry tone was pissing *me* off. I wasn't sure who I was more annoyed at, myself because I had wanted to believe Hicks or Ryan because he saw through it faster than I did.

"I'm thinking that something's up," I said. I told him what had happened with Kim and Rachel. "The way Shauna was talking to Kim in the car? Kim was nervous, really nervous. I'm worried there's something else going on."

"Like what?"

"Like they have a plan—something to get rid of us for good."

"They're not going to kill us, Toni. Nicole was young, they caught her off guard, and Cathy trusted Shauna. That was her mistake."

"And you're too damn confident—that's *your* mistake. They're going to get us one way or another. Back to jail or on a slab at the morgue."

"So what do you want to do?" He sounded as frustrated as I felt. "How are we going to end this thing?"

"We need to lie low, stay away from each other, and see how the next few days go. One of them will make a move, I'm sure of it."

"You can do whatever you want, Toni. But I'm not going away on this. I'm still talking to everyone who was at that party that night, anyone who snorted coke with Cathy over the years, anyone who knows something about anything."

"That's a mistake, Ryan. We need to be careful right now. Let's wait and see if my talks with Kim and Rachel have any effect."

"I'm done with careful. It's time we blow this shit wide open."

"Ryan, that's not—"

He'd hung up.

Still angry and worried as hell about what was going to happen now, I decided to go for a walk on the beach. I'd just left my cabin and was heading down the path leading to the beach when I noticed Ashley's car outside one of the trailers, where loud music was playing. What was she doing here? I paused, and she stumbled down the front steps, the door banging shut behind her. She was giggling as she opened her car door and grabbed some cigarettes from inside. She turned around and tried to light one of them, her cheeks flushed and her eyes glassy. From where I was standing, I could smell the pot smoke leaking out of the trailer.

She cursed at her lighter, gave it a shake, and tried again. She took a drag and glanced up, finally noticing me.

"Toni, hey." She came toward me. "What are you doing here?"

"I live at the campsite." I thought about her standing outside her mom's place, watching. And I wondered if she'd followed me before and already knew I lived here. Had she ever videotaped me? The thought was alarming—especially if she'd seen Ryan there.

"What about you? I thought you couldn't drive without an adult in your car."

"I can't. I snuck out." She nodded back at the trailer. "That's where Aiden lives."

I glanced at the trailer, which was old and filthy, the siding grayed and the awning torn. Plastic lawn chairs circled a fire pit full of beer cans.

"So you're still seeing him."

"Yeah." She took another drag while looking at me from the

side, self-consciously. "Sorry you got sent back." Cautious now. "How was it?"

"Not great."

"Things have been sucking for me too."

She was comparing her life to *my* life? I gritted my teeth, tried to remember she was just a kid.

"How's that?"

"Mom's been freaking out since Cathy was murdered." She sighed, her mouth twisting in a sad smile. "I remember her from when I was a kid. She was funny and she used to come over all the time, then she got messed up and I wasn't allowed to see her anymore. Weird to think she's dead, you know?"

I did know, remembering how I'd sat in Nicole's room after she died, staring at her things and trying to understand that she was never coming back. I kept quiet, knowing the less I said, the more Ashley babbled. And she did.

"My mom and dad are fighting all the time now. Mom's watching me constantly. I can't do anything. We've fought a lot too, about Aiden and you."

"Me?"

"I told her I didn't think you and Ryan killed Cathy, that it didn't make sense. She told me to stay out of it and let the police handle it."

"Good idea."

"There's something up, though. She's spending all this time with Kim and Rachel, but she never even talked to them for years. Now she gets lots of calls. I saw her clearing her cell phone history, but she left her cell on the counter today and she had a text from Rachel saying they had to meet ASAP."

After my little visit.

A guy came out onto the front steps, banging the door behind him. He wasn't much taller than Ashley and had a scruffy goatee. He wasn't wearing a shirt, just baggy jeans that showed the top part of his underwear.

"You coming back in, Ash?" He gave me an odd look, like he was trying to figure out where he'd seen me before.

"Yeah, in a minute, just talking to a friend."

He stared at me again for a second, then went back inside.

"I'm not supposed to be talking to you," I said. "If he says anything . . ."

"He won't. I just thought you should know what's going on with my mom, so you can be careful."

"She's your mother. Why are you telling me this stuff?"

She stared down at the cigarette in her hand and said, "I never thought I'd be a smoker, didn't think I had it in me. But then one day I just started and now I like it. It makes me wonder what else is in me, like maybe I have all kinds of sides I don't know about."

I was still trying to process what she'd said, and what it meant, when she looked up and quickly said, "I think my mom did something bad, like *really* bad."

We stared at each other. I thought about what I should do, if I should just be honest with Ashley. Finally I said, "She lied at my trial. I never fought with my sister that night—lots of other times but not that night. Shauna hated me."

"So it was like how I wrote in my essay? She was a bully?"

"Your mom and her friends were brutal to me, even after they started hanging out with my sister. But something changed that summer in the weeks before she died. I'm not sure what happened between them, but something did."

A pulse was beating hard in the pale skin of Ashley's throat.

"Do you think . . . do you think my mom did it?"

"I don't know what went down that night, but those girls know the truth. Cathy was starting to talk to people about what happened. Now she's dead."

"So you think my mom did something to *Cathy*?" Her voice was scared, lifting up on Cathy's name. "Just because she's a bully doesn't mean she'd murder her, right? Like how you were angry at Nicole, that doesn't mean you'd kill her."

Her expression was almost desperate, and I wondered if the real reason she'd wanted to do the documentary was to disprove her fears that her mother might be a murderer. Would she confront her? I didn't have any reason to protect Shauna, but I still wasn't sure of Ashley's motives—what if she found out somehow we'd talked to the dealer, and threw it in her mother's face? Next thing you know, he'd go missing too. It was better if I didn't reveal too much else.

I said, "You should talk to your mom about that." I'd have loved to see the look on Shauna's face if Ashley did drop that bomb. I caught a motion out of the corner of my eye, a curtain flickering in the window. Aiden was watching. I wondered if he'd figured out who I was yet, if he'd call the police.

"I've got to go," I said.

As I started to walk away, Ashley called out, "I'm sorry."

I didn't know what she was sorry about but I didn't turn around. Later, when I was walking on the beach, I thought about what was going to happen to Ashley when the truth came out that her mother was a murderer. I was sorry too.


When I got back, Ashley's car was gone and her boyfriend's trailer was dark. I hoped I didn't run into her again and considered whether I should move somewhere else. But I hadn't been working, so my money was almost gone.

Back in my cabin, I remembered how Ashley had mentioned her essay. That made me think about Darlene Haynes, who'd had a falling-out with my sister. What had that been about? Could she know something more? Stephanie still had my laptop, so I walked over to the campsite office and did a quick search on the guest computer, happy to see a listing for Darlene in town. Either she hadn't married or was divorced, but I didn't care—it was working in my favor.

The sun had drifted behind some clouds, so I grabbed my jeans jacket and hopped in my truck, with Darlene's address on a piece of paper on the seat beside me. I drove slow, taking alternate routes and checking to make sure I wasn't being followed. Finally I pulled up in front of Darlene's house, which was on the other side of the river. The house wasn't much to look at, just a white single-story box, but it was tidy and there were flowers blooming all over the yard.

I rapped on the door. A cat came running out of a nearby hedge, startling me, then weaved in and out of my legs, purring.

I didn't think I'd get lucky and actually catch Darlene at home, but the door opened and I recognized her right away, though her hair was short now and bleached out. She had a couple of earrings in one ear and was dressed in some sort of uniform, like she worked at a store or a pharmacy. When she saw my face there was a pause as she tried to place me, then shock when she did.

"Are you . . ."

"Toni."

"God, you look like your sister." She was staring at me, trying to take it all in. I saw her eyes drop down to my tattoos, saw the fear as she remembered that I'd been in prison. I wished I'd grabbed my jeans jacket out of the truck.

"Can I come in? I need to ask you some stuff about Nicole."

She looked uncomfortable. "I don't know if that's a good idea."

She'd never been a witness at the trial, which I always thought was strange. If anyone would know about my relationship with my sister, it was Darlene. They'd been close for years. So why didn't the police talk to her?

"It won't take long," I said. "I just need to clear some things up." She was still staring at me. I softened my approach. "I remember you at our house all the time, how close you two were, but something happened. Nicole changed that year, before someone killed her. It wasn't me or Ryan, but that person is still out there. You might know something, something that could change everything. "

Now she looked confused, thrown off guard, like maybe she'd never considered there was another killer.

"It was a long time ago, my memory . . ."

Finally, an opening. "It might not take much, just a small detail."

She still looked torn, like she didn't know what to believe.

"I'm not here to change your mind about me, Darlene. I just need to know what happened between you two, why she ditched you. It must've hurt."

I'd hit the right nerve. Her face was angry as she said, "Nicole turned into a total bitch that year."

Perfect. Anger was good, anger would make her want to tell me more, so she could feel justified. "So why don't you tell me about it?"

She opened the door. "I only have a little while before work."

"That's fine." The cat dodged around my legs, zipped into the house, and raced upstairs.

We sat at her kitchen table. She didn't offer a coffee, but I didn't need one. My nerves were on edge, keyed up from excitement. I was close. I could feel it.

"So what happened?" I said.

"She was seeing a guy, Dave. That's when she first started changing."

"Dave?" That had to be the guy I'd spoken to on the phone, the one she'd been sneaking out to see. "I didn't know she had a boyfriend."

"No one knew. He was four years older than us—already in college. We'd met him at the mall that Christmas and he'd come by school sometimes to talk to her. They hooked up at a party, then she started sneaking out to meet him."

So I was right. "Why did you two fight?"

"She was getting secretive, like she wouldn't tell me stuff about him anymore, and she wouldn't wear certain outfits because he said they were trashy. He partied a lot too, always drinking with his friends. I thought he was a jerk." She stopped and thought back. "I heard him yelling at her on the phone once."

I remembered Nicole crying in the girls' bathroom at school; her fear when I'd picked up the phone. Was he just a controlling asshole with a bad attitude or something more dangerous?

"Did you try to talk to her about it?"

"I told her she should dump him. We stopped hanging out after that for a couple of weeks, then she was with those girls all the time. She started wearing sexy clothes again and going to parties, so I thought she'd broken up with him."

I thought back to that May, how she'd started sneaking out again later that month. Either she hadn't broken up with this Dave guy, or she'd been meeting up with the girls to party, or she was seeing someone else. That summer she'd told me she was in love with a guy who worked with my father. The one who gave her the necklace. She'd said it was the boy from the party, but was that just a lie to cover up for the real person? Then I wondered if she might've been seeing one of the girls' boyfriends. That would've pissed them off, but I didn't think my sister had it in her. Odds were it was this guy.

"Why didn't you say anything to the police about him after she died?"

"I did, and they said they'd look into it. But then you got arrested . . ."

"So you figured we did it."

"I knew you and Ryan got in trouble a lot—and you were always doing drugs, and fighting with Nicole, and there were witnesses. . . ."

"I didn't kill her, Darlene. I don't know if this guy had anything to do with it, but I'd be surprised if the police ever talked to him." I told her about our interrogation, how the police never considered other suspects, how the girls lied.

Darlene looked upset, considering the possibilities but still not willing to believe me completely. "Maybe Dave had an alibi or something."

"Could be, but I'd like to have a talk with him now. Do you know if he's still around? Or his last name?"

She was quiet for a few beats, then said, "I think it was Johnson. No, Jorgensen, something like that, but he moved away."

It was a common enough name and it was going to be hard to find him after all these years, but still, there was a slim chance.

She said, "They weren't friends anymore, you know."

"Who?"

She hesitated, like she was already regretting having said it, but then she went on, in a tentative voice. "Shauna and her group, and Nicole. Those girls were pissed at her before she died. When I heard they'd testified they saw her at the lake with you, I always figured they'd gone there looking for her themselves."

My adrenaline kicked in, everything else slowing down. "You didn't say anything to anyone? At the trial . . ." I was still taking it all in.

She nodded. "They made it sound like they were best friends. I figured they were just doing that for the attention." She shrugged, a small casual motion that enraged me. This information could have changed my life. I took a couple of breaths, gripping my hands together under the table until I'd calmed down.

"What were they upset about?" I said. "How did you hear about it?"

"Nicole called me one night crying. She said Shauna was mad at her and lying to the other girls, saying Nicole had fooled around with Rachel's boyfriend and that she was the one who told Kim's mom that Kim was gay."

I remembered Cathy telling Ryan that they'd been pissed off at Nicole, remembered Kim saying Nicole had gotten her kicked out. I was finally getting close to the truth.

"Did Nicole tell you what Shauna was so angry about?"

"No, just that she'd screwed up really bad and Shauna found out."

I thought over everything, reflecting back on the weeks leading up to the night of the murder. I remembered the white car slowing down outside the house. Maybe it had been Shauna after all. What could Nicole have done that was so bad Shauna turned the other girls on her?

Darlene also looked lost in thought as she stared at the cat, now stalking a fly on the floor. Her voice soft and haunted, she said, "She asked if we could be friends again, said she was sorry for how she had treated me. But I told her she was a bitch and I never wanted to talk to her again. Then I hung up." Her eyes met mine. "That was the last time I ever spoke with her."

Neither of us said anything for a minute. Then she heaved a sigh.

"I've got to get to work now."

"I appreciate you talking to me today." I stood up. "If you think of something else, anything at all, please call me." I gave her my number, which she hastily jotted down on a piece of paper by her phone.

She walked me to the door, her arms hugging tight around her chest, like the conversation had cast a chill over her body.

Out on the front steps, she said, "Those girls, I never could understand why Nicole started hanging around with them."

"Me neither."

"Everyone thought Nicole was so perfect, but she was just good at pretending to be good. We got in a lot of trouble together. We used to laugh about it sometimes. How your mom was always so tough on you but didn't know what Nicole was really up to most of the time."

"It seems none of us knew what was really going on in her life, not in those last few months anyway."

"It's still scary, thinking about her murder. When you're a teenager you don't think stuff like that will happen, not to someone you know. Kids stopped going to the lake, or if they did, her murder was all they wanted to talk about. Everyone pretended they were friends with her, or that they knew you and Ryan. I never went out there again, never even talked about her, but I thought about her all the time. I didn't understand how someone could hate her that much."

She met my eyes, her expression suddenly nervous, like she was worried she'd said too much.

She said, "I have to go," and stepped back inside the house, locking the door behind her.

# CHAPTER TWENTY-EIGHT

## Campbell River

### July 2013

I went back to the campsite and logged onto the office computer, checking to see if I'd gotten any e-mails. There was one about a landscaping job I'd applied for months ago. They wanted to know if I was still looking. I e-mailed back that I was interested and would love to come in for an interview. I didn't know if I'd be on parole for much longer, but I had another meeting with Suzanne coming up and I needed to show her I was trying. Plus, I needed money. I gave Suzanne a call, but she wasn't around. I'd been hoping to get a sense of what might be going on.

When I was finished, I did some online searches for a Dave Jorgensen. Unfortunately, it was a pretty common name, and I didn't see anyone who might be my sister's old boyfriend. I looked up some people we went to school with on Facebook, then checked their friends' lists, but there was no one with that name.

Exhausted from all the stress of the last couple of days, I tried to have a nap but I couldn't stop thinking about what I'd learned from Darlene about that last year with Nicole. According to Darlene, Nicole might've broken up with Dave a couple weeks before she started hanging out with the girls. So why was she still sneaking out? Had they reconnected? I'd assumed her necklace had been lost that night, but maybe the killer had taken it. But if this guy was the real murderer, why had the girls lied at my trial? Just because they hated me?

It was possible, but my gut told me Shauna was involved more deeply in Nicole's death than just lying at my trial, something that seemed even more likely now that Darlene had revealed that Shauna had been angry with Nicole. Could Shauna have been involved with this Dave guy too? She didn't have a boyfriend that last year, not that I remembered. Something had been going on. But what?

I'd hoped talking to Darlene would help me clear things up, but now I had more questions than answers. The only thing I knew for sure was that my sister had had a secret life. One that had probably gotten her killed.

The next morning I headed into town to do some shopping, but when I got to the plaza I noticed Ashley's car in the parking lot. Her boyfriend was sitting behind the wheel, smoking, and Ashley was standing outside the car. Shauna's car was parked beside them, and she was also standing outside. They were obviously fighting about something, their faces angry and their hands stabbing at the air as they made their points. I parked around the corner where I could see them. They exchanged a few more angry words, then Ashley got into her car while her mom was still talking and slammed the door in her face. Ashley and Aiden drove off, Ashley wiping at her cheeks like she was crying, and Shauna staring after them, her face flushed and her mouth an angry line. She got back in her car and started talking to someone on her cell. Whatever Shauna was pissed about, I was sure Ashley's letting her boyfriend drive her car hadn't helped matters. Shauna put down the phone and drove around the corner of the plaza. Curious, I decided to follow her.

This time she pulled into the back parking lot. I kept my distance, but I could see her talking on her cell again, then a man opened the back door of a store. He was around our age, dark hair, with a bit of a potbelly, but nice-enough-looking. Shauna got out of the car. They talked for a moment. Shauna's body language was still aggravated and I got the feeling she was venting about her fight with Ashley. Who was this guy? They looked around, checking to see if anyone was watching. I ducked down, peeking over my steering wheel. He pulled her in for a hug, then kissed her on the mouth. She accepted the kiss but she was the first to move away, pushing his hands off her rear end. He ushered her inside the back door.

I drove around the front of the building to see what store she had entered. A camera shop. Was she having an affair with Ashley's *teacher*? Talk about being involved in your daughter's life. I went back to the campsite and tried to process everything. I had new information, but how could it help me? I considered calling Ryan but decided to keep it to myself for a while. I didn't want him rushing anything.

I thought about everything Darlene had told me. The girls had to know Nicole had been seeing a boy. She would have confided—if nothing else, just to prove how cool she was. Maybe I was right and Shauna had been involved with this Dave guy or was friends with him.

Maybe I was looking at it all wrong. What if they hadn't testified to screw me over? What if they were protecting someone else?

The only person who knew the whole story was Shauna. But how was I going to get it out of her? I couldn't risk following her around. Could I piss her off somehow, make her crack? What would be the best way to get under her skin? Even though she tried to control her daughter's every move, it was obvious she loved Ashley, or at least wanted Ashley to love *her*. I remembered how threatened she'd get when she felt she was losing someone when we were kids. So how would she feel if her daughter were to find out about her affair?

I had to convince Shauna that I had information she wouldn't want her daughter, or anyone else, knowing about. If I could then get her to meet me somewhere private, her ego and her hatred of me might get the best of her and she might start talking. I'd seen that in prison. People who couldn't keep their mouths shut about their crimes because they were so proud of what they'd pulled off that they just had to tell someone. Shauna might relish the idea of telling me face-to-face how she'd screwed my life up. How she'd won.

I thought of Ashley filming her mom talking with Kim. It wasn't a bad idea. My cell phone also had a voice recorder. There was nothing stopping Shauna from trying to attack me, but I had a feeling she wouldn't go one-on-one. She was sneakier than that. I did have a feeling she'd want to meet with me, though, to find out what I knew.

But I wasn't stupid. If she *was* willing to meet with me, I'd make sure I was carrying a knife.

First, I had to speak with her.


I looked up Shauna's number, hoping that Ashley didn't answer. She didn't.

Shauna said, "Hello?"

"It's Toni. I think it's time we talked."

She paused for a long moment. I didn't say anything else.

"You're not supposed to call me," she said.

"And you're not supposed to make out with store owners in a parking lot."

She sucked in her breath, then regained her calm, her voice smooth and controlled as she said, "What's this about?"

"I want to meet with you face-to-face."

"You're nuts. Why would I meet you?"

"Because I know things. Like why you killed my sister. I just had a nice chat with one of my sister's friends from school. A *close* friend. Seems my sister talked with her before she died, about someone she was seeing in secret. But I don't think it was a secret to you."

Silence.

I had to be careful. If I took a step in the wrong direction, I could lose her. I had to make her think I had evidence of something. Then it came to me.

"After Nicole died, my parents gave her friend a box of things, sentimental things, from when they were kids. Like my sister's diary. Now I have it, and something tells me you might want it."

"I don't believe you." She said it firmly, but it was too emphatic, like she was trying to convince herself.

"But you don't know for sure, do you? And the only way you're going to find out is if you meet me at the lake tomorrow night."

"I'm not going to meet a convicted killer at the lake."

I wondered if she remembered that the anniversary of Nicole's death was coming up soon. Did she even care, or had she forgotten the date years ago?

"I think I'm the one taking the bigger risk, don't you? You know that I've never killed anyone, but I can't say the same about you."

"If you have information, why aren't you going to the police?"

She was showing her hand, admitting there was something to be known, to be shown.

"I've already served my time. I don't want to go through another court case and lengthy appeal. I just want to move on with my life, and I need you to back off. So we're going to meet, and you're going to give me a big chunk of cash for this diary. Then I'm going to get transferred out of here, and you never have to see or hear from me again."

"That's all you want? Money?" I could hear her sneering through the phone.

"Thirty grand. Then you never have to see me again."

"What about Ryan?"

I thought quickly. "He's leaving too—we're splitting the money."

She was quiet, also thinking. "What if I can't get thirty?"

"Then your daughter is going to get a call, then your husband, then the police, and then you'll be calling a lawyer."

She sucked in her breath, an angry hiss. "Fine. I'll meet you."

"Eleven o'clock tomorrow night. At the north end of the lake, near the cliffs."

I hung up the phone, then sat in my darkened cabin, my heart thudding. Everything was in play. The only piece missing was Ryan. Maybe he could hide in the woods in case I needed backup. I started to dial his number, then hesitated. I didn't want him to get in trouble, didn't want to risk our being seen together. If something went wrong, and it very well could, I didn't want us both going back to prison. I had to do this alone.

The next day, the hours ticked by in slow motion. I went for a walk along the ocean, thinking of Captain, thinking of Ryan. After tonight things were going to get better, or worse, but I was ready for it.

A little before ten, I grabbed my phone, tested the recording application a couple of times, then put a knife I'd bought the day before in my back pocket. If I was caught with it I'd definitely lose my parole, but the hard metal in my pocket felt solid, reassuring. I'd gotten an e-mail back about the landscaping job and had an interview the following day. For a moment I allowed myself to get excited. It sounded great, working outside all day. Then I shut off the thoughts, not wanting to get distracted, not wanting to think about tomorrow or the next day or anything else. I just had to get through tonight. Suzanne had also called and my heart was in my throat the entire time, but she just asked the basic questions.

There was a strong chance that Shauna wasn't coming alone, that she'd bring Kim and Rachel. Just in case, I wrote a letter explaining everything I'd discovered and who I was meeting, then left it in my cabin. I even wrote out a will, leaving the rest of my pathetic savings and belongings to Ryan, and added a note asking that he adopt Captain and give him the good home he deserved.

After that, I quickly cleaned my room, made my bed, tidied my few belongings, and tried to prepare myself for whatever was coming my way.

# CHAPTER TWENTY-NINE

## CAMPBELL RIVER

### JULY 2013

It was quiet at the lake—no one was out there at this time of night. I had my windows down and the air smelled of pine needles and lake water. It had changed since I'd been there seventeen years ago, more overgrown, trees reaching for each other over the old roads and almost touching on the other side. I hadn't wanted to meet Shauna where Nicole had died, still haunted by memories of pulling her naked body from the cold water. Instead, I'd chosen a spot at the far end, high above the lake where the boys used to drop off the cliffs into the water while the girls screamed in excitement. I was there fifteen minutes early, so I sat in my car with the radio playing and observed the dark woods around me, the shapes and shadows. I thought about how Nicole must have felt that night. Alone and scared, waiting for Ryan and me to come back, but instead someone else had shown up.

Then I thought about the brief note I'd left for Ryan at the cabin. Was that really how I wanted to leave things between us if something happened to me? I fingered the disposable phone in my pocket. Should I call him? I dialed his number.

"Toni, is that you?"

This was a mistake. I should've left things alone.

"Toni? Are you okay? " His voice sounded scared.

"Yeah, hey, I was just thinking about you, and—" I stopped as my throat tightened.

"Where are you? What's going on?"

"Nothing . . . I shouldn't have called."

I could feel him thinking, putting things together.

"Are you meeting someone? Where *are* you?"

"I have to go, call you later." I hung up the phone. Shit.

A couple of minutes past eleven, Shauna's headlights crept up the hill and she parked at the other end of the clearing. I dimmed my headlights so we could see each other but not be blinded. She did the same. She stepped out of the passenger side, holding her hands in front, showing me she didn't have a weapon.

Who was driving? It had to be one of the girls. I hit the recording app on my phone and tucked it into my pocket. I stepped out of my truck, holding my own hands up, though I was well aware of the knife tucked in my back pocket.

I took a couple of steps forward, and so did she. We stopped when we were a few feet apart. "Scared to come alone, Shauna?"

"Where's this diary, Toni?"

"In my truck." I gestured behind me. "Show me the money first." I had to get her talking about what had happened that night, but I wasn't sure how to do it without revealing that I'd never read any diary—and that there wasn't one. Just in case Shauna asked to see something, I'd found a pink diary at a dollar store and had filled some of the pages, but that was only going to get me so far.

She walked to her car and opened the back door, took out a

duffel bag, and threw it a couple of feet in front of her. "Come and get it."

It would look strange if I didn't try for the money. I stepped forward and was reaching down for the bag when I heard a rustling noise. I looked up. Shauna was holding a gun on me. Her arm was straight, the gun unwavering. I held up my hands, stumbled back a couple of steps.

"What the fuck?"

The driver's door opened and a man got out of the car.

It was Frank McKinney. I stared in shock.

"Shauna, get the diary," he said.

How was he involved? Was he going to kill me? My heart started to race frantically. Could I make a run for it? I looked around. The trees were too far away. I'd be shot before I got a few feet. McKinney's eyes met mine.

"What are you doing here?" I said.

"Like you don't know."

He obviously thought I knew more than I did. But what?

McKinney shifted his weight and I caught sight of the gun in a holster on his belt. It also looked like he was wearing a bullet-proof vest underneath his windbreaker, his body bulky. I remembered the phone in my pocket. Could I try to call 911? Before I could do anything, Shauna motioned for me to step away from the truck. I moved to the side, keeping an eye on McKinney, who had his hand hovering near his gun as he watched me. Shauna searched under my seats, in the glove department. She found the diary, flipped through the pages, and laughed. She climbed out of the truck, threw the diary onto the ground.

"It's empty."

"The real diary isn't here," I said. "I've put it somewhere safe."

Shauna looked enraged. "What do you mean, it's not *here*?" She pointed her gun at me again. In the shadows, McKinney also looked furious.

"I knew you'd pull a stunt like this," he said, and took a step closer. McKinney unsnapped his holster and brought out his gun. "Where is it?"

I couldn't stop staring at the gun, the way he held it so casually, his thumb resting on the safety. They weren't going to let me walk away from this, not now. I tried to focus my panicked thoughts. I had to buy myself some time, had to distract them. Shauna turned to look at her father, and I caught a flash of silver from her necklace. It reminded me of something, something I could use.

"I'll tell you, when you tell me where my sister's necklace is. She had a diamond pendant that disappeared the night she died. Like someone didn't want her to have it anymore. Someone who was jealous."

"She shouldn't have had it!" Shauna's voice was high and shrill. "It didn't belong to her."

My breath hitched in my throat. I was close to the truth, and for a moment I wanted to run from it, didn't want to know.

"What happened to it?" I looked through the dark at McKinney, outlined in the headlights, wondering if he'd stop Shauna, but he was silent.

"I took it." Her voice was triumphant.

McKinney spoke now. "Shauna . . ." But his voice wasn't just warning her to be quiet, there was anger in there. Like he was upset with her for taking the necklace—and surprised. What was I missing?

Shauna spun around and faced her father, her voice thick with tears. "You said you were busy, always so fucking busy at the station, but you weren't, not that summer—you were with *her*."

Dread came over me as I finally connected all the pieces. That diamond necklace was too expensive for a teenage boy, too sophisticated.

It had been a gift from someone else.

"Shauna, control yourself."

"Control *my*self? You're the one who was screwing a teenager."

"You *killed* her." McKinney's voice was furious.

There it was. I felt shattered, pulled into a million pieces. I wanted to run at Shauna, wanted to beat her down to the ground like she had Nicole. I started to move forward, then I saw the gun in McKinney's hand.

Anger again from Shauna. "She deserved it. Coming to our house, pretending to be my friend . . . It was disgusting, Dad. She was younger than *me*."

"It wasn't like that."

"What was it like, Dad? Tell me."

"Shauna—"

"God, you were fucking my friend! It was sick and perverted, and—"

"Enough!" McKinney's voice was a roar. "I made a mistake, and I've paid for it every damn day. I'm tired of cleaning up your messes."

The rest of the picture unfolded before me.

"You knew all along," I said. "You *knew* she killed my sister and you helped cover it up."

"I had no choice." His voice was stony.

"Of course you did, you asshole." My chest was tight with anger, my hands clenched. "You lied. You let Ryan and me go to prison—for *years*."

"You two would have ended up there eventually anyway."

"Is that how you justify it to yourself? We were no good?"

"Stop wasting time. Where's the fucking diary?" He raised his arm, the gun pointing straight at me.

I heard another car coming up from behind us. McKinney dropped his arm. I spun around, hand raised to flag down the driver, then stopped when I recognized the red car. It was Ashley.

Shauna gasped.

The car rocked to a stop, and the driver's door flung open. Ashley climbed out, cell phone in hand. "Stop." Her voice was high and panicked.

"What are you doing here?" Shauna demanded.

Ashley looked at me, her face stricken, then faced her mother. "I can't let you hurt Toni."

"Ashley, go home," McKinney said.

"I know what you're going to do. I filmed everything. I called 911. And they know there's a video, but you can't find it—I've hidden the camera."

"Don't be ridiculous. Give it to me." Shauna started toward her daughter.

It was my chance.

I sprinted toward the lake and dove off the cliff, shots ringing out behind me as I crashed into the water, the cold snatching the breath from my lungs. I surfaced spluttering and disoriented in the dark, then saw the long beam of a flashlight shining down from the cliff. I sucked in some air and dove again, hearing more shots, muffled thrums as they struck the water around me.

Gasping for air, I popped back up just in time to see Ashley hit the water a few feet in front of me, near the old floating dock. Shots were still going off, one of them really close. I heard Ashley cry out, and from above, McKinney's voice.

"Shauna, stop! Ashley's down there."

I swam closer to her, whispered, "Ashley, are you hurt?"

"I've been shot." Her breaths were gasps. "My shoulder."

"Can you make it to the dock?" At least we'd have some cover there.

"Maybe." Her voice was high.

"I'm right behind you."

In the moonlight, I could see Ashley trying to dog-paddle with one arm, but she kept going under, gasping and spluttering. She was almost to the dock. I noticed the beam of a flashlight coming down the hill, the light bobbing.

"We're almost there," I told her. "You can do it."

"My arm . . ."

Then she went silent. She was underwater. I waited a moment, but she didn't come back up. I sucked in a breath and dove down to where'd she'd been, feeling through the dark water for her. Nothing. Straining for breath, I swam deeper, closer to the dock, and felt something smooth. Her arm? She slipped from my grasp. I reached out, touched some fabric. I tugged her closer, gripped her arm, and pulled, but she was stuck on something under the dock. Would I hurt her if I tried again? I tightened my grip and yanked hard. This time she floated loose.

We rose to the surface. She was limp. I wrapped one arm under her chin and swam hard for the shore. I couldn't see Shauna or McKinney, couldn't see anything. They could already be waiting for me. But I had to risk it.

My feet touched the pebbled bottom, and I dragged Ashley the last few steps, my arms aching. I glanced down and saw her pale face in the moonlight. The shoulder of her shirt was dark. Blood? How much had she lost?

"Hang in there," I whispered. I eased her down onto the beach and knelt to check her pulse. My hands were cold and wet so it was hard to tell. I put my ear by her mouth and couldn't feel a breath. I was freezing and panting, but adrenaline was still pumping through my veins. I took off my shirt and pressed it against her shoulder, then started CPR while trying frantically to figure out what to do next. I didn't want Ashley to die, but if I tried to alert Shauna and Frank so they could help her, they'd probably kill me. Before I could make a decision one way or another, I heard rustling noises.

Shauna burst through the bushes. "Get away from my daughter!"

"She's hurt," I said. "I'm trying to help—"

Shauna pushed me off Ashley and grabbed her in her arms. "Ashley! Oh, my God!"

McKinney came out of the bushes, dropped to his knees beside Shauna, and felt for Ashley's pulse. "She's not breathing. Lay her down." Shauna started screaming her daughter's name. McKinney pulled Ashley from her arms and laid her down on her back. He started giving her CPR. I should've run, but I was frozen by the image in front of me, McKinney bent over Ashley, her skin pale.

McKinney, panting like he was almost out of breath, said to Shauna, "You have to do chest compressions." But Shauna was just staring down at Ashley now and crying, obviously in shock. I pushed Shauna out of the way, starting chest compressions while McKinney blew into Ashley's mouth.

"Come on, Ashley," he chanted. "Stay with us."

I was crying too, my teeth chattering, the words, *Don't die, you can't die*, repeating in my head as I tried to focus on my task. Beside me Shauna was sobbing Ashley's name, but then she yelled, "Get away from my daughter!" and tried to drag me off. I hit back with one of my elbows, making contact with her stomach. Shauna grunted from the blow, then there were just moans and sobs.

I didn't know how long McKinney and I had been working together, but finally Ashley started to cough and splutter. McKinney rolled her onto her side, patting her on the back, and she coughed up some more water.

"Thank God," he said.

Shauna shoved me out of the way and this time I let her. I got to my feet as she grabbed her daughter to her chest, rocking her back and forth. We were all covered with Ashley's blood—my hands were sticky with it. McKinney was trying to comfort his daughter, his arm around her back. Shauna was saying, "I didn't mean to hurt her. I didn't. She should have stayed away."

There was something in her voice, an odd disconnected quality that made me wonder who she was talking about, Ashley or Nicole. Frank was also staring at her. I took a step back, getting ready to make my escape. My foot came down on a branch. Shauna looked up at me, her face full of hate. "This is *your* fault."

She stood, pulled her gun out of her coat pocket. I made a lunging dive and grabbed her around the waist. She fell, and I scrambled on top of her. We wrestled for the weapon, rolling around in the sand. Finally I felt the cold metal in my hands. I flipped Shauna onto her back, held her down with my arm across her throat, and pointed the gun at her head. My mind filled with rage, a loud roaring in my ears, screaming at me to kill her. Then, a solid blow to my left as McKinney tackled me, and I was thrown to the ground. I lost my grip on the gun and it disappeared into the water. McKinney hit me in the temple with his gun. The world dimmed for a second. I heard another man's voice.

"Let her go!" Ryan.

Now the sounds of fighting, male grunts, fists hitting flesh. I flipped over, my vision blurry, but I could see McKinney and Ryan going at it, fighting for the gun as they rolled around in the dirt, their bodies close, almost in a hug. Shauna was trying to pull Ryan off. I stumbled to my feet, put my arm around her throat, and dragged her away. A shot rang out. Ryan groaned and clutched his side but managed to slam his head into McKinney's nose. McKinney yelled as blood spurted. Now Ryan had the gun in his hand. He pressed it against McKinney's forehead as he straddled his chest, his other hand gripping McKinney's throat. McKinney was still, looking up at Ryan, his eyes desperate and pleading.

"You ruined our lives!" Ryan said.

I yelled, "Ryan, let him go."

Shauna was also screaming. "No!"

Ryan didn't even glance in our direction. His hand was shaking as he held the gun, his arm rigid and his face grim. One side of his body was covered in blood, a spreading darkness. He pressed the gun harder against McKinney's forehead, grinding it against the bone. McKinney closed his eyes. The moment stretched out. Ryan suddenly lowered his hand.

"You're not worth it, you piece of shit."

He staggered to his feet, his body swaying and one hand pressed against his side, the gun hanging limp in his other hand.

The sound of sirens filled the air. I felt a moment of relief, followed by more fear. Who were they going to believe? Cars were pulling up, headlights blinding, colored lights flashing. Voices shouted as flashlights beamed into my face. "Get down. Get down now!"

I dropped to my knees, placed my hands on the back of my head. They came at me, forced me to the ground, grinding my face into the sand. My mouth was filled with it, and I tried to spit it out. One of them was kneeling on my back, pushing my breath out as he wrenched my arms behind me and slapped on the cuffs. Then I was being lifted to my feet. I saw them rush at Shauna and Ryan, telling them to get on the ground. Shauna was fighting, refusing to leave her daughter.

They were patting me down, and one of them found the knife. The cruiser was pulled around and I was shoved in the back. I could hear more sirens now and saw ambulances. I hoped Ryan was getting help. The officer sitting in the front was talking into his radio.

"Frank McKinney and his daughter attacked me," I said. "They shot Ryan—and Ashley."

"We're taking you back to the station," the officer said over his shoulder. "We'll sort it out from there.

"I want to talk to Sergeant Hicks."

The officer didn't answer.

At the station I was locked into a jail cell, still shivering until someone finally brought me a jumpsuit and blanket. I refused to put on the jumpsuit. I didn't care how wet I was, I wasn't wearing that suit. Not yet. I sat in there for hours, and no one would answer my questions about Ryan or tell me whether Ashley had pulled through. Finally, I was taken back to an interview room. Doug Hicks came in.

I watched him warily, wondering what McKinney might have already told him. I hoped Ashley had been telling the truth about the video. I hoped she was okay.

Hicks read me my rights again—another officer had already done it when I was first brought to the station.

"Let's just get this over with," I said.

"Okay, Toni. Take me through last night."

"How are Ryan and Ashley?"

"Ryan's in the hospital but it looks like he'll make it. Ashley's also going to be okay. What were you doing out there? And why were you carrying a knife?"

I'd violated multiple conditions of my parole, but it seemed I was screwed anyway, so I told him everything. How I'd discovered Nicole had had a secret boyfriend, about Shauna's affair with the shop owner, and that I was positive she and her friends had killed Nicole because she was having an affair with Frank McKinney.

"Shauna said you were blackmailing her."

"I told her I had Nicole's diary, but that was just to get her out there. I recorded what happened on my phone." Then I realized my cell was probably at the bottom of the lake. "Ashley said she filmed what happened too, and—"

"We'll get to that in a minute. I want to hear what you have to say."

I told him the rest of my theories, what I'd realized at the lake—that my sister must've been fooling around with Frank McKinney for months. I told him about McKinney driving her home, her sneaking out more after that, how her behavior had changed, about the missing necklace, which Shauna now claimed to have taken. I also told him how Ryan had jumped McKinney to protect me, then McKinney shot him.

At the end I said, "So what's going to happen now? We get blamed for everything again?"

"You're all under arrest. We're taking statements from everyone involved, and we're in the process of reviewing the video Ashley recorded. But you violated at least three conditions, so your parole will be suspended."

"I'm going back to Rockland." I said the words flat, resigned to my fate.

"If everything you're telling me is true, you can appeal on the grounds that you have new evidence."

I laughed. "If I live that long. Someone inside wants me dead."

"We can put you in protective custody."

"I'd rather die. What about Ryan?"

"He'll be in the hospital until he recovers, then he'll go back to Rockland. We know you two met on several occasions prior to this, which is a direct violation of your parole, and we found a knife strapped to his calf."

"He was trying to protect *me*. This is such bullshit. You've seen the video, you know we're innocent." His eyes flicked to my arms, and I glanced down at the scratches. I looked back up at him. There'd been something in his expression, a realization. What was he thinking? Then I got it.

"You see now. You see how Ryan got those scratches the night Nicole died—it was from when we pushed our way through the bushes. I *told* you—"

"We'll get to the truth, and if you and Ryan are innocent, you'll be exonerated in due time. Meanwhile, we have to follow the law, which you broke when you carried a concealed weapon to meet a witness." I hated him for his matter-of-factness, for being part of the system that had screwed me years ago.

"If anything else happens to me or Ryan, it's on *your* head. You sent two kids away for years who didn't do anything. Or is that what this is about? Did you help cover up for your buddy Frank McKinney?"

"I didn't cover for anybody." His face was an angry red. It was the first time I'd ever seen him show a strong emotion. I pushed harder.

"He was your friend. You were together that night."

"He was my partner, but that doesn't mean I won't put him away if he broke the law." Hicks stood up, but before he left, he said, "We *will* get to the truth—and the right people *will* be punished."

# CHAPTER THIRTY

I didn't see Doug Hicks again. I spent the night at the station jail and was flown over to Rockland the next afternoon. Outside the station, media lined the road, trying to get a photo of me and shouting questions: "Toni, did Shauna McKinney murder your sister?" "Are you and Ryan back together again?" "Is it true that you're innocent?" The sheriffs had to shield me from the cameras as they ushered me to the van. I wondered if what had happened at the lake had been on the late news the night before, if the girls in Rockland had heard I was coming back, if Helen was already planning her assault on me.

After I went through the intake process at the penitentiary, I was unpacking my stuff when Brenda and Amber appeared in the walkway outside my cell. I looked up with a smile. "Hey, guys."

Neither of them smiled back, their faces serious. Thinking that they must have news about Helen, I said, "What's up?"

Brenda tried to speak but stopped, tears in her eyes. I was starting to get a really bad feeling. I sat down on my bed.

"Where's Margaret?" I said.

Amber spoke up, her voice high and anxious. "Helen and her haven't been getting along since all that stuff happened when you were in here, and—"

"But it's not your fault," Brenda broke in. "Margaret hated her."

"What *happened*?" I waited in horror, my heart thudding hard in my chest.

Amber's words came out in a rush. "They were watching the news last night and Helen started saying how she was going to kick your ass when you came back. Margaret told her off, then later they met in the yard—we didn't know Margaret planned on fighting her or we would've stopped her. Helen had a shank . . ." Amber was crying so hard she couldn't finish.

"Did she stab her? Is she in the infirmary?"

Brenda was shaking her head, tears running down her face too. "She didn't make it."

I started to cry, deep gasping sobs. Both of the girls were still trying to fight their own tears, all of us helpless to comfort each other with an embrace, the security cameras watching. When I finally got control of myself, my sorrow had turned to pure rage.

"Where's Helen?" I was going to fuck her up good.

"She's in segregation," Brenda said. "They'll throw her into maximum now. She'll never get out of Rockland."

It meant I was safe. I should've been relieved. I got up and paced my cell.

"Why did Margaret fight her? She should have waited until I got back in here."

"I don't know," Brenda said. "She was always telling us to walk away from stuff. And she was really tired lately—and sore. It doesn't make sense that she'd take Helen on by herself."

Amber said, "She left something for you in her cell before the fight. Her roommate gave it to us." She glanced up at the nearest camera. "We'll get it to you later."

The guards called out, "Count!" and the girls went back to their cells, after we promised we'd see each other at chow in the morning.

Later, when lights were out, I thought of Margaret and how she'd managed to avoid fights the whole time she was in prison, until this last one. Then I remembered the last time I saw her, begging me for a massage, saying that she didn't know how much longer she could live in there, her body in constant pain. Had she picked a fight with Helen knowing she'd lose? And knowing that it was the only way to make sure Helen could never hurt me again?

I was devastated, thinking that she might have sacrificed herself for me. Then I remembered something else Margaret had said, when we were talking about Nicole. "You can't blame yourself for something someone else chose to do. You didn't force her into that truck, and you didn't kill her. Blaming yourself is just weak, and it pisses me off hearing you punish yourself, like you don't deserve to ever be happy or something. I don't want to hear that crap out of your mouth again."

And so I tried to think of Margaret now, finally free from pain, maybe dancing with a gorgeous man, spinning around and around in a long, flowing dress, a beautiful smile on her face. She'd told me that death wasn't the hard part, living was. I tried to find peace in knowing that the hard part was over for her.

Amber showed up at my cell the next day with some papers bundled together in a makeshift book. On the front Margaret had scrawled, *For Toni.* After Amber left, I took a breath and opened the book, wondering what had been so important that Margaret had made a point of leaving it for me. Inside the first page she'd tucked a note:

> Toni, if you're reading this, I guess the fight didn't go so well. I just hope I took that bitch down with me!!! I planned on mailing this to you but didn't get a chance to finish. You'll do fine. See you on the other side, kid. Love, M.

My eyes filling with tears, I flipped through the pages and cried even harder when I saw what she had done. She'd jotted down recipes, household tips, life lessons, inspirational quotes, jokes, anything she thought would help me survive on the outside. Anything she thought a mother would tell her daughter.

For the next few days, I spent a lot of time in my cell, thinking about Margaret, how much she had meant to me. Brenda and Amber were also grieving, and we had a makeshift memorial for Margaret in the yard, sharing stories. Now that Helen was out of the picture none of her friends messed with me, but there was still some tension. I wondered how long it would take before my case would go before the Court of Appeals. Angus was trying to get a hearing, but he said it could take up to three months.

One day, when I'd been in for almost a week, I had a visitor. The visit wasn't scheduled, so I was surprised when one of the guards came to get me. I was even more surprised to see my visitor was Suzanne.

"What's going on?" I sat down across from her.

She eyed me from the other side of the table, which was covered with bags of chips, a couple of chocolate bars from the vending machine, and two cans of Coke. "You've lost more weight."

I pulled at my shirt, made a face. "I've been under some stress."

She pushed a chocolate bar and a bag of chips at me. "Here. Eat up."

She was looking at me expectantly and I got the feeling she wasn't going to say anything until I ate something, so I unwrapped the bar and took a small bite. The heavy sweetness made me feel sick. My lawyer had told me our chances of getting out looked good. Did Suzanne know something Angus didn't?

She glanced at the guard watching the room and he gave her a nod. I was also getting the feeling this visit wasn't on the books. Suzanne looked back at me.

Still unsure of what this was about, I kept my mouth shut. She said, "How much do you know about the investigation?"

"Not much. They've been keeping us in the dark." I shared what I knew so far. My lawyer had told me Shauna and Frank McKinney had been denied bail, but McKinney was in protective custody because he'd been a cop. Once the police had reviewed Ashley's tape and all our statements, they pulled in Kim and Rachel for questioning. "We know they were arrested," I said, "but we don't know what the charges were and haven't heard anything since."

Suzanne was nodding as I spoke. "I have some friends on the force. They told me Kim rolled right away on Shauna."

"You know what really happened that night? Were they all involved?"

She nodded again, her eyes sad. "I'm bending the rules, but I wanted you to hear it from me."

I sucked in a big lungful of air, bracing for what was coming next, then said, "How did they get her out of the truck?"

"Kim says that after Shauna told them Nicole had been messing with Rachel's boyfriend, and that Nicole was the one who told Kim's mom she was gay, they were furious. Shauna wanted to get back at Nicole, and the girls agreed."

"Did they plan on killing her?"

"Doesn't sound like it. They were just going to get her alone and humiliate her by stripping her down, taking photos, then spreading them around. They'd been harassing Nicole all week, phoning her, threatening that they were coming for her." I thought of how thin Nicole had gotten those last few weeks, how she'd stolen the pills because she couldn't sleep. I could well imagine how terrified she must have been, how alone she must have felt not being able to confide in anyone, how she hadn't wanted to be home alone that Friday.

"They were waiting outside your house. When they saw you all leaving together, they followed you to the lake." I remembered that night, the heat coming through the windows, Nicole's bare leg brushing against mine, her face serious.

"They parked their car and snuck up on the truck," Suzanne said. "When they realized you guys had left Nicole by herself, they figured you'd be gone awhile. They sent Cathy to lure Nicole out of the truck."

Cathy, who'd spent the next seventeen years smoking and drinking everything in sight. I started tearing at the chocolate bar wrapper, ripping the corner off into little bits, my fingers itching to attack something, anything.

Suzanne's voice got lower, more serious, her gaze flicking to my hands as she said, "Cathy told Nicole she'd been at the party below, seen her drive by, and just wanted to talk so they could clear the air."

I felt sick. "That's why she got out. She thought she could fix everything. . . ." Sunny, sweet Nicole, who wanted to be everyone's friend.

Suzanne paused, letting me gather myself before she continued. "After Nicole was out of the truck the other girls rushed her and ordered her to take off her clothes. When she refused, Rachel punched her. Kim says Nicole tried to hit back, but then both Kim and Shauna attacked her, knocking her down."

I stared at the little pile of ripped plastic in front of me, my eyes filling with tears as I saw my sister falling to the ground, imagined her desperate pleas, her eyes searching for Ryan and me, praying we'd come back and save her.

I could barely find my voice, whispering, "What else? What else did they do?"

Suzanne told me the rest of the terrible story. While Kim and Rachel slapped and kicked Nicole, Shauna grabbed the tire iron from behind the truck's seat. The girls stopped, scared now, but stood frozen while Shauna, in a rage they didn't understand, hit Nicole several times in the head and the face. By the time they finally pulled her off, Nicole was unconscious. Shauna told them they'd all go to jail for assault if Nicole lived, so they had to kill her. She made Rachel hit her with the tire iron too.

I held up my hand. "Give me a minute." The tears were running hard, and I wiped them on my sleeve, fighting the brutal images twisting through my mind.

Suzanne said, "Maybe I shouldn't—"

"No." I shook my head. "I have to know. Keep going."

Cathy and Kim refused to hit Nicole, but once she was dead they helped take off her clothes and drag her body to the water. Kim, hysterical by this point, wanted to go to the police, but Shauna said she'd be arrested as an accomplice. They all snuck back to Shauna's, thinking that they could shower there, that her dad would be working late and no one would ever know. After the trial, Kim fled town and hoped to never come back, but then Shauna tracked her down and told her she had to return to help "clean things up."

Rachel had confessed as well, saying Shauna had delivered the worst of the blows. Rachel had only hit Nicole in the body, never in the head, and she'd been terrified of Shauna. She was also charged with Nicole's murder.

When the police searched Shauna's home they found Nicole's necklace in her jewelry box, with some trace evidence still on it. It made perfect, terrible sense that Shauna hadn't been able to part with the gift, a symbol of her father's betrayal and a trophy of her destruction of Nicole.

After Shauna was confronted with the evidence and the testimony of the other girls, she turned on her father. She hadn't realized that he'd started fooling around with Nicole until later that July, when he begged off from an annual family camping trip, sending Shauna alone with her uncle and aunt. A week later she came home early and discovered her father in bed with Nicole. They'd fought and he swore he'd break it off, but that wasn't enough for Shauna.

"What happened to Nicole's clothes?" I said. "The tire iron?"

"They were in the trunk of the car—along with the girls' bloody clothes. Shauna was supposed to get rid of them, but when McKinney came home in the morning, after the other girls had left, he noticed some sand on the car tires."

"He realized they'd been at the lake?"

Suzanne nodded. "He confronted her, and she told him everything." I could well imagine that fight, Shauna trying to hurt her father with all the vicious details of how she'd killed Nicole. "He dumped the tire iron into the ocean, burned the clothes, cleaned up the car, and they never spoke about it again until Shauna called him, saying that Cathy was starting to talk about that night."

"Did Shauna kill her?"

"Looks like it was Frank McKinney. They found hair and DNA samples on some of his clothes. That might not have been enough, but a witness saw a man matching his description down at the pier the night she was killed."

I remembered how Frank had defended sending us to jail. *You two would have ended up there eventually. . . .* Was that how he justified killing Cathy? She was just a drug addict? I wondered if Cathy had trusted him at the end or just needed the money for drugs so bad she threw caution to the wind. I sat back in my chair, thinking of Nicole, Cathy, Ryan, of all the ruined lives since that night, of all the ways Shauna's hatred and jealousy had destroyed so many people over the years.

Suzanne said, "A lot to take in, I know."

"You're not kidding." My mouth was parched, my head pounding. I grabbed one of the cans of Coke, opened it, and took a long swallow. When I was finished I put it down and looked at Suzanne across the table, remembering how tough she'd always been on me and wondering what was going on with her now. Was it guilt?

"Why are you really here, Suzanne?"

She looked around at the other inmates and their visitors, then back at me.

"Lots of my parolees over the years have claimed they're innocent. . . ." I held my breath, waiting. "You're the first one I believed."

I was glad she'd said it but still angry that I'd been caught up in a system where it didn't matter what Suzanne believed, the law had decided I was guilty and she had to make sure I followed the rules. But there was something else, something she wasn't saying—I could see it in the way she was looking at me, like she was waiting for me to connect the dots. I thought of all the times she urged me to stay away from Ryan, reminded me over and over.

"Did you know Ryan and I were meeting each other?"

"Of course not. I would've suspended your parole immediately." Her face was serious, but she held my gaze a minute too long.

She pointed to my half-eaten chocolate bar.

"Are you going to finish that? Men don't like skinny chicks."

I smiled at her.

A week later, Angus told me Ryan had recovered enough to be sent back to Rockland. This time I sent a letter and we began to write. We were hesitant at first, reserved in our writings, but slowly we began to open up, getting to know each other again as we shared our daily lives on the inside. He talked a little about things he wanted in the future, like a better job and his own place, but he didn't really say much about a future with *me*, like he wasn't sure how I felt about that yet and was waiting until we were released.

I thought about my own life a lot, whether I wanted to stay in Campbell River—with Ryan, I hoped—or go somewhere else and start fresh, especially now that there was so much media attention to our case. But I still had unfinished business in Campbell River. The story wasn't over yet. Not for me, anyway.

# CHAPTER THIRTY-ONE

## CAMPBELL RIVER

## OCTOBER 2013

Three months later, our cases were overturned and our records expunged. There were a lot of media waiting outside the prison for me, but I refused to answer any of their questions and pushed my way through. Stephanie came to pick me up, with Captain. Turns out she'd decided to foster him after my parole was suspended the first time.

"I had a feeling you would come back and I didn't want anyone else to have him," she said.

Captain was ecstatic, jumping over the seat to greet me, his tail whacking both of us, his tongue trying to wash every part of my face. I laughed, then cried into his fur.

We drove to the campsite. The media hadn't found out yet where I was going to be staying. When I'd been arrested the second time and sent back to Rockland, I'd called Stephanie. She'd gone to the campsite and collected my stuff from the manager. Then, when I found out I was going to be released, she paid him to keep his mouth shut. When I tried to thank her, she said, "Don't worry. I'll make you work it off."

A few days later, I took a walk on the beach with Captain, noticing all the fall leaves that now covered the ground, breathing in the crisp air. When I got back, Ashley was waiting on the front porch.

She looked good, with her hair dyed a more natural dark brown. She was still wearing all black but she'd removed the Goth jewelry and only had a silver chain around her neck.

"Hey, how are you doing?" I said as I stepped onto the porch.

"I've been better."

"I bet." I sat on the chair across from her and unclipped Captain. He made his way over to her, nudging her legs. She scratched his ears for a minute.

"It's hard, kind of feels like I lost my mom and my grandpa, like they're dead or something."

I nodded, understanding, thinking about my own parents.

"It's like I don't even know who they are. My grandpa, it's weird hearing everything that happened, what he did. I really loved him, you know?"

"Lots of people have two sides. Maybe everything just got out of hand for him and he didn't know how to stop things once they went that direction. He lost control." I'd thought about that a lot in prison, trying to correlate the Frank McKinney from my youth with the man who'd slept with my sister and helped cover up her murder, then killed Cathy to keep her from talking. I knew how important his career had been and how much he loved his daughter, but I was still shocked at how far he'd gone to protect everything.

"I guess." She was quiet for a minute, then said, "In some ways, I understand my mom more now. Like why she married my dad so young, why my grandpa seemed kind of distant with her, why she was always so jealous if he spent time with me."

"They had a complicated relationship, lots of resentment."

Ashley nodded. "My dad and I are trying to work things out, or at least we're talking about stuff more. I missed the first semester of school. . . . He doesn't want me to stick around here, listening to all the gossip, so he's sending me to a private school in January. It has a really strong arts program."

"That's good."

"Yeah." She glanced in the direction of Aiden's trailer. "And I broke up with Aiden. I think my mom was right about him."

I thought of Margaret. "Sometimes moms are."

She looked back at me, fiddled with Captain's collar, straightening it for him. "What about you and Ryan? Do you think you'll get back together?"

I looked down at the leash in my hand. "A lot happened when we were inside. Prison changes people. It's hard to get back to who you were before."

The night after we were released, Ryan's mother had thrown a party in our honor. It was the first time Ryan and I had seen each other for months and we tried to talk outside in private, but we kept getting interrupted. The moments we were alone felt strange, awkward somehow, like now that we were free to be around each other we didn't know how to act or what to say. His mother pulled him away to talk to some people, and I left the party early. I hadn't heard from him since and I wondered if it was too late for us now. We had changed too much.

"But he's the only other person who sees it the same, right? Who went through almost the exact same thing? I think he still loves you."

"There's a lot that has to get sorted out."

She scratched Captain's ears, her face reflective. After a couple of beats she said, "I understand now why you didn't want to do a documentary. It's real, what you went through. Film can't capture that."

I thought about her video, how it might have saved my life. Then I thought about all my friends on the inside who had no voice, no one speaking for them. Some major news shows had offered big money for an interview, but I'd turned them all down. This felt different, though, talking to Ashley. She was different.

"No, but we can try if you want."

"That would be great." It was the first time I'd seen her smile since I'd found her sitting on my doorstep.

The next morning I woke up thinking about my visit with Ashley. Her mentioning her relationship with her mom and dad got me thinking about my own parents. My dad had written when I was back in Rockland, asking if he could visit and offering financial support for my lawyer. But there was no apology, from him or my mother, and I'd felt my old anger rearing up. Why hadn't they believed me all those years? Why hadn't he mentioned my mother? I told him I didn't need help and that I'd get in touch after I was released, but I hadn't done it. I'd seen his company sign at a house being built in a nearby subdivision, and that morning I finally decided to stop and see him. I wanted to look in his eyes and know that he believed I was innocent—that he'd been wrong about me.

When I pulled up at the site, I spotted him near his work truck, some building plans spread out on the hood. He was studying them intently and didn't hear me walking up to him.

"Hey, Dad," I said when I was close.

He spun around, his expression startled. He reached out a hand, holding it out in the air, his face filling with an odd sort of wonder. Like he couldn't believe I was standing there. "Toni . . . I . . ." His voice caught and his eyes filled with tears. "It's so good to see you."

I'd wanted to be hard, wanted to tell him how shitty they had made me feel, how he had let me down, but now I couldn't say anything, couldn't speak a word, my heart pounding and my throat thick. Then he was standing in front of me. I tried to back up, to push him away, but his arms were around me, his body shaking as he kept repeating, "I'm sorry. God, I'm so sorry."

And then I was crying in my father's arms.

When we finally pulled apart, we leaned on his truck and talked for a while, about where I was living now, my plans for the future. Then, tired of small talk, I cut to the chase.

"I told you I didn't do it, Dad. Why couldn't you believe me?"

"I wanted to, Toni, I really did." He explained that he never thought I was guilty until the trial, then the evidence had been so compelling he didn't know what to think. He told himself if I did it, it was the drugs and the booze, I couldn't have known what I was doing. In a hesitant voice, he said he and Mom had struggled a lot about me and had almost divorced a few years after the murder.

We were still talking when another vehicle pulled up on the other side of Dad's truck. Dad looked nervous, his gaze flicking from me to the car, like he didn't know what to do. Then my mom got out. She was walking over to us, carrying a bag from Tim Hortons and balancing a tray of coffees. When she looked up and saw me standing beside Dad, she stopped still, her eyes wide.

"Hi, Mom." I held my breath. Would she hug me like Dad? Or would she reject me again?

"What are you doing here?" she said. I couldn't read her tone, wasn't sure how she felt about seeing me like this, but she looked upset, almost apprehensive.

Dad said, "Toni came by to say hi."

Mom set the bag and tray of coffees down on the hood of the truck, glancing around to see if any of the workers were watching.

Thinking that she might be expecting an angry confrontation, I said, "It's good to see you. I've missed you."

Now she was staring at her feet, shaking her head back and forth. Was she crying?

"I want you to know that I'm not angry—not anymore," I said. "I can understand how things looked, how much trouble I caused you as a teen. It hurt, a lot, but I'd like us to start over if we can. Maybe spend some time together—"

My mom finally looked up. She wasn't crying. She wasn't sad. She was furious.

"I don't care what the courts said. *You* took her there, *you* left her alone." Now there were tears, but they weren't for me—they were for Nicole, always for Nicole. Her breath was ragged and she was sucking at the air, her grief and rage making her body shake.

"You *knew* she was sneaking out, you *knew* what was going on for months. And you didn't say anything. She's dead because of you and I never want to see you—"

"Stop!" my dad yelled. "Just stop."

Mom glared at him as tears leaked down her face. "And you, Chris. You let Toni get away with everything. If you'd just been firmer with them—"

"Stop it," Dad said again. "Stop blaming everyone. She's gone, Pam."

"You don't think I know that?"

"You still can't let go."

"She was my *daughter.*"

"She was mine too, but we still have one daughter and she's standing here with us. You have to accept that Nicole is never coming back."

"No, no." She was shaking her head again. "You can do whatever you want, but I'll never forgive her." She turned and faced me. "Do you hear that? I will *never* forgive you."

She ran back to the car, slamming the door behind her and spinning the wheels as she burned out of the driveway.

Too shocked even to cry, I stared after her, my legs vibrating with nerves while her words echoed in my head. *Never forgive you . . .*

My dad reached out and laid his hand on my shoulder, making me flinch.

"I'm sorry, Toni. She's never dealt with it. Nicole's room is still the same, and she won't let me pack anything. She can't move past it. The therapist said the only way your mom can cope is by staying angry and blaming everyone, or else she finally has to face that Nicole's gone."

I spun around. "How can you still be with her?"

He looked surprised. "I love her."

"Well, she doesn't love me."

"She does, she's just stuck blaming you. Otherwise, she'll start blaming herself, for not seeing what was going on with Nicole that last year. I did the same thing but I worked through it, and I want a relationship with you."

"She won't like it."

He sighed. "I know, and I'll deal with that, even if it means losing her. But I'm not losing you again. You're my daughter."

I looked back at the road, still seeing my mom's car drive off, seeing the hatred in her eyes, and I felt anger rush through my body. She was my *mother*. She was supposed to love me no matter what, and my father had let her treat me like crap for years. He'd let her push me away.

Then I remembered Shauna crouched over Ashley, so full of hatred for me that she couldn't see I was trying to save her daughter, couldn't see anything past that anger. I didn't want to be like that. Didn't want to be like my mother. I wanted to forgive.

I turned to my father. "Do you need a helper?"

———

That afternoon I worked side by side with my dad again, banging nails, and a couple of days later I started a new job at the shelter—one of the long-term people had left. Mike had called and offered me my old job, said Patty was sorry for not believing me, but I said no thanks. I needed a fresh start. His buddy also offered me my boat back, but I was still pissed about how he'd kicked me out, so I passed. It's good, working at the shelter, hanging out with the dogs. I don't make much money, but whatever. My lawyer says I can sue for false conviction, but it'll be a long haul. Meanwhile, I'm just doing my thing. Dad suggested I work with him, but for now I'm just going to help out on weekends while we get to know each other again.

Doug Hicks came by once when I was walking home with Captain. It startled me, seeing the police car sitting in my driveway, couldn't help but get my heart rate going. He got out.

I said, "Haven't you heard? I'm a free woman," and walked past him.

"That's why I'm here. I want to apologize."

"For what?" I stepped onto my porch, blocking the steps with Captain by my side, making it clear he wasn't welcome any farther.

He sat on the hood of his car. "For not believing you seventeen years ago."

"What about Ryan?"

"Him too. You guys caused us a lot of trouble . . ."

"It didn't mean we murdered my sister."

"No, but with the witnesses, all the evidence? It didn't look good."

I leaned against my railing. "Yeah, I know."

He looked tired as he said, "Frank McKinney, I looked up to him when I started out. Thought he was a great guy—a really good cop."

"Everyone did."

"He's starting to come clean now that he knows he doesn't have much chance of beating this. Admits things got out of hand with your sister."

I felt a stab of anger. "He had no business messing around with her. I don't understand how they even connected."

"He pulled her boyfriend over for drunk driving one night. Nicole was in the passenger seat."

"That Dave guy?"

"Looks that way. Nicole didn't want anyone to know, so he kept it quiet. After that, Frank kept an eye out for her, made sure she stayed away from the boyfriend. They developed a friendship of some sort. They'd drive around, apparently just talking. Then one night the girls had a party at his house, he drove her home, things progressed. He says he was in love with her."

"She was sixteen."

"This job, it gets to all of us. Some cops start thinking the rules don't apply to them anymore. And I guess when Frank's wife died, he just went off the deep end. After that all he cared about was the job."

I could fill in the rest. Shauna had a hard enough time accepting that daddy dearest was always at the station. When she realized he was spending what spare time he had with Nicole, a girl even younger than herself, she flipped. It probably wasn't that hard to fill Rachel's and Kim's minds with lies and turn them against Nicole, which led to her death. And it wasn't hard to see why Nicole might have fallen for McKinney—how he had seemed so powerful back then.

"I don't feel sorry for him."

He met my eyes. "I don't either. I'm just sorry this all happened."

"That won't give me years of my life back."

"No." He stood up. "But you still have years left. Do good things with them."

He got in his car and drove off.

———————

That night I heard a knock on my back window. I woke up with a start, Captain barking beside me. I pulled back the curtain. It was Ryan. He motioned for me to open the window. I gave Captain a command to quiet down and slid open the lock. Ryan grinned at me.

"Want to go for a drive?"

"Where are we going?"

"Wherever we want."

# ACKNOWLEDGMENTS

There never seem to be enough words to express how much I appreciate the following people, how they made all the difference—even if their role was a small one, it was huge to me. But I'll try my best.

With enormous gratitude to my editor, Jen Enderlin, who told me I could do it, then helped me get there. I've learned more from you than I can even begin to acknowledge. Your insights, encouragement, and advice have helped me grow as a writer with every book we work on together.

For the team at St. Martin's Press: Sally Richardson, Matthew Shear (who wrote me the loveliest e-mail, which I will treasure forever), Dori Weintraub, Lisa Senz, Nancy Trypuc, Kim Ludlam, Kelsey Lawrence, Laura Flavin, Elizabeth Catalano, Stephanie Hargadon, Caitlin Dareff, and the entire Broadway and Fifth Avenue sales forces. Also, thanks to Dave Cole, who has now done a stellar job copyediting three of my books, and Ervin

Serrano, who designed this amazing cover. I hope you all know how grateful I am.

Deepest thanks to Mel Berger. Your ongoing support, sense of humor, and guidance has been invaluable over these past years. I couldn't ask for a better agent and friend. Thanks also to Kathleen Breaux, Ashley Fox, Tracy Fisher, Laura Bonner, Raffaella DeAngelis, Annemarie Blumenhagen, Covey Crolius, and the rest of the fantastic team at William Morris Endeavor Entertainment in New York and L.A.

In Canada, thanks to Jamie Broadhurst, Fleur Matthewson, and the entire group at Raincoast Books. I'm lucky to have such wonderful cheerleaders in my corner. I'd also like to thank all my foreign publishers around the world. One of my greatest pleasures is hearing from my foreign fans.

As always, endless appreciation to my lovely and wise critique partner, Carla Buckley, who can bash around story ideas for hours, understands my craziness, and convinced me to try Skype. How did we live without it? Your friendship and humor has helped me out of many dark corners and snarled plots.

For their professional advice I'd like to thank in no particular order: Bert King, Chris Lucas, Constable J. Moffat, Renni Browne, Shannon Roberts, Virginia Reimer, C. Saffron, M.L., Canadian Prison Consulting, Kim Brown, Lori Hall, and Stephanie Paddle. Any mistakes are most certainly mine.

For their constant support and love, my husband, Connel, who is truly the best man I know; my daughter, Piper, who was tucked securely in the womb during most of the writing of this book (and blessed our lives in a million ways since her arrival); and little Oona, who keeps me company in my office every day.